Praise for AC Benus
from the members of gayauthors.org

The sea has got to Redburn, and good. In that one voyage he's experienced more life in every extreme way than in all his previous years combined. It's got him hooked like a narcotic, but I feel his good nature will serve him well and prevent him from falling into the chasm of hatred and anger that consumed Jackson.
— Stephen *(Redburn)*

The unveiling in this *Typee* gives the reader an extra dimension that readers in Victorian times might have missed (or could very well have understood). Great script, AC!
— J.HunterDunn *(Typee)*

After a conflict between Jarl and An'natu, Redburn comforts Jarl, who breaks down. Their discussion about the bigotry of society is as valid now as it was in Melville's days. It ends with these beautiful words spoken by Redburn:

> *"Into the love of equals, we are bound –*
> *You and I are just alike –*
> *One to the other, unbroken."*

Thanks, AC. Another great script.
— J.HunterDunn *(Omoo)*

You've captured the spirit of Victorian novels quite well – not a jot of happiness anywhere, and conventional morality reigns supreme. Where may we expect to see the workhouse, or the beadle, or grimy smokestack belching out noisome vapors to settle over brick tenement terraces?

More please, and pass the opium so I can have a pleasant dream.
— ColumbusGuy *(Pierre)*

I like symmetry in architecture; music. It has an aesthetic appealing quality. And I find it in *Pierre* as well. Redburn, Emily and Sara make one side of the building, while Pierre, Lucy and Isabelle form the other, completing the symmetrical structure of the whole script.
— J.HunterDunn *(Pierre)*

Also Available from AC Benus

MOJO
Post-Modern Satire and Sex-comedy: this hilarious novel up-dates Petronius' Satyricon by setting it in Trump's America's of grifters, the ultra rich, and truth-deniers
ebook: **ISBN 9781734561074**; paperback: **ISBN 9781734561050**

Summer 2020 – Hell in a Handbasket
A contender for the Pulitzer Prize in poetry, 2021, this collection grapples with the year of pandemic, racial justice and environmental crisis
ebook: **ISBN 9781953389015**; paperback: **ISBN 9781953389008**

The Thousandth Regiment
This scholarly work is a translation of and commentary on Hans Ehrenbaum-Degele's First World War poems "Das tausendste Regiment"
ebook: **ISBN 1657220583**; paperback: **ISBN 9781657220584**

The Easiest Thing in the World
And other poems: marking the third anniversary of the Pulse Nightclub attack
ebook: **ISBN 9781734561029**; paperback: **ISBN 9781734561036**

Same Love
Short Story Anthology: a compendium offered during this time of pandemic, D.K. Daniels, Editor (Contributor)

THE SECRET MELVILLE SERIES, Volume 1

7 Filmscripts

AC Benus

an AC Benus Impression
San Francisco

*Grateful acknowledgement is here offered
for the support and encouragement I've
received on the literary site www.gayauthors.org,
especially Parker Owens and J.HunterDunn
for their help with this series*

THANK YOU!

ISBN 978-1-953389-02-2 (ebook)
ISBN 978-1-953389-03-9 (paperback)

THE SECRET MELVILLE SERIES: 7 Filmscripts, Volume 1
Copyright © 2021
by AC Benus.
All rights reserved.

*Cover photo: Pixabay
https://www.pexels.com/@pixabay*

*Title Page photo: Mark McCammon
https://www.pexels.com/@markmccammon*

*Vignette: printing-block sketch from
original 1840s Melville novels*

Library of Congress Control Number: 2020918357

Table of Contents
Secret Melville, Volume 1

Introduction to the Secret Melville Series

I. Objectives

> What I feel most
> moved to write,
> *that* is banned —
> Yet, altogether,
> write the *other* way
> I cannot.
>
> —Herman Melville [1]

My goals for this Introduction are not fancy or complex.

I hope by the end of it a reader will see Melville is not so scary. And you will in fact find his "truths" are familiar to our continuing struggles of the present day: environmental and cultural sanctity; freedom *from* religion (especially all those judgmental, and purporting to be Christian); same-sex love as a natural and ubiquitous element of life on Earth; love's supreme strength to stir heroics in people; and the universal power of forgiveness.

A second ambition of this Introduction is to show that screenplays are not so scary either. Like all the writing forms you are already familiar with, to read them you basically start at the top left-hand corner of the page, read right and down — and the story unfolds before your eyes. In fact, it is a hallmark of all well-written filmscripts that they play out in your mind as a series of images and dialogue.

To boost this confidence in simply being able to pick up a script and start reading, I've provided a brief "how to" essay as Series Appendix 1 (Volume 3, page 263)

A third objective might merely be to get you ready for the great adventures which lie ahead. It's no accident that most open-minded scholars readily admit Melville wrote *the* greatest novel that exists in the English language. His importance as an artist is multifaceted, and this arguably shows best in his characters. Everyone you are about to meet are as real as living people, and each of his many, many sailors stands unique and highly differentiated. Just how successful our author is at doing this only recently struck me. For last year I picked up the novel *Sea-Wolf* by Jack London. In comparing the two writers' sailors, the older maestro blows London out of the water. Melville creates flesh-and-blood "people," while Jack never manages to lift his personalities above the drub of highly undifferentiated "characters." For London, they are called to fill a role and don't strive for anything more.

At this point I need to be clear and state for the record I admire London. In fact, I hold him in supreme regard as a writer, which is why it turned into such a surprise to encounter *Sea-Wolf* after all of my deep immersion into Herman Melville's maritime novels. Criticizing Jack London is no attempt at character assassination on my part, for he *is* great, but even his importance must by comparative necessity pale next to Melville's.

Acknowledging his skill as a writer can now allow me to show you in more detail what inspired me to create the "Secret Melville."

II. Justification for the Series

My personal journey with Melville began in high school. We were given segments of *Moby-Dick* to study, including Chapter 4, "The Counterpane." What an eye-opening introduction! I suppose my fifteen-year-old self read this intimate, yet humorous, installment of the book thinking "Is this chapter saying what I think it's saying?" Being totally uneducated then about the ways and means Gay artists in the Western tradition both hid and openly discussed same-sex love, I told myself there was a *possibility* Melville was saying (what he is so clearly saying), and Ishmael and Queequeg have indeed formed a love-match akin to marriage. It's one that's meant to endure until death.

This youthful suspicion of mine concerning a possible plot mechanism to spring the entire novel forward was confirmed in my full reading of *Moby-Dick* after I graduated from college.

That was a period where my time constraints were lifted from purely academic pursuits, and I purposefully went back to re-read the literature that most piqued my interest in high school: the short stories of Jack London; *The Scarlet Letter*; *Catcher in the Rye*; anything by James Thurber; *The Great Gatsby*; *The Grapes of Wrath*; and most particularly of all, *Moby-Dick*.

Nearly a decade later, I was in the used book shop a couple of blocks from home, and chanced upon a 1929 reprint of *Pierre, or The Ambiguities*. The introduction mentioned this Melville novel was the one immediately published after *Moby-Dick*. So I bought it, eagerly hoping to enjoy it.

What actually happened upset me deeply, because I wasn't able to read *Pierre*; it was entirely impenetrable. And after two or three concerted efforts to start again at the beginning and really *focus*, I put the book aside feeling like a failure. Later I found out Melville too must have had this experience, for he condensed it nicely. "[E]very incomprehended idea is not only a perplexity but a taunting reproach to one's mind[.]" (*Pierre, or the Ambiguities* Book 21)

It was this sensation of being inadequate, coupled with the guarded praise contained in *Pierre's* introductory remarks, which triggered my naturally tenacious instincts to "solve" my shortcomings.

The solution I eventually stumbled upon changed my life. Because I had decided the best way to penetrate the 'mystery' of *Pierre* was to start with Melville's first novel and read my way up, in sequence, until I could look *Pierre* in the eye as a tamable adversary.

The used bookstore near my workplace had copies of *Typee* and *Omoo*, and I was bowled over. Casually, across the span of the next few years, I acquired and read the six Melville books preceding *Pierre*, and then went into an easy reading of my own personal white whale of print.

Why do I go into all of this detail? To show that my discovery of Melville was almost accidental, and assuredly that of a regular guy with a broad literary interest. And the justification for this Series lies in realizing Melville's narrator for these six sea novels is the same young man. We follow his life from age nineteen to about twenty-five, at which point, he quits the sea and takes up a vocational pen instead. I recognized the life of our multi-book hero would make a fantastic sequence of movies, all culminating in the young man's first "New York novel" of *Pierre*.

Only in preparing my notes for this Introduction did I discover John Brooks Moore, a Melville advocate, spoke about how all the sea books tie together to tell one, unified narrative. He wrote the following in his prefatory remarks to one of Melville's novels:

> *Moby-Dick* [...] is extremely confusing unless read as a chapter in the work of Melville, not the most important chapter necessarily, however masterful[.] [...] How can this [segment] be understood if the reader of *Moby-Dick* does not know the preceding experiences of the man, chronicled in *Typee, Redburn,* and *White-Jacket,* and the later experiences shadowed in *Pierre*. The novels of Melville may be said, in general, to present a crescendo of protest, rebellion, disillusion, quiescence – the end of all incurable anguish. The steps in what was certainly the almost intolerable process of development to Melville ran fairly well represented by four books of his: *Redburn,* the first questioning of the world and the first disgust for its ways; *Typee,* the partial escape from that repulsive world; *Moby-Dick,* the indictment of life and of things as they are; *Pierre,* the revulsion complete and refusal to make any terms of concessions. [2]

Perhaps now is the time to mention an aspect of Melville's writing concerning names. In the vast area of Melville scholarship, this phenomenon probably has a title, but I'll artlessly call it "the Name Thing." For even though we follow our eponymous hero from his late teenage years onwards, Melville is cagy with letting us know his true name (and / or identity). Remember, the opening line to *Moby-Dick* is "Call me Ishmael"; meaning that's not his name, but as far as we're allowed to get close to him, it's all he'll give us. This guardedness – as if saying "You, reader, may hurt me if I exposed my *true* name to you" – repeats over and over; new novel, new name for the same main character / narrator. For this Series I have called him "Redburn" because this is what the boy we first meet is called in the opening filmscript of the sequence. [3]

Another feature of the scripts might be thought of as story reconstructions. I show events from the books in the imagined way the real life scenes may have unfolded; these lived experiences were later used by our author in the 'non-secret' print versions. Naturally, my motivating impulse has been to uncover the truth of the sea novels, rather than obscure the contents of the books, which – trust me – are plenty explicit on their own.

In general, *The Secret Melville Series* breaks down like this:

Movie One:
Redburn's introduction to darring-do and the privations of sea life; his first taste of love.

Movies Two through Five:
Redburn's hero-quest, seeking what was taken from him; love, his motivation to keep moving forward and not give up.

Movie Six:
The homeward-bound journey; struggling with the will to live a loveless life.

Movie Seven:
The consequences of being changed by the search for one to have and hold; love as a means of redemption.

With this in mind, we can look more closely at some of the recurrent themes and objectives of Melville's first seven novels.

III. First, "the Gay Thing"

How 'secret' could all of these men forming partnerships in Melville's novels really have been to a 19th century audience? The answer is a resounding "Not very." However, like most artforms creating material in the public sphere primarily intended for Gay eyes, there is a (usually dazzling) surface appearance — offered up for mass consumption — veneered above great substance for the initiated. A Gay code if you like, but one that is not now or has ever been mysterious or 'secret' to those in the Community.

As mentioned earlier, my first encounter with Melville was reading certain chapters of *Moby-Dick*. One enigmatic, lost-in-translation moment that struck me even then was why on earth Ismael would wander into a nighttime church service as he looked for lodgings, at the start of his travels, in New Bedford, Massachusetts. The answer to the initiated is as plain as can be, but our high school teacher either did not know herself, or felt it inappropriate (sadly) to toss it out to us. Ishmael goes into the church because its glowing "smoky light" must have been burning an inviting shade as familiar as the "Gomorrah" mentioned in the same breath. A dusky purple-shaded tint; mauve; lavender. A color-coded lantern lit above its open doors. The Gay traveler in Ishmael expected gay-friendly room and board behind the walls of what turned out to be a church. That the man stumbled into an African American religious service is part of the wry sense of humor Melville appeared to delight in inserting "between the lines" for his Gay readers — a sense of humor more often than not known by the name of *camp*. [4] But for non-initiated readers, the 'secret' simply stays a 'mystery.'

It's a topic Melville was bold enough to address to his readers directly:

> In the cold courts of justice, the dull head demands oaths; and holy writ, proofs; but in the warm halls of the heart, one single, untestified memory's spark shall suffice to enkindle such a blaze of evidence, that all the corners of conviction are as suddenly lighted up as a midnight city by a burning building[.] *(Pierre Book 4)*

But back to Ishmael on his night of arrival alone in New Bedford; what confirmation do we have he was seeking out the equivalent of a modern Gay B&B? First off, the signal of a classic red lantern (or, the red lights of a red light district) are well known. Melville mentioned this 'straight' color code specifically in *Moby-Dick*. After our hero-couple Ishmael and Queequeg have joined forces in New Bedford, they move on to Nantucket to locate a whaling vessel to take them as crew. In optics none too subtle, Melville has the pair's next innkeeper be a certain "Mrs. Hussey," whom the boys first glimpse arguing with a dissatisfied male customer in her establishment's doorway; above them blazed a dull-red lamp said to resemble "a blackeye." Likewise, in the earlier book of *Omoo*, Melville dropped the presence of politeness altogether and flatly told us about a French madam on Tahiti who worked out of a tent with a red lantern above her flap.

And then, to return to the specifics of a purple-colored lantern in this context of accommodations, the novel Melville published not long before *Moby-Dick* — *Redburn* — contains one of the most remarkable same-sex love sequences in all of English-language literature. A high-end callboy Redburn meets in Liverpool 'kidnaps' the American teen for a train journey and overnight visit to the capital in a chapter

Melville titled "A Mysterious Night in London." There, on the tab of the working boy's aristocratic client (nicknamed by Harry and his fellow hustlers as "Lord Lovely"), they stay at an exclusive Gay gentlemen's club, which, as you can guess by now, has a lavender lantern burning above its entrance.

Moving back from the specifics, arguably more important than just where Gay people would congregate to let their hair down, socialize and *meet* one another, is what Melville shows us once these enduring love-matches are struck between his characters.

I'll go into some detail later concerning Ishmael and Queequeg's partnership, but theirs is merely one among many in Melville's writings. These Gay couples are more heroic than not in our author's hands, so they must have been welcome inspiration to the LGBT+ readers of his age.

In addition to Ishmael and Queequeg, there's Captain Claret and the Master-at-Arms in *White-Jacket;* Chips and Bungs in *Omoo;* Blunt and his deceased partner in *Redburn;* Cabaço and Archy in *Moby-Dick;* Shenley and Pierre in *White-Jacket;* Jermin and Bembo in *Omoo;* Flask and Daggoo in *Moby-Dick;* and Charlie Millthorpe's devotion to Pierre Glendenning in *Pierre*. This is by no means an exhaustive list but it will serve nicely as preamble to mentioning Zeke and Shorty.

Zeke and Shorty, "whole-souled fellows" who "got along famously," are a contented pairing of retired sailors on Mo'orea, a satellite island of Tahiti. Sharing what Melville implies is their 'nuptial hammock,' they represent an extraordinary thing to readers of the 19th century: a same-sex couple's *happily-ever-after*. They have literally found a piece of paradise where societal pressures will never be able to break them apart. You will find this "a place of our own" aspiration a common theme in nearly all of the 19th and early 20th century's Gay literature, and it's reasonable to speculate Melville himself provided the literary *beau idéal* of a same-sex love HEA in the works to follow by such Queer authors as Bayard Taylor, Charles Warren Stoddard, and Edward Prime-Stevenson.

However, these authors had no monopoly on themes of same-sex marriage in their times. W. S. Gilbert — of Gilbert and Sullivan fame — wrote a long poem about an established male couple going to get the paperwork finalized for their union (via a joint Last Will and Testament), and who wind up crushed in the machinations of a heatless legal system seeing only money existing between them and not love. [5] As a satirist and social reformer, Gilbert wrote *Damon v. Pythias* (London 1870) as a way of questioning how "The Law" had even the slightest justification for imposing itself on the contentment of any Lesbian or Gay 'marriage of true minds.' For marriage is a fundamental right, even if only legally protected through private contracts or public Wills. [6]

But despite Zeke and Shorty's ideal of being able to make it together, the cold reality for most 19th century Gay men and women was of a society forcing them to marry people of the wrong gender. Even so, male love found ways to shine through adversity, and one of the most publicly prominent methods to show a great love for a former (pre-marriage) partner was in the naming of one's firstborn son. This practice seems to have been a genuine feature of Community knowledge, as Abraham Lincoln wanted to name his oldest boy after his partner of four years, Joshua Speed. (Mary Todd had the boy named after her father instead.) Tennyson did get the naming of his eldest child after Arthur Hallam, his partner who died abroad and for whom the poet labored over the tragic love poem *In Memoriam* for eleven years. And not one but *two* of Melville's partners named their firstborn boys after him, gifting the world a Herman Melville Greene and a Herman Melville Williams!

So, despite the cruel pressures to conform many if not all Gay people felt in the 19th century, the premise of how an abstract 'fictional' possibility of a happily-ever-after — which you may call a sentiment — relates to the absolute symbol of two equals joining up, leads me to the topic of which school of thought motivated Melville's big-picture themes.

IV. What is Transcendental Thought?

The best way to hash out the details of a Transcendental School of consciousness is to provide context through a compare / contrast method; this can show what artistic move-ment it rebelled against.

In time, trends repeat, and most contemplative schools arise when shallower ones ex-haust their credibility. One can observe this pendulum phenomenon again and again starting with the Italian Renaissance. The surface-obsessed early Renaissance painters, for example, gave way to the Manneristic complexity of Michelangelo (a Manneristic complexity that carried into that man's poetry, by the way). In 16th century English verse, the Cavalier School of epicurean, live-for-the-moment poetry gave impetus for the Metaphysical School to be born in the works of Katherine Philips and John Milton.

Likewise, the dominant School of early 19th century writing, the Romantics, yielded to Transcendentalism. In each of these artistic revolutions, we can perceive the same intellectual step moving from the personal to the representational.

For English-speaking authors, the writers of the Romantic era were interested in re-straining thought to the familiar, maudlin kind. Thus, the *personal* of their times might be better termed the sentimental to us. Thinking of it this way, the contrast is clearer: Wordsworth's

> "...I saw a crowd,
> A host of golden daffodils..."

As compared against Tennyson's

> "...Tis better to have loved and lost
> Than never to have loved at all...."

Tennyson's *In Memoriam* – perhaps the greatest love poem of the language – explores diverse topics like Creationism versus Evolution, and Existential wondering what role God has, if any, in the modern industrialized world. Tennyson's unifying objective was expansive; if in *In Memoriam* he picked up on a theme touching the clichéd, he did so to reach his readers' intellect, via the heartstrings, and to enlarge his message to an all-inclusive understanding.

Like the sentimental gesture of pressing a flower in a book, a Romantic School artist sought to press *my* flower in *my* book as a means, through words, to remember *my* attachment to a memory. They seemed focused on surface preservation; as if encasing an idea in amber. Or, thought about in another way, they sought to contract the remnants of experience into a few, trifling words – which, more often than not, reverted to tropes.

So what then is the Transcendental version of the self-centered Romantic form of sentimentality? Follow the same scenario above, and imagine our new type of writer has also picked a meadow flower. For them, the flower of interest is a stand-in for *every* flower, pressed in a book of *everyone's* ownership, to remember a shared moment of existence with *all* moments of existence. Or, in other words, the merely "pretty" nature of the Romantics becomes for the new school Nature, imbued with Her all-powerful language of humanity's shared experiencing of Her. We see this in the way the important-but-neglected poet Lucy Larcom phrases it:

> Nature's book is never sealed.
> Its pages are ever unfolding
> With new and delightful instructions, [...]
> Gaining nearer glimpses
> Of heaven through the bareness
> Which follows the summer glory
> Of human pride. [7]

If we reject the flower in amber aesthetic, we can see Larcom's objective is to conjure the image of a blossom recreated each time it's viewed with greater significance.

Larcom, like her better-known admirers Emerson and Thoreau, headed a generation of American poets rebuking mawkish English upper-class poetic taste, which was carefully censored to be free of any 'taint' of democratic thinking, lest it incite the oppressed to rise up against Whitehall's empire. Self-representational government, equality, justice – these are nowadays the Transcendentalist topics best known to the public mind through exposure to Walt Whitman. But, perhaps we should also know that Whitman only became Whitman through his assimilation of Melville. Few people seem to realize Whitman's best-remembered line, which is from his collection of tribute poems to the assassinated Abraham Lincoln, "O Captain! my Captain!" is a quotation from Chapter 132 of *Moby-Dick*.

Whitman embraced him because Melville as a poet and writer of fiction represents the supreme rejection of the personal in favor of the universal. In his novels particularly, and in his sea novels most explicitly, Melville illustrates time and time again an interest not in the sentimentally compressed, but in the unfetteredly expansive. He's creating democratic tools to connect public ideas to the great unknown; perhaps to show Man's relationship to cosmic connectedness itself.

And what "proof" is there that Melville belonged with Transcendentalists like Larcom? Well, here is just one quote, from among many dozen possible examples, to give you an idea of where our author's heart and mind stood:

> I am of a meditative humor, and at sea used often to mount aloft at night, and, seating myself on one of the upper yards, tuck my jacket about me and give loose to reflection. [...] And it is a very fine feeling, and one that fuses us into the universe of things, and makes us a part of the All, to think that, wherever we ocean-wanderers rove, we have still the same glorious old stars to keep us company; that they still shine onward and on, forever beautiful and bright, and luring us, by every ray, to die and be glorified with them.
>
> Ay, ay! we sailors sail not in vain. We expatriate ourselves to nationalize with the universe[.] (*White-Jacket* Chapter 19)

V. Bigotry and the Power of Gay Heroics

Knowing now what we know about Transcendental artistic purpose, sometimes using stock items — like flowers — to represent large-scale ideals, we can examine one of the ubiquitous features of Melville's sea novels: the Gay hero. Each of his protagonists stand up for what is fair and just in his books, and heroism in general is an archetypical characteristic among many of his fictional people. To be a hero when called upon is an omnipresent element of all of his work.

Likewise, one of the ever-present villainies Melville's hero must confront is intolerance. He takes on misogyny, racism, religious-based discrimination, and naturally, homophobia. [8]

Now, I imagine many readers of this will not be able to "picture" Melville as anti-racist, but I'd argue any preconceived baggage we carry was saddled on us by Hollywood. We must not confuse the prejudiced, and oftentimes downright grotesque, film views as having anything to do with Melville. The movie representations, both new and old, cop racial attitudes that impose their respective ages' narrow-mindedness upon the text. One fact to show this is that Ishmael marries Queequeg in the book, so how racist could *Moby-Dick's* narrator be? And a second fact to confirm this people-phobia is, how many of these movie versions of the book have the couple marry? None. And omission is arguably the worst imposition on any text.

The portrayals of Queequeg in film have not been of Ismael's savior and partner — the one whom the protagonist of *Moby-Dick* tells us possessed "a spirit that would dare a thousand devils" and "a lofty bearing" (Chapter 10) — but of hateful, and possibly anti-gay, representations of a mentally-challenged brute. The 1930 movie version of the Polynesian shows him as a grunting microcephalic sideshow freak. Why? Clearly whatever reasons filmmakers chose to limit Queequeg's role – which carries over to the pigeon-spoke, black-faced portrayal ("brown face," really) seen in the John Huston / Ray Bradbury "Moby Dick" [sic] of 1956 – they reflect the political mandates and mass biases of when the films were created. Ironically, of course, these prejudices of 20th century moviemakers were the exact hatreds Melville's 19th century books exposed to exacting ridicule and condemnation.

So, concerning what we think we know, we'd better clear our heads before reading what Melville had to say in regards to racial or religious discrimination.

In terms of approaching these novels, we should be extra-cautious about any pro-Christian biases we may drag into our interpretations.

Therefore, to continue along the *Moby-Dick* path of example, we have to acknowledge the ethnically diverse secondary officers of the *Pequod* are not the 'savage' pinheads movie versions have been most comfortable showing, but more simply non-Christians. This distinction is represented well in the scene where Ishmael is presenting his partner to get signed up on the ship he scouted out earlier. This is a "Papers, please" scene, literally, because the financial organizers of the whaling venture demand to see paperwork saying Queequeg has been formally, certifiably, converted to Protestant beliefs. Ishmael responds by insisting his partner belongs to the "First Congregational Church"; a very Transcendental stance, as you can now see. In so doing, Melville is saying Tashego, Daggoo and Queequeg – the *Pequod's* junior officers – come from a worshipful congregation that has never parted ways with the Garden of Eden, which is the Earth itself. They are pure (which is why Ahab needs *their* blood oath in a later scene), in utter contrast to the hypocritical, self-styled Christians among the whale boat's men and senior officers – especially Captain Ahab. The non-Christians' presence on the *Pequod* becomes one of world-witnesses to Ahab's Christianity-based bloodlust.

Conceive of the bloodlust against the white whale as being based in Christian belief, you ask? Judeo-Christian-Islamic belief, yes. Because if you come to see the junior officers as pure, spotless witnesses, then you can perceive Ahab as a surrogate for Cain, who, through the shame-ridden concept of 'Original Sin,' is driven mad by the so-called-religious demand of guilt. In this way, Ahab is an allegory for all *civilized* men and women made crazy by the conflicting notions of repentance versus lust for power, wealth, fame, etc. It's a theme Lucy Larcom also gave thought to when she wrote:

> Have you ever seen a Soul,
> A Heaven-born one, suffocated
> By earthly prosperity, dying of too
> Much sunshine, its pinions
> Clogged and weighted down
> By the drossy ashes
> Men call gold,
> Until it could not flutter
> Towards immortality? [9]

This then is the burden of every Son of Cain, and which in *Moby-Dick,* becomes part of what has driven the *Pequod's* captain mad, and dooms all aboard to a living hell. But the so-called pagans – which eventually includes our "heathenish" looking Ishmael – are exempt from the clash of Cain. Ultimately this selflessness leads to Ishmael's redemption through Queequeg's heroic love and sacrifice, which is the only genuinely Christian display in a book Melville himself termed "wicked." [10]

In the broader environmental and social justice themes of the novel, hopefully it now becomes apparent the bloodlust itself is sign and symbol of the entitlement Ahab and most likeminded Judeo-Christian-Muslims felt towards enslaving, and polluting, and slaughtering their way across the natural environment, because "God gave it to us to profit off of it as we see fit."

Needless to say, Melville is a vociferous critic of this self-entitled hubris. No decent Transcendentalist could be otherwise. And perhaps it's this conflict of egotistical "mine" versus a universalist "ours" that gives rise to the hero archetype in Melville's writings. He needs brave ones who damn consequences and rush in to do what's right, despite the modern world's blind spot concerning humility.

A willingness to do quixotic battle with windmill giants ties in perfectly with the not-so 'secret' world he builds for his Gay characters. This element of bravery, if you like, is part of what makes the aforementioned Zeke and Shorty's quiet enjoyment of life together so powerful. This couple — with their eternally safe and bucolic 'nuptial hammock' — display giant-killing heroism simply by denying 19th hypocritical mores the power to split them up. Their mythical greenwood is real and unmolested by homophobic hatred.

In *Pierre*, it's this exact type of primal, agricultural existence that Charlie Millthorpe would most like with his belovèd Pierre in the Hudson River Valley. Melville goes to pains to imbue Charlie with a noble pedigree, along the lines of George Washington, descending from a knightly family in England who, through the centuries, is reduced to toiling for a living. But like Washington, Millthorpe does not mind rolling up his sleeves, and shows the 'aristocracy' of his blood by staying faithful to his love right down to the final pages of the book.

We see this same grounding in love from the heroic way Jermin (Jarman, in this series) supports Bembo, and Bembo — a Polynesian — supports his alcoholic partner in *Omoo*. Theirs is another 'private' relationship in Melville's oeuvre where real heroism is on display as just the way Gay partners live and breathe to support one another (as perhaps all spouses should). Their union is but one of at least a dozen pairings in Melville's sea books shown as akin to full marriage. These love matches are uniformly presented as equitable and harmonious, without any displays of petty rancor from within the couplings.

Fully compatible traits are also the attributes Gilbert gave his same-sex couple in *Damon v. Pythias*. But Gilbert's satire is not on the couple or their companionability — as that's a given, being together as they have been for decades — but rather on The Law's capricious ruining of lives, which in the 19th century it certainly did for Frederick Park, Ernest Boulton, Arthur Pelham-Clinton; and later, Alfred Douglas and Oscar Wilde too. These men, lest we forget, were all arbitrarily persecuted merely for being Gay.

In this context, Melville's un-whitewashed voice speaks to us eloquently from the pages of his book about naval life, *White-Jacket*. He proclaims — from the year 1850, mind you — The Law's illegitimacy to intrude upon the lives and imprison Gay people. With clarity breathtakingly heroic for his position and era, he tells us:

> Oppressed by illiberal laws, and partly oppressed by themselves, many of our people are wicked, unhappy, inefficient. [...] We have a brig for trespassers; a bar by our main-mast, at which they are arraigned; a cat-o-nine-tails and a gangway to degrade them in their own eyes and in our own. These are not always employed to convert Sin to Virtue, but to divide them, and protect Virtue from legalized Sin from unlegalized Vice. [...]
>
> Yet the worst of our evils we blindly inflict upon ourselves[.] (Chapter 94 – "The End")

And also, from the same book:

> Besides, though we all abhorred the monster of Sin itself, [...] we were in a good degree free from those useless, personal prejudices, and galling hatreds [...] which so widely prevail among men of warped understandings and unchristian and uncharitable hearts. No; the superstitions and dogmas concerning Sin had not laid their withering maxims upon our hearts. We perceived how that 'evil' was but good disguised, and a knave a saint in his way; how that in other planets, perhaps, what we deem wrong, may there be deemed right[.] We perceived that the anticipated millennium must have begun upon the morning the first worlds were created; and that, taken all in all, our man-of-war world itself was as eligible a round-sterned craft as any to be found in the Milky Way. And we fancied that though some of us of the gun-deck were at times condemned to sufferings and slights, and all manner of tribulation and anguish, yet, no doubt, it was only our misapprehension of these things that made us take them for woeful pains instead of the most agreeable pleasures.
>
> I have dreamed of a sphere [...] where for one gentleman in any way to vanquish another is accounted an everlasting dishonor; where to tumble one into a pit after death, and then throw cold clods upon his upturned face, is a species of contumely only inflicted upon the most notorious criminals. (Chapter 44)

The author's words viewed here, in the appropriate perspective-granting context of this Introduction, will disempower any gay-erasing detractors' attempts at convoluted obfuscation to 'explain away' the obvious. They are wastes of breath. Melville's meaning, despite tortured BS to say otherwise, will remain just as clear in the future as it is now, and as it was when he wrote it. In an unarguable way he states "Let me people go." [11]

The Queer person as hero in the master Transcendentalist's work is all-present. The ones who are outsiders, because they see the world from a Gay-as-outcast POV, time and time again selflessly save the day. Besides the most familiar heroics of Queequeg's making of a coffin to save his belovèd's life, the Māori harpooner saves the life of a disrespecting punk *after* the bigot had said racist and homophobic things to Ishmael and Queequeg on the ferry taking them to Nantucket. These actions almost perfectly mirror the heroics of Jarl in the *A Voyage Thither* section of *Mardi*. The man also saves the life of An'natu after she'd taunted Jarl and his partner with hate-laden anti-gay comments.

These examples are just a few among many in Melville's writings. The opening book in this series, *Redburn*, is a perfect initiation into the not-so 'secret' way Melville discussed same-sex love. We glimpse this fearlessness in the story not only between the Greenlander and the title character, but also with Lavender, Blunt, Harry Bolton, and — on the return voyage — a sexy Italian teenage immigrant boy singing about men who want to share his bed for money. Sex, in addition to love, is everywhere in a seaman's life, Melville says and writes to show it to us. The way this open 'secret' plays into the unfolding of these people and their relationships involves our author crafting prose so the initiated will nod their heads and feel satiated by Melville's honesty. However, the same sections of prose might give an outsider momentary pause for wonder, but which he'll soon brush off and move on — like the 'mystery' of the purplish lantern lights.

With this grounding in place, let's take a look at the two screenplays presented in Volume 1. Volumes 2 and 3 will also have brief story setups for the scripts in those respective installments.

VI. Remarks: the Volume 1 Scripts

I will present plot summaries, hopefully avoiding any spoilers for first-time readers.

Redburn

The opening adventure of this series is an appropriate one. *Redburn* is among Melville's best work, and sold very well, despite the author not thinking terribly much of his efforts. Part of the novel's success as a work of art stems from its being a classic hero's tale. To paraphrase folklorist Joseph Campbell's definition of this most-ancient genre of fiction, it's about a young person going over there; doing something; and then coming home again.

The point of such tales is to show how the journey itself alters a person, and the motivations which initially launched them on their individual quest may not be the same ones leading them back again.

In our story, nineteen-year-old Redburn has led a rather sheltered, protected — and perhaps, women-heavy — existence. He *will* go to sea to challenge his self-reliance and prove it to his sick older brother Peter. Redburn also seeks out the freedom many Gay men have always found in being a sailor.

Peter finds a suitable ship making the relatively quick passage from New York to Liverpool, and back. The brothers go onboard for an interview.

Separated, the teenage boy gets his first taste of ribbing from the *Highlander's* crew. He can hold his own in a good-natured give and take, but one sailor — Jackson — immediately proves his nature as a world-weary sailor is anything but good. In a Melvillian twist, it soon becomes apparent Jackson suffers from the same fatal disease as his brother: tuberculosis.

So the voyage "over there" does not go by without incident, but Melville pulls in his considerable skills at humor to lighten the journey. He also begins to supply the lad with lovers and potential mates. Lavender — close to Redburn in age, but with more street smarts — initiates the sheltered boy into sailor sex, while the sexy Greenlander has more serious intentions on the protagonist's heart.

Landed in Liverpool, the middle section of this classic hero's journey involves one heck of an epic boy-boy romance. For soon, Redburn — distinctive in the red hunting coat — draws the attention of high-class callboy Harry Bolton. Both young men are taking advantage of the city's Gay cruising ground, The Exchange, and strike up a friendship that immediately deepens. A romantic day in the countryside causes Harry to invite Redburn with him to London. But Bolton is not entirely upfront concerning the overnight stay in the capital. Perhaps afraid he'd alienate the sweet American boy if he told him the reason for the trip; Harry has to work. Unbeknownst to Redburn, Bolton has secured his patron's permission to stay with the sailor at the client's exclusive Gay gentlemen's club in London. Redburn wakes up the next morning not entirely sure what happened, but he can see Harry's distressed about lying to him.

Now the young couple sees "escape," and Bolton — who had seafaring experience in his boyhood — signs up for the homeward journey of the *Highlander*.

The trip back, as one might predict, is not as smooth as anyone hoped.

Typee

Redburn's initial seafaring planted wanderlust firmly in his heart, especially as home-life presented nothing to match the sexual freedom onboard ship.

He signed up for a South Seas whaling voyage, and when our story opens, he'd had enough. The *Dolly's* captain has shown little interest in providing Redburn days off on Polynesian tourist spots, so the sailor hatches a plan.

He draws Toby, his partner — and the love of his life — into an escape plan. They will hike up the central mountain range of the tropical paradise Nuku Hiva, and down again into the Valley of the Happar — a group friendly to Westerners.

This trip up proves difficult and frays the relationship just a bit, but the descent on the other side is even harder.

Finally arriving where the *Dolly's* search party cannot look for them, the boys settle down to a new and unfamiliar way of living. For one, to their utter surprise and delight, they quickly find out same-sex love is respected among Polynesian culture; what's more, it's expected and rolled into the everyday concept of family.

Another thing for which the young couple was not prepared was landing into a political powder keg. The French have set their sights on colonizing Tahiti and the Marquesas Islands, of which Nuku Hiva is a part. The locals, naturally, are willing to fight for their independence, and some in the community look askance at Toby and Redburn as possible agents of the would-be French occupiers.

Tensions are inevitable, and the inevitable results in changes for the Americans.

Despite all of this, Melville's novel is ultimately one about the strength of family to pull through adversity. And because of it, *Typee* too is among Melville's best books.

VII. Apologia – "the Format Thing"

Since their emergence in the early 20th century, screenplays have followed a strict set of rules governing layout. This is because of widespread faith that a "properly" formatted script will yield one minute of movie runtime for every page. Thus, a 90-paged screenplay is the goal for most moviemakers who do not wish for a film to go more than an hour and a half.

The first rule of formatting assumes an 8 ½" x 11" paper size. Publishing these filmscripts in book form immediately negates all other rules concerning page-count and movie length.

However, there is another metric to use, and that is wordcount. I can compare the seven screenplays in this series against word-length / runtime for several well-known films.

First a word-count breakdown of *The Secret Melville Series:*

Redburn = 28,700
Typee = 32,650
Omoo = 29,950
Mardi = 18,050
Moby-Dick = 32,075
White-Jacket = 26,500
Pierre = 30,375

And now some films with their screenplay wordcounts and runtimes: [12]

2001: A Space Odyssey (1968) = 18,230 = 2 H. 29 mins.
Body of Evidence (1992) = 21,325 = 1 H. 39 mins.
The Apartment (1960) = 31,000 = 2 H. 05 mins.
Adaptation (2002) = 35,118 = 1 H. 55 mins.
Saving Private Ryan (1998) = 40,140 = 2 H. 49 mins.
The Abyss (1989) = 41,000 = 2 H. 20 mins.
Aliens (1986) = 43,790 = 2 H. 17 mins.
Lord of the Rings (2001) = 44,235 = 2 H. 58 mins.
Chinatown (1974) = 46,755 = 2 H. 10 mins.
Schindler's List (1993) = 47,525 = 3 H. 15 mins.
Traffic (2000) = 53,155 = 2 H. 27 mins.
Titanic (1997) = 63,312 = 3 H. 14 mins.
Magnolia (1999) = 66,055 = 3 H. 08 mins.

As you can see, despite faith in the page-number method (and the resulting wordcount), film lengths are entirely dependent on the director's vision. The shortest screenplay analyzed here resulted in a film that is longer than the ones with almost double the wordcount. *2001: A Space Odyssey* is good to mention in the context of *Mardi*. The nominal 18,000 words of *Mardi's* filmscript does not mean I intended a short film; only that I conceived of Redburn's exploits in this movie to be weighted towards the visual.

Dialogue has purposefully been cut back to allow the director broad sweeps of South Pacific grandeur as the central characters travel from island to island.

Taken together as a matrix, the information given here shows the seven films of *The Secret Melville Series* can each come in at around the 2-hour mark, give or take a few dozen minutes. But again, runtime will be entirely up to the director's artistic vision.

VIII. Conclusion

Having your first taste of what type of stories Melville wishes to relay from the preceding "Remarks," I feel you've gained the last tool you'll need to wade into what I'm sure you'll find are excellent adventures and romances.

Working with each of the seven books, my confidence of purpose tells me any open mind reading these scripts and *then* going back to read the originals will see my interpretations are not only sound, but the most directly honest way of understanding the action as documented by Melville.

He lived Redburn's trials and triumphs and then fictionalized them for broader, more Transcendental purposes than just making personal keepsakes.

As you come to the end of the series, you will encounter a brief appendix where I've gathered some choice quotes about the quality of Melville as a writer. Hopefully, you'll see for yourself through these screenplays just how vital Melville's legacy is to us today.

AC Benus,
San Francisco
November 21, 2020

Polynesian Text Note

Melville spelled Polynesian words and placenames in the best way to assure his readers pronounced them correctly. Therefore, as an example, he spells Taipi as "Typee."

I have retained Melville's spellings in script places where he's denoted a proper name and one of his characters speaks it. For the descriptions and notes I have tried to use the standard spellings now in use. When encountering these words or names, please remember the 'rule' on pronunciation more or less follows the 'every letter pronounced' standard English-speaking students of Spanish are taught. The vowels present the largest hurdle — which is why Melville spelled them as he did — but they too follow the general precepts familiar to most people from studying Spanish: a always equals an "ah" sound; e = "eh"; i = "ee"; o = "oh"; u = "oogh".

Introduction Text Endnotes

[1] Melville quote: from letter to Nathaniel Hawthorne, September 1851. See the Series Appendix 5 (Volume 3, page 277) for the full battery of surviving love letters Melville wrote to Hawthorne.

[2] John Brooks Moore quote: from "Introduction" to *Pierre, or the Ambiguities* (New York 1929), ps. xxi-xxii.

[3] The Name Thing: Redburn is an unusual moniker to be sure, and a few months before Melville's first novel of *Typee* was released in England, a long anonymous poem was published in New York called "Redburn: or the Schoolmaster of a Morning." As its composition follows a time period corresponding to Melville's stint as a boys' schoolmaster, it seems this Redburn too belongs to the author, although scholars continue to debate the possibility. The poem in its entirety can be found here:

https://archive.org/details/redburnorschoolm00melvrich/page/n3/mode/2up

[4] Camp humor: this same section of *Moby-Dick* indulges in 'wicked' wit concerning the name of the Inns Ishmael encounters: they are all overtly phallic. There is the *Sword-Fish*, the *Crossed Harpoons*, and ultimately the place our hero is looking for, *The Spouter!* Almost to prove the anatomical point of the joke, the one possible place of accommodation that is not wanted is *The Trap*.

[5] Gilbert's *Damon v. Pythias*: another secret-not-so-secret Gay work of art shows up in the early repertoire of composer Arthur Sullivan. The comic imbroglios of J. Maddison Morton / F.C. Burnard's *Cox and Box*, which Sullivan set to music in 1866, are too detailed to go into here, but the story deals with another Gay trope of the 19th century — the "confirmed bachelor." Messrs. Cox and Box belong to this category and have a HEA with each other by the end of the operetta. For this is when they declare themselves to be "brothers," and hilariously confirm they are not actually blood-related. They intend to live harmoniously with one another for the rest of their lives (away from the grasping women who lured them into unwanted betrothals). The term "brothers" of course means same-sex partners, and at least in 19th century American farming, "brothers" of this type dotted the agricultural landscape. They would buy land together in some corner of a place they did not come from and live out their own Zeke- and Shorty-style *happily-ever-after*.

The libretto for *Cox and Box*, a "Triumviretta in One Act," can be found here:

https://www.gsarchive.net/sullivan/cox_and_box/cox_box.pdf

[6] 19th and early 20th century Gay marriage conventions: in addition to contracts and Wills, a third legal means couple had to protect their joint assets was through adoption. The older partner legally adopted the younger to make him his closest living relative for a post-mortem retention of wealth by the survivor. A famous example is Walter Plunkett, costume designer for *Gone With the Wind*, who adopted his partner Lee in the mid-20th century.

[7] Lucy Larcom quote: from *Similitudes* (Boston 1854), ps. 36-37.

[8] "He takes on…" bigotry: it's interesting to note that a project Melville pitched to write jointly with Hawthorne involved a woman who would take on the role of hero. This was, or would have been, his second land novel. The project is usually denoted as "the Agatha story," and it's possible the book was finished and published under the title "The Isle of the Cross." For more information, see here:

https://en.wikipedia.org/wiki/Isle_of_the_Cross

[9] Second Larcom quote: from "Butterfly in the Dust," *Similitudes* (Boston 1854), page 26.

[10] *Moby-Dick* as a "wicked" book: from letter to Nathaniel Hawthorne, September 1851. See the Series Appendix 5 (Volume 3, page 277) for the full battery of surviving love letters Melville wrote to Hawthorne.

[11] "Let me people go": in Chapter 89 of *White-Jacket*, Melville speaks of rape, in guarded tones, aboard naval vessels. As the biblical Lot's neighbors were destroyed for attempting to rape unwilling male visitors, the author's remarks harken to the traditional view of what 'the sin of the cities of the plains' truly refers to. Sadly, Melville relays that reports of forced sex were unwelcomed by the authorities: "More than once, complaints were made at the mast of the *Neversink*, from which the desk officer would turn away with loathing, refuse to hear them, and command the complainant out of his sight." Perhaps the reason for this was the lack of a means — or willingness — to establish consent. Which would mean since discreet consensual sexual contact was ignored, so too must be that which may have started mutually but went awry; and then drags in the last category of out and out rape as a blind spot to this lenience. That regular crewmembers, like Melville in the voice of his White-Jacket protagonist, would not associate sex with their equals in age and status as an infraction is borne out by many other passages in the book. I'll briefly give two more of them:

> From the wild life they lead, and various other causes (needless to mention), sailors, as a class, entertain the most liberal notions concerning morality and the Decalogue; or rather, they take their own views of such matters, caring little for the theological or ethical definitions of others concerning what may be criminal, or wrong. (Chapter 10)

And this:

> You see a human being, stripped like a slave; scourged worse than a hound. And for what? For things not essentially criminal, but only made so by arbitrary laws. (Chapter 33)

[12] Wordcount and runtime data: wordcounts are per Microsoft Word; runtimes are per IMDb. All tallies are approximate.

SECRET
MELVILLE

The only real journey, the only true 'Fountain of Youth,' is not to eternally seek out new destinations, but to view them as if with refreshed eyes; to see the universe with the eyes of another, of a hundred others; to see the hundred universes that each one of them sees, that each one of them is.

—Marcel Proust

Secret Melville 1:

REDBURN

From Man to Boy – His First Voyage

———————∿∿∿∿∿∿∿———————

"Then I was first conscience of a wondrous thing in me . . . and was lost in one delirious throb at the center of the All. A wild bubbling and bursting was at my heart, as if a hidden spring had just gushed out there; and my blood ran tingling along my frame, like mountain brooks to spring freshlets."

—Chapter 13

Based Upon the Novel:

Redburn:
His First Voyage

Being The
Sailor-boy Confessions
and
Reminiscences of the
Son-of-a-Gentleman,
in the Merchant Service, 1849

by Herman Melville

———————·····~~~~~~~~~~~·———————

[Part 1 — Letting Go — I: A Soul to the Sea]

EXT. VILLAGE ON THE HUDSON — MORNING

A descending view unfolds over rooftops and smoking chimneys; over trees in early summer fullness; down to the riverbank; a quay, and along the berthed side of a green-hulled paddle wheeler. This is one of many ferries that ply the Hudson. A whistle **BLOWS**. [1]

EXT. QUAY AND GANGPLANK

From a low angle, **REDBURN** and **PETER** bump their way through the crowd and rush up the gangplank. The whistle **BLOWS** again, and **MEN** hoist the gangplank onboard.

INT. CROWDED PROMENADE DECK OF FERRY

The back shoulders of Redburn and Peter make their way through a chatty and festive crowd. They are not as well dressed as the other passengers. Redburn wears a red hunting jacket, a billowy cap, and has a homemade calico bag slung over a shoulder. Under his left arm is a rectangular mahogany case about 24" by 10", by 4" high. Redburn's long hair is tied back with a black ribbon. They push ahead; the opening and blue sky of the foredeck is in front of them. [2]

EXT. BOW OF FERRY

Out in the open, Redburn and Peter catch their breath and lean on the railing over the now-advancing prow. Redburn is nineteen, and Peter, a tall and comely man, is in his late twenties. Peter's glance is one of concern for his kid brother; he knows the teen is not prepared for the world. Redburn beams in expectation, and both turn to watch the river be cut by the ferry's prow. Redburn puts his right arm around his brother's waist and hugs him. Peter raises his arm and places it on Redburn's far shoulder, then squeezes him closer two or three times.

EXT. SURFACE OF WATER

The paddlewheel slaps still water into foam and raises soaking blades into the air. The prow creates whitecap wakes on the Hudson.

FADE IN: TITLE CARD: "The Secret Melville, REDBURN, From Man to Boy — His First Voyage"

While credits roll, shots of the water lift to show a perfect early summer day. Old-growth trees along the riverbank arch branches far over the water. Behind them, a blue plate-glass sky shines with cotton candy clouds. A rising shot of the branches, and slow ascent into the leaves, shows all of them in varied animation from the June breeze. Under the images and text of the credits, the title SONG "Loomings" plays:

Just as rill to rivulet
A creek to a torrent
A stream to a river hike
And a delta rushing waters free —
Follow any path you like
They all lead a soul to the sea.

A boy follows his own image —
Just where Narcissus had a seat —
Where fair heads will encourage
The moving waters to meet
His inextricable fortune
Where good and bad join again.

For as rain melts into the land
Gathered by pull of gravity
Channels swell to meet demand
That grow still more forcefully
To find their way to the ocean
And start the cycle again.

(recap: "Just as rill to rivulet..." etc.)

[Part 1 – II: Arrangements]

EXT. LOWER MANHATTAN WHARF STREET – NOON

A small square is faced on two sides by low, old buildings, much neglected and battered by exposure to the bay. Cobblestones lead back to storefronts and taverns. One shop sports three gilded orbs on a rusted iron frame. The sign above it reads: **"Port-Of-Call Pawn Shoppe."** To the left of the square, a street skirts the Hudson. Docks jut out where several green and white ferries are moored. There is a great deal of wheeled and foot traffic. By the ferries, well-dressed **MEN, WOMEN** and **CHILDREN** rush to and from the boats and hail cabs. In the square and by the shops, **SAILORS, HUSTLERS,** female **PROSTITUTES** and street **URCHINS** meander about. The barefoot urchins hawk newspapers, apples, etc. Working **MEN** push barrows and drive wagons and **WHISTLE** and **HOOT** at the rent- boys and girls. [3] Redburn and Peter come through the crowd, intent on what is unseen behind us. They pause, free of the crowd, and stare.

EXT. LOWER MANHATTAN WHARF

From their point of view, the street bends around, and tall ships line dock after dock. Their yardarms and rigging cut across a blue and summery sky, while behind and over them, seagulls sail and cry.

INT. SAILORS' TAVERN

The large room is bright from mullioned windows onto the square. Redburn and Peter stand facing each other, one elbow each on the bar. Over Redburn's shoulder is the door and front window; over Peter's, the room, which Redburn surveys with open curiosity. Older **SAILORS** sit in groups of three and four at tables, while hovering near them, and leaning against walls, younger **SAILORS** chat and stay attentive to the older ones. Redburn's eyes follow a few choice specimens. Between the brothers on the bartop is a plate of sugared donut-holes and two open ginger beer bottles. Redburn's case sits on the counter by Peter, his hat rests by the teenager's elbow, and his bag is tossed to his feet. Peter has to strike Redburn's arm to get his attention. Redburn grins and pops a donut in his mouth.

PETER
It looks good on you.

Redburn stops chewing — a few grains of sugar fall from his mouth as he looks puzzled.

REDBURN
Huh?

Peter picks up and shakes the loose-fitting shoulders of the hunting jacket.

PETER
**This old shooting jacket of mine; it's just the thing. A bit big,
but you'll have room to fill it out.**

Redburn continues chewing through a grin. He takes a swig of ginger beer, and his eyes follow a handsome sailor walking past him. He wipes his mouth with the back of his hand.

PETER (CONT'D)
**Look, I know it's not sailor garb, but it's warm; it saves you the
expense of another; it has fine long skirts...**

Peter pokes his brother's gut.

PETER (CONT'D)
...Stout horn buttons...

Peter tickles him a moment.

PETER (CONT'D)
...And plenty of pockets.

Peter dives his hands into the front pockets on the skirt of the jacket. Redburn playfully shoves him away and they wrestle for a moment. A sick cast creeps across Peter's face. He stands upright, pulls out his handkerchief and coughs into it. It is a hollow, consumptive cough. Redburn's grin is instantly gone. Peter stops, looks into his hankie, and quickly hides the slight hint of blood there from his brother.

PETER (CONT'D)
**If we had the money — we'd send you out in the finest sailor
gear: a new cap and monkey jacket — for a monkey boy — but,
as it is...well, that's why you have toted father's fowling piece**

down the Hudson. Pawning it will at least give you pocket change.

Weighed down with worry for his brother, and the responsibility of reclaiming a family heirloom, Redburn's eye is suddenly caught by the frank stare of a young sailor. Despite himself, he inhales in excitement. **TOBY**, with dark curly hair, and in his early twenties, leans on a wall and holds his gaze. Emboldened by the spirit of adventure, Redburn partially smiles and nods at Toby. Toby, abashed, looks into the mug in his hand. Peter knows what his brother is doing behind his back, and blinks a few sad times as he takes a drink of ginger beer.

PETER (CONT'D)

It's hard to believe. Some boys at nineteen are men already; others, still boys. It's difficult to conceive that my kid brother is ready to venture into the rough world.

REDBURN

(excited)

You know for months I've been poring over the New York papers – the shipping columns – and the ads that possess the strangest, most romantic pull on me are the South Sea voyages; maybe on a whaler!

Peter shuts down Redburn's excitement.

PETER

Not for a brother of mine. Your mother and I agree: a quick passage on a clipper or schooner and a lively trip back to us from England is best.

Redburn is crestfallen, but Peter jocularly punches his shoulder.

PETER (CONT'D)

I've found a ship – the *Highlander* – set to sail tomorrow for Liverpool. We'll see if she is right for you.

Redburn has a great deal of affection for his brother as substitute father.

REDBURN

Do you remember how Father, some evenings by the fire after telling us of Paris and London, with quickening breath, would say one day I was destined to be a great voyager – just as he had been.

PETER

One day always stays one day. Had you only heeded that – but today – today, you leave us. I only pray it won't be a leave-taking for good.

Redburn chuckles and fingers a donut.

REDBURN
Too dower, brother — too dower. Soon enough, like Father, I'll
be back to our cozy drawing room relaying my adventures to
an eager auditory.

Redburn pops the donut in his mouth; grins.

PETER
You go to sea a boy, mounted with dreams of glory, and leave
no heavy hearts but those in your own home. You take with you
the one and only true supporter of your actions — the heart that
beats strains of wanderlust in your bosom.

Redburn smiles at his brother with warmness.

REDBURN
Too dower...

PETER
Your mother and I know there is no misanthrope like a boy
disappointed, no December blast so bleak as his looks. So, go
your way. Adventure yourself enough to want to come back to
us.

Peter stands upright; pats his pockets.

PETER (CONT'D)
Look, now. You have the stationery I gave you?

Redburn nods; picks up his bag.

PETER (CONT'D)
Use it. Write your mother at least once a week.

REDBURN
I won't be able to post—

PETER
Never mind that. Write to her every week; every day, if you can;
even if you have to hand-deliver them to her yourself.

REDBURN
Yes, brother.

Peter starts buttoning his coat and drops a nickel on the counter.

PETER
Look lively, boy. We have to get you shipped!

Peter walks past Redburn towards the door. Redburn shoulders his bag, pops his cap
on, and drains his ginger beer. The bell attached to the door **RINGS** — Peter is leaving.
Redburn sloshes his brother's bottle and drains it too. Glancing at the door, he uses his

cap and tips the plate of donuts into it. He turns and jogs to the door. Then, a slow descent comes to rest on the mahogany case on the counter. The bell **RINGS**. In another moment, Redburn's hands come and grip the case. He lifts it, but Redburn stops; an odd expression creeps over his face. Through the room, Toby walks towards him with a half-smile. Toby seems like he intends to walk past him, so Redburn reaches out and arrests him by the arm. Toby pauses, but says nothing.

REDBURN
I...just tell me – what is your name?

TOBY
(warm smile; shy look)
Toby.

[Part 1 – III: Save me the Pleasure]

EXT. DOCK OF THE *HIGHLANDER* **– AFTERNOON**

Turning off the street, **PETER** leads **REDBURN** along a wharf. Redburn's cap is on his head; the donuts transferred to his pocket. With wide eyes, to his right is a ship with sparkling clean rigging: a clipper. On the left is an aging tub – a midsize barque – with dingy rigging and stained hull. Redburn's gaze tracks the approaching figurehead on the dingy ship: a six-foot-tall Scotsman in 'full fig.' A bit overly manly, he is thus tipped to the fey side. He's arrayed from head to toe with a blue cap; a mass of strawberry blond hair, curly beard and mustache; a fearsome face with a crooked nose apparently broken in a bar brawl; a ruffled shirt; a tight-fitting blue waistcoat with brass buttons. In addition, his right elbow is extended and bent to end in a fist near his heart. Under his left arm is a bagpipe with the reed in his mouth. His kilt is yellow and blue plaid; his left knee is raised; and he has yellow calf-socks and blue pumps. He is surprisingly vibrant compared to the ship he heads. Redburn trails past 'Donald,' and scans the name of the vessel: **HIGHLANDER**. [4]

EXT. MAIN DECK OF THE *HIGHLANDER*

PETER steps on deck from the gangplank. The **SECOND MATE**, an African American in his mid-thirties, is caulking a hatch nearby. He stands and pushes his knit cap back a bit on his forehead. Peter sees him and strides up to him confidently. **REDBURN** sheepishly appears at the head of the gangplank, and **JACKSON**, a skinny man in his mid-thirties with no hair, jaundiced skin, and one twitchy wall-eye, stares at the boy irritably. He starts to move towards him.

PETER
Good morning. Is your captain, Captain Riga, on board
at this time?

SECOND MATE
Aye.

Peter points astern.

PETER
Is that his cabin?

SECOND MATE
Aye.

PETER
Thank you. Good day.

Peter glances over his shoulder, expecting to find his brother there. He is not. He sees him still by the gangplank.

JACKSON
What'ye want, baby-boy?

Peter steps up and takes Redburn by the elbow. He gives a friendly nod to Jackson.

PETER
Let's go.

Peter leads the way to the cabin. Redburn glances back at Jackson, who makes a show of hocking phlegm and spitting on the deck. He never takes his eyes off of Redburn.

INT. CABIN OF THE *HIGHLANDER*

Paneled in mahogany, the room has a desk and smaller round table. The table is covered, and a place setting is laid for lunch. Along the wall opposite the door is a built-in credenza. **CAPTAIN RIGA** works at his desk with his head down. He is in his fifties, well-fed and wears clothes better suited to a high-priced lawyer. **LAVENDER**, with a long yellow silk scarf tied on his head as a turban, arranges dishes of food on the credenza. He wears a slightly big snuff-colored swallowtail jacket and breeches with taupe stockings and shoes. He is a light-skinned African American teenager. **KNOCK; KNOCK.** Lavender looks to the Captain, who flicks some downward fingers at him. The Steward opens the door, and **PETER** strides in with a nod and smile. As Peter moves to the desk, **REDBURN** trails in, lingering by the door. Lavender returns to stand by the credenza, and Redburn makes eye-contact with the handsome young man.

PETER
Good morning, sir!

CAPTAIN RIGA
(rising)
Good morning to you, sir.
(to Redburn)
Good morning, lad.

REDBURN
Good morning, sir.

CAPTAIN RIGA
Steward, bring chairs for the young gentlemen.

PETER
(to Lavender)
Oh, never mind. We are fine.

Riga is miffed. This bit of impoliteness means he will have to stand too. Redburn comes deeper into the room; leaves the door open.

PETER (CONT'D)
(to Riga)
I merely called to see whether you want a fine young lad to go to sea with you. Here he is.

Peter needlessly gestures to Redburn.

PETER (CONT'D)
He has long wanted to be a sailor, and his friends and family — for I am his brother — have concluded to find a quick first passage to test his resolve, and — well, frankly — his fitness for a life at sea.

Riga puts his hands behind his back and paces up to Redburn.

CAPTAIN RIGA
Ah. Indeed?

Redburn stiffens as Riga moves behind him. Suddenly Redburn's cap is knocked from behind and falls into his hands. Lavender snickers, and Redburn tries to suppress a smile. Riga emerges from the other side.

CAPTAIN RIGA (CONT'D)
I like him. He seems to be a fine fellow.

Riga suddenly turns and comes close to Redburn's face.

CAPTAIN RIGA (CONT'D)
So, you want to be a merchant-sailor, my boy, do you?

As Redburn opens his mouth, Riga turns and singsongs back to his desk.

CAPTAIN RIGA (CONT'D)
It's a hard life, though — a hard life.

Redburn thinks the Captain is playing with him.

REDBURN
Well, sir, I am ready to prove myself; more than ready, sir.

CAPTAIN RIGA
(to Peter — confidentially)
I hope he's a country lad. These city tykes are mostly 'hard cases.'

PETER
Oh, yes! He's from the country, and of a highly respectable
family. His great-uncle died a senator.

Riga grows half hostile; half sardonic.

CAPTAIN RIGA
But his 'great-uncle,' the senator, won't be shipping with
the lad, will he?

PETER
Oh, no – OH...

Peter thinks it's a joke; laughs.

PETER (CONT'D)
...No...!

Riga mimics Peter's laugh; turns to Redburn.

CAPTAIN RIGA
You know there's no country-life of coddled eggs and jugs of
milk onboard a ship.

REDBURN
Yes, sir, I know. My father crossed the ocean, even if I haven't.

PETER
Yes, our father was a gentleman of one of the finest families in
America, and he crossed the Atlantic several times on important
business.

Riga's insolent tone reasserts itself.

CAPTAIN RIGA
Ambassador, extraordinary?

Peter hardens at the realization of Riga's mock.

PETER
No. A fine and prosperous textile merchant.

CAPTAIN RIGA
(incredulous)
A son of a gentleman?

Riga gestures to Redburn, but intentionally slights both brothers. Peter draws in a deep
breath to suppress his growing anger.

PETER

Certainly. He is only going to sea for the humor of it. We wanted him to travel with a tutor, but he is an erring and headstrong boy — so he <u>will</u> go as a sailor. You'll sign him on as a ship's 'boy?' Or, do we need to find better passage?

CAPTAIN RIGA
(sits)
Well. It so happens, we are in need of a 'boy' —
gentleman's son or not.
(to Redburn)
Shall you and I finish the paperwork?

PETER
(sitting too)
I shall sign for him, as he is still a minor.

Riga opens his desk drawer and makes a great show of extracting the ship's articles. He and Peter bend heads and begin to go over details. Redburn glances at Lavender, who seems to be suppressing riotous laughter. Redburn turns, sees the open door, and noiselessly exits.

EXT. MAIN DECK OF THE *HIGHLANDER*

Sailors stand around. **DUTCHIE,** a short, red-haired man in his mid-forties; **BLUNT,** a dark-haired and sprightly twenty-five-year-old with clothes too big for his body; **THE GREENLANDER,** a tall Nordic type, twenty-eight, with long strawberry-blond hair in a ponytail and a commanding build — all talk to **JACKSON.** As **REDBURN** wanders forward, they cling around the boy.

DUTCHIE
Twig that coat of his! Tell us, sonny, how'd ya Pa pay
for buttons like those?

The sailors laugh. Dutchie whips off his cap and squeezes it while genuflecting before Redburn. He holds out supplicant hands.

DUTCHIE (CONT'D)
Oh, please, sir. Just one for the baby, sir. Just one for the poor!

Blunt helps Dutchie stand.

BLUNT
Leave off 'im, boys — that chappy ain't going to sea. No, not
dressed like that he ain't.

Blunt puts his arm around Redburn's shoulder.

BLUNT (CONT'D)
He must be setting out to 'do a spot of hunting' — sea elephants
I suppose!

Redburn raises his arm and detaches Blunt, but Dutchie is right back in front of him, pinching his lapel and fingering a button.

DUTCHIE
Say, matey — lookie here — tell a chap how one goes about liquidating heirlooms like those — scrap 'em by the pound?

Dutchie yanks on a button. Redburn looks down, and Dutchie's finger comes up to flick the tip of Redburn's nose. The others laugh, except Jackson who refuses to join the merriment. Now it's the Greenlander's turn. He sidles up and grabs Redburn's shoulders as Blunt had.

THE GREENLANDER
Now — you ruffians — leave off the lad. Leave off, do ye hear?

The Greenlander partially smiles and holds steady on Redburn's eyes.

THE GREENLANDER (CONT'D)
I suppose his ma wouldn't let Little Darling here go to sea without stuffing those great big pockets with sweetmeats — hand 'em over!

The Greenlander shoves his fingers in Redburn's front coat pockets. Redburn twists and shoves The Greenlander's hands out of his private region. The Greenlander is utterly surprised to be holding a donut. He laughs and holds it up for everyone to see; the sailors laugh riotously as The Greenlander pops it into his mouth. He chews and gleefully eyes Redburn. The commotion leads the **FIRST MATE** and the **SECOND MATE** to storm over. The First Mate is a big man, about thirty, dresses like an expensive accountant, and has good humor written on all his features. The sailors back off a bit, fully exposing Redburn.

FIRST MATE
(to the crew)
Hush, you rascals! The night shift is trying to get some shuteye.
(to Redburn)
And, you! Ashore with you, young loafer! There'll be no stealings on this vessel. Sail away, ya hear!

REDBURN
I ship tomorrow with you.

SECOND MATE
As what, Pillgarlic — as what!

REDBURN
A ship's 'boy,' sir.

The Mates are amazed, and dismayed.

FIRST MATE

Be gone with ye, I say. You and your shooting jacket. Ship tomorrow? What as, a games-keeper? As a hound-runner? — Disassemble I say, young one, disassemble!

REDBURN

But I do. My brother signs the ship's articles as we speak.

SECOND MATE

If you're going to sea, then where's your sea chest; your gear?

Redburn peevishly holds up his bundle.

SECOND MATE (CONT'D)

Well, lad, if that's all you prepared for; all you think worthy for a hard life at sea, chuck it over the bulwarks — you won't need it anyway!

The sailors laugh.

FIRST MATE
(slowly warms)

Now listen here, my fine punky lad, whatever your doddering old dam christened you with — it won't do onboard this ship. You need what the French tars call a *nom de mer*, get me? And I'm the one who gets to pick it.

SECOND MATE
(laughs)
'Doddering ole dam!' You know what a
dam is, pogue?

REDBURN
A dog's mother

There is a riot of laughter from the sailors.

SECOND MATE
(scolding)
'A dog's mother.' Well, what the First Mate is calling you son,
in a sophistic's way, is a son of a—

The First Mate slaps a hand on Redburn's shoulder and roughly half-turns him. He flicks Redburn's ponytail, and spins him back around forward.

FIRST MATE (CONT'D)
As for a name.... Long hair, eh? Red shooting jacket, eh? From
now on...
(announcing it to the crew)
...You will be known as 'Redburn.'

The First Mate bends down, half-squints and winks so none can see but Redburn.

FIRST MATE (CONT'D)
Fathom?

REDBURN
(bucking up)
Yes, sir.

FIRST MATE
First lesson, lad: there are no 'yes, sirs' on ship! You will say
'Aye, aye' from now on. Got it?

REDBURN
Yes... Aye, Aye. Sir!

FIRST MATE
And save the 'sir' for Captain Riga.

The First Mate walks away, telling the sailors:

FIRST MATE (CONT'D)
Green as grass — a regular cabbage-head.

Redburn is surprised and stiffens to find Jackson suddenly right next to him. Jackson speaks slowly, with menace.

JACKSON
Hayseed in your hair; cow shit behind your ears. It's greenhorns
like you that have been the death of many a sailor like me.

Jackson jerks his chin to the bulwarks.

JACKSON (CONT'D)
Go to. Follow the Second Mate's maxim and chuck yourself
overboard — save me from the pleasure.

Redburn starts as his brother's hand rests on his shoulder.

PETER
Come along. This ship will do nicely.

Peter compels Redburn to the gangplank. There he pauses and makes Redburn look at him.

PETER (CONT'D)
Now we must turn Grandfather's piece into some useful cash.

Peter taps the box and nearly dislodges it from Redburn's grip.

[Part 1 — IV: Yellow Pawn Ticket]

INT. "PORT-OF-CALL PAWN SHOPPE" — EARLY EVENING

The **PAWNBROKER**'s hands grip the mahogany case. He is a man in his late fifties, dressed in old-fashioned tails, and sports an embroidered smoking cap on his head. He sets the case on the counter with care and opens the lid. A hand-forged fowling rifle is disassembled in fitted and green felt-lined compartments. The inside lid is taken up by an enormous white label with a Royal Warrant. The Pawnbroker's face, despite effort, cannot conceal his wonder that such a piece walked into his shop. He eyes his clients **REDBURN** and **PETER** with shrewdness. [5]

PETER
It's worth twenty dollars. What will you
lend on it?

PAWNBROKER
(sour-face)
Twenty dollars...?

There is a commotion at the next window. The **ASSISTANT** hands the Pawnbroker a man's large diamond signet ring and gestures to the **HUSTLER** standing nervously at his window. The Hustler is an Irish-looking lad, 16 or 17, with slightly pimply face, a cap tightly squeezed in his hands, and rough clothes, but his neck is flourished with a colorfully tied scarf. The Pawnbroker browbeats him.

PAWNBROKER (CONT'D)
**And where would a rapscallion pogue like you get a grown-
man's signet ring?**

The Hustler looks around, not wanting Peter and Redburn's scrutiny.

HUSTLER
I ain't stole it. He give it me.

PAWNBROKER
'Give it,' for what?

HUSTLER
(steely)
That's 'tween me and the gentl'man.

The Pawnbroker sets the ring coldly on the counter in front of the Hustler.

PAWN BROKER
You stole it.

HUSTLER
(gets heated)
I ain't. I works for it. He paid me with it.

PAWNBROKER
Work?

The Hustler gets anxious, grabs his ring and makes for the door.

HUSTLER

I ain't took it!

PAWNBROKER
(shouts)
**Don't come back. <u>Your</u> kind aren't welcomed here! Tell your
little-birdie *faygeleh* friends too!**

The Pawnbroker calms himself by straightening his smoking cap by the tassel. He
remembers the gun.

PAWNBROKER (CONT'D)
Now — such an old-fashioned piece, made…?

PETER
Eighteen Hundred Five.

PAWNBROKER
OH — So old; but — not old enough….

PETER
**It's worth every penny of twenty dollars. What will you
lend on it?**

The Pawnbroker purses his lips; eyes the piece covetously.

PAWNBROKER
Um…three dollars.

PETER
Five dollars!

PAWNBROKER
OH — So hard to bargain with. Four dollars.

PETER
Four dollars.
(to Redburn)
It's less you have to pay back.

EXT. "PORT-OF-CALL PAWN SHOPPE" – DUSK

PETER stands facing the ferries; he peers at his watch. **REDBURN** closes the door
behind him. He has four dollar bills in his hand. Peter presses a yellow pawn ticket into
his brother's palm with the cash.

PETER
**Here. You keep it safe. If something delays you — if you decide
not to return — then both of you will be away from the family,
possibly forever.**

Redburn holds the ticket up to his brother's eye level. He makes a show of putting it in
his inner coat pocket.

REDBURN
I will keep it safe.

Peter lurches for his handkerchief; a coughing fit overtakes him. Redburn steps forward to support him, but Peter waves him off.

REDBURN (CONT'D)
Brother...take care...

Peter holds up his hand for Redburn to wait, then catches his breath. He can't contain his emotions anymore.

PETER
It's I who should bid you 'take care of yourself.' And hear another 'take care' from your mother's heart, if but from my lips.

Redburn hugs his brother's waist hard. Peter slowly lowers his hands onto Redburn's back to hug in like kind. Redburn pushes back to hold his brother's eye.

REDBURN
You bid me do what I must, and I ask you to do likewise. For who among us, self-imposed castaway or not, would not solemnly promise to look after himself, seeing that no one else will.

The ferry whistle **BLOWS**. Peter forces a handshake, and jogs across the street. He disappears in the crowd.

REDBURN (CONT'D)
Farewell, brother. You do not know the magic of your kindness upon me yet — but I swear — you will one day. Take care....

Redburn turns to gaze upon the forest of masts. Behind them, the sky is edged in crimson, and seagulls crisscross the air.

[Part 2 — The Passage Over — I: Water-Rat]

INT. FORECASTLE OF THE *HIGHLANDER* — NOON

Like a Turkish bath, thin columns of light pierce the dusty air from bottle-bottom skylights. More light comes through the open hatch. Wide bunks line the bow section, with sea chests tucked below. The uprights between the bunks each sport a tin whale oil lamp on a gimbal, several of which are lit. **REDBURN** sits barefoot in the middle of the floor. To his side is a pile of rope scraps; in front of him, a piggin. He pulls apart the fibers and stuffs them into the piggin. **DUTCHIE** and **BLUNT** sit in their bunk facing each other; **THE GREENLANDER** sits on a sea chest to the side of them. He wears his favorite green and white scarf. The three play cards. **JACKSON** broods alone in the bunk no one will share with him. **MIGUEL** lies face up and motionless in another. He is down to his tee-shirt and trousers, and a large serpent tattoo snakes up his forearm. The light from the hatch falters; the **SECOND MATE** takes a few steps down.

SECOND MATE
(shouts)
Seveda! Get your scurvy-ridden carcass on deck, now!

There is no reply.

DUTCHIE
Miguel ain't roused yet. He's still where the shore crimp dumped him yesterday, a'fore we sailed.

THE GREENLANDER
Drunk as a skunk...

The Second Mate retreats, muttering to himself.

SECOND MATE
I have to run this goddamned ship by myself...

DUTCHIE
(knowingly)
Maybe the lad's too hot.

Dutchie gets up to undress Miguel.

JACKSON
(commandingly)
Leave off. He ain't in need of a sea-ma. Let him sleep it off in peace.

Dutchie gives Jackson a cold sneer, but sits back down. The Greenlander sniffs around.

THE GREENLANDER
Ain't you fellows smell that?

DUTCHIE
Must be bilge water shaken up by the ship's fresh roving.

BLUNT
I suspect it's a rat — one caught and died among the hollow spaces in the side planks.

Blunt raps on the hull.

JACKSON
Could be. They smoked out this forecastle a couple of days ago, sending all our rat companions straight to hell. Had to shovel them out of the hold....

Jackson climbs out and goes over to Miguel. He makes a show of kicking Redburn's scraps around.

THE GREENLANDER
Blast that rat! Blast all goddamned rats!

Jackson leans towards Miguel's mouth; his bad eye narrows and twitches.

JACKSON
He's blasted, for sure.

Jackson rights himself and turns.

JACKSON (CONT'D)
No land-variety dead here. It's a fellow water-rat,
shipmates, that's dead.

Jackson lifts Miguel's arm and lets it fall lifeless to hang below his bunk. Simultaneously, Redburn and the men stand up. Redburn steps in his piggin and makes a mess. He squats to his knees to gather, and Dutchie nearly trips over him.

DUTCHIE
Don't be sittin', still picking your infernal oakum!
Move aside, boy.

Redburn stands like he's been stabbed, and presses his back against the far bunk.

DUTCHIE (CONT'D)
Let me see.

Jackson steps away, to under the hatch, and Dutchie pulls a lit lamp off of its holder. He slowly leans the light to Miguel's face. The **FIRST MATE** calls from the top of the hatch.

FIRST MATE (O.S.)
Where's that damned Miguel?

JACKSON
He's gone to the harbor where they never weigh anchor.

Jackson begins to cough.

JACKSON (CONT'D)
Come down! See for yourself.

As seen from Miguel's face, Dutchie nears with his own face and the lamp. The hatchway **FLUTTERS,** followed by loud **STOMPING**; the First Mate descends. Dutchie speaks as if to himself.

DUTCHIE
Ho. He's not dead.

Dutchie brings the lights close to Miguel's lips, and a methane-blue jet of flame sparks from Miguel's nostrils and the corner of his mouth. In a horrible moment, his whole body is on fire with the same smokeless fire, and Dutchie reels back.

DUTCHIE (CONT'D)
My God...

Everyone in the forecastle sees; Miguel's eyes are open; his mouth curling into a scowl as the flames consume his remains. Now his clothes catch, and smoke begins to blanket his form. **HISSING** crackles as water begins to vaporize. Redburn is horrified. He sees the blue flame spread down to animate Miguel's snake tattoo into a writhing omen of hell.

FIRST MATE
Don't stand there — smother him!

The Greenlander grabs a blanket. He covers and pats Miguel.

BLUNT
Saints alive.

JACKSON
Take hold of it.

Jackson and the First Mate rush over to the Greenlander's side.

JACKSON (CONT'D)
He must go overboard.

The Greenlander pulls the sheets from Miguel's bunk over the body and the men lift up the bundle.

JACKSON (CONT'D)
A few moments more and he can sparkle all he likes with the phosphorescent jewels of the dark sea.

Jackson goes out of his way to approach Redburn with the body.

JACKSON (CONT'D)
Out of the way, pogue!

Jackson elbows Redburn's chest and sends the teenager to the floor reeling in pain; Redburn smacks the back of his head on a bunk rail. Dutchie, like waking from a dream, eyes the fallen boy confused. He realizes he still holds the lamp and puts it up. Dutchie goes to work, telling Blunt.

DUTCHIE
Here, Blunt, take this too.

Dutchie strips the mattress and shoves it at Blunt.

DUTCHIE (CONT'D)
Send it overboard.

BLUNT
(crosses himself)
Heaven have mercy.

Blunt bundles the bed gear; Dutchie tosses two pillows on top. He goes to the hatch and asks Redburn.

BLUNT (CONT'D)
Did you see him burn? He burned like those Protestants lining up to roast in that Calvinistic Hell of theirs.

From halfway up the ladder, Blunt turns and says before he goes.

BLUNT (CONT'D)
God pity the bastard – God pity us all.

Redburn stands; rubs the back of his head.

DUTCHIE
Redburn, you go along. Run to the cookhouse. Tell the Doctor what's happened and fetch a pot full of red-hot coals.

REDBURN
Yes...aye, aye.

From halfway up the ladder, Dutchie stops him.

DUTCHIE
And, boy – get a fistful of coffee beans too. Go!

EXT. DECK OF THE *HIGHLANDER*

From a low vantage, **REDBURN**'s feet and lower legs come running up. After a cut, the same angle shows Redburn going back more carefully. In one hand he has a saucepan held away from his body; in the other, a tied bandana full of coffee beans.

INT. FORECASTLE OF THE *HIGHLANDER*

DUTCHIE is alone and busy stacking a few boards. **REDBURN** cautiously descends the ladder.

DUTCHIE
Good lad. Now, see, in cases like this, we always smoke out the bunk...

Dutchie takes the pot. Sets it in the center of Miguel's cleared out bunk.

DUTCHIE (CONT'D)
You've got the coffee beans?

Redburn gives him the bandana. Dutchie unties it and pours beans over the coals.

DUTCHIE (CONT'D)
Now, we let it work.

Dutchie sits on the floor; pats the floor next to him. Redburn sits.

DUTCHIE (CONT'D)
That poor fellow was one of the regular crew, but prone to drink himself stupid. That's why we had him rounded up by the crimps. Know ye what a crimp is, son?

Redburn shakes his head.

DUTCHIE (CONT'D)
A crimp's an agent. If you know who you're looking for, they're handy. But out in England they're different. It's big business there. There they haul any 'able-body' onto ships that need crew, then they walks off with cash, and the boob wakes up bound for Borneo, or Malacca, or God knows where. Some of 'em, the crimps that is, dump men they drugged — dope or laudanum — and the captains don't care. After they wake up, what are they going to do? Walk home?

Redburn laughs, which causes him pain. He touches the back of his head.

DUTCHIE (CONT'D)
Speaking of England, lad, can ye dance?

REDBURN
Dance?

DUTCHIE
Aye! When we put ashore in Liverpool, you'll have to hold up the honor of the *Highlander*.

Redburn is lost.

DUTCHIE (CONT'D)
See, we'll have to train you up proper so you don't disgrace the whole ship's company. When we go to some sailor tavern, the various boys of various companies dance. The best company gets a round all around for the best dancing lad. See?

REDBURN
I see. I'm willing to learn.

DUTCHIE
Good spirit, lad; good spirit.

Dutchie stands and regards Redburn with ominous intensity.

DUTCHIE (CONT'D)
As for that Jackson, stay away from that lot, boy. He's like a rabid slave-catcher's hound dog. Don't let him smell the fear on you. He'll cut ya to shreds. To shreds. Up! We must nail the unfortunate's bunk shut for the duration. It's tradition.

Dutchie grabs a board. Redburn grabs the other end and they position it. Dutchie draws back the hammer.

DUTCHIE (CONT'D)
Death. Ain't we all slaves to you....

He drives the first nail.

[Part 2 – II: Storm]

EXT. MAIN DECK OF THE *HIGHLANDER* – TWILIGHT

Squalls of intermittent rain sheet across the deck. **SHOUTS** from members of both the day and night **CREW** on the main yard make **REDBURN** look up to them as lighting turns them brighter than daylight for a brief moment. Above them, the higher sails are still set. Various other members of the **CREW** dash about deck. **THUNDER** rumbles. Redburn goes up to different groups to help, and each time is told to go away. The **FIRST MATE** bumps into him as he is giving orders.

FIRST MATE
Come on, lads, lively! We still have the topsails to reef. The storm is soon upon us!

Redburn's attention is drawn by **CAPTAIN RIGA**, already in his nightclothes, but with an overcoat on top. He stomps and paces the quarterdeck as he shouts at the **FIRST MATE**. While thus employed, **LAVENDER** comes out with an umbrella, which he opens, struggles with in the wind, and positions over and behind Riga's head.

CAPTAIN RIGA
God damn it! Why'd I hire a nursery-school marm instead of a First Mate?! Get those goddamned sons-a-bitches to haul the yard around!

Riga feels the umbrella smack the top of his head. He knocks it out of Lavender's hand, and the wind takes it to sea.

CAPTAIN RIGA (CONT'D)
You stupid mulatto! You want to get us struck by lightning!

Redburn slowly shakes his head in disappointment; Riga is not the man he thought he was. Lightning flashes again and the deck tilts from side to side. Redburn tries to steady himself, but begins to look green in the gills. He rushes to the bulwarks, pushing **THE GREENLANDER** out of his path, who in turn watches Redburn bend himself over the side and vomit. **THUNDER** rolls. Recovering and trying to right himself, Redburn whips around and steps right in front of **JACKSON** and two other members of the **CREW**. The other sailors sidestep him, but Jackson grabs the teenager by the lapel. The Greenlander knocks **DUTCHIE**'s arm and gestures to the unfolding scene.

JACKSON
Don't cross paths with me, boy!

Jackson glowers at Redburn with his bad eye.

JACKSON (CONT'D)

What business do you, pogue, have going to sea? Eh! Taking bread out of the mouths of honest sailors; nicking a good seaman's place? Punk, if you ever get in my way again, so help me Beelzebub, I'll be the death of you. If you chance to stumble in the rigging near me, I'll pitch you in the drink without so much as a second thought. Try me.

Redburn punches Jackson's grip away.

REDBURN
(slow)

You try it, old man. I may be a boy, but if being a man means I'm ground down to a wretch like you, may I always stay a kid. As for your threat, do your worst. We'll see who comes out on top.

JACKSON

Watch it, boy. Though your sail may be ascending and mine descending, I could still do you a nasty turn on the way down.

Seemingly out of nowhere, Dutchie is there pulling at Redburn's arm. He speaks to him in a loud voice for all to hear.

DUTCHIE
Come with me, young scapegrace. It's high time you
prove your mettle.

Dutchie bends his head and whispers in confidence.

DUTCHIE (CONT'D)
Rub this in Jackson's face.

Dutchie spins Redburn to face the assembled crew. He raises his arm and slowly points an arc up the mainmast.

DUTCHIE (CONT'D)

That sail, the fifth, the highest — that's the main-skysail. I know it looks no bigger than a cambric handkerchief, but, my boy, it must be furled. Yes, that little sky-scrapper, just behind them clouds — well, tumble up there, Redburn, and take him in, I say. That's work fit for boys, and not 'old men,' like me.

All the crew cheer on Redburn, except Jackson, and buoyed by the adrenalin still in his system, he jumps onto the rope ladder.

THE GREENLANDER
Careful, boy — that yard is fixed at the top, not the bottom.

Redburn nods and climbs through the increasing wind and rain.

EXT. MAINMAST OF THE *HIGHLANDER*

REDBURN climbs fast. Below him, the **CREW, CAPTAIN RIGA**, and **MATES** watch him. At the point where the rope ladder ends and 'Jacob's ladder' begins — straight up the mast — he looks down, and looks sick. He pants slightly, draws in fresh air and heads up. Rain falls into his eyes that are trained on their goal. Lighting flashes.

EXT. LOWER YARD OF THE SKYSAIL

THUNDER peals. Peering down, the deck seems miles away as **REDBURN** sways with the mast. Straddling the yard on one side of the mast, he holds on and squats. He undoes the pins securing it. After they are out, he pauses a moment, looking out to a horizon edged in crimson/orange light; dark clouds overhead. As seen from above Redburn, the rain falls flat on top of him. He raises his head to it, closes his eyes and delights in the sheer thrill of it. There is shouting from below.

FIRST MATE (O.S.)
Loose it, boy! Loosen it!

Redburn stands. With his free hand, he cups his mouth.

REDBURN
(shouts)
Hoist away!

In a near-instant, the yard under him begins to rise, taking Redburn with it. Seen from above, he rides it like a bull; one arm waving in the air for balance. As the lower yard comes to rest on the top yardarm, lighting flashes and Redburn punches the sky in triumphal defiance.

REDBURN
(shouts)
Yes!

EXT. MAIN DECK OF THE *HIGHLANDER*

THUNDER peals as the **CREW** gathers around give **REDBURN** backslaps. **DUTCHIE** and **THE GREENLANDER** lead him forward. Redburn's adrenalin quickly fades and he begins to look greener than ever. Dutchie talks to him in warm tones.

DUTCHIE
You need some little better outfit to wear. We'll see what my chest can spare. That cap of yours won't do — just won't do.

Redburn stops; puts a hand to his mouth and runs to the bulwarks. He nearly folds himself in two — backside in the air — hurling over the sides.

DUTCHIE (CONT'D)
Greenlander, minister to the boy's queasiness.
You've got 'medicine' to spare.

Dutchie slaps the Greenlander's back and moves away chuckling. The Greenlander eyes Redburn's backside, licks his lips, and says to himself.

THE GREENLANDER
My pleasure.

[Part 2 — III: Tender Ministrations]

INT. FORECASTLE OF THE *HIGHLANDER* — NIGHT

Miguel's bunk is boarded shut. All the lamps are lit. The ship rises a bit fore and aft with the inclement seas, and **REDBURN** lies in his bunk with **THE GREENLANDER** standing by his side. He puts the back of his hand to Redburn's forehead, and the boy stiffens at the man's touch. However, he melts again looking into those clear blue eyes.

THE GREENLANDER
Seasick, lad?

REDBURN
Aye.

THE GREENLANDER
Sit up, now. Sit up — I have just what your head needs.

The Greenlander pulls out his sea chest, opens it and extracts a silver hip flask. He smiles at the teenager, closes the lid and stows the chest. He comes up, opens the flask and wipes the mouthpiece on his sleeve.

THE GREENLANDER (CONT'D)
Nurse on this, baby-boy. It's kinder than any mother's milk.

Redburn takes it; sniffs it; glances blankly at his shipmate.

THE GREENLANDER
(knowingly — half laughs)
What?

REDBURN
(gulps air)
I signed the anti-drinking pledge, at our village
temperance meeting.

The Greenlander comes in close; looks around; winks.

THE GREENLANDER
I won't tell, if you won't.

Lovingly he pushes the flask to Redburn's lips. The boy sips deep and smiles sheepishly.

THE GREENLANDER (CONT'D)
Sip on it, boy. Some of that does more good than many
nights' sleep.

Redburn sips on his own, and The Greenlander grins and musses the front of the lad's hair. He turns and goes to a shelf near the hatch. Redburn's eyes follow his well-built back. The Greenlander pulls down a sealed tin, opens it and pulls out several sea biscuits. He comes back holding them up.

THE GREENLANDER (CONT'D)
Nibble on three or four of these while you sip, and you'll be
shipshape by morning.

Redburn reaches out, but instead of taking the biscuits, he touches The Greenlander's fingers. The Greenlander sets the food down, and holds his hand open for the boy to systematically explore its rough and soft spots. Redburn pauses on one of The Greenlander's silver rings.

REDBURN
Are you really from Greenland?

THE GREENLANDER
Aye, lad.

REDBURN
So far away...

As Redburn gently twists the ring, The Greenlander pulls back a moment. He pulls it off, and drops it onto Redburn's thumb. Redburn watches as he rotates it in his other hand, then returns his attention to the now-sad-looking gaze of The Greenlander. Redburn reaches out the hand with the ring on it, gently stroking the man's cheek with the back of his fingers.

REDBURN (CONT'D)
Greenland...hard to believe.

THE GREENLANDER
Aye, I'm from Greenland; Dutchie is from Holland; and you
Yanks are from the wilds — Perspective, lad, is just a matter of
being close enough to see yourself in others.

REDBURN
You see something, in me? Something familiar?

THE GREENLANDER
Aye. Very familiar.

Redburn's fingers move back to The Greenlander's earlobe. He feels the gold loop with the anchor on it, and then lets go to renew a long sip from the bottle. He laughs freely, just like the boy he is.

REDBURN
Do your earrings mean anything?

THE GREENLANDER
Aye, lad.

The Greenlander reaches down and grabs Redburn's right lobe with some force.

THE GREENLANDER (CONT'D)
Right is for rounding the Cape of Good Hope; left, Cape Horn.

REDBURN
(admiringly)
You've been around the world...
(slyly)
...Gold looping your ears, silver banding your fingers; I'd a thought a sailor left his jewelry at home.

Frowning affectionately, and licking his lips, The Greenlander comes in close. He grabs Redburn's cheeks from below – around the chin – and rocks his head from side to side.

THE GREENLANDER
We will see, nug. [6] **One day you may be man enough to let me pierce those virgin ears of yours myself.**

The Greenlander slaps the boy's cheek; just hard enough so Redburn will remember it. He hears a noise, turns and sees **LAVENDER** halfway down the ladder. He stands upright and advises Redburn.

THE GREENLANDER (CONT'D)
Get some rest.

Lavender is down, and The Greenlander pushes past him going up the ladder. Redburn watches his backside; smiles.

[Part 2 – IV: Good Night]

INT. FORECASTLE OF THE *HIGHLANDER*

LAVENDER strides over to **REDBURN**.

REDBURN
You're not wearing your fancy – I mean – colorful clothes.

LAVENDER
Off-duty. That's only in the cabin.

REDBURN
No turban?

LAVENDER
That's only when we're berthed, or onshore. Sea air ain't too
good for silk.... Say, it's best we two bunk up. You don't want
to get put with Jackson.

REDBURN
Don't say his name.

LAVENDER
He don't bunk with nobody anyhow; too distrustful. So?

Redburn smiles broadly and pats the mattress next to him. Lavender hoists himself up,
and slides in over Redburn's legs. The two lie in a comfortable, chatting position.

REDBURN
I hear the fellows call you Lavender — why do they do that?

LAVENDER
Smell.

Lavender tips his head to Redburn's nose.

REDBURN
Um.

LAVENDER
Captain likes it. I first got in the habit working as a brush-up boy
in a barbershop on Broadway. Barber would dress my hair with
nice smells. You like it?

REDBURN
(sly smile)
I do.

LAVENDER
How old are you?

REDBURN
Nineteen.

LAVENDER
Really — a year older than me — you seem younger. Well, share
your medicine, son.

Redburn and Lavender enjoy a hefty swig.

LAVENDER (CONT'D)
The Greenlander is always talking about the ladies. He knows
what a good-looking fellow he is. If you credit what he says,

seems he's some sort of 'Lady Sailor' — on about one here, one there — each port, a lady waiting for his lovin'.

REDBURN
But, you think otherwise...

LAVENDER
Think?

REDBURN
Know, then.

Lavender changes the subject.

LAVENDER
I saw you there — this evening. It looks like you were born to the sea, like you've got brine in your blood.

Lavender takes a swig; Redburn frowns in concentration.

REDBURN
We all do. Someone — well, one book of mine — says our blood has the exact saltiness as the sea. We're told God crafted us from a bit of mud and a dab of His own spit. I fancy God's spit is plain old seawater to you and me.

LAVENDER
(sympathetically)
The seamen treat all greenhorns rough. Don't take it to heart — they think it's their job.

REDBURN
I haven't seen any of them — the sailors — treat you badly. On the other hand, the Captain...

LAVENDER
Look, for the sailors, I do what I can to keep...mutual trust. I can be their friend or their enemy, and they get more being a friend to me. But they sure don't have no respect for you.

REDBURN
When Jackson attacked me — it was all I could do to keep holding my breath — to choke down the rising sobs, for what could I help feeling then — any boy in the world would have felt the same. I don't want to be full of hate...

Redburn's mood shifts; he slowly twists the ring on his thumb, drawing Lavender's attention to it.

REDBURN (CONT'D)
But — some of them are nice.

Lavender grabs Redburn's thumb and draws it and the big ring to his face.

LAVENDER
The Greenlander's one of them respects me the most.
We get along.

Lavender drops Redburn's hand; turns serious.

LAVENDER (CONT'D)
Don't let that Jackson get to you. He may be a big bully, but that's only because his great days as a sailor are behind him. He's the weakest man — bodily; spiritually — of the whole crew.

Redburn scans the earnestness of Lavender's face with his own intensity.

REDBURN
I have no doubt, though young as I am, I can throw him down. But he has such an overawing way about him; such a deal of brass, and...recklessness; such an unflinching face — withal one so hideous — that Satan himself would run from that mortal.

They laugh; drink.

REDBURN (CONT'D)
But, tell me, why has he no beard, no eyebrows, no hair?

LAVENDER
Have you not seen a walking corpse? He had the Yellow Fever, and survived — in a manner of speaking.

REDBURN
That's why his skin is so sallow? So, saffron-colored?

LAVENDER
That's why his nose is broken down in the middle. But worse, stay your distance, for now he's got the hollow-ringing cough of a consumptive. Don't breathe his deadly breath.

REDBURN
But what explains that eye? I'd defy any oculist to turn out a glass eye half as cold; a third as snaky; a quarter as deadly. By rights it must have first lodged in the head of a she-wolf, or some lank and starving tigress.

LAVENDER
It's looking on his own mortality, and he's too ornery
to die on land...

REDBURN
...Nothing left but the foul dregs of a man – I would pity him,
but he's still dangerous. But why, why does he hate <u>me</u>?

LAVENDER
Don't you see? With each second you become a piece of the
sailor he was. His hate of you is his grip on life – he lets loose
of one, the other falls too.

Lavender takes Redburn's hand again, this time he doesn't let go.

LAVENDER (CONT'D)
And, because you are young, and handsome.

Redburn turns a half-smile into Lavender's too serious eyes. He takes his hand away
and musses the front top of Lavender's head the way The Greenlander had his. He
turns his head back, and rests his hand on his tummy. Lavender slowly laces his fingers
with those on Redburn's stomach, and slides his other hand below Redburn's waistband.
Redburn turns back, offers mild surprise, but soon closes his eyes as Lavender expertly
pleasures him. Soon his breaths are labored and choppy. As he begins to climax, he
arches his back, and silently pleads with Lavender, but as the other does not desist,
Redburn rolls his eyes back helplessly. While he orgasms, Lavender rests his lips on the
side of Redburn's mouth to catch his out-of-control breaths. Before Redburn can recover,
or even fully open his eyes, Lavender has withdrawn his hands, and rolled onto his side
away from Redburn.

LAVENDER (CONT'D)
Good night, Redburn.

[Part 2 – V: Breakfast]

INT. FORECASTLE OF THE *HIGHLANDER* – MORNING

Through the darkness, sounds of men's **VOICES** come to **REDBURN.** He opens his eyes;
blinks. His head is heavy, but his stomach is fine. Members of the **CREW** stand at the
counter by the hatch. Some shave, other with soap and washcloth stand naked and
bathe. There is jocular camaraderie. Redburn quickly puts his hand on Lavender's side
of the bunk. He is gone.

DUTCHIE
Up, boy.

THE GREENLANDER
Leave him be – he's sick.

Redburn sits. He feels fine, though he wonders why he is covered in crumbs. As he
brushes them off, his voice is gruff; no one listens to him.

REDBURN
I'm well...

> JACKSON
> Damn it, Blunt! Last night ye were at it again.

Blunt is massaging in hair oil before a mirror.

> JACKSON (CONT'D)
> You sleepwalked right to the damn mirror and rubbed your
> scalp for an hour. Can't you recall?

> BLUNT
> (shrugs)
> Didn't hurt you none.

> JACKSON
> Yeah, but sometimes you shout in your sleep — like the dead's
> after you — then it bothers us.

> DUTCHIE
> Why are you riveted to that hair tonic anyway, boy?

The Greenlander grabs Blunt's head in a friendly way and tilts it to Dutchie's inspection.

> THE GREENLANDER
> Can't you see? Young Blunt here is graying down the center!

Blunt pushes free. Redburn launches himself down, stretches, shivers and puts on his jacket.

> DUTCHIE
> Vanity — thy name is youth…

> JACKSON
> Looks like he goes about with a badger skin cap on his head.
> Better suited for the hills of Kentucky than the plains of the
> Atlantic.

> DUTCHIE
> Run, lad; go and fetch our breakfast.

Redburn blinks.

> DUTCHIE (CONT'D)
> To the cookhouse. Go along. Run!

EXT. DECK OF THE *HIGHLANDER*

From a low vantage, **REDBURN**'s lower legs and bare feet come running up with determination.

EXT. COOKHOUSE OF THE *HIGHLANDER*

A schoolchild's slate with attached cord hangs by the door. On it is neatly chalked: **Dr. Thompson, Esq.** The door is open. **REDBURN** braces both hands on the frame and stares inside.

INT. COOKHOUSE OF THE *HIGHLANDER*

The **COOK** is at his stove, stirring a pot and whistling to himself softly. Opposite the stove is a fixed bunk. **LAVENDER** sits on it, eating from a bowl. Both look blankly at **REDBURN.**

REDBURN
(explains)
I'm here to fetch the porridge.

Redburn glances at Lavender; cops a half-smile.

REDBURN (CONT'D)
Morning.

Lavender nods and glances at the Cook, then into his bowl. The Cook stands akimbo, a dripping spoon at his hip.

COOK
You mean 'Burgoo.' Never was any 'porridge' on ship.

REDBURN
Yes, sir.

COOK
**You will not call me 'sir.' Call me what all ship's cooks are
called — Doctor — or, Mr. Thompson.**

The Cook pulls down a shallow eighteen-inch-round tub from the shelf over the bunk. While talking, he pours the steaming contents of the pot into it, eventually picking it up and shoving it into Redburn's arms.

COOK (CONT'D)
**They need to teach you proper argot — words — ain't none of
them teaching you? Now, take this here 'kid' — the tub, not you
— down to your mates, and tell them to start teaching you the
vocabulary — get it? — the lingo.**

EXT. DECK OF THE *HIGHLANDER*

From a low vantage, **REDBURN**'s feet and lower legs go back more carefully. He has the kid balanced on both arms.

INT. FORECASTLE OF THE *HIGHLANDER*

All members of the **CREW** are now dressed and sitting on stools in a nearly complete circle. In the center is an empty stool. **JACKSON** presides from the bow. Each sailor has a tablespoon at the ready. **REDBURN**'s shadow darkens the hatch, and **DUTCHIE** jumps up.

DUTCHIE
Hand it, boy.

Dutchie takes the kid and places it on the center stool. As Dutchie sits, and Redburn walks up, Jackson stands with all eyes upon him. He bends over the kid and spoons out a large hollow on the center of the burgoo. The Greenlander hands him a quart-sized redware jug, and Jackson pours a stream of molasses into the cavity. Redburn salivates.

JACKSON
All right, boys, dig in.

From the kid's point of view, the sailor-spoons scoop burgoo and dip themselves into the molasses. There is concord, as no spoons vie for the same space. Redburn stands dumbfounded.

REDBURN
(to himself)
I don't have a spoon. Why don't I have a spoon?

A frantic Redburn turns and runs up the ladder. The sailors eat contentedly. Soon Redburn is back with a small stick he found on deck. He pushes his way into the circle and sticks his twig into the food, close to the molasses. All the sailors stop and glare at an unaware Redburn. Jackson stands, and knocks the stick to the floor.

JACKSON
Is twigs what they stir their tea with in the country?

The sailors laugh.

JACKSON (CONT'D)
Sticking splinters into our burgoo! Son of a gentleman, my ass.
Couldn't that gentleman Pa of yours afford a gentlemanly spoon
for his offshoot?

The sailors laugh again. Redburn sits and dejectedly watches the burgoo disappear. Blunt glances over, sighs and sticks the whole bowl of his spoon in his mouth by way of cleaning it. It offers it to Redburn.

BLUNT
Here, Pillgarlic — puppy dog eyes belong
on land, with those sticks of yours.

Redburn grins broadly and surveys the contents of the kid. There is only a little on the far side; by Jackson. Redburn stands and stretches his reach. Jackson raps Redburn's knuckles with his spoon. Redburn recoils in pain.

JACKSON
Rules, boy. Learn 'em! You help yourself from your side;
your side only.

Redburn rubs his knuckles and scraps the bottom and sides of the kid near him. Finally he pops a measly portion of Burgoo into his mouth as the others laugh. Redburn hands the spoon back to Blunt.

REDBURN
Thank you.

THE GREENLANDER
Up, boy – fetch us our coffee.

INT. FORECASTLE OF THE *HIGHLANDER*

Members of the **CREW** smoke, each with a cup in hand. **REDBURN**'s shadow darkens the hatch. He descends carrying a large tin coffee pot. Dutchie takes it and put in on the center stool. The Greenlander pours a cup, stands and hands it to Jackson. Then he pours another and presses it into Redburn's hand.

THE GREENLANDER
Blunt, take over.

The Greenlander goes over to the biscuit tin, comes back and has Redburn sit next to him. As Redburn sips, The Greenlander opens the tin and produces a couple of biscuits. He passes the tin on and takes the cup for a drink, handing it back.

THE GREENLANDER (CON'D)
Lad, break it like this.

The Greenlander fractures the hard cracker atop Redburn's head, then presents his own scalp for Redburn to reciprocate. He does, and everyone laughs, except Jackson. Round the circle, the breaking of bread continues. A smiling Redburn musses a few crumbs out of his hair; then shakes himself like a dog. The Greenlander puts his hand on the back of Redburn's neck affectionately, and gives him a couple of gentle pulls.

[Part 2 – VI: Slush]

EXT. MAIN DECK OF THE *HIGHLANDER* – AFTERNOON

It is a chill day with intermittent sunbursts. Members of the **CREW** go about their business. The **SECOND MATE** comes up to **REDBURN**. Redburn now wears a proper brimmed hat, loaned from Dutchie.

SECOND MATE
Redburn! Slush down the maintop sail.

Redburn blinks at him blankly.

SECOND MATE (CONT'D)
We must grease it so it hoists smoothly. Run to the cookhouse.
Doctor Thompson will give you what you need. Run.

EXT. MAINMAST RIGGING

REDBURN climbs with a small bucket in his left hand. A brush dangles from a cord tied to the bail handle.

SECOND MATE (O.S.)
Not a drop! Not a single drop on my beautiful deck,
you hear, boy!

EXT. ABOVE THE MAINMAST TOPSAIL

REDBURN arrives at where the yard meets the mast. He situates the bucket, then sniffs it, making a repulsed grimace. He slushes carefully, watching his footing.

EXT. MAIN DECK

JACKSON and **BLUNT** watch Redburn working.

BLUNT
Looks like that greenhorn was born on water. He already hops
about the rigging like Saint Jago's monkey. The kid's fearless.

JACKSON
(scoffs)
Says you, Irish Cockney.

Jackson thumbs his nose at Blunt, coughs a few times, then his one evil eye drifts in profile back up to Redburn.

EXT. MAINMAST TOPSAIL

As **REDBURN** slushes, he spots something dark under the surface of the water. He pauses, soon more dark objects join the first. He stands and hangs as far over the yard as he can with one hand on the mast. As sunshine bursts through, the objects grow lighter and break the surface in arching succession. Blowholes send jets of water skyward one by one.

REDBURN
(shouts down)
Sea-elephants! Starboard side!

EXT. MAIN DECK

Members of the **CREW** run to the starboard bulwarks. They **SHOUT** greetings at the breaching whales.

EXT. MAINMAST TOPSAIL

REDBURN smiles uncontrollably.

> **REDBURN**
> I'll be damned.

EXT. SURFACE OF THE WATER

Whale flukes gently glide into the foaming water and disappear.

[Part 2 – VII: Of Mermaids and Sailor Love]

INT. FORECASTLE OF THE *HIGHLANDER* – NIGHT

Members of the **CREW** sit, smoke, and delicately pick the last remains of dinner from their teeth.

> **REDBURN**
> What kind of whales were they?

> **DUTCHIE**
> Pilot whales.

> **JACKSON**
> No.

> **THE GREENLANDER**
> Sperm whales.

> **JACKSON**
> No – have none of ye shipped on a whaler before?

A look goes around; no one volunteers a positive reply.

> **JACKSON (CONT'D)**
> Sperm whales are monstrous things, like mountains on the sea
> – hills and valleys of flesh! Regular krakens meant to create tides
> high enough to inundate continents when they descend the
> depths to feed. The only thing more monstrous is what they hunt
> on the bottom – that's why they have teeth like ivory pegs, and
> faces scared from battle.

> **REDBURN**
> What do they hunt?

> **JACKSON**
> (glazing over)
> Worse than our worst nightmares...

Jackson comes to.

JACKSON (CONT'D)
But what we saw today weren't no sperm whales;too small!

THE GREENLANDER
Right whales

JACKSON
Not so. Their spouts ain't bushy enough — it wouldn't be right to
say so. I tell ye, men, them Crinkkum Crankum whales.

Jackson breaks into a black smile; he hates gullibility. A series of knitted eyebrows pass
from sailor to sailor.

BLUNT
(under his breath)
Blarney. Pervert.

REDBURN
Why, what's he mean?

Blunt smiles lewdly and eyes Jackson as he tells the boy.

BLUNT
'Crinkkum Crankum' means something special, boy. Not that
you would know, but it refers to a woman's, um…shall we say,
'bill of goods.'

Redburn makes a dumbfounded face. The other sailors laugh.

BLUNT (CONT'D)
And 'bill of goods,' lad — well, somewhere I read, that means
'the private parts of a decent woman, and the public parts of a
gay one.' A prostitute.

REDBURN
(pause - still dumbfounded)
What's that got to do with whales?

The men double over in laughter. The Greenlander rocks Redburn's shoulders in
affection. Eventually Dutchie gathers himself.

DUTCHIE
(to Redburn)
Don't ship with a whaler, boy. That's the lesson! It's a hard life
— blood and guts — decks awash with it — and boiling of fat night
and day; the stench of death. It does something to the heads of
them whalers.

BLUNT
But, you do get to see far corners — the Indian Ocean, and
Madagaskey where they wear no togs at all. No, all they need
is a bowline 'round their midship.

JACKSON

And what would you, Bog-jumping Limey, know about the Indian Ocean? Have ye sailed her? – No, not like me. See, I was shipped at age eleven, like this, to Liverpool, then put aboard an East Indiaman. Six blasted months at sea! There is nothing worse, so in Bombay I runs away, only out there it's tough, so I sign on a Portuguese ship. Any you lot even catch a whiff of a slave-runner? I thought not – hell afloat. As a boy it was my job first thing every morning to poke a stick tween the lines of them, stacked like knives in a box. The ones that didn't move, were dead during the night; suffocated or starved – it's the way them slave-running bastards pick off the weak ones. So we had to unmanacle them – weed the dead out from the living – and toss seawater over the rest to wash down the chained-up filth.

BLUNT
(to Redburn – half jokes)

His whole life is like this: full of pirates, plagues and poisonings. Aye, few men could have so long plunged into such infamous vices, and clung to them so firmly, without paying the death-penalty.

Blunt laughs openly, making Dutchie and The Greenlander uneasy. The Greenlander tries to placate Jackson by playing to his ego.

THE GREENLANDER
You've been chased a lot in your life, ain't you? But, you always outrun 'em.

JACKSON

Hell itself ain't as swift as vessels I've been on – opium clippers, where more than dope was traded – women for the whorehouses of Chinatowns 'round the world; slaves themselves. Ain't no pity on them – on none of us. Even the self-appointed do-gooders of this world kill and mangle. Afore I came down with the fever, I was on a slaver, just off Cape Verde, when a British cruiser starts to chase us down. As we pulls away, she sends three shots through our upper deck – their 'good deed' raked through file after file of chained human carnage. We out-sped her, but shoveling out the mess took days.
(laughs)
I'd like to have seen 'Mr. Riggs' among 'em.

REDBURN
(quietly to The Greenlander)
Mr. Riggs?
DUTCHIE
Our Second Mate.
(to Jackson)
You have a lot to atone for – don't add fresh insult.

Redburn goes ashen; The Greenlander tries to distract him.

THE GREENLANDER (CONT'D)
Here, you need it. The smoke produces a certain mellowness.

The Greenlander holds his pipe to Redburn's lips. The teen inhales and immediately breathes it out. The Greenlander purses his lips a bit and shakes his head. The crewmen continue to talk, but fade out as Redburn and The Greenlander speak in private tones while smoking.

REDBURN
Greenlander — no one talks about Miguel. Why?

The Greenlander stiffens; wonders if he should be honest.

THE GREENLANDER
They feel it just as bad as you — they don't talk about it so
Death won't notice them. It's all around us, son, Death is.

Redburn shudders — he can't believe it's true.

THE GREENLANDER (CONT'D)
Sailor superstition — learn not to show you give it a thought.

Dutchie rises and stretches.

DUTCHIE
Go to, lads. Let's clear. It's time for our
boy's lesson.

They push back, stack the stools, while Dutchie goes to his chest and pulls out a squeezebox. Coming back, he takes Redburn by the hand and leads him to the center. The men fall back. Dutchie begins to play a slow jig and stomp away. Redburn stands there not knowing what to do. The sailors begin to beat time with hands and feet, and The Greenlander jumps in with Redburn and begins to jig. He has Redburn following his steps. Soon the tempo increases, and Redburn is matching the man step for step. Darkness falls and the sounds begin to seem farther away. As the music comes to a crescendo, the men cheer.

INT. FORECASTLE OF THE *HIGHLANDER* — MIDNIGHT

The **MUSIC** transitions into the melody line of **BLUNT**'s upcoming song. Only a few of the lights are lit. Members of the **CREW** lie in their bunks; two by two, except Jackson. Gentle rhythmic **SNORING** laps the stillness. Blunt sits on his chest with a far away and pained look. He holds an open ledger and pencil. He starts to sings quietly.

BLUNT
(SINGS)
"For young men all, heed now this cry
That as ye replace; be prepared —
For though you stall, even you too will die,
And then a lad, takes your place — golden-haired.

We drop our dead in the sea,
The bottomless sea; the bottomless sea —
Each bubble a hollow sigh,
As it sinks forever and aye.

If you, mermaid, chance to find,
Please to him be kind; please to him be kind —
'Cause sent with him from the top,
Comes my love wrapped like a teardrop.

Tis night above all around,
Still without a sound; still without a sound —
Find that rest ye long have sought;
I remember, though the sea gives you not a thought.

So young men all, heed here this cry
That as ye replace; be prepared —
For though you stall, even you too will die,
And then a lad, takes your place — raven-haired."

Near the beginning of Blunt's song, **REDBURN** opens his eyes. **LAVENDER** is climbing into their bunk, looking pooped. Once he is settled, Redburn turns to him and grins. Lavender starts to lay his hands on Redburn, but Redburn gently pushes them back. Instead, Redburn's hand sinks beneath Lavender's waistline. Lavender seems surprised, but soon knows Redburn is not the novice he thought he was. As his breathing becomes labored, Redburn raises a hand and covers his lover's mouth. Lavender stiffens, and his eyes convey that he is near climax. Redburn takes his hand away and replaces it with an open mouth to share Lavender's breaths in silence. Task completed, Redburn whispers in Lavender's ear, before he turns his back on him.

REDBURN
Good night, Lavender.

[Part 2 — VIII: Playing Chicken with The Greenlander's Heart]

EXT. DECK OF THE *HIGHLANDER* — MORNING

From a low vantage, **REDBURN**'s lower legs and boots come trudging along. He is tired and stiff with soreness. He wears The Greenlander's favorite green and white scarf with the man's ring as a pass-through above the scarf's knot.

INT. COOKHOUSE OF THE *HIGHLANDER*

The **COOK** is dishing out the burgoo. **REDBURN** nods at **LAVENDER** cupping hot coffee. Lavender offers him a warm smile.

REDBURN
Doctor? How many days now have I been fetching the morning burgoo?

COOK
Oh — bout two weeks' worth of days. Or what them Limeys call a 'fork-knife.'

REDBURN
(crestfallen)
When do we reach Liverpool?

The cook raps his spoon authoritatively on the side of the full kid. He half chuckles, catching Lavender's eye. He sets his spoon down.

COOK
Not till you've doubled your morning walks.

REDBURN
(amazed)
Another two weeks...?

The cook laughs, comes forward, and wipes his hands on his apron.

COOK
It's not so bad. Land — that's about a week off.

The Cook puts a fatherly arm on Redburn's shoulder and leads him out on the deck. Lavender gets up and leans in the doorframe, spoon in mouth, to watch.

COOK (CONT'D)
And don't go around thinking 'Land-Ho' means we're in port. First, it's Ireland, son. That's when you hear 'land-ho.' It ain't the same as hearing 'Liverpool-Ho!'

The cook turns him to examine him closer.

COOK (CONT'D)
They teaching you the proper words
for things?

REDBURN
Proper?

COOK
Yeah — sea words!

He looks around; alights on a bucket.

> **COOK (CONT'D)**
> Take that. What's that called?

> **REDBURN**
> (shrugs)
> A pail?

> **COOK**
> Where? On land — that's a pail all day long. At sea — they
> all buckets, son. Get me?

Lavender chuckles and comes out to join them. The Cook winks at him slyly.

> **COOK (CONT'D)**
> What about a 'chicken?' They tell you what
> a 'chicken' is?

Lavender laughs openly; Redburn blinks at him in confusion.

> **REDBURN**
> Not the ones on land....

> **COOK**
> A 'chicken' ain't a chicken on land — there's a different term
> for him there.

> **REDBURN**
> So, what's a 'chicken?'

> **COOK**
> You is! — Well, I mean, you could be one — but first you got to get
> aligned with an older seaman. One who can look after you. Why
> — a sailor'd do anything for his young man. Do the boy's
> washing, mend his breeches — Hell, he'd comb the lad's hair, or
> stitch his buttons back — he'd do anything the 'chicken' don't
> want to do for hisself. Get me?

> **REDBURN**
> Like a...protector?

The Cook makes a sly glance at Lavender.

> **COOK**
> Yeah. Yeah — like that. And — what the boy wants to give back
> for that 'protection' — Well — that's up to him, and his sailor.

The Cook straightens The Greenlander's scarf.

> **COOK (CONT'D)**
> You The Greenlander's 'chicken,' son?

REDBURN
(reddens)
I....

COOK
Don't make no never mind to me.

REDBURN
He hasn't...asked—

COOK
Don't work that way. A sailor's boy has all the power – he gives
what he gives to his chummie – depends on how attached he
feels to the sailor. That's between you and him – I mean – tween
a 'chicken' and his seaman.

Lavender laughs again, but it slowly trails into distraction. He walks to the bulwarks;
horror spreads across his face.

LAVENDER
(shouts)
Sound the alarm!

[Part 2 – IX: Shipwreck]

EXT. QUARTERDECK OF THE *HIGHLANDER* – MID-MORNING

CAPTAIN RIGA looks with a glass. **LAVENDER** and the **MATES** stand by his side.

EXT. WRECK OF A SHIP

From the waterline, a inundated hull of a large vessel lolls in the waves. The entire
superstructure is splintered and floats about the wreck still attached by rigging, lines,
ropes *etc.* Most the bulwarks are gone, showing bare stanchions which rise about four
feet above the waves. Waves wash across her deck, and her open main hatch belches
violent breaths with every push or pull of the sea. The stump of the foremast rises about
four feet above deck; the mainmast about ten feet.

EXT. QUARTERDECK

The view from **CAPTAIN RIGA**'s glass lingers on the mainmast. A torn and bloody coat
sleeve appears to be nailed there. He can see a disembodied and shriveled hand rise
from the cuff. Panning, he pauses on three grassy-green lumps lashed and slumped
over the taffrail. These are dunked in and out of the water with each wave. He hands
the glass to the **FIRST MATE.**

CAPTAIN RIGA
They must have been dead a long time.
(to the Second Mate)
Log our current position.

EXT. MAIN DECK

Members of the **CREW**, including **BLUNT, DUTCHIE, JACKSON** and **REDBURN** gather at the bulwarks to stare at the wreck. Jackson walks behind Redburn without him noticing. He bends into the lad's ear.

> JACKSON
>
> Looky here – hie yourself to land and stay there, boy. That –
> that is a sailor's coffin. Do you see?

> REDBURN
>
> But – what are those? Those mossy things that bob like
> moldy lumps of soap.

> JACKSON
>
> Idiot. Those are them – the dead.

Jackson laughs as Dutchie and Blunt become hot; Redburn gets sick to his stomach.

> JACKSON (CONT'D)
>
> Wouldn't you like to sail with them 'ere dead men? Eh,
> pinchcock, wouldn't it be nice?

Jackson's hollow laugh turns into a coughing fit. An angry Dutchie pushes Redburn out of Jackson's way.

> DUTCHIE
>
> Don't laugh at them poor fellows.
> (to Redburn)
> You see their bodies, but their souls are farther off than the
> Cape of Good Hope.

> JACKSON
>
> (mocks)
> Good Hope. Good Hope! There is no hope, good or bad, for them,
> Dutchman. They are drowned. They are as damned as you or I
> will be one of these dark nights.

> BLUNT
>
> (crosses himself)
> No. No –
> (to Redburn)
> All sailors are saved. We may suffer squalls here below, but fair
> weather aloft. That's why so many wear an anchor on their skin;
> a seaman's cross.

Jackson forgets Redburn and circles Blunt like a shark.

> JACKSON
>
> And did you get that out of your silly dream journal, you
> Greek bunter; Gany Boy.

Blunt narrows his eyes in barely controlled wrath. He clinches his fists and tries to keep them below his waist. Redburn blinks at Blunt — he is surprised this particular insult is used in regards to him.

> **JACKSON (CONT'D)**
> Don't talk of heaven to me...
> (coughs)
> ...It's a lie...
> (coughs)

...I know it — and you're all fools who believe in it. Do you think, Grecian pogue, that there's any heaven for <u>you</u>? Will they let <u>you</u> in there with your tar-stained hands and oily slick of hair? Mind you, Irish Cockney, there's no peace for <u>your</u> kind.

> **BLUNT**
> (deliberate)

I know your fears. That some day soon a shark will gulp you down a toothsome hatchway, and you will find death only a passage from earthly gale to hellish blast. There's no forgiveness on those who can't forgive — that's your fate.

Jackson wants to attack, but stumbles away with renewed coughing.

> **DUTCHIE**
> He grows worse by the day — body and mind.

> **BLUNT**

He argues — would with the devil himself — that there is nothing to believe in; nothing to love; nothing worth living for in another person—

> **DUTCHIE**
> A Cain afloat, grudging every heart that dares course with
> life next to his.

> **BLUNT**
> (to Redburn)

Pity him, boy. There is more anguish about that man, maybe about all men, than wickedness. His evil — man's evil — springs only from his woe.

EXT. QUARTERDECK

CAPTAIN RIGA slams his glass shut. He glances at the **MATES,** before taking **LAVENDER** and going to his cabin.

> **CAPTAIN RIGA**
> Sail on. Poor wretches can't be helped by
> the likes of us.

FIRST MATE
(aside to the Second Mate)
Would he were lashed to some rotting timber for the
world to sail him by.

[Part 2 – X: Man-of-War's Man]

INT. FORECASTLE OF THE *HIGHLANDER* – NIGHT

The ships lists slowly from side to side; **RAIN** pounds the deck and closed hatch. Occasional **THUNDER** peals. All the lights are lit. **REDBURN** and **BLUNT** are alone. Blunt sits on a stool, writing in his journal; Redburn sits on a chest, writing a letter to his mother.

REDBURN
What's that you keep? Is that...

Redburn becomes self-conscious.

REDBURN (CONT'D)
...Your dream book?

Blunt does not pause in his writing. He replies without looking.

BLUNT
Do you believe you can be visited? By those we love, but
taken from us?

REDBURN
I believe my father watches over me...

Blunts raises his eyes; pleased.

BLUNT
Good lad. I'm sure he does.

Blunt leans elbows on his knees, preening towards the teen.

BLUNT (CONT'D)
Why are those doubters gloomy at the thought of the dead? What comfort is in their stone-cold 'belief?' – Belief that those we love are departed from all of our joys and sorrows; belief that those gone are indeed nothing but dead to us; that they revisit us not; that their voices no more shimmer in the air about our heads; and that even though spring must inevitably come, they cannot feel the sap renewing green life that rises in the very marrow of our limbs. Why believe at all, if not to believe <u>in</u> something?

After a pause, Blunt feels he can trust Redburn. He calls him over to sit by his side.

BLUNT (CONT'D)
I write my dreams here. This is my dream book, and I believe love can guide not only when near us, but from far on the other side too. We keep them here; as long as we need them.

Blunt places the open book in Redburn's hands. The teen cradles it and scans a passage.

BLUNT (CONT'D)
When I was a lad, a bit younger than you, I shipped on a British Man-of-War. After a year or so, we came upon a French sloop who opened fire on us. We drew alongside and had a proper battle, all guns blazing, and my — my Man-of-War's man — gave his life pushing me out of harm's way.

During a long pause, Redburn closes the book and watches Blunt's profile relive the horror of that long-passed moment. Blunt sighs, regarding Redburn squarely.

BLUNT (CONT'D)
But, if he were here today — I know he'd want me to
watch after you too.

Blunt looks at his hands.

REDBURN
(softly)
Blunt? Is that why your clothes are all too big? You
wear his gear?

Blunt rocks his head for a helpless moment; he smiles uncontrollably,
which forces out a tear.

BLUNT
Boy, when the last of his clothing is threadbare and gaunt — and can no longer shield me in the elements — I'll know. Then he'll be telling me it's time to let go — to let go of him and retire to the land.
(cheerfully)
But for now, with proper mending, his weeds will clothe me a proper lifetime at sea — and so I'll wear them with pride.

The ship lurches port; the men almost topple off their stools. The ship's bell **RINGS** violently. The hatch slams open; rains falls in with the sound of the **STORM**.

SECOND MATE (O.S.)
All hands on deck!

[Part 2 – XI: Bow and Cringe]

EXT. QUARTERDECK OF THE *HIGHLANDER* – NIGHT

The alarm bell ceases to **RING**. Periodic sheets of rain pummel the lolling deck. The mainmast topsail is ripped and flaps in the intermittent gale. The **MATES** survey the damage.

FIRST MATE
This storm squalls and rests so it's like a troop of wild horses
before the flaming rush of a burning prairie.

SECOND MATE
Hoping to be done with it – we must bow and cringe to it
for a while more.

BLUNT, JACKSON and **THE GREENLANDER** run up on the main deck to receive orders.

FIRST MATE
Take in the canvas to double-reefed-top-sail, and take the boy!

SECOND MATE
Tumble up there, my hearties, and take
in that sail!

EXT. HALFWAY UP THE MAINMAST

Ascending the port side rope ladder, **JACKSON** leads the way, followed by **BLUNT** and **THE GREENLANDER. REDBURN** trails behind. Jackson points to the yard above and yells down.

JACKSON
The sail has ripped! Run her in boys.

Jackson steps on the yard and Blunt and The Greenlander pass him quickly going up to the next yardarm. As Redburn approaches, he tells him.

JACKSON (CONT'D)
Go and tighten the spars.

Jackson points to the starboard side of the yard he is on. Redburn hurries past him to do as told. The ship lists to-and-fro slightly. From Jackson's point of view – Redburn bends to check the ropes binding the sails. A flash of lighting licks Jackson's evil eye, and his wet hand extracting his jackknife. From Redburn's view, the rain runs sideways into his face. He hears a nearby sound, turns to it. **THUNDER** snarls. Jackson is five feet away with a wild murderous intent – his knife glinting in the dull light from below. Redburn slowly rises, extending arms for balance. He glares at Jackson, daring him. As lightning again lights Jackson, a terrible smile grows desperate. As he starts to lunge, **THUNDER** roars, and Blunt swings on a rope from the higher yardarm.

He kicks the knife out of Jackson's hand. Jackson nearly topples, but gains his balance. Blunt on the return swing is helped by Redburn to stand on the yard with him. Jackson begins to back up with loathing for Blunt's interference. The Greenlander is coming down the starboard rope ladder, and Blunt guides Redburn to him.

BLUNT
Get on deck.

The Greenlander takes Redburn and helps him down. Blunt warns Jackson.

BLUNT (CONT'D)
(low tone)
This ain't over.

EXT. MAIN DECK

REDBURN jumps on deck from the rope ladder, quickly followed by **THE GREEN-LANDER**, who grabs his shoulders and looks him over head-to-toe.

THE GREENLANDER
(trembles)
Did he hurt you!

The sick-with-worry frown from The Greenlander, and raw emotion in his voice, confuses Redburn.

REDBURN
No. I...

Unaccountably to Redburn, The Greenlander hugs him just as **BLUNT** lands on the deck. Redburn spots Blunt and thoughtlessly pushes The Greenlander off of him. He goes to Blunt all smiles. As Blunt slaps his back, and the boy responds with jocular action in-kind; heartbreak seeps across The Greenlander's face.

[Part 2 – XII: Blood on the Floor]

INT. FORECASTLE OF THE *HIGHLANDER* – MORNING

The day is fine; sunlight pours down the open hatch and through the bulls eyes. Breakfast is over. Members of the **CREW** finish up dressing, and their coffee. **BLUNT**'s and **THE GREENLANDER**'s conversation becomes an argument.

BLUNT
Oh – toss off with ye. You know I shipped as a lad – how
could <u>you</u> have more sea-experience?!

THE GREENLANDER
Your time as a powder monkey don't count as seamanship. All
you did was run grunt from magazine to gun deck. There's no
shipping in that!

Blunt stiffens his spine, throws his shoulders back and swaggers before the bigger man.

BLUNT
Daft! What's come over you? Now you hate me, or something?
(sincerely)
Tell me what I've done to you — eh?!

As seen from Blunt, The Greenlander's face washes over with a micro expression of sheer sorrow. Then, he sees **REDBURN** over The Greenlander's shoulder.

JACKSON
Cease your clamor! You talk in circles. I will decide the matter.

Jackson goes up menacingly to Blunt.

JACKSON (CONT'D)
Lend us your jackknife. I've had mine misplaced for me...

Blunt looks wary, but grins and hands it over. Jackson takes it with obvious hate, but says to The Greenlander.

JACKSON (CONT'D)
Now. You come into the light.

Jackson walks to stand under the hatch. The Greenlander turns an accusation on Redburn, then grudgingly follows Jackson.

JACKSON (CONT'D)
I can tell who's been to sea longer — like a trader with
a horse. Kneel.

The crew stiffen, hating this intentional act of humiliation. The Greenlander reluctantly kneels.

JACKSON (CONT'D)
Throw your head back and open your gob.

The Greenlander swallows hard, then as he begins to open his mouth, Jackson grabs his chin hard with his left hand.

JACKSON (CONT'D)
Open all the way!

Now fear spreads across the kneeling man's face as Jackson raises the knife. It glints as it goes into The Greenlander's mouth. There is a terrible **SOUND** — steel on tooth enamel. The Greenlander closes his eyes, and Jackson speaks as if to himself, peering intently.

JACKSON (CONT'D)
I can tell a sailor's life by the wear on his teeth.

The crew are holding back; waiting for any sign of pain to leap into action against the crazy man.

DUTCHIE
(aside to Redburn)
Like a baboon peering into a junk bottle.

Jackson extracts Blunt's jackknife.

JACKSON
You're done.

The Greenlander stumbles to his feet and goes to Blunt. Jackson waves the knife loosely.

JACKSON (CONT'D)
(to Blunt)
Now you.

Blunt never takes his eyes off Jackson as he goes and kneels. With defiance, he yawns wide. Jackson grabs his chin and forces his head back. Jackson's evil eye trains on Blunt's look as he sticks the man's own knife into his mouth. A moment later, Blunt's hand comes up with force and grabs onto Jackson armed hand. He stands and a steady trickle of blood falls from the corner of his mouth. He lets Jackson go, and spits a glob of blood at his feet. Jackson turns and tells the crew with coolness.

JACKSON (CONT'D)
The Greenlander's been longer to sea.

Jackson sheaths Blunt's knife in Jackson's holster, and turns a wicked grin on his victim. Blunt purses his lips and draws back his right fist.

JACKSON (CONT'D)
Do it, bender. I'll lash you Peg Boy to mincemeat myself at the mainmast. You know the Captain would let me do it too. Well? Punk.

There is a clamor from the deck above; **FOOTFALLS, SHOUTING,** then several voices ring out one by one: **"Land-Ho!"** The crew look at one another a brief second and scamper up the ladder.

EXT. MAIN DECK

Members of the **CREW** crowd the port side bulwarks. Everyone except **JACKSON** cheers and congratulates each other. **DUTCHIE** puts his arm around **REDBURN**.

DUTCHIE
Ireland, boy. Ireland!

From the bulwarks, the rocky and verdant shore glints in dappled sunlight. White shore birds pepper the air with crisscross patterns and loud cries.

[Part 2 – XIII: Figurehead]

EXT. BOW SECTION OF THE *HIGHLANDER* – MID- AFTERNOON

The weather is clearing up. Clouds move east, the same as the ship. Near the bowsprit, **DUTCHIE** has a hammer and is nailing loose boards on the bulwarks. **REDBURN** stands by with the nails from a small bucket.

> DUTCHIE
> What do you think of Donald?

> REDBURN
> Donald?

> DUTCHIE
> The Highlander, boy – our figurehead!

> REDBURN
> I don't know. He rather frightens me.

> DUTCHIE
> Good. That's his job – to fright the sea; to defy Poseidon Himself with his bravery. Our Highlander – dressed in 'full-fig,' as they say – is game to his wooden marrow.

EXT. FIGUREHEAD

Donald rides the ripping water below his feet with sunshine glinting off of his glossy features. While **DUTCHIE** continues, Donald's details are shown.

> DUTCHIE (CONT'D – V.O.)
> In a strong gale he is glorious to watch – trekking through; ever daring the waves, upwards and down again, over vales and the heights of watery lowlands and highlands. He guides the ship that she might go foaming on her way fearlessly.

EXT. BOW SECTION

REDBURN and **DUTCHIE** continue.

> REDBURN
> But, his face – it's awful. His nose is
> out of joint.

> DUTCHIE
> Oh, lad, it's because he's scrappy.

> REDBURN
> He got a broken nose?

>   DUTCHIE
> Aye, and far worse too. Why, a few trips back, a Liverpool tree
> surgeon had to tend to his sea-brawl and sea-fight wounds. The
> good doctor proclaimed that like many an old sailor, his leg had
> to come off.

EXT. FIGUREHEAD

While **DUTCHIE** continues, Donald's replaced leg and other patched areas are seen in
detail, ending with a lingering pause on his broken nose.

>   DUTCHIE (CONT'D – V.O.)
> The surgeon worked and worked – off came the useless
> appendage – on went a new leg – a proper wooden leg, of
> course! He is a sailor after all. I'm sorry to say, as fine a
> carpenter-doctor as he had, Ol' Donald's new leg – and his new
> nose splint – never quite set right, for if you watch right close,
> you might perceive a slight limp. But, a trophy that is, and one
> that every old sea-veteran from Siam to Siberia would be proud
> to troop though any sea tavern.

EXT. BOW SECTION

REDBURN and DUTCHIE continue.

>   DUTCHIE
> No need to fear Donald, son. He watches out for us. Now – go
> fetch me some twelve-penny nails, these little ones won't hold
> here.

INT. TOOL SHOP

The door is open to the deck. **REDBURN** comes into the doorframe and stops. From
Redburn's view, **THE GREENLANDER** leans against the opposite wall. His hands are
raised over his head and holding him away from the wall. His eyes flutter open and
shut; he makes little mouth movements. Looking down, Redburn sees the back of
LAVENDER's head at The Greenlander's waist. He kneels with his hands resting on the
man's thighs, his head moves closer and away from The Greenlander in a regular
rhythm. The Greenlander opens his eyes; sees Redburn watching. He slowly lowers his
hands and presses on the back of Lavender's head, increasing his tempo. He grows
more vocal; his breaths becoming choppy; his eyes stay focused on Redburn, until he
stops pushing Lavender's head and his eyes roll back in his head. A moment later, he
guides Lavender away and does up his trousers. The Greenlander walks straight
towards Redburn, gets close enough to whisper something, but only winks slyly, which
Redburn sees with a sparkle from the diamond in one of the man's earrings. The
Greenlander shoulders past him, hitting Redburn hard. When Redburn turns back,
Lavender is leaning just as The Greenlander had been, and eyeing Redburn. Redburn
turns without saying a word.

[Part 2 – XIV: A Fair Night – The Least Puddle]

EXT. QUARTERDECK OF THE *HIGHLANDER* – NIGHT

Set sails billow and lightly rap in a fair breeze. Beyond them, a full moon sets off a dramatic skyscape. Here and there stars peek out between the rigging. The **FIRST MATE** slowly paces and looks out over the main deck; hands behind his back; a lit cigar in his mouth. Later, **LAVENDER** comes out of the cabin and climbs the ladder to the quarterdeck. He stand off a pace, taking in the sea air.

EXT. MAIN DECK OF THE *HIGHLANDER*

DUTCHIE, BLUNT, REDBURN and a couple of other members of the **CREW** lounge by the windlass. A hip flask furtively passes from hand to hand, with cautious glances towards the First Mate.

DUTCHIE
A pleasant watch. I wish I had my squeezebox.

Redburn glances aft. **LAVENDER** has moved to lean on the railing above the main deck. He catches his eye; Lavender stands, folds his arms, and an angelic voice emerges as Lavender **SINGS** the three verses of Blunt's Mermaid song. **THE GREENLANDER** comes strolling up to the windlass. He carries the lit stub of a candle and a flat box. The Greenlander's hands pulls back from a cigar box as he sets it on the windlass. A moment later, his fist comes down and breaks the top. He reaches in and brings a cigar to his teeth; biting and spitting off the tip then lighting it with the candle. He puffs contentedly, then passes the candle and cigars around as he sits.

THE GREENLANDER
(smirks at Redburn)
None for young Pillgarlic, there. His mama don't want baby-
boy to smoke – among other vices.

The sailors laugh. Redburn steels his resolve and takes a cigar. He does what he has seen and spits. The candle comes to him and he inhales deeply, immediately producing a coughing fit. The men laugh again. Blunt reaches over.

BLUNT
I'll take it.

Blunt smokes contentedly and leans back on his elbows. Above him the sails and the evening enfold peacefully over Lavender's singing.

BLUNT (CONT'D)
Such a fine night, lads. It beats all the cold and rain and
makes it seem endurable.

DUTCHIE
(to Redburn)
So, boy, we near our travel's end. Will you ship back with us?

REDBURN
Certainly.

DUTCHIE
Will ye ship again once back in New York?

REDBURN
I...

THE GREENLANDER
Take my advice, youngin — as soon as you ever get home, pin
your ears to your head so they never take wind again. Sail
straight away into the interior of the country. Don't stop until you
are deep in the bush — far from the least running river, stream or
brook — never mind how shallow — hie ye out of sight of even
the least puddle, lest the water lead you back down to the sea.
You are no sailor.

DUTCHIE
(offended)
Oh! No, you go too...he's a regular rigging monkey. Why, I
never...what's gotten into you lately, you....

As Dutchie speaks, The Greenlander casts a cold eye on Redburn, who holds his gaze,
while a single tears stains the boy's cheek.

[Part 2 – XV: A Social Call]

INT. FORECASTLE OF THE *HIGHLANDER* – MORNING

Breakfast is over. Members of the **CREW** finish up dressing and their coffee. **REDBURN**
is preening in a mirror. He is not wearing The Greenlander's scarf; The Greenlander
is; the ring back on The Greenlander's finger. Redburn wears his best trousers, a blue
shirt, and a huge scarf barrowed from Blunt, which is tied like a bow under his chin.
JACKSON is in his bunk, watching and occasionally coughing. He does not move from
there.

BLUNT
(laughs)
Must be going ashore, eh, Redburn? Just watch that first
step off the deck. It's a big one.

DUTCHIE
And wet.

REDBURN
I'm going to pay my respects to the Captain.

THE GREENLANDER
(incredulous)
'Respects?'

REDBURN
Aye. When we first met, he seemed cordial enough, and as my brother arranged for Riga to be my watch on board, I expected to be invited to the cabin — perhaps for a Sunday lunch — but now, I see the onus is upon me to make the first social call. Time is running out on this voyage, so....

All the men are wide-eyed. Blunt hush-fingers them; gesturing to play along.

BLUNT
Yes. Yes — I'm sure he'll be delighted at you calling on him.

The men round a chorus of 'Um' and head nods.

THE GREENLANDER
Aye — let him go — let him go! I suspect the Captain will have some nice nuts and raisins for him. Maybe even a donut!

BLUNT
But lad, look at your hands! Your nails are yellow from tar. Tisk, tisk — that will never do. Here — wait.

Blunt throws open his chest, roots and pulls out thick sealskin mittens.

BLUNT (CONT'D)
Not kid leather, but here, slip these on. A gentleman does not go out without his gloves.

REDBURN
(puts them on)
Thank you.

DUTCHIE
(about to whistle)
Shall I call you a carriage?

As Dutchie lets loose with a piercing whistle, The Greenlander stuffs some oakum in Redburn's pocket.

THE GREENLANDER
Don't forget your calling cards—

Blunt plants both hands on Redburn's face and smooches him loudly.

BLUNT
Present my best to our skipper.

EXT. MAIN DECK OF THE *HIGHLANDER*

REDBURN strides confidently aft, members of the **CREW** trailing in suppressed laughter. As he passes the cookhouse, the **COOK** comes out. **BLUNT** whispers something in his ear. The Cook cracks a huge grin, goes inside for a moment, then comes running with a long flesh fork. He presses it in Redburn's be-mittened hand.

COOK
Don't forget your walking stick—

As Redburn approaches the cabin door, the **FIRST MATE** stands akimbo. Redburn touches the brim of his cap with the flesh fork as he tries to pass by. The First Mate grabs Redburn by the scruff of his collar and hauls him back.

FIRST MATE
What in the name of Davy Jones' locker is the meaning of this!

He drops the lad, who straights his clothes.

REDBURN
My brother intended the Captain to tutor me aboard ship — circumstances being what they were — I have been delayed — but, this morning, I intend to visit my friend.

The First Mate is slack-jawed; the sailors laugh uncontrollably.

FIRST MATE
What do you mean playing such tricks on a ship I am the chief mate of? If I thought you even half serious, I'd lash you to the bowsprit myself.

The cabin door opens. **CAPTAIN RIGA**, face half-shaven, napkin tied around his neck, and an apple bouncing in his hand, comes out on deck. **LAVENDER**, razor still in his hand, follows.

CAPTAIN RIGA
What is this ruckus?!

Redburn runs up to the Captain. He doffs his cap clumsily due to his hand coverings. It winds up halltree'd on the meat fork.

REDBURN
It's a very pleasant day, isn't it, sir?

The Captain draws in a deep breath of shock. In a moment it flashes into rage. He throws the apple hard at Redburn's chest. Redburn is stunned, but like a ninny, he runs after the apple and returns. He holds it open-mittened before a crimson Riga, and bows.

CAPTAIN RIGA
(to the First Mate)
You will have to ripen this greenhorn.

The Captain looks like he is about to box Redburn's ears, when the **LOOKOUT** calls from above: **'Liverpool to starboard!'** The First Mate pushes Redburn aside.

FIRST MATE
Make everything aright! We are fast upon the mouth
of the Mersey.

As the crew rush about their duties, Redburn wanders to the port side bow. He leans over the bulwarks. Before him is a gloriously cloudy sky where sunbeams break down to the water and on the landscape behind. The orange-laden waterscape is fringed with whitecaps, darting puffs of seagulls, vessels with sails large and small, while beyond them, the sun-gilded spires and slate roofs of Liverpool shimmer in the wet air. [7]

[Part 3 — A Trip Overland — I: Baltimore Clipper]

EXT. STREET BEFORE "THE BALTIMORE CLIPPER" — NIGHT

The *Highlander's* **CREW** make their way through the greasy and crowded streets of Liverpool near the docks. Some streetlights and door lanterns make the scene even drabber to **REDBURN**, who trails behind. The denizens of the street are prostitutes, hustlers, street urchins and sailors from various nations. The beggars catch Redburn's eye particularly, for they trudge in the gutters barefoot and in rags. The crew pool in front of a storefront and makes a show of 'after you' as they file through the door. Redburn looks up at the sign: **"Ye Baltimore Clipper."** Above the text is a ship in full sail on a choppy sea. As he is last to go in, he notices a youth standing in a doorway two doors down on the opposite side of the street from the tavern. **HARRY BOLTON** leans heavily on the wall, both hands shoved in his breeches' pockets. He is a young man about Redburn's age, with chestnut hair and soulful eyes. He wears youthful clothes, and has an extravagant red silk scarf billowing under his chin. His gaze follows a small group of sailors passing his door; then he sees Redburn. Harry slowly stands upright. Redburn nods a greeting, and Harry touches the brim of his cap with a sly half-grin. **THE GREENLANDER** comes out and slaps Redburn's back.

THE GREENLANDER
Disassemble, Pillgarlic. Disassemble!

Redburn ducks under The Greenlander's arm. The Greenlander glances toward what Redburn had been looking at. Harry stiffens. The Greenlander slowly smiles at him lewdly, adjusts his trousers by the front of the crotch, then spits and goes into the tavern.

INT. TAPROOM

The **CREW** stand in the middle of the room, waiting. **THE GREENLANDER** pushes past **REDBURN**, and the men gather at the bar. Redburn's eyes widen, glancing around. Plush red curtains are drawn across the front windows, while every inch of wall space is plastered with old shipping notices, one on top of the other. By the time Redburn inspects the bar, the **BARMAN** has placed pint tankards before each man. **BLUNT** waves him over, and Redburn arrives to find a half-pint glass of beer on the bar for him. Drinks in hand, everyone except the teenager lifts them in the air and glances to **JACKSON.**

JACKSON
To a safely sailed voyage.

CREW
Hear; hear!

Jackson drinks; the men follow his example. After they've all drained their tankards, plunked them on the bar, wiped mouths with sleeves, there is a slowly gathering look to Redburn. He reluctantly picks up the brown ale, holds it to his nose, then sips it gingerly. He lowers the glass with a sour face and squinting eyes. The men laugh, and Blunt slaps Redburn's back, causing him to spill some beer on the counter.

INT. UPSTAIRS DINING ROOM – NIGHT – LATER

The **CREW** file in and takes seats at a large central table. **REDBURN,** last to come in, nearly gasps. The room has the same drawn curtains as downstairs, but the walls are neatly papered with hand-colored prints of ships; all in full sail and in sunny weather; the blue of all the tropical skies brightens the room. Above the table hangs a large model ship in full detail. From her hull, branches of brass arms come out to hold lit whale oil lamps. Redburn finds his seat close to the door, and sees the table is loaded with pots of mustard and horseradish, dishes of relishes, pickles, and cold cuts. Upside-down mugs are at each place setting. Tavern **BOYS** arrive with the feast. First in, to raucous **APPLAUSE, HOOTS** and table **BANGS,** is a lad with a platter overladen by a huge slab of roast beef. He goes to the head of the table and Jackson. Next in, a boy with a platter of cut squares of Yorkshire pudding, and a great sauceboat of gravy. Behind him, another carries bowls; one with steaming new potatoes topped by parsley, the other with spring peas and pearl onions. The food goes on the table, and the serving boys leave. As all quiet down, Jackson stands. He picks up the large knife and fork and slices a piece of roast beef. The first boy returns with large jugs of ale. **CHEERS** go 'round the table.

INT. UPSTAIRS DINING ROOM – NIGHT – LATER

The meal is over. Empty bowls and platters litter the center of the table. The **CREW** drink and pats their bellies. **BLUNT** scans **REDBURN**'s plate, and speaks to **DUTCHIE.**

BLUNT
Well, he might not be able to drink with the least of us, but he
can pack it away with the best of us.

REDBURN
Why does Lavender not join us?

DUTCHIE
When he goes ashore, it's never with one of us.

BLUNT
Who knows where he goes, or whom he accosts!

REDBURN
What about Doctor Thompson?

DUTCHIE
He never spends his money on shore – nor at sea, for that
matter. That old skinflint hoards every shilling for a rainy day.

BLUNT
And, when it does rains, he comes out of his cookhouse just to
see if it ever really pours pennies from heaven.

THE GREENLANDER
He must have enough money secreted away in his pot sand
and piggins to buy the *Highlander* and all her crew and cargo!

REDBURN
(amazed)
Doesn't he want a change from salt pork
and hardtack?

DUTCHIE
As for want of change, remember, the Doctor and Lavender
have ceaseless variety in the emptins from Riga's sideboard.

INT. UPSTAIRS DINING ROOM

The table is cleared; the cloth removed. Trays with short candles, tobacco jars and
pipes lay here and there. The **CREW** lean back and smoke. Some have hands behind
their heads and inspect the ceiling; others have loosened trousers, and have lifted boots
to rest on the table edge. **DUTCHIE** becomes animated. He rises and fetches something
from near the window. Pulling up his squeezebox, he speaks to the men with excitement.

DUTCHIE
Boots off, boys! Clear the table. Now, do you hear! It's time
young Master Redburn shows he's ready for the taproom.

Dutchie motions for **THE GREENLANDER** to lift the teen boy onto the table.

DUTCHIE (CONT'D)
Let's see if he can dance to do the *Highlander's* crew proud.

Dutchie plays a lively version of Bach's jig in G major. [8] The men beat out the time on
the table as Redburn dances freely. Soon the men **HOOT** and **WHOOP** in time with the
music. Redburn's face grows flush with exhilaration and pride. But from the head of the
table, **JACKSON**'s hateful glare tries to sear into the lad.

EXT. STREET BEFORE "THE BALTIMORE CLIPPER" – NIGHT – LATER

The **CREW** file out and heads back to the ship. **REDBURN** is last. Once out the door, he
looks to the doorframe Harry had been leaning against. It is empty. Dejectedly, he
lowers his head and, as he does so, catches something in the doorway exactly opposite
the tavern. **HARRY** is standing, backed against the doorframe, his hands behind him
by his rear end; standing in front of the working boy is **THE GREENLANDER**. The sailor
has his right hand on his hip, and the left extended possessively over the boy's right
shoulder to lean in close to the boy with the supporting aid of the doorframe. He is
chatting in easy low tones, but Harry appears uneasy; suppressing a desire to glance
at Redburn. In a moment, The Greenlander rights himself, drops his arm, and Harry
tries to take a half-step out of the doorway. The Greenlander purposefully knocks his

shoulder into Harry to block him. The Greenlander leaves first, and begins to stroll in the opposite direction from the ship. Two paces later, Harry turns to follow the man. He offers Redburn a shy and momentarily sad glance. Redburn watches Harry go up the street, in the wake of The Greenlander's steps.

[Part 3 – II: Of Dockwall Denizens and Sewer-Squatters]

EXT. STREET ALONG THE DOCKWALL – MORNING

A summer day in Liverpool; **REDBURN** has shore leave and is anxious to go exploring. He strolls with a glowing report from his shoes and swings an old book in his hand; his father's guidebook. But as he walks along the base of the wall, the number of beggars increases. They sit on the dirty cobblestones in motionless groupings, sunburned and with pock-scared faces. Their gnarred hands reach out to him and his clothes. As he moves along, they become packed together, sitting shoulder to shoulder, then two deep, then three deep. He begins to run, as if from a circle of Dante's Hell.

EXT. WAREHOUSE STREET

REDBURN walks on an empty street. He glances in at open loading doors, sees bales of cotton and dusty air; no people. Suddenly he hears a faint, womanly **CRY**. He pauses. There is no one to be seen. He hears it again, and locates its source. He crosses to an iron sewer grate; squats and peers in. Slowly a **WOMAN**'s filthy face emerges from the gloom. Redburn starts. She thrusts out a shriveled hand, and Redburn recoils, right onto his backside.

> **WOMAN**
> **Penny for the baby, sir.**

Redburn scrambles backwards on hands and heels till he can rise and run.

[Part 3 – III: The Exchange and Parting]

EXT. BIRDSEYE VIEW OF "THE EXCHANGE" – LATE AFTERNOON

A slow descent from the summer sky surveys a stately Georgian building with central courtyard and arcade. From top to bottom: the lead roofs glint dully, while white statues of Regency-style-dressed females stand in the cornice balustrade; down the walls, reflective window glass separates full Corinthian columns; and below them, the arches of the arcade are banded with uninterrupted horizontal molding that circle the whole court. Men in top hats and business suits mill about the enclosed plaza. **REDBURN** stands below the main arch of the gate, guidebook in hand. He knocks his cap back in wonder. [9]

EXT. CENTRAL COURT OF "THE EXCHANGE"

From **REDBURN**'s perspective, the court is large and dominated by an off-center monument. He becomes aware that many **MEN** and **YOUNG MEN** are taking note of him. He shuts both mouth and book. He slips the book into the front skirt pocket of his coat, and proceeds into the light of the plaza. He veers right, and walks along the arcade. Here in the shade, he notices that many of the young men are well-dressed, and each appears decorated with a colorful flourish of some kind; a scarf, a colorful vest or shirt, etc. As they stake out columns of their own and eye the conservatively dressed businessmen, they make a strong, hands-in-pocket, contrast. Some of these teenage boys seem to accent the quality of their idle youth by leaning shoulder blades on the columns. Many have raised thighs on display, facilitated by a foot braced on the column behind them, and a rakishly bent knee out in front. As he walks, Redburn notices the small groups of businessmen seem unaware of the boys around them, and talk 'cotton futures,' but occasionally, after concluding business with a handshake, one of these men steps up to a youth. Then, after an impossibly short exchange, the man heads for the gate. The boy invariably waits a few moments, then follows the him out to the street. Something draws his attention across the yard. Someone seems to be matching his pace in the opposite arcade. He continues walking but watches the figure. Redburn can't see detail; just that the person is the same height and size as he is. Redburn walks straight into the chest of a **MAN** standing in front of him. Redburn jolts back and instantly removes his cap.

REDBURN
I am sorry, sir. I—

MAN
Pinks, eh?

REDBURN
Sir?

MAN
Your costume – hunting gear – properly known as 'pinks.'

Redburn is desperately confused. His vision darts.

REDBURN
I...from my brother, sir.

MAN
Cunning smile. Oh, must be a strapping fine fellow, your 'big brother.' You a Yank? No one calls anyone 'sir' around here.

REDBURN
Aye....Yes, sir.

Redburn's flickering sight only partially registers a figure running across the plaza towards him. The Man creeps into a wicked smile, and bends into the American's ear.

MAN
What about it, Yank, feeling up to sorts?

REDBURN
(puzzled)
I feel fine, sir.

The figure darts into the arcade, and out-of-breath, **HARRY BOLTON** jams himself between man and boy.

HARRY
Leave off, guv'nor — he's a sailor.

The man looks around, unwanting to draw any attention. Harry pulls Redburn into the sunlight. They stop by the monument and watch the man trail through the arcade and beneath the arch. Harry smiles warmly and scans Redburn frankly.

HARRY (CONT'D)
I thought it was you. Don't see many sailors out for a fox hunt.

Harry takes off his cap to match Redburn, who is momentarily lost in the youth's lovely curly chestnut hair. He half melts in Harry's big hazel eyes before recovering himself.

REDBURN
You...outside 'The Baltimore Clipper' — what are you doing here?

Harry smiles broadly; a hand goes to the back of his head.

HARRY
Like you — out for a stroll.

REDBURN
Oh.
(pause)
I wanted to speak to you last night...

HARRY
Mutual. I as well.

After another shy pause, Harry pops his cap back on, then lifts Redburn's hat and carefully arranges it on his companion's head. He links their arms and turns them towards the gate.

HARRY (CONT'D)
Let's go exploring.

They take two steps, and then Harry swings them around one hundred eighty degrees.

REDBURN
What is it?

Harry takes them to an unoccupied column. He places Redburn against it and stands in front of him so Harry's back is to the court.

HARRY
Don't look yet...but, there's someone I do not wish to encounter. Do you see him? That man in mauve?

Redburn sees **LORD LOVELY** across the yard. He is maybe twenty-five, sports a stiff attitude and a tall walking stick. He is handsome and aristocratic.

HARRY (CONT'D)
He's an acquaintance of mine. A friend.

REDBURN
Why do you avoid this 'friend?'

HARRY
He's a London Chum.
(clearly lies)
He doesn't know I'm in Liverpool – don't know what he's doing
here himself – but it's best we don't reconnect until back in
London.

Redburn inspects this singular dandy again; the man begins to move into the
arcade opposite.

REDBURN
What is his name – is he royalty?

HARRY
(sham sigh)
Can't say. We lads call him 'Lord Lovely,' for obvious reasons.

Harry darts a glance over his shoulder, sees Lord Lovely looking the other way,
and garbs Redburn's elbow.

HARRY (CONT'D)
Come. Enough of 'The Exchange.' Let's see the rest of Liverpool!

EXT. STREET IN FRONT OF "THE EXCHANGE"

PEOPLE rush about. REDBURN and HARRY emerge though the Exchange gate.
Redburn looks at the sky and the approaching twilight. He stops.

REDBURN
I'd like to explore more with you, but I must report to my
ship. It's getting late.

HARRY
(comforting smile)
I'll walk back with you.

To Redburn's growing grin, Harry replies by linking their arms again. They head
towards the docks.

HARRY (CONT'D)
How old are you?

REDBURN
Nineteen.

HARRY
Same as me! Well, just turned Twenty. Where are you from?

REDBURN
The Hudson River Valley.

HARRY
(excited)
New York!

REDBURN
Near. Where do you come from?

HARRY
Sussex.

Redburn makes a puzzled face.

HARRY (CONT'D)
Near London.

REDBURN
Why are you in Liverpool?

HARRY
I've shipped before, you know. I thought I might get back into it.
As a lad, the orphanage placed me on an East Indiaman. Do you
know what they call boys on long haul vessels? Guinea pigs!
(momentarily pained)
And, such was I.

They start along the dock wall, and now none of what bothered Redburn earlier
seems to matter.

HARRY (CONT'D)
Do you like shipping?

REDBURN
Yes – no.
(sighs)
It's lonely. I have no experience and do not know who or what
to trust. Sometimes, though, when I'm busy, when I do not need
to 'think,' then I am very happy at sea – and not lonely in myself.

EXT. BULWARKS OF THE *HIGHLANDER*

REDBURN steps off the gangplank, and goes to look down on the dock. He is relieved
HARRY is still standing there, hands in pockets, though he appears anxious, like he
doesn't want to be seen.

REDBURN
Are you still here?

> **HARRY**
> What will you do tomorrow?

> **REDBURN**
> Same as today.

> **HARRY**
> No. Come walk with me, through
> the countryside!

Redburn smiles uncontrollably and leans over the bulwarks to get as close to Harry as he dare. Harry's features lose all tension. He is warmed by just how open and genuine Redburn is.

> **HARRY (CONT'D)**
> I'll...
> (choked)
> I'll be here early. So be ready!

Harry gathers steam as if to run. Redburn calls out with earnest.

> **REDBURN**
> Wait! I...I don't know your name...

> **HARRY**
> Bolton, Harry Bolton. And you?

> **REDBURN**
> (pausing a moment)
> Call me – Redburn.

Harry nods his head up to his new friend, then turns and jogs off like the boy he is. Redburn's eyes follow, and smile in the dimming light.

[Part 3 – IV: Dappled Shakespeare]

EXT. COUNTRY LANE – MID-MORNING

Trees, thatched cottages and hedgerows are intermingled with open spaces blooming in July color; iris, hollyhock, wild rose, yarrow *et al*. Behind fences, fat sheep and cows graze, and in fields, **PEOPLE** bend to their farming tasks. **REDBURN** and **HARRY** stroll along; Harry with a green straw roving in his mouth. As they pass by homes, rosy-cheeked **CHILDREN** come up to them and talk hurriedly. They trail along a few steps and then run off to their own devices. Birds sing in the air, and bright splinters of sunlight hit the young men when they look up into the sky.

> **REDBURN**
> The air is sweet with the breath of buds and flowers. It's so like
> home! It's hard to believe <u>this</u> is really England.

Redburn laces his fingers behind his head.

> **REDBURN (CONT'D)**
> Now I know what English poets through the centuries meant by
> 'greenwood' and 'green splendor.' It — it ravishes me.

Harry laughs and sends an affectionate elbow to Redburn's gut. Redburn's hands come
down and ride Harry's shoulders.

> **REDBURN (CONT'D)**
> Think of it. This scene of soft air, one that fairly tingles with the
> green of the grass and the smell of the thatch — I might be
> inhaling the very breath of Rosalind and Orlando.

Redburn runs out in front of Harry, and recites to him walking backwards.

> **REDBURN (CONT'D)**
> 'O Rosalind! These trees shall be my books,
> And in their barks, my thoughts I'll character.'

Harry smiles warmly; punches Redburn's chest with playful sincerity.

EXT. HILLTOP OVERLOOK – NOON

The plate-glass sky is streamed with dreamy clouds. The view looks down on lanes,
fields and homes. Wheat bends slowly in the summer breeze. **REDBURN** takes his eyes
off the scene and turns around. An ancient oak crowns the hilltop. **HARRY** is taking off
his jacket and rolling up his sleeves. Redburn slaps his pockets and pulls out a few sea
biscuits. He smiles, joins Harry and rips off his coat. They sit with backs against the trunk.
Harry gives a sly look, then extracts a wine bottle from his jacket. They laugh; Harry
pushes in the cork and takes a swig. Redburn exchanges the biscuits for the bottle and
drinks himself.

EXT. HILLTOP OVERLOOK

The afternoon shadows are gaining length. The bottle is empty and overturned.
REDBURN and **HARRY** lie, nearly touching, head to foot beneath the oak tree, hands
behind their heads. Harry begins to sing.

> **HARRY**
> (SINGS)
> *"Under the greenwood tree,*
> *He who loves to lie with me,*
> *And who tunes his merry note*
> *Sweeter than a sweet bird's throat —*
>
> *Come ye hither,*
> *Come so hither ye —*
> *Come ye hither,*
> *Come and laze with me."*

Redburn slaps Harry thigh with the back of his hand. He sits up astounded.

REDBURN
Why didn't you reveal you like Shakespeare as much as I do?

HARRY
(shrugs)
Some mystery is good....

REDBURN
That's from the same play I quoted earlier.

HARRY
Amiens' song to his love, Jacques.

REDBURN
From 'As You Like it.'

HARRY
(wry grin)
I like it indeed; you, indeed.

Redburn lies back, but this time he rests his elbow and forearm on top of Harry's knees and thighs.

REDBURN
How did you become so well-read. I mean—

HARRY
The orphanage taught me my A,B,Cs. But the rest is due to a patchwork sailor in the East Indiaman. He took me under his wing; read to me by the hour, at night; taught me, and taught me well. I knew I loved to learn under his watchful protection; learned about myself too. Learned about love, how it works.

Redburn's hand slowly creeps across Harry. He slips it into Harry's grip. Harry takes it and squeezes it warmly. Above them, leaves rustle; pom-pom clouds flattened on the bottom roll by. Harry and Redburn have sat up. Their hands have gone to behind each other's waist. Birds light in and out of the tree, chirping. Redburn and Harry close eyes and lean into each other. Their lips touch with near disbelief, then, a moment later, they kiss with tender passion and kindred trust.

EXT. COUNTRY LANE – MID-AFTERNOON

REDBURN and **HARRY** stroll back to town; arm in arm, their jackets tossed over shoulders. They pass a small church with open doors. Next to it is an inn with a fenced yard. Here **PEOPLE** sit at tables eating, drinking and carousing. A newlywed **COUPLE** bend heads together. As the boys pass by with obvious interest, a jolly and pudgy-cheeked **MAN** comes to the fence.

MAN
Good day, lads!

> REDBURN and HARRY
> Good day.

> MAN
> Where to – Birmingham?

> HARRY
> No. Back to Liverpool.

> MAN
> From Liverpool, then?

> REDBURN
> I guess so.

> HARRY
> We've come to look at the countryside.

> REDBURN
> And mighty fine it is too.

> MAN
> Come and sit a spell, lads! Join us.

Redburn and Harry glance at each other a moment – each daring the other to laugh – they know they don't fit in.

> REDBURN
> Thank you, but we must be on our way.

They move on. After they clear the inn, Redburn glances over his shoulder.

> REDBURN (CONT'D)
> Look at us. You stroll about with me, and I with you, in perfect abandonment. You don't seem to mind the reckless cut of my shooting jacket. And you don't care who might stare at so singular a couple.

Harry stops dead; he swallows and chokes on a racking sob.

> HARRY
> You don't mind being seen with...me?

Redburn starts with open mouth. He misunderstands; thinks he's hurt Harry.

> REDBURN
> No – that's not what I mean. I...

Harry takes Redburn's hand in some kind of amazement.

> **HARRY**
> I know.
> (feeble smile)
> I know.

They continue walking. After a long pause, Harry tries to ask.

> **HARRY (CONT'D)**
> Do you think you might consider leaving your ship? Not go
> with them – stay here – with...me....

> **REDBURN**
> You mean, abandon ship? I don't think I could ever do that...not
> go back to my family? I don't...but, there is another way. You
> could ship with me. We'll tempt all rough weather – together.

The tilting light slices itself though the green leaves as it falls on rooftops, on the backs
and shoulders of Redburn and Harry stopped in the road, on the flowers and grass at
their feet. They kiss and their heads slowly fall on each other's shoulders. Birds **SING**.

[Part 3 – V: Kidnapped]

EXT. MAIN DECK OF THE *HIGHLANDER* – EARLY MORNING

Off her port bulwarks, Liverpool's docks and church spires glisten in the damp morning
air. **BLUNT** and **THE GREENLANDER** are chinking a section of deck where it meets the
bulwarks. Father forward, **REDBURN** is coiling rope. **HARRY** bounds up the gangplank
onto the deck. He pauses and looks for Redburn. Harry is in long trousers and a jacket.
Under the jacket is a vibrant silk tartan vest. A starched scarf is tied into a stiff bow
that sticks out beyond the lapels. His usual cap is replaced by a dapper and youthful
sporting hat. As he walks past them, The Greenlander does not see Harry, but Blunt
does. Blunt stands, knocks the brim of his cap back and gawks akimbo. [10]

> **BLUNT**
> (to The Greenlander)
> **Catch a sight of the Fancy Boy!** [11]

> **THE GREENLANDER**
> Huh?

The Greenlander glances up in time to see Harry bounding up to Redburn. Redburn
does not see Harry's approach.

> **HARRY**
> Lad!

> **REDBURN**
> Harry! Why, you're dressed debonair today—

Harry pulls Redburn in for a quiet conference.

> **HARRY**
> And so shall you be, my boy. Traveling clothes. I'm taking you to London. I'll meet you at 'The Exchange,' then we'll go by train. Hurry! Come as you are; I'll bring a bag and dress you in my duds.

Harry gently pushes Redburn towards the forecastle. Redburn walks, then runs. As Harry turns to go to the gangplank, he walks into The Greenlander's chest, and the man roughly grabs the boy's arm.

> **THE GREENLANDER**
> Well, well — can't enough of me,
> eh, toffer? [12]

Harry jerks free, but his professional demeanor is on, so he responds by playing to the compliment just paid him. Harry edges around The Greenlander; a lively foot and lewd grin disarming the sailor.

> **HARRY**
> Sure guv'nor. And you're a regular indorser, but this ain't a festival night, so I'm not sportin' right now. We'll get together and a make a real wedding night of it, eh? Soon. [13]

> **THE GREENLANDER**
> (grabs own crotch)
> You like romance, eh, boy?

Harry bolts for, and then down, the gangplank. The Greenlander goes to the bulwarks. He watches the youth run along the dock and licks his lips.

INT. LIVERPOOL TRAIN DEPOT – MORNING

Smoke and steam waft over the heads of **PEOPLE** rushing about. A train of yellow and black carriages waits at a platform. Most the doors are closed and passengers lean out of windows talking to well-wishers. **HARRY** pulls **REDBURN** along looking for an open door. Redburn carries a bag over his shoulder and is dressed as a near twin to Harry; but wears his old cap. **LORD LOVELY** walks unconcernedly towards them. Redburn points. [14]

> **REDBURN**
> Wait! Isn't that 'Lord Lovely?'

> **HARRY**
> (not stopping)
> Oh. Really?

Harry finds a coach, and bundles Redburn inside.

INT. TRAIN COMPARTMENT

HARRY follows **REDBURN** and slams the door shut. In a moment the whistle **BLOWS,** and the train lurches forward. Harry smiles in exhilaration.

> **REDBURN**
> What manner of friendship do you have
> with him?

> **HARRY**
> (chuckles)
> A strained one, Redburn – strained.

EXT. LONDON, A WEST END STREET – NIGHT

A cab rolls through a cobblestone street of mansions. Gaslights are lit, but there are no people or other traffic about.

INT. CAB

HARRY half hangs out the open window, carefully eying the passing houses. **REDBURN** strains to see anything outside the window on his side.

> **HARRY**
> Here, driver! Here!

EXT. SIDEWALK BEFORE A GAY GENTLEMEN'S CLUB

The cab pulls away, revealing **HARRY** and **REDBURN** standing before the steps of a large building. Redburn scans the somewhat plain-looking structure. The most unusual feature is a large lantern arched over the steps by an iron trellis. The other houses have white lights by their doors, but this lantern burns a decidedly lavender color.

> **REDBURN**
> It all seems so beyond the real. Is this London?

Harry goes up the steps like he owns them.

> **HARRY**
> Come along, Master Redburn.

When the American gets to the top, Harry puts his arm around Redburn.

> **HARRY (CONT'D)**
> Now, when we get inside, act posh. I'm going to act posh, so don't be surprised. But if you cannot manage it, it's better you just keep quiet. I didn't kidnap you to make a fool out of myself.

Harry winks.

[Part 3 — VI: A Night of Mystery]

INT. CLUB'S HALLWAY — NIGHT

As **REDBURN** and **HARRY** approach, liveried **FOOTMEN** open the doors in silent unison from the inside. They are young and handsome. From the guest's eyes, the hall is a magic arbor. Marble floors and wainscot end in smooth plaster walls that concave up into a flat ceiling. The plaster is completely covered in *trompe l'oeil*. The walls are painted as arbor columns and lattice panels; the ceiling, a lattice arbor roof — and both are interwoven with leaves and vines in full fruit with purple grapes. A verdant landscape and blue sky are in the background. There are three gasoliers suspended from the ceiling, spaced evenly down the hall with branching and lit arms. Their center posts drop from polychrome plaster roundels that seamlessly form vine branches out of the ceiling painting. Shading the lights are purple crystal grape clusters. Redburn gasps; there is nothing about the outside of this building to give a hint of its interior luxury. [15]

INT. RECEPTION

At the end of the hall, an open space forms. Here a desk houses a standing **MAN**, but **REDBURN**'s attention immediately goes to the huge painting behind the desk. An eight-foot-tall Guido-like Apollo wears rays of sunlight behind his head, and nothing else but a lyre, and a slip of strategically placed red cloth. As they get to the open space, the Man raises arms in warm welcome to **HARRY**.

HARRY
(low to Redburn)
Wait here a moment.

Harry steps up to the man, and Redburn turns a slow circuit of wonder. The space he is in is a buffer area. To the right and left are matching large openings to salons that stretch back to the street. The lintels are supported by heroic-scale telamons; youths, facing each other with raised hands and bent elbows, wearing only a mini-slip of fur to cover the front. On their heads are massive wreaths of grain and flowers. These four titans are painted to look like highly honed and polished gray granite. The walls of the salon to the right are hung with crimson silk, and the upholstery matches. Groups of ornate soft seating are peopled with well-dressed **MEN** and **YOUTH** engaged in spirited conversation. The furniture supports positively writhe in carved forms of classical men, like the Laocoön Group. The salon to the left is appointed in green silk. Here mahogany pedestal tables are laid for dinner of small groups. More men and young men sit, eat, smoke and converse. Harry touches Redburn's elbow and leads him into the dining salon. [16]

INT. DINING SALON

REDBURN and **HARRY** sit at a table. Harry looks around, and speaks to a **WAITER**.

HARRY (CONT'D)
Malmsey.
REDBURN

(whispers)
What do you call this place?

HARRY
(whispers back)
You don't have to whisper. It's safe here.

Harry leans back; speaks in his regular voice.

HARRY (CONT'D)
This is 'The Club' – <u>very</u> exclusive.

REDBURN
Beats 'The Baltimore Clipper.' But how can you afford—

HARRY
Friends, Redburn. Friends.

REDBURN
Like, Lord Lovely....

HARRY
Like Lord Lovely!

The waiter arrives with a silver tray. He sets it down, and his gloved hand reaches for the stopper. Harry waves him away, and pours two glasses himself. He hands one to Redburn, raises the other, and drains it. He refills it while Redburn takes a sip. On the second glass, he offers a toast.

HARRY (CONT'D)
To – To the mysteries of adventure; and romance.

After drinking half, Harry sets his glass down. While his is topping off Redburn's wine, he seems distracted by something in the hallway. He stands.

HARRY (CONT'D)
Remain where you are. I must withdraw
for a moment.

As Redburn opens his mouth to speak, Harry strides confidently back to the Man behind the desk. Harry exchanges a few words, gesturing towards Redburn, and the Man looks disconcerted. However, the man slowly nods, then bows and extends a 'right this way' arm. They disappear though a nondescript door at the side of Apollo. Suddenly Redburn feels very out of place. He glances about the room, then sinks into his chair. He takes the wine glass and sips some more, feeling eyes upon him; curious eyes. Now he notices this camouflaged door is quite busy. Couples go from the salon through this door, and other groups emerge from it to stand a moment in the hallway — the men heading for the front door, the young men back to the lounge. Harry reappears, seeming flushed.

HARRY
Come along, young Master Redburn. Our chamber is ready.

REDBURN
(rises)
Are you all right?

HARRY
(false laugh)
Of course! Come along.

INT. RECEPTION

HARRY pushes the side door open and walks through it. **REDBURN** follows and stops again in wonder.

INT. STAIR HALL

A large square room, with a wide staircase hugging three walls, rises to a columned second story with concaved skylight above. A massive and gaily lit gasolier with thousands of crystal prisms hangs from the center of the skylight. As **HARRY** starts up, **REDBURN** sees the steps are marble with a Turkish carpet runner. The newel is a worked bronze plinth topped with a gilded bronze sculpture. He looks at it closely: like the Three Graces, three youths interlock arms with a shared garland of fruit and flowers draping between their hard naked bodies. Yellow silk lines the walls and is bordered with heavy embroidery of laurel leaf ropes in gold thread. Two enormous framed copies of classical frescoes — both from Herculaneum — dominate the walls. As Redburn climbs, he cannot take his eyes off the vibrant color and riot of images of the first one: "Hercules and Telephus," and especially the spiritually transcendental face of Arcadia. Her repose — the abundance of the fruit in a basket by her side and of the wreath crowning her head, and the impishly sly grin of the baby Pan behind her — intrigues him. From her, his eyes trail to Telephus being suckled by a doe, then up to the strong profile of Hercules. Redburn passes eye level with Hercules' gloriously bronzed, and demi-divine backside, making the boy brush. Moving on, he pans the second painting: "Chiron and Achilles," from the tender and fatherly face of the centaur, down his powerful arm to the face of the doting youth in his embrace. He lingers on the boy's soft features, then trails the S-curve of his torso to the lyre in his hand. [17]

INT. TOP LANDING AND HALL

In front of **REDBURN** is a dim hall leading back to the front of the building. He peers and sees **HARRY** moving down it, so he follows. From Harry's POV, he looks back to see the stair-hall gasolier glows like a halo around Redburn's head. When he gets to the end of the hall, Harry lightly pushes on a pair of rosewood doors. They glide open, blinding Redburn for a moment. As he shields his eyes, he can make out a chamber fronting the entire width of the street.

INT. SUITE

On the far wall in front of **REDBURN** is a marble bracket. On top of this is a classical bust of Antinoüs, the lovely youth with his right shoulder raised and his eyes cast downwards to his left. On the walls, a dark blue French paper provides richness. This paper is bordered with wide and narrow stripes of flocked velvet in tones of snuff color. [18] As Redburn enters the room, he wobbles on the thick French carpet, and sees this part of the room is a sort of antechamber; to his left is a lintel with draperies, beyond which is tucked a bed tucked. It's surrounded on three sides by snuff-colored silk floor-to-ceiling Vienna blinds. The right side is a sitting room with fireplace and soft seating like the salon downstairs. Between the windows on either side of the bust are paintings. One is of Alexander cradling his dying love, Hephaestion; the other, Hadrian holding the expiring form of Antinoüs. Redburn stands below the bust's left side, and gazes into the youth's eternally pained eyes. **HARRY** comes up behind him, intoning softly.

HARRY
Deaf. Mute, to all he's seen. But, mind you, whisper no secrets
into his stony ear, lest another hear.

Harry laughs and slaps Redburn's back, then goes to close the door. Redburn looks at the seating area more closely. Above the mantel hangs a copy of Broc's "Death of Hyacinthus." A pair of sofas are 90-degrees to the fireplace and a sofa table is pulled to one. On it is a tray with decanter and three glasses.

HARRY (CONT'D)
They've drawn us a bath. I'll go first.

Redburn turns to see Harry already stripped to his trousers and kicking off his shoes. Harry steps through a door at the side of the bed. Soon Redburn hears water **SPLASHING**, and Harry **SIGHING**.

REDBURN
(as if to himself)
They're all tragic.

HARRY (O.S.)
What...?

Redburn goes to the foot of the bed.

REDBURN
They're all tragic. Every picture here is of love destroyed by
another's jealousy; outright intolerance. Or hate.

INT. SUITE SEATING AREA – NIGHT – LATER

REDBURN, with just a towel on his head and another around his waist, sits on a sofa. He rubs his hair a moment, then lets the towel fall to his shoulders. He looks to find **HARRY** smiling at him. The working boy sits on the other sofa wearing only a towel around his waist. Two poured glasses of wine wait near him.

HARRY
Let's drink

Harry rises and picks up the glasses. He walks one over and puts it in the American's hand.

HARRY (CONT'D)
To love — tragic or otherwise.

They clink. Harry drains his glass; Redburn sips. Harry pours himself another and sits next to his companion.

HARRY (CONT'D)
Drink up. You can't stay a lightweight forever.

Redburn casts dark forebodings on the floor. Harry scoots in so their thighs are touching their entire length. He puts a concerned arm around Redburn's shoulders.

HARRY (CONT'D)
What's the matter, Redburn? You're not afraid of me, are you?

REDBURN
No.
(perplexed)
No — I was just thinking what a dog's life I lead in the stinking forecastle of the *Highlander*.
(sadly — holding his gaze)
What kind of life do you lead?

Harry swallows; makes no reply. Instead he guides Redburn's glass to Redburn's lips.

HARRY
Relax. This place is just an illusion, a short and pleasant diversion. A place for just us. Here, despite what they think and devise to keep us isolated on the outside, we can join each other and recognize a perfect union — heart to heart, or as Billy said — a marriage of true minds. These pictures are reminders that the way it has been, is not the way it has to be, despite the world's threat hard upon our doors. Believe me, if we stick together, it's the world that will change.

Redburn feels a drowsy warmth, mixed with a kindling of youthful love for Harry, sink into his bones with leaden insistence.

REDBURN
I believe in you.

HARRY
(sad)
Drink up.

Harry guides the bottom of the glass upwards, draining the contents beyond Redburn's innocent lips. Redburn's sight falters; lingers on the painting over the fireplace; a close up of Apollo's lips in a near kiss on his dying love.

BEGIN 'REDBURN DRUGGED; HARRY AT WORK' SERIES OF SHOTS:

A) Redburn opens his eyes; is he being carried. He looks up into Harry's face.

B) Redburn feels himself plopped on the bed. He looks up to the ceiling. Here the painting is a riff on Griepenkerl's "Theft of Fire." A vigilant Jove caresses Ganymede, who sleeps leaning on his chest and outstretched arm. Redburn sleeps.

C) Redburn opens his eyes; it is darker now. He feels the bed jostle in a regular rhythm. He turns and perceives Harry's face close to his. Harry is breathing hard, arms tossed over his head, and his features are tormented in ecstatic pleasure. Something is hovering over the lad. Redburn struggles to focus on the moving image. It is a naked Lord Lovely; a determined look is on his handsome features. Harry's hand goes up to the back of Lord Lovely's head; they both cry out in some sort of muffled release. Redburn sleeps.

D) Redburn opens his eyes; Harry is sleeping with his head on Redburn's chest; his arm thrown over him and holding his hand. The American looks to Jove and Ganymede above; their tender sleep. He picks up Harry's hand and brings it to his lips while he has visions of the classical faces he has seen: the mystic Arcadia with her garland; the impish Pan; the sad Antinoüs kissed by a tear-stained Hadrian; Apollo passionately kissing Hyacinthus, and above him, a placid Ganymede asleep, forever protected by the king of the gods. Redburn gently brushes the soft curls from before Harry's eyes. He kisses the boy's forehead with a lingering pain. Harry rouses – they begin to kiss passionately; Harry's hand goes beneath Redburn's sheet.

END 'REDBURN DRUGGED; HARRY AT WORK' SERIES OF SHOTS.

[Part 3 – VII: Not a Word]

INT. SUITE BEDROOM – MORNING

Through **REDBURN**'s darkness, an insistent tone repeats something indistinct. Each time **HARRY**'s voice becomes a bit clearer, and finally Redburn opens his eyes.

HARRY
Redburn! Wake up.

As seen from above the bed, Redburn is naked, an arm tossed over his head, and the satin bed sheet, just a slip over his crotch. He looks like the Apollo downstairs. Redburn turns his head; the windows are open and the blinds are up and rustle softly. From outside, **BIRDSONG** and **TRAFFIC** wafts in from the street. He has disturbingly brief flashes of what went on last night: Harry's face in ecstasy; the inward introspection of Arcadia; Harry and Redburn kissing; the sly grin of Pan. Harry is suddenly standing on the bed over him.

HARRY (CONT'D)
Wake up. We have to catch our train.

Redburn sits. Harry is already wearing his shirt and trousers.

INT. SUITE SEATING AREA

REDBURN walks with the sheet held to his waist with one hand; the other is at his temple. His clothes are tossed on the sofa. He reaches for his drawers and slips them on. Then the sofa table distracts him. The three glasses have all been used. He knits his eyebrows a moment, picks up Harry's glass and sniffs it. He sets it down and picks up the glass he used. He sniffs, and immediately pulls back, making a sour face.

INT. TRAIN COMPARTMENT – NOON

HARRY sits opposite REDBURN, who still has a hand to his head. The train rumbles through the countryside.

> HARRY
> (wry grin)
> So, what did you think of London?

> REDBURN
> London? All I saw was Euston Station and the interior
> of a cab. And, and, 'The Club.'

> HARRY
> I know. Better than any guidebook.

Redburn lolls his head back on the seat, closes his eyes and speaks as if from a dream.

> REDBURN
> What was that, Harry? It's as if you ran through my soul – in and
> out, at every door I put up, you burst it open, forcing me to
> unshutter everything to your vehement onrush.

Redburn raises his eyelids. Harry is staring out the window, and appears about ready to sob.

> REDBURN (CONT'D)
> What is it? What was that, Harry?

> HARRY
> (somewhat frantic)
> Look...

Harry fishes a wad of pound notes from his inner jacket pocket. He flashes it before Redburn.

> HARRY (CONT'D)
> Let's run away. You pick where – I don't – I don't—

> REDBURN
> Where did you get that?

Harry remembers Redburn's reluctance to not go home again. He feels he's made a mistake; shoves the money out of sight.

HARRY
I...I've made my mind to leave England.

Harry reaches and takes Redburn's hand. He implores for Redburn's trust.

HARRY (CONT'D)
What would you say about me shipping to New York, on
your vessel — with you?

A hopeless grin of joy spreads across Redburn's face.

REDBURN
Truly? You would do that?

HARRY
Yes. You could show me about America. I could meet your
brother; your family.

REDBURN
Nothing would make me happier.

Harry sits back in the seat as an utter wave of despair washes over him.
Redburn rises and sits next to Harry.

HARRY
I'm glad you will have me. But swear, swear an oath to me right
now, you will never speak of last night again. Not to me, not to
anyone, even to someone who asks.

REDBURN
Who would ask?

HARRY
Just say you swear.

Redburn swallows hard.

REDBURN
Smoking; drinking; and now swearing. What would the Junior
Temperance League think...? Not to mention, my brother.
(serious)
Not another word. I swear it.

Harry hugs Redburn's waist, looking much relieved.

[Part 3 — VIII: Shove off]

EXT. MAIN DECK OF THE *HIGHLANDER* — AFTERNOON

The **FIRST MATE** stands akimbo by the cabin. In front of him is **REDBURN**, cap wrenched in his hands. A few paces behind him, **HARRY** waits, bag over his shoulder. The young men are back in their regular clothes.

FIRST MATE
(to Redburn)
So, you've turned prodigal, eh? We flattered ourselves you had
made a run of it — for good!

LAVENDER, wearing a turban, steps out of the cabin door to watch.

FIRST MATE (CONT'D)
(to Harry)
**And what do you want, Pillgarlic? There'll be no stealings
on this here vessel—**

REDBURN
He wants to sign up.

FIRST MATE
(incredulous — to Harry)
Any experience?

HARRY
Aye — on an East Indiaman.

FIRST MATE
A guinea pig, eh?

HARRY
(stands to attention)
Aye, aye!

The First Mate walks up to, then around Harry, looking him over. Finally, he slams a
hand on Harry's shoulder and roughly compels him towards the cabin door.

FIRST MATE
We'll see about that.

As the First Mate and Harry disappear into the cabin, Redburn and Lavender exchange
an awkward glance. Lavender burns with coldness towards him.

[Part 4 — The Way Back — I: A Fresh Start]

EXT. MAIN DECK OF THE *HIGHLANDER* — TWILIGHT

The ship exits the Mersey estuary. **REDBURN** and **HARRY**, newly arrayed in sailor
garb, work together happily. They go up the bulwark, lean over and catch a last
glimpse of Liverpool: of masts, spires, birds and dramatic clouds.

BEGIN 'SMOOTH SAILING' MONTAGE:
(different clothes each time — series of days)
   ■ **EXT. MAIN DECK — MORNING**

Redburn and Harry scrub the deck, barefoot and in shirtsleeve — more playing than working.

■ **EXT. RIGGING – AFTERNOON**

Redburn and Harry horse around and laugh in the sparkling sunshine. The water looks tropical from up here.

■ **EXT. QUARTERDECK – DUSK**

Harry stands and sings by the rail overlooking the main deck. The crew pause, listening to Harry's beautiful voice.

■ **INT. FORECASTLE – NIGHT**

Harry climbs over Redburn getting into their bunk. Harry sidles up and rests his head on Redburn's chest. Redburn plays with Harry's curly locks.

■ **INT. FORECASTLE – LATE NIGHT**

Blunt sleep-massages his scalp in front of a mirror. Redburn and Harry hush-finger each other, suppressing laughter.

■ **INT. FORECASTLE – MORNING**

Redburn and Harry break biscuits over each other's head. The crew laugh.

■ **INT. OF THE LONGBOAT – NOON**

Redburn rests his head on Harry's chest. Harry picks biscuit crumbs out of Redburn's hair.

■ **EXT. MAIN DECK – AFTERNOON**

Redburn and Harry coil rope together as a team, while Blunt and Dutchie make 'ain't it cute' gestures.

■ **EXT. MAIN DECK – AFTERNOON**

From another angle, Jackson's invidious eye glowers on the same scene.

END 'SMOOTH SAILING' MONTAGE.

[Part 4 – II: Relief]

EXT. MAIN DECK OF THE *HIGHLANDER* – EVENING

HARRY works alone chinking, stooped over by the bulwarks. **THE GREENLANDER** comes up behind him, glancing around. He touches Harry's backside with a bit of force. Harry looks up into his eyes, then stands to face him.

THE GREENLANDER
(licks his lips)
How about it?

HARRY
I ain't in the game anymore. Stop asking me.

THE GREENLANDER
(clicks his tongue)
Who's gonna believe that? Once a three-shilling wagtail, always one. Don't make me ask you again. I might not be so nice the next time I feel sporting.

Harry looks both ways; turns sad eyes on The Greenlander.

HARRY
You want to hurt Redburn? Or are you just looking
for some relief...?

The Greenlander is momentarily taken aback, but slowly recovers with a grin. As he steps closer to Harry, his tone grows sweet.

THE GREENLANDER
Whichever one you want to believe, nug.

Harry looks around again; nods. The Greenlander leads him to the tool shop.

[Part 4 – III: Ahab's Tormenter]

EXT. COOKHOUSE OF THE *HIGHLANDER* – AFTERNOON

The slate says: **"Rev. Doctor Thompson, 16 Forecastle Sq."** A bright day, the sails **SNAP** cheerily above. The **COOK** bustles about. He's laid the skirt of an old coat as a doormat, and **LAVENDER** leans on the wall watching **REDBURN** pick oakum. Lavender tries to sound disinterested.

LAVENDER
Your new bunkmate suit you? He better than me?

REDBURN
(looks up)
Not better – different – we're equals. We don't play games.

The Cook comes out with a ringbolt. He noisily attaches it to the doorframe. He loudly knocks it several times.

LAVENDER
(to Redburn)
Careful what you wish for. Others could take it away for sport.

As the import of what the boy has threatened hits Redburn, the Cook calls out.

COOK
There! Now, boys, if you wish to call on me, just
use my knocker.

The Cook stands back to admire it in pride. He suddenly remembers something.

COOK (CONT'D)
Oh, Redburn, you are a learnèd boy. Let me ask <u>you</u>....

The Cook disappears into the cookhouse; pots and pans **CLANK**.

REDBURN
(to Lavender)
Being equal means you trust equally.

Lavender chortles in contempt. The Cook comes out with his well-worn bible; it is tied with a cord. He grabs a stool and sits by Redburn.

COOK
Now — let me find it....

He opens the cord and pulls on a bookmark. He asks as he flips through pages.

COOK
Tell me what I'm supposed to think of this here lesson. Yes — 2 Chronicles — this one.
(READS)
'Now therefore, behold, the LORD hath put a lying spirit in the mouth of these thy prophets, and the LORD hath spoken Evil against thee.'

The Cook closes the book and leans into Redburn with earnest tones.

COOK (CONT'D)
He's talking to Ahab. God's decided Ahab ain't fit no more to be a leader. But — and this is what I puzzle over — can God 'speak Evil?' If God can 'speak Evil,' then what chance do any men have in this world to do what's right? You tell me what I'm supposed to think.

REDBURN
That assertion of God doing evil deeds against those he created, his children...

Redburn glances at Lavender.

REDBURN (CONT'D)
...Is a mystery no one can explain. It's like saying a father would delight in the ruin of his son over any effort to guide him.

The Cook appears downcast; his worst fears confirmed.

COOK
We don't stand a chance. If God decides to do us an Evil; an Evil is done. Done in His name.

REDBURN
But, if you're really asking my opinion....

The Cook nods.

REDBURN (CONT'D)
...We'd all do best to head Saint Paul, and set that 'old' testament stuff aside. We should take the saint's advice, and turn our lives charitably to live with others, in faith, hope...

Redburn silently pleads with Lavender.

REDBURN (CONT'D)
...And love.

Lavender stands and starts to stalk off. The Cook has a breakthrough of spirit. He stands too.

COOK
Yes. Old Ahab was misled — but we
don't have to be.

The Cook deftly puts his hand out and stops Lavender. He spins him and sits him forcefully on the stool by Redburn. Lavender looks up at the Cook like the doctor's a dangerous man. But the Cook is more sympathetic than anything else.

COOK
(to Lavender)
Now, you, young man — I know you to be a sad profligate and
gay deceiver ashore, addicted to every youthful indiscretion—

Lavender tries to rise; his mouth hard in determination to get away. But the Cook only holds Lavender's shoulders in place.

COOK (CONT'D)
I worry about you, son. I want you to live content, without
burden. You understand me?

Lavender's face changes; the Cook unhands him.

COOK (CONT'D)
Both of you boys — listen up.

The Cook begins pacing like a preacher, his bible getting thoroughly thumped in the process.

COOK (CONT'D)
See how we act? We look down upon the Turk; abhor the
cannibal; but may not some of them gain the heaven we seek
before us? We fancy, because of what we wear, we have
civilized bodies, but these fancy clothes house barbarous souls.
We may have eyes, but be blind to the real sights of the world;
ears, but deaf to its voice; life, but dead to its deaths.

The Cook raises Lavender's chin.

COOK (CONT'D)
And not until we know that one grief willfully paid to another
outweighs ten thousand joys stored for ourselves, will we
become what Christ was striving to make us. You lad, break too
many hearts...

The Cook glances at Redburn.

COOK (CONT'D)
...Both on land, and at sea.

Lavender rises with the slow wrath of the falsely accused. He teeters between racking sobs and violent anger.

LAVENDER
And what it's true? What's that got to do with me! I'm not the one going after anyone, so why blame me if <u>they</u> feel like I'm fair game? Hell, no. Take your blaming and shaming and use on yourself if you want. Or better yet, use on the ones who go after kids like me! Why blame me and try to shame me when it's them; when it's their 'sin,' and not mine.

Lavender leaves, but turns back to Redburn and the Cook, his mouth nearly foaming with rage.

LAVENDER (CONT'D)
Blame God for making them that way —
not their victims!

[Part 4 — IV: Get the Benches, Boys]

INT. FORECASTLE OF THE *HIGHLANDER* — NIGHT

A couple of lamps are lit. One is balanced on the knee of **REDBURN** sitting on a stool and writing to his mother. Sounds of peaceful sleep spill from the bunks, except one. Miguel's bunk is now open; **BLUNT** tosses there and mutters with increasing loudness. Redburn cautiously rises and takes the light to peer into Blunt's face — the sleeping man is anguished.

BLUNT
(asleep)
The benches boys, get the benches. Judgment...day...

Blunt bolts up and knocks Redburn back on his heels. Blunts wakes himself as he shouts.

BLUNT (CONT'D)
...Is coming!

Blunt is frightened to see how afraid Redburn looks in the lamplight.

REDBURN
You were dreaming. You all right?

Blunt shakes his head a moment like a dog. He grabs onto the top of Redburn's shoulders to help him while he jumps out of his bunk.

BLUNT
It was awful. The last day, boy. No more chance to get it right —
no more chances. But that's not all.

Blunt whispers in Redburn's ear.

BLUNT (CONT'D)
A portent — one of us must die before we reach New York
— one of us.

Blunt glares and nods frightfully at Harry who is sound asleep. Redburn is horrified.

[Part 4 — V: Love in a Longboat]

INT. LONGBOAT OF THE *HIGHLANDER* — AFTERNOON

An ascending view shows blue skies through the rigging. The sails flap in gentle midday languor. A descending view into the bottom of the boat shows **REDBURN** and **HARRY** lying head to foot, but with their heads aligned with the other's thighs. Their jackets are spread below them, their sleeves are rolled up and their feet are bare. Harry is humming a lovely melody, softly so just Redburn can hear. Redburn sighs, locks his arm around Harry's legs and uses his thigh for a pillow. He makes up lyrics for Harry's song. He begins to sing softly.

REDBURN
(SINGS)
"A sweet thing is a song
Gentle and liquid
As it meanders along
Through thoughts the softest,
Drawn to be the sweetest song.

Tis a musical brook
That winds and wanders
To pied by the grassy nook
Where grow the tallest
Margins of the heart forsook."

HARRY
You make me sound like Orpheus, taming panthers and
tigers with song.

REDBURN
More like Bacchus — who stole aboard a ship, a boy like us, and
when the sailors deemed to have him, he trans-morphed into a
black leopard to rip them apart.

Redburn lets loose of Harry, and props himself on elbows.

REDBURN (CONT'D)
You have been afforded the respect I was denied coming on
board this ship. I'm glad. You don't realize how miserable I was
going over. Alone, forlorn, I found myself a sort of Ishmael.
Without a single friend or companion, I began to feel a hatred
growing for the whole crew. So much so, that I prayed against

it; that it might not master my heart completely; that it not make a fiend within me — something hideous, like that within Jackson.

HARRY
So you would have <u>me</u> be the Bacchus leopard?

REDBURN
(chuckles)
That's all over now.

Redburn spins around, lies down with his armpit just higher than Harry's head.

HARRY
Let's switch out Ovid for a topic with New York. Soon we'll be there.

Redburn forces his arm under Harry's head. He rolls Harry's head onto his chest. Redburn strokes Harry's locks. Harry, unseen by Redburn, looks utterly desolate.

REDBURN
Soon.

HARRY
I don't want the voyage to be over. It's always the going that matters, not the getting. You deserve better than my kind. I don't warrant the blessings of your goodness on me.

Redburn kicks back with a leg and rolls Harry firmly on his arm. He wipes Harry's tears with his thumb.

REDBURN
Who's luckier than I? You tell me that.

Redburn kisses Harry tenderly. Then with equal reciprocation, they make out with sustained and happy abandon.

EXT. LONGBOAT OF THE *HIGHLANDER*

JACKSON presses his ear to the hull of the boat. He rights himself and plots his treachery.

[Part 4 — VI: In the Center of the All]

EXT. HELM OF THE *HIGHLANDER* – TWILIGHT

THE GREENLANDER is instructing **REDBURN** on how to steer. The setting sun falls before the prow of the ship.

THE GREENLANDER
Hold your hands just so — easy motions now — and keep your eyes on the compass.

The Greenlander takes his hands off of Redburn's and steps back akimbo.

THE GREENLANDER (CONT'D)
Easy with her....

REDBURN
(after a long pause)
I hope you haven't hardened your heart against me.

THE GREENLANDER
(looks around agitated)
Hush, boy. Don't let others hear you talk that way — not to me.

REDBURN
I was young; green. I didn't know I was doing anything at all.
I just hope you understand.

The Greenlander gazes at the back of Redburn's head, longing to comfort him — to turn back the clock — instead he toughens his voice.

THE GREENLANDER
Luff, boy. Not too much. Gentle tillage is always called or.
(pause — softly)
You're still green.

REDBURN
I know.

THE GREENLANDER
Do ye? Do you know what they call a tar who cannot merely hand, reef or steer — a mariner better than his ability to run aloft, furl sail, haul ropes or stand at the wheel? It is nothing fancy, but to a true seaman's heart, it is the proudest thing he can be named — a sailorman. Though we despise his hatred, such a man is Jackson. Lesser would shrink off to waste away on land, but he wants to push off standing at duty; to die a hero; a sailor. Do you think you could be such a sailorman, young one?

REDBURN
Aye. I am learning, but still I give my crewmates the goodwill of my muscles and backbone — small as it is — as a lever to use as they need. Archimedes said he could move the world itself, as long as he had a lever meant to the task.

THE GREENLANDER
Archimedes? What did he know of a sailor's life? Sailors, boy, are a certain reckless lot prone to sentiment and sensuality. We are borne aloft on the tides friendless, save a rare special case, and carried beyond the reach of the good influence of family, and love, and after the privations of a long journey, set adrift in a foreign port to seek solace, alone. Most old tars are old drunks

because of it. If not drunk of body, then drunk with hate for both
breeze and calm — hate for both good and evil — like Jackson.
(brightening)
You want to be a sailor, nug? Harangued by dockside, soul-
damning clergymen; robbed by barmen and hustlers; regarded
by gentlefolk as but little above a brute.
(tender)
You want to be a sailorman, boy?

Redburn can feel the heated words of The Greenlander soaking the nape of his neck
along with the pull and shudder of the tiller through his palms. He squints at the disc of
the sun nearing the horizon, and inhales a smiling breath of sea air.

REDBURN
Aye, for times like these. For times when sailors can be honest
with themselves as with no one else. Times when the ship
bounds like a horse, wind-impelled to plunge along and cut the
foam from her prow. Every mast and timber pulsing with life and
joy. I feel it as a wild exulting in my own heart: one delirious
throb at the center of the All, bound around this world, to go
reeling with the planets in their orbits, to respond in my heart
with peace to the wild commotion of the outer circles. Yes. Yes,
I want to be a sailor.

After a pause, The Greenlander places his hand on Redburn's shoulder.

THE GREENLANDER
Good, lad. A sailorman you shall be.

From over the backs of their heads, a rising view shows the rigging of the ship sway;
her prow piercing the heart of the orange heart of the setting sun, and how small the
Highlander is on the watery vastness.

[Part 4 — VII: Holy Orders]

EXT. MAIN DECK OF THE *HIGHLANDER* – NOON

Tar simmers black and fuming in an iron cauldron. It is set in the open on a brazier.
JACKSON stirs it and broods how it seems a precursor to hellish torment. There are
several small buckets at his feet. The **SECOND MATE** strides up, with **REDBURN** and
HARRY in tow.

SECOND MATE
Aloft with that. Take the boys and show them how to seal any
cracks in the main-top-yard.

JACKSON
(spite-laden)
Aye, aye, Mr. Riggs.

Redburn steps up and takes a bucket. Jackson ladles in some tar, and Redburn moves off towards the mainmast rope ladder. Harry takes a bucket and holds it level with the cauldron. As Jackson stirs, he speaks into the blackness.

                    JACKSON
You should enter into Holy Orders when you get to New York.

                     HARRY
                    (puzzled)
                     Why?

Jackson's head slowly turns on him — his bad eye glinting.

                    JACKSON
Because, pogue, you are a profane coward. Just the type to think dropping to your knees before Christ absolves all your other knee-dropping before men; those who are hard, with pieces of silver bulging their pockets.

Jackson 'accidentally' splashes a drop of tar on Harry's hand. The boy screams, drops the bucket and rubs the tar off with his sleeve. He turns pained eyes on Jackson, silently pleading 'why?'

                 JACKSON (CONT'D)
A foretaste of the hellfires that await you — and all your kind —
          punk. Would I had some feathers....

Jackson laughs manically, which turns into a lung-churning fit of coughing. He uses the back of his hand to wipe his mouth — it comes away smirched with black blood.

EXT. MAIN-TOP-YARD

HARRY, with bandaged hand, is slushing tar on the yard near the port side.

EXT. MAIN-TOPGALLANT-YARD

JACKSON, on the yard above, peers down on **HARRY**. He is positioning himself to be directly over the boy. From Jackson's point of view, Harry is oblivious to his presence. He begins to tip his bucket of steaming tar.

EXT. MAINMAST TOPGALLANT SHROUDS

REDBURN, on the rope ladder just above **JACKSON**, shouts out.

                    REDBURN
                Look out below!

EXT. MAIN-TOP-YARD

HARRY looks up, and nearly falls, avoiding the burning tar. Harry looks down to see members of the **CREW** scramble as Jackson's tar and bucket splatter and sizzle on the deck.

EXT. MAIN-TOPGALLANT-YARD

REDBURN has jumped on, and is forcing **JACKSON** backwards; out to the end of the yard. Redburn unsheathes his jackknife and holds it up. Jackson begins to cough; each cough lessening his supply of balance and oxygen. Jackson fumbles to pull Blunt's knife out, but once he does, it slips from his hand. It falls towards the moving ocean far below. Finally, Jackson stops; he's run out of yardarm. He looks down a moment; at the blood on his hand, then rights himself defiantly.

REDBURN
I said I could throw you over, if need be.

JACKSON
(coughs)
Come and do it, baby-boy.

Redburn takes a step, but stops. Jackson's coughing grows violent; he is barely able to stand. His sputum horrifies Redburn as it stains the sail with increasing sprays of putrid red. Jackson stops, catches his breath in desperate wheezes, and eyes Redburn. He rises, wipes his mouth and pulls back a hand coated in blood. Blood smears his chin, and trails down his neck to tinge the collar of his tee-shirt. A maniacal calm suddenly washes over the dying man — his plot can come to a kind of success.

JACKSON (CONT'D)

I said it lad, your sail may be rising; mine falling, but I can yet do you a harm. See this? See this blood of mine staining your memory — treat it with the gall and enmity that my humor has against the whole world you inherit. Grudge it, boy, as I have done, like mankind does you wrong as if one person. From now, it rankles and festers in your heart, as it did mine. It's for you, boy — you who kills me. Live with it, until you come to your own wheezing last breath, like mine.

Jackson steps off the yardarm. Redburn rushes over. He sees Jackson plunge in the water, and the *Highlander* placidly glides by the foaming spot he disappeared beneath.

[Part 4 — VIII: Quiet to Unquiet Men]

EXT. MAIN DECK OF THE *HIGHLANDER* — NIGHT

In the space before the quarterdeck, **BLUNT, DUTCHIE,** and **THE GREENLANDER** play cards, smoke and furtively pass a flask around. Their cards are on a wooden crate between them. **REDBURN** and **HARRY** sit off a bit. They hold hands shielded by their bodies, so that the others cannot see.

THE GREENLANDER
(squints — cheroot clenched in his teeth)
**Oh, what I wouldn't bet to win a reprieve from looking
at you ugly lot.**

BLUNT
(under his breath)
Here we go.

The Greenlander slams a card down, extracts his cigar and exhales in gloating triumph.

THE GREENLANDER
**I'd much rather be looking at one of the lovelies I keep tucked
away in port. You should see my gal in Stockholm...**

The Greenlander makes a buxom gesture.

THE GREENLANDER (CONT'D)
...And my Copenhagen lass; as sweet as honied-wine.

DUTCHIE
**As for the 'ladies' that interest your raggedy sort, I have nothing
to say. For women are like creeds — if you cannot speak well of
one — don't speak ill of any!**

BLUNT
Amen!

Redburn pulls up Harry's hand; examines his burn. It is healing. He sets Harry's palm openly on top of his thigh, puts his hand on top of it.

HARRY
Don't let...his...memory trouble you.

REDBURN
(means it)
I don't. Live by the sword...live with hate, die with it too.

Blunt glances at the boys. He smiles and winks at them.

BLUNT
**But, Dutchie, correct my misperceptions, but I believe I've seen
you with <u>wives</u> too? Yes, in New York, Redburn, you'll see a
certain 'Molly' is one of the first persons aboard, smelling of
grass and sweet water. And you should see, Harry, in Liverpool,
an 'Abigail' grabs and pinches Dutchie in the most shocking
spousal affection.**

REDBURN
(laughs)
What are you Dutchie, a Joseph Smith at sea?

Dutchie stands in sham peevishness.

DUTCHIE
(remarks directed at Blunt too)
**Watch it, boys, you're none of you too big for me to
bend over my knee.**

The Greenlander stands as well; stretches.

THE GREENLANDER
Let's have a song. Harry...

The Greenlander pulls him up.

THE GREENLANDER (CONT'D)
...You sing. Remind us old men what it means to be young!

The Greenlander lifts Harry onto the case. The Greenlander winks and smacks Harry's backside in genuine affection. The men line up in a semi-circle facing Harry and the quarterdeck. While Harry sings, **LAVENDER** strolls up to the quarterdeck railing to watch. As the song concludes, a lingering view of the faces of the men reveal a melting of crusty personas; while a final shot stays on Redburn. He looks miserably sad as he realizes just how much in love he is.

HARRY
(SINGS)
"Now, music is a holy thing –
Its notes, its rumble,
However humble,
Cannot touch a single heartstring
If played by a hand unwilling,
For those who will bruise
Pan's poorest reed, abuse
The God of Song's horned voice to sing.

For young and old I have a song:
Love-airs, which women think the best;
Gay tunes, where the sad most belong;
Sad sounds, upon the agèd rest.

When'er I draw a crowd, I know
Which face from whom the mood will suit,
And from who the silver might flow
To show I please such feelings mute.

I ply sad songs to the merry,
Light airs to the morose who stay,
While the rich for low tunes terry
And the poor sop ballads all day.

Yet, men there are who'd rather me
Share my room than the voice they find —
To them I know the value be
Quiet to an unquiet mind."

(recap: "Now, music..." etc.)

When Harry finishes, the men clap heartily. After Harry takes a bow, he hears Lavender clapping behind him. He turns, and in a close view of Harry's profile, a lecherous grin spread his lips. A wicked sparkle lights his eye as he winks.

[Part 4 – IX: Servicing]

EXT. MAIN DECK OF THE *HIGHLANDER* – AFTERNOON

Members of the **CREW** go about their duties. **REDBURN** searches among them. He asks a group of them including **DUTCHIE**.

> **REDBURN**
> Have you seen Harry?

> **DUTCHIE**
> Aye, lad. I saw him aft.

INT. DOOR OF TOOL SHED LOOKING TO DECK

REDBURN walks on deck towards the door; he has not a care in the world. He comes into the doorframe, bracing his hands on either side. His face slowly sinks.

INT. TOOL SHED

On the opposite wall from the door, **LAVENDER** leans back as **HARRY**, on his knees, services him. Neither sees **REDBURN**.

INT. DOOR OF TOOL SHED LOOKING TO DECK

REDBURN runs from the door. He staggers like he can barely see.

EXT. STARBOARD BOW SECTION

REDBURN stumbles up to the bulwarks. He braces his hands on it, then from elbow to fingertip wipes his eyes with his sleeve. Still the tears roll freely, and he pounds the top rail with clenched fists, but then he blinks a few times. More eye-wiping and concentrated focus is given to something far away. He swallows hard.

REDBURN
(softly to himself)
Land...
(top of lungs)
Land-Ho!

A chorus of '**Land-Ho**' rockets back along the deck. Redburn leans as far over the bulwark as he dare, grabbing some rigging for support.

REDBURN (CONT'D)
(softly to himself)
Home.

EXT. LAND IN THE DISTANCE – DAY – LATER

Rocky green cliffs linger in the hazy distance. White dots of seafowl rove the air in what appears from this distance to be slow motion; blue skies and painterly white clouds drift above all.

[Part 5 – Home – I: Take It/Take Care]

EXT. MAIN DECK AT GANGPLANK OF THE *HIGHLANDER* – AFTERNOON

HARRY, with his bag, runs up to the edge of the gangplank. He excitedly calls and waves his arm.

HARRY
Come on, lad!

Harry goes down, making heavy **FOOTFALLS.**

EXT. MAIN DECK LOOKING STERN

REDBURN comes running, bag on shoulder. He begins to slow down, seeing something by the gangplank.

EXT. MAIN DECK AT GANGPLANK

REDBURN slows. In front of him, **THE GREENLANDER** holds up his right hand like a stop sign, while his left slowly extracts something from his waistband. He meets Redburn's gaze as he slowly hands over his favorite green and white scarf.

THE GREENLANDER
Take it.

The Greenlander presses it into Redburn's hand. He steps back.

THE GREENLANDER (CONT'D)
Remember me, sometimes – when you stand at the helm.

The Greenlander is almost emotional; he glances about the deck.

                    THE GREENLANDER (CONT'D)
                         Just — take care.

Redburn forces the man to hold his eyes. He slowly brings the scarf to his nose and inhales deeply. A moment later, he runs down the gangplank.

EXT. BULWARKS BY GANGPLANK

THE GREENLANDER leans over, watches **REDBURN** join up with **HARRY** on the dock below.

                    THE GREENLANDER (CONT'D)
                              (quietly)
                    I'm sorry he broke your heart.

[Part 5 — II: My Oyster]

EXT. LOWER MANHATTAN WHARF STREET — NOON

The same small square as before, only today it is bright. The area looks cleaner; there is less traffic. The **PEOPLE** are fewer and seem happier; more optimistic.

EXT. LOWER MANHATTAN WHARF

REDBURN and **HARRY** walk towards us. Behind them rise the masts and riggings of tall ships. They are both eating pork pies from newspaper wrappers. They drink from a shared ginger beer bottle.

EXT. LOWER MANHATTAN WHARF STREET

REDBURN and **HARRY** stop before the square. The funnels of the green and white ferries are off to their left. The boys finish up their pies and toss the wrappers in the gutter. Harry takes a swig, and pans around broadly with the bottle.

                             HARRY
    I do believe this <u>New York</u> of yours will be my oyster. Yes. I do
       have an inkling my wits will be a match for the place.

                            REDBURN
                         (grabs the bottle)
    I have no doubt you will be master of your domain, Harry
                         Bolton. No doubt.

                             HARRY
                          (mood deflates)
    You are a good, fine-natured fellow, Redburn. Too good for
                         the likes of me.

                  Redburn jocularly elbows him.

REDBURN
Don't I know it!

HARRY
(takes Redburn's hand)
And – I need not tell you how sorry I am to be
leaving you so soon.

REDBURN
(heartily)
We'll see each other again! We might even ship together. I fear
I've gained my sea-legs, and will soon be land-sick and queasy.

Harry blinks in the sad acknowledgement that they will never see one another after
this.

HARRY
Farewell, old chum.

As seen from close to their hands, Harry extracts his fingers from the still-grasping touch
of Redburn's. Harry runs across the street, into the heart of the square. He meets up
with **LAVENDER,** and throws his arm around his shoulder. As he leads Lavender off,
Lavender turns and glances at Redburn. The retreating pair melt into the crowd. A ferry
whistle **BLOWS** and breaks Redburn's stupor. He sets the bottle down, and pats coat
pockets with both hands. He opens a flap and withdraws a battered and faded yellow
pawn ticket. He dashes across the street.

[Part 5 – III: Not Enough]

EXT. "PORT-OF-CALL PAWN SHOPPE" – AFTERNOON

The door opens; the bell **RINGS. REDBURN** comes out with the gun case under his arm
and closes the door behind him. As he turns around; he freezes in his tracks. **PETER**
stands in front of him.

REDBURN
(shy half-smile)
Good afternoon, brother.

PETER
You look well; well-tanned, at least.

Redburn holds the fowling piece for Peter to take.

PETER (CONT'D)
You keep it. You've earned the right. But now we have a ferry to
catch, and your mother is expecting some reading material from
you.

REDBURN
(grins)
Oh — I've got enough for a book — one hell of a book....

PETER
Swearing, brother?

Redburn shrugs. Peter steps up and puts an affectionate arm around Redburn's shoulder. Redburn responds by hugging his brother's waist, hard. Peter lowers his other arm and hugs him back.

REDBURN (CONT'D)
It's good to be home.

EXT. STREET ALONG FERRY DOCKS

REDBURN and **PETER** walk away with their backs to us; Peter with his hand on Redburn's shoulder, Redburn with his arm around his brother's waist.

PETER (V.O.)
Well, brother — have you had adventure enough?

REDBURN (V.O.)
Adventure?! More than expected, but not enough. Not enough for a lifetime. I fancy I must hie me to the sea again: to the sea, brother! To the sea.

END CREDITS.

While the credits roll, another version of the title **SONG** "Loomings" plays, starting from the second strophe. There are shots of a blue plate-glass sky with cotton candy clouds. A forest of tall ships in their berths stands against the azure with arms and rigging akimbo. Over and above them, seagulls course and cry.

———————~~~~~~~~~———————

Redburn Appendices

The updateable nature of the internet means some material documented here may have been moved or deleted. If so, copy the name of the content & content-creator and search online. Alternates will most likely be easy to find.

Redburn Script Notes

1) Time Setting: June to August, 1839.

2) Character and Costume Notes:

REDBURN: From the Hudson River Valley; 19-20 years old. Redburn's education is of the highest class. Personal tutors opened his mind in all directions, but in his heart, a love of learning and books competes with a desire to be among men; to grow to be respected by them, as one of them. He is a young Gay man yearning for freedom; freedom from his family, from their expectations for him, from their pressures for him to marry. So he, like many 19th century Gay men, is led to the sea for its autonomy; for its out-of-sight camaraderie that more often than not leads to love and reciprocal physical relationships. He is no novice to physical love, having proceeded his way through many 'boyish romances' in his village. These contacts, though reciprocated, were limited to touch. Thus, when he lays a hand on Lavender for the first time, Lavender knows he's dealing with experience. Lavender's placing his mouth near Redburn's as Redburn climaxes grows into a lifelong love of this maneuver, but Harry is the first person he kisses and is kissed by. He is not prepared for the emotional world he is thrust into. First, learning of Blunt's lifelong devotion to his dead partner's memory affects his soul deeply – the ancient Greek myths of same-sex love as the noblest form of human devotion is exampled in a stinky forecastle in the summer of 1839, by a slight and totally modern young man. Secondly, he is disoriented by the sincerity of The Greenlander's interest in him – he does not recognize it as love. Once he does, it is too late; he does not feel the same way for him. Thirdly, the passion of hate from Jackson is unexpected, but quickly gives him focus. Redburn's attitude to his crewmates, other than Jackson, is one of fear-based caution mingled with a full-on erection to be among them and learn from them. In stature, he is average height, but has a well-developed body from working on his relatives' farms. He is vivacious and jocular, and laughs and smiles with the freedom of most teenagers. He has shoulder-length brunette hair which he usually wears tied back with a black ribbon. He has soulful 'Spanish' brown eyes. (For more information, see Series Appendix 2 – "Redburn's Sexual Expressions" (Volume 3, page 267).

> **CLOTHES:** He brings very few pieces of clothing on ship, all of a working nature: two pairs of long trousers (with patched knees), one pair of knee breeches, which he wears when first coming onboard. He has four pairs of

shirts: white, red, indigo and navy. He wears a billowy leather Scotch cap (no pom-pom on top) of the type that will evolve into the baseball cap. Later on, Dutchie lends him a proper seafaring tarpaulin hat with a brim. Over all he wears his brother's red hunting jacket. Since he has no jumper (a seaman's "frock"), he must wear this jacket even when it is only slightly chilly. For their trip overland, Harry dresses Redburn in Harry's 'working' clothes: full-length light-colored trousers, a dark-blue baize jacket, a flashy silk plaid vest and a starched vermillion cotton scarf tied into a huge lineal bowtie. After Harry comes onboard, he borrows freely from this boy's brand-new seafaring kit, and is seen wearing duck trousers and navy and indigo jumpers instead of his coat. In Liverpool he buys a jackknife and holster. For a time, early in the passage over, he wears The Greenlander's green and white scarf around his neck, with the man's silver ring as a pass-through above the knot. He begins the voyage with a pair of high farm boots, which he finds totally unsuitable for the work. He cuts off the tops and folds the ends down, but mostly, when the weather permits, he goes barefoot. Later, Harry buys him a pair of sailor pumps.

PETER: Redburn's brother. Born in New York City, moved ten years previous to a village on the Hudson; 28 years old. Peter has watched his immediate family's fortunes fall precipitously. With a recession, his father's textile import business waned, forcing the family to live in the cheaper hinterlands, near other relations who could help out. From bad to worse, his father died suddenly, and the business being heavily leveraged, could not go on. Whatever he could do, he did to make sure his brother and sister continued to receive their education, but in the course of this grueling work, he became exposed to tuberculosis. He is aware of his brother's affectional orientation, but as long as he sees his younger brother being discreet about it, he can avoid bringing it up. He is the same way, but has never had the sort of freedom of sensuality that his brother has enjoyed, and thus never initiated or exchanged mutual love with a romantic partner. In many ways he envies the boldness of his brother's spirit. Peter also fears its recklessness, but he cannot live Redburn's life for him. He feels the early stages of the disease tapped the strength out of Peter, and invests in his brother the hopes of the happy life he can never enjoy for himself. Peter is deeply moved by the filial affection his brother showers upon him.

> **CLOTHES:** He wears conservative business attire, and a low-sloping top hat that was in fashion circa 1825.

TOBY: Born and raised in New York City; 21 years old. Sparked by mutual love-at-first-sight, neither Toby nor Redburn know when they first bump into each other that they are destined to be the love of the other's life. Toby reappears in the following film, *Typee*, and thereafter. Toby is an inch or two shorter than Redburn and of a slightly more wiry build. He is lithe and jocular in the extreme; handsome, with fine dark curls, and placid blue eyes. He has been toughened by a life at sea since the age of sixteen.

> **CLOTHES:** He is meticulous and trim in his spotless sailor garb. He takes pride in his appearance, and is first drawn to cruise Redburn because of that young man's odd and flamboyant attire.

CAPTAIN RIGA: Latvian-born; mid-50s. Bushy haired and dapper in full beard and mustache, Riga is officious and sardonic. While at dock or on land, he wears his finest clothes and polishes his finest manners. At sea he wears outdated and worn clothes, and only speaks to the ship's officers and his steward. When first seen, his hair is dark, then quickly grays at sea, where it stays gray until land is sighted. It suddenly turns jet-black again, and Lavender's hands look stained for a few days. He is fond of Lavender and sees that the lad always looks nice wearing his hand-me-down clothes.

> **CLOTHES:** In public he dresses like a lawyer, and uses Lavender in his silk turban as a sort of accessory to draw people's attention to him and his high status. He likes a bit of color flash in his neckwear, and he likes to see color on the back of his cabin boy. At sea he wears what is warm and serviceable; mainly clothes he has had for twenty years.

LAVENDER: (aka *the Steward; cabin boy*) African American New Yorker; 18 years old. An orphan boy apprenticed to a Bowery barber, Lavender became the victim of sexual usage by the barber, and of men who paid the barber as pimp. At fourteen, he ran away and signed up as 'boy' on a ship. Here the Captain took notice of the handsome youth, and groomed him to be a steward. Captain Riga signed him away to join him on the *Highlander* about 18 months ago. Riga makes no sexual demands on him, which Lavender finds to be both a relief and troublesome. If Riga is not attached to him, Lavender could be replaced by another boy who captures Riga's eye in the future. Lavender is accustomed to using his sexual appeal to obtain what he requires. He knows most men find him intriguing, and uses that knowledge as needed. In Redburn he encounters, for the first time, a 'type' like he is. He wonders what Redburn's game is, seeing the other teen does not use his obvious appeal for mercenary advancement. Redburn puzzles him, but also attracts him. The Cook is his only true friend onboard, which hurts him when Doctor Thompson lectures him on 'profligate' ways. He is a couple of inches taller than Redburn, lean, smooth-complected and has gray eyes.

> **CLOTHES:** On duty, Lavender wears the colorful clothes from Riga's youth: swallowtail jackets, vests and knee breeches with stockings. These are out of date, but in vibrant Regency colors: mulberry, snuff, crimson, etc. While berthed, or on land with Riga, he ties a long yellow silk scarf around his head in a turban. At sea, he wears no headgear at all. Off duty, he wears his own clothes, which are current, tasteful and restrained: long trousers, plain shirts and an indigo monkey jacket. On his right ring finger he wears his most valuable possession: a man's baguette diamond ring in gold. This is the only thing the barber ever gave to him. [19]

FIRST MATE: Pennsylvania-born son of a preacher; 35 years old. He is at the point of his career where he needs to be noticed by ship-owners. He does this by being the consummate business manager of the *Highlander,* counting the days he can receive his own commission and see the backside of Riga for good. He accepts things the way they are for as long they function, and will advise the Captain with what he believes he wants to hear. His clothes in port speak to his professionalism. He has dark hair, is tall and thin, and has a drawn-out face.

CLOTHES: In sight of land, he wears clothes better suited to a rakish accountant than a sailor. When first seen, he is jacketless, wears a striped calico shirt with sleeve garters, vest, snuff-colored trousers and a beaverskin hat. During the voyages he wears jerseys, a tight pea coat and a red wool toque cap.

SECOND MATE: (aka *Mr. Riggs*) African American New Englander; mid-40s. A terse man who is bulky and not overly tall. He is generally curt and offers one piece of advice for most occasions: "Chuck it overboard." He feels the ship cannot run without him, and that the bunch of dandies onboard the *Highlander* makes his job all the harder.

CLOTHES: From first to last, he is seen in a loose pea coat and a tight-fitting blue stocking cap. He is a man of few words, and even fewer clothes.

THE PAWNBROKER: New Yorker: mid-60s. As a religiously-inclined Jewish man of his age, he has little patience for the hustlers and prostitutes who frequently come in his shop. Stolen goods are a constant problem, because the nascent NYPD routinely comes in and 'shops' for whatever they fancy with the 'testimony' that it was stolen. Much of his profits are siphoned off for protection from the beat cops' superiors. He lives for the rare gentleman bringing him true valuables, of the fowling piece type.

CLOTHES: Being a frugal man, he wears fashions current in about 1825: a black squaretail jacket, vest and high ruffled shirt. His head is covered by an embroidered and tasseled smoking cap.

HUSTLER: (in pawnshop) Irish-born Bowery Boy; 16 years old. A freckled, and slightly pimpled strawberry-blond youth doing what he has to to-get-by without resorting to robbery, or cheating, or anything 'bad.' He went out of his way to come to lower Manhattan to liquidate a ring his 'husband' gave to him. [20] His own Bowery neighborhood being none too safe to attempt the same. His pride is hurt by the Pawnbroker's accusation, but he's relieved the man did not outright steal the ring, claiming that he needed to hand it over to the police.

CLOTHES: The unique hustler uniform on both sides of the Atlantic is the same; a trademark by which their clients may know them. This Bowery boy looks overly youthful in beige corduroy knee breeches and pale-blue stockings with a sportingly tight jacket in dark-blue baize. He has a jocular clerk's cap in tan tweed. Billowing under his chin, and layered about his neck, is a red silk scarf. This piece of wealthy extravagance, as part of an otherwise boyish ensemble, is the signal to his clients that he is 'sporting.' In later generations, this will evolve into the visual code of hustlers wearing red neckties to signal themselves to their potential clients. [21]

JACKSON: Bowery Boy; mid-40s. A career sailor who contracted yellow fever while on a long-haul tour and was discharged about seven years ago. He partially recovered his health, but never recovered his hair or full liver function; thus he appears thin, totally bald, sallow and jaundiced. An old acquaintance of the First Mate, he enjoys his 'senior sailor' status, knowing that he can kick back when he needs a rest. Because of his compromised health, he has battled tuberculosis for the last several years. He is in the final stages of the disease, and every day wakes feeling his body die a bit more than the morning before. He has a lot in his past to atone for (slave running; opium smuggling; a long list of rapes; and hate crimes), and no time in which to do it. Men in his position either repent and aim the remainder of their life to doing good, or they break bad and fully embrace the notion of going out with a bang as their final legacy. He's gone bad: resents robust life as exhibited in the others around him, fears usurpation by better-bodied sailors, and hates love in any human manifestation. He uses intimidation to hold onto position and his sanity (so he doesn't have to face the fear of after-life retribution for his wrongs to other people). He is average-build, with only one remarkable physical feature: a walleye. He has one hefty gold earring in his right ear (signifying he has rounded the Cape of Good Hope).

> **CLOTHES:** He has several pairs of overalls: some in nankeen; others in denim; some in duck. Under these he wears several pairs of colored shirts all at one time – one because he has shrunk in his clothes, two so he appears to still be bulky, and three because he is constantly chilled in his waning health. On his hairless head he wears a "large white wool hat, with a broad rolling brim." [22]

THE GREENLANDER: Sailor of Viking stock; 28 years old. A man who went to sea for the usual reasons of freedom and male-male camaraderie. He is borderline between believing he will find a mate, and be settled at sea with him, and a doomed feeling that such 'accidents' are rare. Redburn has no idea the hopes his actions fan, nor can he relate to the motivations for The Greenlander's self-preservation turn of a cold shoulder on him after the youth breaks his heart. He likes sex, and he likes to talk about sex, though he couches his experiences in feminine pronoun. He is genuinely turned on and intrigued by Harry, and after an initial wish to hurt Redburn, he grows fond enough of Harry to be respectful, and to wish the lads best of luck in their partnership. He hopes that what he says about Harry's 'type' is wrong and that the boys can build a lasting relationship. But Redburn's heartbreak tilts him firmly back to the hope side of things – seeing how Redburn was broken just like he was. With rare, and lavish detail, Melville paint a vivid physical picture of The Greenlander: tall and slender-waisted, but muscular on top with broad shoulders and chest, wavy flaxen hair, fair and smooth skin, and clear blue eyes. He wears a pair of gold earrings with a diamond-studded anchor on each. On his fingers he has several thick silver bands, some plain, some with sea motifs like leaping dolphins. His hair is long enough that he sometimes ties it back with a colorful ribbon.

> **CLOTHES:** A typical Gay sailor, he is fastidious to a fault, both on land and at sea. He has a large wardrobe, and all items of clothing look brand new because he maintains them with love. He dresses "...very tastefully too, as if he knows he is a good-looking fellow." Every day a new ensemble: he has pairs of trousers in white duck, indigo cotton, navy wool. He has shirts in light-blue flannel, red and blue wool, and natural linen. When he wears a jersey, he has French striped tee-shirts on under them, and his jerseys are white with indigo collars and flaps, or indigo with white collars and flaps. Over these he wears a leather belt. He has two monkey jackets, one in green baize and one in navy wool. Around his neck, he has

an endless variety of scarves, some in fine wool flannel with paisley patterns, others in solid colors of silk — but his favorite — the one he wears more than the others, is green and white with a check pattern in lustrous silk. To hold the ends of the scarves in place as they ride his chest, he uses a polished shark vertebra. His preferred headgear is a broad brimmed hat "bright as a looking glass" complete with a pair of long-trailing green ribbons.

DUTCHIE: From the Hook in Holland; mid-40s. He comes from a sailing family, and from a young age listened with intent to his uncles and older cousins talk about Batavia, Curaçao and all the other corners of the Dutch trading world. Frankly, he finds the conditions and freedom on American ships much more to his liking. He is investing his money and in a few years he'll have to decide where to settle down, and which of the women he is in long term relationships with will be invited to his new home. He is good-natured, rather optimistic, and looks to find the best in the people he has to work and live with, even Jackson. He is not too tall, and has thinning vivid red hair and a freckled complexion. He is a stout man with well-developed legs and arms that sport a couple of fading tattoos beneath his abundant freckles.

> **CLOTHES:** A second thought at best, his clothes are worn and faded from long use at sea. He favors red shirts and dark wool trousers. He has a medium-blue monkey jacket and faded navy pea coat. He lends Redburn a worn, but sensible canvas sailor's hat. He wears the same model, only newer, and with a red ribbon to identify it as his.

BLUNT: An English-born Irish Traveler; 25 years old. Given to an orphanage near London soon after being born, his young mother was forced to abandon him due to family pressure to keep the baby secret. In the orphanage, several other Irish kids made sure he knew about, and was proud of his heritage — knew it was superior to the one surrounding him. This early-life sheltering amongst one's own set Blunt on a path to a life of strong attachments. At eight years of age he was signed over to the Royal Navy as a powder monkey, or one of the little boys who supply the gun decks with gunpowder when under attack. A teenage boy became his protector and family on ship, and as the two grew up together, love and reciprocal devotion blossomed. After ten years of life together, this young man sacrificed himself to push Blunt out of the way of exploding ordinance. Blunt feels guilty; sometimes wishes they had died together, rather than one live on and feel the pain he does. After his partner's death, Blunt became increasingly spiritual. Several visits of his partner to his dreams prompted Blunt to begin a journal, and plummet the depths of dream symbology. These records provide great comfort to him in his ongoing despair. He consults with spiritualists in Liverpool and New York who look into crystals to try and soothe the causes of his cares. Tough young, he cannot conceive of a time when love will be a comfort to him, if it comes from somebody else. Far from being morose about it, he lives each day as one closer to reunion, and is grateful. Outwardly he believes he hides all his inner turmoil, but he is wrong. His nightmares, and his prematurely graying hair let everyone close to him know he is far from happy. His physicality is extreme. Lithe and quick, he is on the smaller side, prone to desperately far-away looks broken by self-abashed grins and a hand to the back of the head, as well as long periods of quiet introspection and flashes of anger. He has a love of language first born by his 'family' in the orphanage, then expanded many fold by the diverse characters around him in the navy. He speaks with a 'standard' London accent, but can turn on a dime to cant a lilting Irish, or a tough Bowery Boy accent — or anything else he fancies. He has a bushy head of dark straight hair, graying along the center. It is medium length, and because of his hair product, he wears it spiky.

> **CLOTHES:** His look is particular; all of his clothes are too big for him, and make him look boyish. But, they are lovingly darned, cleaned and kept safe from over-use. The style is somber, of the type approved in the Royal Navy. These are in fact the clothes of his deceased partner, ever and always about him. He wears a gray fisherman's sou'wester in inclement weather; a naval cap at other times. In bad weather, his partner's boots come up to his knees and rattle about on his feet; otherwise he wears pumps or goes barefoot.

COOK: (aka *Doc; the Doctor; Mr. Thompson; Dr. Thompson*) African American New Yorker; 55 years old. A religious man, who might have been content to be a preacher if his early circumstances had allowed, he is not fond of the sea. His cookhouse gets much of the worst of the weather, and the constant drafts reminds him how his career is winding down due to advancing age. Frugal in the extreme, he has a tidy sum waiting for him in a New York bank, and never ventures off ship when in port to spend money. He is content with his few books, and the company of Lavender, whom he genuinely likes and worries about. After Lavender and Redburn split, Lavender returns to the Cook's bunk, where he knows he is safe. Cook is not judgmental; humbly he believes one cannot remove the splinter from a neighbor's eye without first removing the plank from his own. He has a warm face, usually dressed in a half-smile and sly eyes that invite a person into the joke.

> **CLOTHES:** To suit the dignity of being the ship's 'doctor', he wears long sleeve shirts and vests with his apron over them. The shirts are fashioned from bed ticking; his vests are long and old-fashioned waistcoats, and generally appear worn and faded. A maroon one is his favorite. He wears dark trousers and has a buff-colored jacket for when he steps away from the cookhouse. Usually his sleeves are rolled up. On his head, in the best of chefly fashion, he wears a massive single toque with a heavy tassel.

HARRY: (aka *Harry Bolton*) From Bury St. Edmunds, Suffolk; 22 years old. He is a very accomplished Artful-Dodger-type hustler, and a practiced fabricator of the truth he believes his hearers want to believe. He tells Redburn he is 20, and grew up with a well-off aunt in Bury before shipping as a 'boy' on an India-man. In fact, he was given up to an orphanage and apprenticed against his will at age 13 for the grueling voyage. In circumstances similar to Blunt, Harry was protected by an older sailor and had his education finished on board ship. Unlike Blunt however, Harry's 'protector' grew disinterested in him on the long return voyage and exposed the lad to usage for money to line the older sailor's pocket. On this leg of the journey, Harry professed a passionate hatred for shipping to the first mate, and afterwards, the officer introduced Harry to a high-class London 'big brother' (a pimp of male prostitutes) who saw Harry's potential. Excelling at entertaining posh clientele, he soon graduated to the upper echelons of 'The Club' and the cultivated tastes of the ruling class of Britain. Harry is super attentive, witty and very well-read. He entertains as much with his mind as with his form. As his profession demands, he is an inveterate liar, and leaves Redburn constantly wondering who and what this remarkable boy might be. He likes sailors for fun, and this is initially what led him to "The Baltimore Clipper," and drew him forcefully to the innocence of Redburn. His vitality commands the attention of everybody in the game, but leaves him wondering if Redburn is attracted to his 'game,' or to the real Harry. His budding love for the American takes him by as much surprise and wonder as it does Redburn, and he starts the *Highlander's* return voyage in the sincere hope of getting a fresh start with Redburn. But, pressures mount, and he reverts to what he knows best. He has no intention of breaking Redburn's heart, but like Lavender, he feels others' reaction to him is not ultimately his doing. Among many other things, he is an accomplished singer and dancer. Physically, he is the same height as Redburn — if a few pounds lighter — lean and described by Melville as having "silken muscles." He has longish and youthfully cut chestnut hair, an evenly dark complexion, and large hazel eyes.

> **CLOTHES:** His 'sporting' attire for the docks is much like the Bowery boy Hustler: knee breeches, stockings, shirt, baize jacket, bright scarf under his chin, and a clerk's cap. For the trip to London, he wears his high-class working attire: full-length light-colored trousers, a snuff-colored baize jacket, a bright silk plaid vest, and a moss-green starched cotton scarf tied into a huge bowtie. On his head he wears a youthful brimmed hat, like a low-profile cowboy hat. His sea wardrobe is instinctively calculated to appeal to sailors: two "Guernsey frocks" (corded knit sweaters), one in white, one in indigo; light-colored jumpers and trousers, a sea-green monkey jacket, and all his various scarves. His headgear is a billowy tweed fisherman's cap with visor. All his clothes look new and clean.

3) As part of a photo montage for The Secret Melville No. 5, two the sailor couples in Redburn should have formal, early 19th century-style pictures taken and mounted in gutta percha cases with gilt frames. For this screenplay, the couples are: Blunt and Partner; Harry Bolton and Lavender. See Moby-Dick Text Endnote No. 20 (Volume 2, page 332) for a gallery of authentic sailor wedding-type portraits for staging inspiration.

Redburn Text Endnotes

[1] Hudson River ferries: the "St. John," 1840s:

https://3.bp.blogspot.com/-4r1MYWJrZAo/TtOP-
E5Cmpl/AAAAAAAAAVs/MsJmcvhge8I/s1600/Hudson+River+St
eamboat+ST.+JOHN+-Currier+and+Ives+Print.jpg

The "Francis Skiddy," 1859:

https://i.pinimg.com/736x/36/44/1d/36441dd5d5a6398eef3c
c81e0c31f63a.jpg

[2] Redburn's red shooting jacket: is the same in detail to this example, except Redburn's has horn buttons and is square in the front (i.e., not a 'cut-away' example as in the pictures):

https://www.nma.gov.au/__data/assets/image/0011/654725/
MA46105548-Hunting-coat.jpg

https://www.nma.gov.au/__data/assets/image/0009/734724/
MA46106401-Hunting-coat.jpg

[3] The Battery and environs of lower Manhattan, 1830s:

https://h7.alamy.com/comp/3/1f944dc5cf95411d84e548a546
f92d4a/2ba445p.jpg

https://media.wnyc.org/i/800/552/l/80/2020/05/800px-
Park_Row_and_Park_Theatre.jpg

Hustlers of the Bowery, 1830s:

https://www.boweryboyshistory.com/wp-content/uploads/2008/06/boweryhydrant.jpg

[4] The *Highlander* of New York: When Melville wrote "Redburn" there had never been a ship registered in New York under the name *Highlander*. The book became one of his best sellers, and the keel of the *Highlander* illustrated below was laid in the Brooklyn Shipyards within a matter of months after the 1849 release of *Redburn*. It is more than probable this vessel was named in tribute to the fictional *Highlander*. As per Melville, her figurehead was named Donald, and outfitted remarkably like the author's description. A very similar figurehead from another vessel survives; see the next illustration.

"The *Highlander* of New York" by Louis Roux:

https://imgc.artprintimages.com/img/print/highlander-of-new-york_u-l-e81yy0.jpg?h=900&p=0&w=900

Figurehead of the 1855 *Donald McKay*:

https://newenglandnomad2015.files.wordpress.com/2017/09/img_01761.jpg?w=490

[5] Cased fowling piece: English examples from about 1805:

https://www.christies.com/lotfinderimages/D54592/a_cased_34-bore_double-barrelled_percussion_sporting_rifle_by_j_purdey_d5459286g.jpg

https://images.bidsquare.com/item/l/9518/95183.jpeg?t=1ENuki

[6] Nug: rough term of endearment from man to boy (like 'kiddo,' 'bugger' or 'sport').

[7] Arrival in England: "Port of Liverpool" by Samuel Walters, 1836:

https://www.shipspottersteve.com/uploads/1/6/9/2/16921916/wp-20150502-14-58-48-pro-2_orig.jpg

[8] Dutchie's 'Baltimore Clipper' dance music: Bach's Gigue in G, BWV 577:

https://www.youtube.com/watch?v=KsYwi8FP2E4

[9] The Exchange: Liverpool's cruising grounds:

http://streetsofliverpool.co.uk/wp-content/uploads/Exchange-2.jpg

[10] American Teen sporting Harry and Redburn's 'London' look, early 1840s (author's collection):

https://i.pinimg.com/564x/25/05/76/2505766c33f7779ccf43
43bdf5ad136a.jpg

Harry and Redburn's silk plaid vest: 1840s example:

https://1tq45j21k9qr27g1703pgsja-wpengine.netdna-ssl.com/wp-content/uploads/2020/03/ma-29932.jpg

[11] Fancy boy: hustler; young male sex worker.

[12] Toffer: a superior sexual service provider.

[13] Indorser: a passionate lover. Festival night: sex-worker's hours of operation. A wedding night: a romantic sexual date.

[14] An 1834 railway carriage:

https://blog.railwaymuseum.org.uk/wp-content/uploads/2013/11/bodmin-carriage.jpg?w=507

[15] Flavor of "The Club": London's 'Reform Club' in 1841:

https://upload.wikimedia.org/wikipedia/commons/4/48/Reform Club. Upper level of the saloon. From London Interiors %28 1841%29 %28cropped%29.jpg

[16] The Telamones supports in 'The Club': Leo von Klenze's examples for the Hermitage in St. Petersburg:

https://www.thenationalnews.com/image/policy:1.320990:1499
472910/image/jpeg.jpg?f=16x9&w=1200&pf$w=dfa40e8

https://previews.123rf.com/images/rostislavv/rostislavv1210/ros
tislavv121000229/15840332-atlas-titan-who-held-up-the-
celestial-sphere-statue-1846-at-entrance-of-new-hermitage-st-
petersburg.jpg

'The Club's' sofas, based on Kedleston Hall examples:

Overall view:

https://media-cdn.tripadvisor.com/media/photo-
s/19/d9/20/2c/the-kedleston-drawing.jpg

http://images.ntpl.org.uk/hppa-
zooms/00000000658/cms_108607_1.bro

End support:

http://images.ntpl.org.uk/hppa-
zooms/00000000658/cms_108608_1_2_.bro

[17] The Stairway Paintings "Hercules and Telephus":

https://upload.wikimedia.org/wikipedia/commons/3/3d/Hercule
s-and-telephus.jpg

"Chiron and Achilles":

https://upload.wikimedia.org/wikipedia/commons/6/6e/Chiron_i
nstructs_young_Achilles_-_Ancient_Roman_fresco.jpg

[18] Three shades of snuff for reference:

https://ramsay.arthistory.wisc.edu/static/Snuff.jpg

[19] Monkey jacket:

https://cdn.shopify.com/s/files/1/0050/1275/0447/products/d
ouble-breasted-sailor-jacket_sj-
159_web_p1730561_1_2400x.jpg?v=1571714811

[20] Husband: a regular client who favors a particular hustler over all others, and who may make the arrangement semi-permanent and exclusive; analogous to situations where men provide housing and income to a beloved mistress. This term, along with all the others in this series, comes from *Grose's Classical Dictionary of the Vulgar Tongue*, London 1823 – a slang guide full of Gay terms. An unabridged facsimile is available here:

[21] The Hustler's neck scarf: Melville relays in graphic tones that the young man's neckwear is soiled — with what, he does not explicitly say — but he adds suggestively that it: "looked as if it were going to seed." (Chapter 4)

Secret Melville 2:

TYPEE

In the Valley of the Shadow of Death

————·····∿∿∿∿∿∿∿∿∿·····————

"But with the inconstancy of a despounding mind that speculates in the dark as to the causes that have produced the misery under which it languishes, I would often experience the most bitter remorse after indulging in these reflections, & again & again would seek to pierce the mystery that hung over the sudden disappearance of my companion."

—Unpublished portion of
Typee manuscript [i]

Based Upon the Novel:

Typee:
A Peep at Polynesian Life
during
a Four Months' Residence
in
a Valley of the Marquesas, 1846

and its supplement

Sequel:
The Story of Toby, 1847

by Herman Melville

EXT. LONGBOAT OF THE *DOLLY* – MORNING

The boat glides across sunlit water: oars cut a tropical bay and come up glinting, only to fall and repeat the process. **GROANS** of exertion alternate with the beat of the oars. **REDBURN**'s hand skims the moving surface near the prow, and cuts the water into diamond-like sparkles.

INT. LONGBOAT

REDBURN rights himself, and with a quick and friendly smirk, flicks water in **TOBY**'s face. They sit next to each other in the bow of the boat, and are dressed like twins — both in clean work clothes; white tee-shirts, navy-blue jumpers with scarves, white cotton duck trousers, and broad-brimmed hats with trailing ribbons. Toby has an extra, yellow bandana, tied around his left bicep. They feel they are watched. On the other side of the boat, four members of the **CREW** are rowing hard, while **JIM** and three other members of the crew sit two-by-two. In contrast to the boys, the other passengers wear colorful scarves tied like bow ties, starched shirts, clean trousers, and various fancy jackets. The *Dolly* is behind them at anchor. Jim elbows his compatriot, and gestures with his chin.

> **JIM**
> Get a gander at those two...dressed like they're going aloft,
> not going ashore.

While the other sailors laugh heartily, Redburn and Toby exchange a silent unease.

> **TOBY**
> (blusters)
> And look at you assorted lot. Dressed in your finest church-going
> togs, when the nearest proper church is six weeks to the east.
> We wouldn't go fishing to the bottom of <u>our</u> sea chests to impress
> a parcel of un-britcheded natives. Why — out of the sight of you
> rabble — I might venture a time in the buff to match the best of
> them.

The sailors laugh good-naturedly, and Toby gives Redburn a wink unseen by the rest. Redburn turns and faces the breeze. Ahead lies the shore of Nuku Hiva and its mountain peaks rising thousands of feet above the water. Tropical lushness is peppered with dark rain clouds. A flash of lightning strikes the mountaintop.

EXT. LONGBOAT

The oarsmen **GRUNT**. The water sparkles as the oars cut it. **REDBURN**'s hand skims it into diamonds.

[Part 1 – II: The Escape]

EXT. STEEP TRAIL ON NUKA HIVA – NOON

A light tropical rain is falling. From a low vantage – close to the foliage growing along the trail – **REDBURN**'s and **TOBY**'s feet come running past. Their trouser legs are wet and already stained at the hems with mud. They continue up the path; shoes slipping on bits on muddy patches.

EXT. HIGHER UP THE TRAIL – EARLY AFTERNOON

It rains steadily now. The trail is less clear than before. **TOBY** leads by slapping the soaked overgrowth out of the way. **REDBURN** stops; stoops; braces his hands on his knees trying to catch his breath. Both now have their jumpers tied around their waists, and Toby has his bandana tied around his neck. Redburn struggles to call out.

REDBURN
Toby!

Miffed, Toby turns and comes back to Redburn. He re-shoulders the pack he is carrying.

TOBY
(hoarse whisper)
No more lingering! Let's shove ahead while we can. We have to make it to higher ground, where no one can see us from the village.

Toby looks over the trail's edge. The village – a gathering of buildings with its harbor – is a couple of thousand feet down. In the bay, a French black-hulled warship, la *Reine Blanche* dominates, while several smaller vessels anchor at a distance around her, including the *Dolly*.

TOBY (CONT'D)
(tone becomes more open)
**Come on, mate. A few hours more, and we can laugh
fortune right in her face.**

REDBURN
(stands upright)
**All right, brother. Quick's our play – only – let's stay close
together. That's all. All right? Stop leaping around like a young
roe on this treacherous terrain!**

TOBY
(akimbo)
**Why...remember, Redburn – brother – this is your idea
of adventure. Not mine!**

Toby turns and walks off, going fast up the path. Redburn inhales sharply and follows.

FADE IN: TITLE CARD: "The Secret Melville, TYPEE, In the Valley of the Shadow of Death"

While credits roll, there are shots of **REDBURN** and **TOBY** continuing up the trail: foliage moving, rain falling with more menace, flashes of lighting and thunder, and the men jumping rivulets fast growing into streams. They are soaked and miserable.

[Part 1 – III: The Assessment]

EXT. A CLEARING – MID-AFTERNOON

The sun begins to peek warmly through the receding clouds. Off the trail is a large, level meadow with some flat rocks in the center. **REDBURN** and **TOBY** come through a thicket into the clearing. Wearily they make their way to the rocks, and spread themselves out like lizards to dry in the sun. They gaze up at the clouds turning from gray to white as they roll overhead.

REDBURN
Let's assess what we've brought.

Redburn sits up, cross-legged. Toby tosses him the bag without rising. Redburn lifts the flap and extracts the items one at a time. He arrays them to dry between him and Toby. First, a shaving kit. Toby rolls on his side, propped on one elbow, to watch. Redburn frowns as he opens the straight razor and flashes it in the sunshine. He sets it down. Next, a flat wooden box with notebooks and several pencils in it. Then, a ditty bag with needle and thread; a pair of pipes; a small tin box with firesteel, flint and tinder; several strings of beads; two folded bolts of calico fabric. Toby turns back to the sky with a hand behind his head. Redburn is about to set the bag down when he hears one more thing rattle in it. He reaches in and is surprised to be holding a three-and-a-half inch square photograph case. [1] It is cast gutta-percha with a simple rolled edge and a large raised scallop relief in the center. He glances at Toby, who pretends to pay no attention. Redburn opens the case. The picture is of Redburn and Toby in a studio, sitting with their hands linked. He swallows hard and wordlessly closes it. It goes with the other items. The bag is now empty. He sets it aside, then remembers more. Redburn pats his chest and moves to the pockets of his jersey. Toby rises and sits like his partner. Lifting a knowing eyebrow to Toby, Redburn extracts from his right pocket a mushy fistful of sea biscuits reduced to a pulp. He plops it down. Toby sees it is covered in flecks of brown, runny tobacco. Redburn does the same with his left pocket and extracts a fistful of tobacco likewise flecked with biscuit. Redburn motions for Toby to do the same, and he produces two identical lumps which go next to their twins.

REDBURN (CONT'D)
Well – at least we brought something to eat.

TOBY
(aghast grimace)
We should pick the tobacco out....

REDBURN
No time.

Redburn smashes the two pulpy bread masses together. He holds it in front of Toby's face.

REDBURN (CONT'D)
Want some now?

TOBY
(turns his head)
Ugh...

REDBURN
Aye. Me neither.

Redburn plops it down. Toby catches sight of Redburn's stationary box.

TOBY
(incredulous)
You brought pencil and paper...? What for! Did you bring
envelopes and stamps as well?!

REDBURN
You brought a shaving kit? Planning on presenting a
headhunter with the gift of a straight razor?

The humor is lost on Toby. He answers honestly.

TOBY
No. I brought it to shave.

REDBURN
Oh, and you think to borrow a shaving mirror from the
local, tribal hairdresser?

TOBY
Well...

REDBURN
I brought my notebook to record observations; special
explanations on our privileged peek into Polynesian—

It dawns on Redburn.

REDBURN (CONT'D)
Oh. I'm the one chosen to play barber to your stubble, am I?
No mirror needed.

TOBY
(grins hopelessly)
And, I've shave you.

REDBURN
(laughs)
We come to another Eden, and your vanity wills out. Let your
beard grow! God mentions nothing about two-bit barbers in

paradise. You're the one joking about trudging about in the altogether...or...was that just an idle threat?

Toby again lies back, this time with both hands behind his head.

TOBY
Maybe. Maybe not.

Redburn puts the items away in the bag.

REDBURN
Think they're looking for us yet?

TOBY
Not till seven, when the boat launches back to the ship. I might miss the *Dolly*. She wasn't a bad vessel.

Redburn stands and brushes the seat of his trousers. He shoulders the bag, then goes over to Toby's rock. He looks down into Toby's face, which is half squinting in the sunlight.

REDBURN
We better go.

Redburn extends a hand, and Toby takes it. Redburn helps Toby stand, then while Toby is brushing himself, gets their hats. He plops Toby's hat on Toby's head, and they head back to the trail.

[Part 1 – IV: Shipboard Hardships]

DISSOLVE TO:

TIME CARD:

"ONE MONTH EARLIER"

EXT. MAIN DECK OF THE *DOLLY* – NOON

A scorching sun beats through rigging to bleach the deck of the ship at sea. The sails rap in a light breeze. **JIM** and **REDBURN** are coiling rope next to the Captain's chicken coop. In it, a solitary rooster broods motionlessly on one foot.

REDBURN
Six months at sea!

Jim does not reply. Redburn coils harder with frustration.

REDBURN (CONT'D)
Six months at sea! Six months, without even a glimpse of a blade of grass; six months without one snuff of loamy earth raised to greedy nostrils.

Jim stops working and fishes out his pipe and tobacco pouch. As he fills it, he sets one foot on the coop.

> **REDBURN (CONT'D)**
> Look at us. The sky above; the sea below; and nothing else. There's not a sweet potato left on board; not a yam to be seen — and those spots of color – the green to yellow bananas, the sacks of oranges that spangled out stern yards. They've all been plucked — mainly by that Captain Vangs.

Jim has deftly lit the pipe, and now grins at Redburn though a smoke halo.

> **REDBURN (CONT'D)**
> Jim, what? You think this is a matter
> for levity?

> **JIM**
> No, Redburn, my boy; no. See here? Here. The chicken coop.
> This is your signal, lad. We'll be port-bound soon enough.

Redburn stops working. He comes up to stand akimbo by Jim. Redburn looks like Jim has lost his mind.

> **JIM (CONT'D)**
> You think it cruel of me to wish this little fellow a goner?

> **REDBURN**
> I don't see what this has to do with—

> **JIM**
> Well – you should. Pray, lad, for the decapitation of so
> forlorn a tyke as little Pedro.

Jim rights himself and stands next to Redburn. He points at the coop with one hand, and puts the other on Redburn's shoulder.

> **JIM (CONT'D)**
> The Captain will never point the prow of the *Dolly* landward
> while he still has the anticipation of a mess of fresh meat.

Jim removes his hat in faux solemnity.

> **JIM (CONT'D)**
> Alas, Pedro is the last of the crew that can furnish it to his
> praiseworthy belly.

Jim knocks off Redburn's hat from behind. It falls into Redburn's hands.

> **JIM (CONT'D)**
> Cheer up, boy! See? Look how he's but the last and solitary tenant of the coop? Remember Pedro as he was — a gay and dapper young cock — strutting as a king amongst his harem of

coy hens. But now? Now – pity him that he stands there, moping the day along on that everlasting one leg of his. He turns with disgust from the moldy corn set before him; huffs at the brackish water that sloshes in his little trough. Anyway, my boy, why? He mourns the loss of his companions. He saw them one by one, snatched by that great hard-hearted hand of fate. One by one, his partners were taken from him, to points unknown.

Jim sits on the coop. Redburn looks dubious.

JIM (CONT'D)
Soon we'll have to land. I predict that by Sunday, our formerly lithe little fellow will be laid out before Captain Vangs with all due ceremony – and, that before night falls, Pedro will be buried beneath the vest buttons of that very worthy individual.

REDBURN
(shakes his head)
We'll see, Jim. We'll just see.

EXT. MAIN DECK OF THE *DOLLY* – AFTERNOON

The sun in the sky is partially blocked by rolling tropical clouds. **REDBURN** and **TOBY** are greasing tackles by the bulwarks. Redburn pauses; stands; wipes his hands on a yellow bandana, and leans over the bulwarks. He grows philosophical.

REDBURN
Listen, Toby. Just listen.

Toby pauses. He looks up at his mate.

TOBY
I don't hear anything.

REDBURN
Exactly. Why is it that when a whaler sails the line as we do, all grows so quiet? It's like sound is replaced by a rhythmic lullaby that laps along with the tiny waves, breaking them into shards of broken quiet sunlight. Have you ever heard such silence anywhere else on this globe?

Toby rises, stands next to him and snatches Toby's bandana out of Redburn's hand. He wipes his hands clean.

TOBY
There's more to hear – listen. There. I can hear the sometimes breaths of the grumpus. Forward, I can hear the *Dolly* ripping the water cut under by her prow.

Redburn smiles, remembering how alike he and Toby really are.

TOBY (CONT'D)
You hear it too?

REDBURN
(serious)
There's something I wanted to tell you. This trip's been hard—

JIM interrupts them by calling from the quarterdeck.

JIM
Hurrah, my lads! It's a settled thing!

As Redburn and Toby turn to Jim, he's coming down the ladder to them.

JIM (CONT'D)
The Captain's had enough. We shape our course
for the Marquesas!

REDBURN
What? Impossible...

JIM
I predicted it! Remember! The Captain's hungry—

TOBY
Ain't we all...

JIM
So we head for land. Why, just now I was manning the helm,
and Vangs comes out. I says to him: 'It's no good, sir. D'ye see?
Why, Captain, I'm as good a helmsman as ever put hand to
spoke, but it's no good – not even I can coax this old ship to
windward anymore. Any why, sir? Because *Dolly* knows the
land is under the lee.' And then you know what old binnacle-
eye tells me? He says: 'Aye. I believe you. And why shouldn't
she drift leeward, Jim? Didn't every one of her stout timbers, and
the very lashings surmounting her, all grow on shore? She has
sensibilities for 'home,' and like the rest of us, wants to return to
it for rest.'

TOBY
But, to the Marquesas?

Toby turns wide eyes on Redburn.

TOBY (CONT'D)
Why, the very name spirits up outlandish visions...

REDBURN
(tries to outdo Toby)
Maidens, like the lovely *Houri* of classical Greece –
and just as naked....

TOBY
Coconut groves and bamboo temples. Sunny emerald vales
awash with ripe fruit trees....

REDBURN
Tattooed chiefs and beau-ideal warriors....

TOBY
Canoes dancing on flashing blue waters. Forbidding
woodlands guarded by horrible-looking idols....

JIM
Pots of chopped up stew, and a feast laid – fit for a cannibal.

Redburn and Toby share a 'that's a good one' look, but they frown as Jim makes it
clear he is all too serious.

JIM (CONT'D)
Study up, lads. Nukahiva is like a fan deck. Some twenty-miles
round, give or take. A high peak forms her pinion. Out from that
are three vales. Nukahiva, the port, is the largest, and sectioned
off from the others by craggy mountains running straight to the
sea; next the Happar, and these two groups are as fresh and
clean, and friendly as Eden itself. But the far vale, they are to be
feared. Typee – the very name is a slur by the other tribes: for it
denotes a lover of human flesh. And aye, inveterate gour-
mandizers of the stuff they are too.

Jim pokes Redburn's tummy.

JIM (CONT'D)
They fancy the white man's flesh the tenderest veal available.

Then seriously to Toby.

JIM (CONT'D)
You never want to cross into their valley. Like the shadow of
death, no one will cross it to rescue you from there.

Jim laughs at the two slack jaws before him.

JIM (CONT'D)
But, you'll love the rest of it, lads. It's the South Pacific's own
secret garden – even though the snake has been turned loose by
the devil. The French new 'empire' includes poor buggers who
can't fight against their own enslavement.

Jim spits on the deck, and rubs it in.

JIM (CONT'D)
I've heard tell French war ships lie at anchor all across Tahitian waters, and at Nukahiva too. Imagine it? Being mastered by a rabble of frogs? Poor bastards!

[Part 1 – V: The Cave Scene]

EXT. ROCKY LEDGE ON NUKU HIVA – EVENING

A faint footpath through low grass ascends further up a rocky outcrop. Over the edge is a fall of several hundred feet. **REDBURN** and **TOBY** pause at the start of the path, looking worn-out.

REDBURN
It looks a sort of footpath....

TOBY
If so, we better beat a path away from any unwelcome encounters.

REDBURN
Don't you have any curiosity. Would Robinson Crusoe, finding a footprint on the beach, as he did – run away from it?

TOBY
(without humor)
We are not alone on this island.

REDBURN
Come on.

Redburn edges past Toby and heads up the path. Toby reluctantly follows. They skirt their way halfway along the path, and Toby peers over the ledge. He shoots an angry look at Redburn's back.

EXT. OPENING IN CAVE ROOF

REDBURN and **TOBY** come to a high spot where the path ends in thick overgrowth. They gently press through this, and find a flat area that forms an opening to the roof of a cave. The foliage is lush, and any number of tree roots shoot straight down the hole into semi-darkness. They come up to the rim, and cast their eyes downward.

REDBURN (CONT'D)
I suppose this was no path...

TOBY
Right – or else everyone who takes it, comes here to jump.

REDBURN
Not so.

Redburn has an idea. He goes to a safe spot, grabs ahold of one of the roots, and tugs on it hard to test its strength.

REDBURN (CONT'D)
They who come here manage a descent without a leap of faith.
Shall we attempt the same feat?

Redburn doesn't wait for a reply. As Toby makes his way to him, Redburn grabs the root and steps off the ledge. He looks up into Toby's concerned face standing above him where he had just been.

TOBY
(amazed)
And what in the name of dirty coal-holes everywhere do you
expect to find at the bottom? A broken neck!

Redburn motions for Toby's help in rejoining him on top. He does so and they stand together on the ledge.

REDBURN
No, Toby, I expect to find a place to shelter. The sun goes down.
Do you have another idea?

TOBY
I'll tell you what, my pleasant fellow, if you intend to pry into
every damn nook that catches your magpie fancy, we'll quickly
get knocked on the head by petulant locals. And that – even by
your standards of adventure – would not be welcomed.

Toby becomes sincere and urgent. He takes Redburn by the forearm.

TOBY (CONT'D)
For God's sake – just, for once, take my advice. Steer clear! We
need to find a place to moor ourselves fast for the night – before
it gets too dark.

REDBURN
(extracts his arm)
That's just what I've been driving at. I wager that the cave is –
roomy, dry – and decent shelter from the rain.

TOBY
Aye. And, no doubt, shelter from any decent sleep too.

REDBURN
(peevish)
Very well, my brother...

Redburn sits on the ledge next to the tested root, and looks up into Toby's eyes.

REDBURN (CONT'D)
...I suppose then, I will see you in the morning. Looks like I'll
have to spend the night on my own...

Redburn takes hold, and swings himself out. He begins a slow descent.

REDBURN (CONT'D)
...Good night.

Toby starts to pace with his hands on top of his head. He mutters angrily.

TOBY
Robinson Crusoe – My Ass!

Toby pauses and gingerly peers into the hole. He paces again, this time not knowing what to do with his hands. He stops; looks skyward; draws in a hostile breath then shakes a cockeyed head at heaven. He quickly goes to the edge, where he squats, selects a strong-looking root, and steps off.

INT. CAVE

From the cave floor, the opening in the ceiling is forty five feet up. The roots cascade down from the aperture like wild fringe to a few feet above the cave floor. Water drips from the opening like a slow-motion fountain. **REDBURN** is carefully sliding down his root, and is about eight feet from the floor, when **TOBY** slides down past him on another root, and plops with heavy feet on the cave floor. Toby turns and reaches up to grab his mate's legs, then helps him down. The two momentarily assess any damage to each other, then as if first becoming aware of it, their faces turn to the orange light of sunset coming in through the cave opening at their side. They walk up in amazement – through the roomy cave – to the precipice of the cave door. Starting from the back of their heads, and then over them, a high vista looks over a super-lush valley falling away from the cave. Far below them a stream meanders, with several rivulets feeding it, through the valley and off to the sea about ten miles away. On the sea, at the horizon, the orange disc of the setting sun is half submerged.

INT. CAVE – NIGHT

A mellow fire is calmly crackling. Above it, **REDBURN** and **TOBY** are standing and warming their hands and backsides.

TOBY
Does the valley of the Happar lie before us; that is the question.

REDBURN
Or of the Typee? What's to be done now?

TOBY
(matter-of-fact)
Descend into the same valley we ascended from today.

Redburn looks shocked. Toby stares into the fire.

TOBY (CONT'D)
What else remains to us that we can be sure of? We'll starve if we stay in these barren highlands.

REDBURN
Starve, agreed. But we can't go back to Nukahiva. By now Vangs has bribed all the natives with prospects of flowing bolts of calico to turn Judas to us, and return us to the hard kiss of the lash on board the *Dolly*.

Redburn pauses.

REDBURN (CONT'D)
You saw the valley today — could the residents of such a lovely place be anything but fine-mannered, and good-hearted fellows?

TOBY
(peevish)
How can we risk it? You heard Jim: Cannibals!

REDBURN
Jim spun some tired nursery-tales for us. He treated us just like we were milk-toast boys tucked into our bed for a winter's night. Nonsense. I don't believe anyone would fancy our scrawny, salt-brined bones for dinner.

Toby drops his hands in an incredulous gape.

REDBURN (CONT'D)
I, for one, prefer to chance a bold descent and brave risking of the consequences, than molder away in these sloppy caverns.

Toby raises his voice — Redburn backs up involuntarily, but Toby matches his step.

TOBY
Consequences?! This whole scheme was you mooncalf brainchild. If it were up to _me_, we'd still be in our bunk on board ship. You'd risk my neck as carelessly as your own?

Redburn tries to placate Toby's temper.

REDBURN
Right — don't get hot...It's my fault. It _is_ my fault.

TOBY
And who will pilot us thither — to your paradise valley; possibly of death.

Redburn grins from ear to ear. He stoops into a boxing stance, and playfully punches a one-two into the center of Toby's chest.

REDBURN
Why — you, of course! I follow your lead.

Toby glares at Redburn, who self-consciously stands erect and lowers his hands.

REDBURN (CONT'D)
Look. We follow the streams. They flow right into the river that
cuts through your 'valley of death.'

Redburn gives Toby a playful cheek smack. Toby overreacts. His arm flies up and angrily knocks Redburn's hand away. Toby's sight narrows, and he puts up his dukes; one foot going back to brace himself. Redburn, after a pause, looks remotely sad. He parts his lips in regret, and then slowly lifts open palms which he gently encloses around Toby's nearest fist. Redburn slowly closes his eyes and draws Toby's fist to his mouth. He punches himself gently with it, then opens his eyes and kisses Toby's knuckles. All heat is instantly gone from Toby, who now looks equally sad. Background **MUSIC** softly introduces Redburn and Toby's love theme. [2]

REDBURN (CONT'D)
I'm sorry.

Redburn opens Toby's fist and interlaces his fingers with his. He leads Toby to a spot close to the fire and gestures for Toby to sit. Toby sits with his back against the cave wall, and Redburn pauses. Toby beckons with double open arms, and Redburn falls into his embrace. He rests his head against Toby's chest, and Toby's arms enfold him.

REDBURN (CONT'D)
This is turning out not to be the adventure I had hoped.

Toby is lost in his own thoughts.

TOBY
You are the only person in the world that can handle me. You
know just how to tamp down my temper, and keep me safe.
How many times on shipboard have you defused me from
wrecking my face on the fists of bigger sailors? How many.

Redburn plays with Toby's fingers.

REDBURN
You brought our photograph.

TOBY
(matter-of-fact)
How could I leave it behind? Remember — remember the day in
New Bedford we had it taken? We were to ship out soon...

REDBURN
The day was overcast. But the photographer rigged some lamps.
Do you think he...knew?

TOBY
He sees many sailor David and Jonathans. All he knows is,
their money is good.

REDBURN
Do you remember my first sight of you?

TOBY
Tavern in New York. Only two years ago? Seems a life already.
You finagled my address from me, cheeky boy — wrote to me
ceaselessly — how we should ship together. How glad I was you
pestered me. How glad I am you can handle me.

Toby moves the hair off of Redburn's forehead. He bends in and kisses Redburn's brow.

TOBY (CONT'D)
I wouldn't leave you — not if all the headhunters of Polynesia
tried to force me. I hope you know that...

From the fire, Redburn's eyes glaze over as he speaks almost from a trance.

REDBURN
Destiny decided our fate long before we met — where we would
go — how we would travel there — wherever — together.

[Part 1 — VI: The Hawaiian]

EXT. PORT OF NUKU HIVA — MORNING

The *Dolly* approaches the mouth of the bay, and above her fly a bevy of seafowl. A
fine day flashes off the lush green peaks rising thousands of feet in the center of the
island. A mile in, the large French warship la *Reine Blanche* centers the harbor, and
smaller vessels — minding a respectful distance — surround her. La *Reine Blanche* flies an
unnecessarily large French flag. A longboat is coming out to the *Dolly*.

EXT. A YARDARM OF THE *DOLLY*

TOBY is at the end of a yard. The breeze hits his face as he stoops to secure a lashing.
When he stands, he grips a rope and leans into the breeze facing land. He shields his
eyes as he carefully surveys the island. He wears a French striped sailor shirt, indigo
trousers, and is barefoot. Birds circle overhead.

EXT. BULWARKS OF THE *DOLLY*

REDBURN sends a rope ladder over the side. He looks down to the longboat and
makes sure they can reach the ship's ladder. The **CREW** of the longboat steadies the
end of the ladder, and **KARAKOI'I** begins to climb. Redburn extends a hand and helps
him on deck. He is instantly taken with the appearance of the man, for Karakoi'i wears
a green shooting jacket with big brass buttons. The two stand in momentary silence,
recognizing kindred spirits. **JIM** stands at the rail of the quarterdeck.

JIM
Welcome aboard, *monsieur* Pilot. To the helm, if you please.

Jim waves Karakoi'i over, and the man begins to go. Redburn takes a hold of Karakoi'i's lapel.

REDBURN
I shipped my first voyage with a shooting jacket much like your own — only, mine was red.

KARAKOI'I
You like, lad? It was a gift from an admirer on board la
Reine Blanche, there.

Karakoi'i needlessly points, but wants to delay the parting.

KARAKOI'I (CONT'D)
And what do they call you?

REDBURN
(holds out his hand)
Redburn.

KARAKOI'I
(takes it — holds it too long)
Karakoi'i. Redburn, eh? Not easy for Polynesian tongues. You should consider an easier name — like, Tom—

REDBURN
You are from...?

KARAKOI'I
Oahu — Hawai'i

Jim calls from the head of the quarterdeck ladder.

JIM
(peevish)
This way, *s'il vous plaît*.

Karakoi'i bows elaborately to Jim *à la française*.

KARAKOI'I
Après vous, le grand seigneur de la mer.

Karakoi'i slaps Redburn's shoulder and steps towards the quarterdeck.

KARAKOI'I (CONT'D)
I'll see you later, Redburn.

Karakoi'i winks at Redburn, and Redburn watches him go up and join Jim. Those two disappear as **TOBY** jogs up to Redburn.

TOBY
Who was that?

REDBURN
Our harbor pilot – a native of Hawaii – one of us, I fancy.

Redburn quickly turns and looks over the bulwark. The longboat is shoving away. Redburn gestures for Toby's help, and they haul up the ladder. The *Dolly* begins to glide to a spot to anchor in the harbor. Redburn and Toby lean over the bulwarks and watch the smaller vessels glide past. Soon they pass the brooding hull of la *Reine Blanche* and her enormous *Tricolor*.

REDBURN (CONT'D)
What's the point of those ships? It's like bringing a cannon to a cricket match. What for?

TOBY
Domination, is what for.

Once clear of the French ships, the shore becomes visible and so too a flotilla of small native boats, apparently rowing towards the *Dolly*. As the ship settles into an anchorage spot, Redburn and Toby hear the anchor winch release; a chain **RUMBLES** followed by a loud **SPLASH**. The canoes come closer, all rowed by solitary, smiling, young **MEN**. They begin to jostle around the hull of the *Dolly*, vying for better positions and holding up their produce. Some boats are piled high with brown coconuts; some with green coconuts; others with ripe breadfruit and smaller bright-colored fruit. Now other members of the **CREW** begin to crowd the bulwarks. Toby knocks Redburn's elbow and points halfway towards shore.

TOBY
Look! A string of coconuts is swimming out to us!

They watch amazed as a bobbing line of twenty coconuts bound with light cords moves towards them on its own. Soon, a **BOY**'s shaved head pops up at the leading end of the string. He smiles and waves, so the couple wave back.

REDBURN
But what's that – a school of fish?

Redburn points, and moving out from the shore, a silvery flash of multiple ripples seems to be advancing on the ship. As the 'school' approaches, members of the crew begin to **HOOT** and **WHISTLE**. Several young **WOMEN** are swimming out to the *Dolly*. As they watch in wonder, Karakoi'i comes up behind Toby and Redburn with some urgency.

KARAKOI'I
Lads! Let down the ladder. Get to – or you'll drown those
***wahine*. Lively now; lively!**

Redburn and Toby lower the ladder. The crew gather in a broad semi-circle, and Jim comes down to watch. Soon Redburn and Toby help dripping girls step on deck. The sailors stand with akimbo-awe, and the ladies move to a spot below the quarterdeck laughing and chatting. They help each other straighten up their hair, etc., and the crew form a new semi-circle around them. Jim licks his lips and pushes the brim of his hat back.

JIM
Break out the calico, boys! We're about to
do some trading.

Redburn and Toby exchange an uneasiness, and Karakoi'i, standing next to them, laughs shamelessly at their discomfort.

[Part 1 – VII: Hula – Cannibal Talk – Debauch]

EXT. MAIN DECK OF THE *DOLLY* – NIGHT

MUSIC scents the warm air. Across the waters of the bay, light reflects from houses on the shore and from the ships at anchor. Looking up, the rigging of the *Dolly* is festively strung with different colored, multifaceted, glass oil lanterns. These small cup-lights are in pastel colors – pale blue, clear glass, amber, white – and sparkle like a man-made constellation in her rigging. In the area before the quarterdeck, the native **WOMEN** are dancing the legends of their people. They wear broadleaved skirts and headbands of flowers and leaves. A few **BOYS** sit at their side playing drums and flutes, and they too wear floral headbands. Arrayed in front of the women are the **CREW** of the *Dolly*. Some stand in groups of two or three, arms draped over compatriot shoulders, while others sit on the deck in a broad crescent. **JIM, TOBY** and **REDBURN** sit front and center with legs kicked out in front of them. **KARAKOI'I** sits on his haunches next to Redburn, with arms braced on his knees and hands clenched. He smiles to see Redburn and Toby enjoying themselves. Jim fancies the Hawaiian is some kind of vague threat.

JIM
I don't cotton to primitive ways.

Redburn and Toby exchange a suppressed snicker.

JIM (CONT'D)
Seems young ladies should brook some underwear.

Redburn and Toby laugh.

TOBY
(to Karakoi'i)
Aye. If Jim was cappy of the French Fleet, they'd all be locked
away in corsets.

JIM
Not what I mean – cheeky. You know-it-alls better tread lightly
when you get shore leave. Remember – some of them's cannibals.

KARAKOI'I
(good-natured)
And what do you know of that?

JIM
(hostile)
I know it means a savage eats the most plentiful meat on this
here island — his fellow man.

KARAKOI'I
(laughs — to Redburn and Toby)
If it happens, it happens rarely.

Karakoi'i reaches out a 'peace offering' hand to Jim, who only glowers at him.

KARAKOI'I (CONT'D)
It's respect.

Jim huffs at Karakoi'i's statement. Karakoi'i frowns, and withdraws his hand. He tells Redburn and Toby.

KARAKOI'I (CONT'D)
Respect for your vanquished foe — a warrior, and only a warrior, honors the warrior spirit of his enemy by taking a piece of that spirit into himself — carrying that brave spirit forward in the world a bit longer.

JIM
(to his shipmates)
Stay away from Typee, lads, despite what 'good intentions' you are spoon-fed. Word is, about twenty years ago, a hapless whaler put in at Typee, and every last man of them was murdered — their heads cured in savage style as a mementos of this 'bravery' and 'respect.'

Jim stands in disgust, spits at Karakoi'i's feet, and Karakoi'i rises defensively. Jim ignores him, and instead lectures Redburn and Toby.

JIM (CONT'D)
Savages. Watch 'em, milk-sops. You can't trust none of them.

Jim skulks off. Toby waves a beckoning hand at Karakoi'i, and pats the deck where Jim had sat. Karakoi'i's smile returns, and he sits next to Toby.

TOBY
Don't let him get to you. His type is a
fading breed.

The men return their attention to the hula, but Karakoi'i notices Toby elbows Redburn, and exchanges an odd look with his mate. Soon Toby stands, brushes the seat of his trousers and wanders off. Karakoi'i scoots next to Redburn. Redburn pretends to watch the dance, but feels the heat of the Hawaiian's gaze on him. He turns frankly into it.

REDBURN
(in POLYNESIAN, with subtitles)
Are you enjoying yourself?

Karakoi'i is flattered, and impressed. Holding his gaze.

KARAKOI'I
(in POLYNESIAN, with subtitles)
I like what I see...
(in ENGLISH)
Who taught you?

REDBURN
I've known some sailors – like you.

KARAKOI'I
A quick learner – eh?

REDBURN
Aye.

KARAKOI'I
(in POLYNESIAN, with subtitles)
**Looks like you and Toby won't be fancying any of
the girls tonight.**

Karakoi'i leaves Redburn's startled gape for the dance, but in a moment, he laughs
and turns back.

KARAKOI'I (CONT'D)
Some of us don't.

Karakoi'i winks at him, and playfully elbows Redburn to make him laugh.

[Part 1 – VIII: Love in a Longboat]

EXT. MAIN DECK OF THE *DOLLY* – NIGHT

REDBURN walks forward alone on the deck. The **MUSIC** of the hula fades behind him.
As he passes a secluded area, he hears faint and muffled **VOICES**. He turns and sees
two members of the **CREW** – one bare-assed – with a young native **WOMAN** against
a wall. As the half-naked sailor thrusts, the other giggles along with her and pivots a
hipflask to the girl's smiling lips. Redburn assesses the woman is a willing participant,
and moves on. At the stern davit of one of the longboats, Redburn pauses. He looks
around and assures himself he is unobserved.

EXT. FORWARD RIGGING OF THE *DOLLY*

The **MUSIC** sounds, and glass oil lanterns twinkle. [3] Slowly we descend through the
lights and ropes to see **TOBY** lying in the longboat. His head is near the bow with his
hands propped behind it.

INT. LONGBOAT ON BOARD THE *DOLLY*

From **TOBY**'s vantage, the rigging with the lanterns and faint stars beyond, looks magical. It is a perfect tropical evening. He hears a sound, and looks up to see **REDBURN** climb on board from the stern. Toby half rises and pats the spot next to him. Redburn lies next to Toby. The two silently look at the beauty floating above them for a moment. Toby rolls to face his mate, then scootches around and positions his head in Redburn's lap. Redburn absent-mindedly strokes Toby's curly hair.

REDBURN
Have you given much thought to my plan?

TOBY
Plan? To jump ship. That's what you call a plan?

REDBURN
No, I mean – once we go ashore on leave, we head straight up the mountain and make our way to the valley of the Happar – we stay there unbothered till the *Dolly* sails. Then we ship with a decent crew later.

TOBY
To 'Happy Valley,' huh?

REDBURN
Toby, I hate it here. When we signed the ship's articles, the Captain made a contract with us too. One, to feed us – properly feed us; two, to expedite the voyage with haste and prudence – but he has broken that compact.

Toby sits upright.

TOBY
I told you – back in New Bedford, on the other side of the world – a South Seas whaling trip is arduous. I said, it's long, we should ship on the Atlantic crossing, but you – you…. So tell me, isn't this the adventure you were looking for? The adventure you levered my decision with?

Redburn sits up too. He reaches out and picks up a few of Toby's fingers.

REDBURN
Toby. Mate, listen to me. I have a presentiment that Vangs will keep us to sea for years to come. We chase whales that consistently run before us. This voyage is to end badly. Brother, you know it as well as I do. Some of these New England captains run the crew on crumbs for months, then insanely put into port in Chile or Peru to restock and drive right back out to the hunting grounds. Madness! They can't escape their own ambition for slaughter – the blood does something to them—

TOBY
And so you would make a criminal of me? Of us?

REDBURN
We have rights to do this. I'd rather place my future prospects in the hands of islanders we don't know, than be manipulated by the sorts of 'christians' who have sore abused us already.

Toby pulls his hand out of Redburn's grip. He folds his arms and looks down. He blinks a few, slow, times.

REDBURN (CONT'D)
All right. I will have to go alone.

Toby drops his arms. He looks frankly at his partner.

TOBY
You win. But, maybe someday you will listen to me, someday important. After all, I only want what's best for you; what's best for us.

To the look of infinite sadness from Toby, Redburn reclines halfway back and opens his arms. Toby folds himself in his embrace, and they settle down together. The sound of the hula momentarily asserts itself.

TOBY (CONT'D)
I don't seem to have a choice – you're all the family I've got. I can't let you go without me.

They turn eyes back up on the twinkling lights over them. Redburn rises on an elbow and kisses Toby. At first, they kiss tenderly, but as the music grows in their ears, they become lost in passion.

[Part 2 – Hard Reality Dawns – I: Morning in the Cave]

INT. CAVE OVERLOOKING THE VALLEY – DAWN

TOBY stands at the entry. Below him stretches a landscape barely coming alive in sunlight. Crimson edges the ridges facing east, and all seems animate with movement from the breeze and running water. Behind Toby, the remains of the fire lightly smoke. REDBURN sleeps close to it, lying on his side, in a near-fetal position. Toby's hand goes to Redburn's shoulder and rouses him.

TOBY
Awake, brother.

Redburn only half opens his eyes at Toby, and frowns. He speaks in a husky voice half-choked in sleep.

REDBURN
Awake, mate?

He struggles to sit up.

REDBURN (CONT'D)
If I am awake, then my top lights have gone out. It's darker
with my eyes open than shut.

TOBY
Nonsense. You're just not awake yet.

Redburn scratches his head, stretches and yawns.

REDBURN
You intimate that I've been asleep.

Toby reaches down with both hands, and Redburn grabs on. Toby hauls him to a standing position.

REDBURN (CONT'D)
It seems you've had a steak and egg breakfast — by the
mood of you.

Toby musses Redburn's hair.

TOBY
Don't be peevish — child. Up with you!

Toby rubs Redburn's cheeks.

TOBY (CONT'D)
Let's away. You plan on dozing through your adventure?

Toby spins Redburn, and brushes off his mate's back, seat of his trousers and legs.

TOBY (CONT'D)
Where's your hat...?

REDBURN
(mumbles)
Our adventure.

Toby gathers their things. He plops Redburn's hat on Redburn's head.

TOBY
What?

REDBURN
(gruffer)
OUR...

(softer)
Adventure — together.

Toby stops his busy work. He sighs open-mouthed, and holds Redburn's eye.

TOBY
I'm here, aren't I?

Toby gently forms a fist and brings it to rest on the side of Redburn's cheek.

TOBY (CONT'D)
Now. Let's go.

[Part 2 — II: Waterfall and Tree]

EXT. STREAM — MID-MORNING

The sun is burning hot in a cloudless sky. **REDBURN** and **TOBY** follow the course of the growing stream cutting through the high canyon. They have to wade in it in places; at other areas, they have to clamber over boulders along its bank.

EXT. THICKET — NOON

REDBURN and **TOBY** follow a low **RUMBLE** through a maze of six-foot-high swamp grass and reeds. The sound becomes more distinct the farther they go. By the time they break through to a clearing, the **ROAR** of a waterfall is loud and clear.

EXT. WATERFALL

REDBURN and **TOBY** skirt their way along the line of grass to a rocky promontory overlooking the falls. They stand and peer down at the straight descent of a three-hundred-foot cascade. Following the course the water takes from there, they scan a mild river running through fields of taro and orchards of breadfruit trees. Farther along, roofs of thatched structures multiply as the stream nears the sea, about 5-miles away. The partners are stunned with amazed disbelief.

REDBURN
Well, Toby — What's to be done now?

Toby glances back over his shoulder. A steep grade covered with foliage blocks all sense of direction.

TOBY
Since...we can't beat a retreat, I suppose we must shove forward.

REDBURN
Very true, dear brother, but how do you propose to accomplish such an amiable ambition?

TOBY
We ride the waterfall straight down.

REDBURN
It's the easiest thing in the world to jump, hothead, but the hard
thing will be the report of rocks on our limbs when we land.

Toby doesn't listen. He focuses on the flank of the waterfall. Toby motions with his head.

TOBY
Look. See those roots? They fall straight off the cliff.

Redburn turns to see various tree roots cascading in clumps, like dark and mossy icicles, continually sprayed by mists from the falls. Suddenly Toby clamps a hand on Redburn's shoulder. He croons right in his ear.

TOBY (CONT'D)
Are you ready to venture it?

Redburn's gaze glides into Toby's big baby-blues, only inches away.

REDBURN
I am.

EXT. TOP OF CLIFF FLANKING WATERFALL

TOBY leads the way as he and **REDBURN** edge over the tops of slippery tree roots. At a likely spot, he stops and carefully sits. He reaches down, and by feel, selects a sturdy root. Toby grabs ahold, and swings his legs out to lock them around the root. He begins to lower himself. Redburn moves to where Toby had started, looks down on the top of Toby's head, and beyond to the craggy terrain beneath his partner. Redburn slowly sits.

EXT. CLIFF FACE

TOBY's progress is halted. His root is getting too thin. He spies and tugs on a nearby root. Toby transfers to this one. He looks up and yells at **REDBURN.**

TOBY
Come on! It's fine – do as I do.

EXT. TOP OF CLIFF FLANKING WATERFALL

REDBURN grabs the same root Toby is on, and inches his way off the cliff. He frantically wraps his legs around the root and begins a not-too steady descent. After a couple of controlled movements, Redburn begins to slip.

EXT. CLIFF FACE

REDBURN slides uncontrolled. He can see **TOBY**'s hat below him. He yells out.

REDBURN
Toby! Heads up!

Redburn clamps down with all his might, but by the time he is able to stop, he is precariously close to the top of Toby's head.

TOBY
Mate! Do me the kindness of not falling until I get
out of your way.

Toby swings onto another root. Redburn gets the notion not to use the roots already 'cleaned' by Toby. He transfers and continues down. Finally, Redburn seems to have backed himself into a corner. The roots he tries are thin and snap off in his hand. He spots a good-looking candidate, but it is four feet to his side. Toby has paused below and watches. Redburn feels around on the cliff wall for a toe footing, and slipping once or twice, finds one. He eyes his target, inhales sharply, and kicks off. He flies toward the root with outstretched arm, and just as he grabs it, the root he was on snaps loudly, and plummets past Toby's head with only inches to spare. The root splashes into the roiling water at the bottom of the falls, still a hundred feet below. Toby shouts up congratulations.

TOBY (CONT'D)
Good job, lad. You are nimbler than I supposed!

REDBURN
Heads up, Toby. I may beat you to the bottom yet!

EXT. NARROW LEDGE IN CLIFF FACE

TOBY, standing on the ledge, helps **REDBURN** down from his root. Both keep their backs pressed against the cliff wall. All the usable roots are gone. They inch their way over, away from the falls, and Redburn gingerly gawks over the ledge. They are still fifty feet above the ground. Redburn rights his view and stares straight ahead. Toby squats and peers over.

REDBURN
Well, my boy, what's to be done now?

Toby stands erect. He wears a grin.

TOBY
Exit as soon as possible.

REDBURN
And how, mate-o-mine, do we <u>do</u> that?!

TOBY
Something like this.

Toby steps off the ledge.

REDBURN
Toby!

Redburn makes his way to where Toby had been, and looks down. The top of a palm tree is twelve feet below. A rustle of palm fronds, and Toby stands wobbly. Toby laughs and whoops in a rushed inhalation. He waves for Redburn to join him.

TOBY
Come on, me hearty! There's no other way!

Toby gauges Redburn's hesitation.

TOBY (CONT'D)
You can do it. I know you can!

Toby changes position and the fronds rustle as Toby sinks from sight.
His voice drifts up.

TOBY (O.S. CONT'D)
Come on! Don't leave me....

Redburn holds out his hands in a 'hold on' gesture. He gulps air, and leaps.

REDBURN
Christ Almighty...!

EXT. TOP OF PALM TREE

REDBURN lands amongst the fronds, but instantly roils in pain. His left knee jerks up to his chest, and he desperately grabs his left ankle. He grimaces as he touches it.

REDBURN (CONT'D)
Toby?

TOBY (O.S.)
You're fine. Start climbing down.

Redburn rolls over to see **TOBY** climbing down the trunk. Redburn turns onto his back, clutching the brim of his hat: he can't stay here, but can he make it down? He turns again; Toby is on the ground, looking around impatiently. Redburn inhales sharply and disappears from view.

EXT. BASE OF PALM TREE

TOBY has antsy feet, but he raises his arms, and **REDBURN** falls the last few feet into them. Redburn won't let go, and hops a few times, giving Toby the idea that the left leg is a problem. Toby helps Redburn sit at the base of the tree. He plops down next to him. Redburn lifts his trouser leg and Toby inspects an ankle bruised and beginning to swell. Toby leans back against the tree. Before them spreads a quiet valley.

TOBY
Well. We made it.

REDBURN
Yes, but made it where?

[Part 2 – III: A Trip into Town]

EXT. HIGH VALLEY PATH – MID-AFTERNOON

Trudging downhill, **TOBY** has his arm under **REDBURN**'s armpit, and is supporting him while they walk.

> **REDBURN**
> **Toby, mate, this is serious business. We can't intone willy-nilly the name of tribes that might be enemies here. Mum's the word till we know where we are.**

> **TOBY**
> **Aye, lad. Aye.**

They begin to perceive a looming clearing on their left. As they near its entrance, both stop in wonder. From the path, a mighty forty-foot-high Tahitian gooseberry tree is carpeted with ripe yellow fruit that grows like bunches of grapes straight from its branches. A two-hundred-foot clearing surrounds the tree.

EXT. CLEARING

REDBURN and **TOBY** rush towards the tree. Toby un-shoulders his pack to better aid Redburn's speed. Toby deposits Redburn against the tree trunk, then runs bedlam looking for a stick. He finds one and begins to swing at the fruit. It falls, and Toby yells in exhilaration. He drops hard to his knees, and uses his jersey to hold the collected fruit. He pops one in his mouth and stumbles over to his mate. The two sit and contentedly gorge themselves.

EXT. CLEARING – LATE AFTERNOON

REDBURN and **TOBY** lie beneath the tree and stare up at a constellation of pale yellow fruit. Toby suddenly misses his bag. He sits, then stands and spots it. He casually goes up to the bag laying near the perimeter of the clearing. Redburn sits up and watches. Toby bends down unconcernedly to retrieve the bag. He stops. Something catches his eye in the undergrowth.

> **REDBURN**
> Toby? What is it?

Toby, while still bent, waves his hand for Redburn to stay away. Redburn gets up and hobbles over to Toby. He looks where Toby is looking. A couple of feet in, a small **BOY** and **GIRL** stare out at them. The boy's hand is covering the girl's mouth. They wear woven belts with fresh green breadfruit leaves hanging down as kilts.

> **TOBY**
> (half-mouthed)
> **What do we do?**

> **REDBURN**
> (in POLYNESIAN, with subtitles)
> **Hello!**

The boy and girl do not react, except with wider eyes. Toby gets an idea. He sits cross-legged facing the children. He makes a show of rooting in the bag, and slowly extracts one string of beads, which he holds up. He acts surprised, and pulls out a second string. The boy drops his hand from the girl.

REDBURN (CONT'D)
(in POLYNESIAN, with subtitles)
A gift for you. Come, get it.

The children exchange an expectant glance, then the boy pushes the girl forward, and follows her out into the clearing. Redburn takes one string and places it around the neck of the boy. He repeats this with the girl. The kids pick up the beads and look at them.

REDBURN (CONT'D)
(in POLYNESIAN, with subtitles)
Where are the older people?

The kids point down the path.

REDBURN (CONT'D)
(in POLYNESIAN, with subtitles)
Let's go.

[Part 2 – IV: The Welcoming Committee]

EXT. VALLEY PATH

TOBY supports **REDBURN** as they walk. The **BOY** and **GIRL** are trooping in front of them, but turned to watch the men. Toby smiles at them with a head nod.

TOBY
(low tone)
**I think we try to learn what we can before the grown-ups
appear. I'm going to...**

Toby asks the children loudly.

TOBY (CONT'D)
(in POLYNESIAN, with subtitles)
Happar, good?

REDBURN
Toby! I said don't.

The kids look at each other amazed.

TOBY
See. It means something to them.

TOBY (CONT'D)
(in POLYNESIAN, with subtitles)
Happar good?

BOY
(in POLYNESIAN, with subtitles)
Happar? Good....

TOBY
(in POLYNESIAN, with subtitles)
Yes — Good?

The boy turns to the girl like Toby is nuts. Giggling, he asks.

BOY
(in POLYNESIAN, with subtitles)
What's he babbling?

GIRL
(in POLYNESIAN, with subtitles)
He likes the Happar!

Both kids turn to Toby and nod as if placating an unstable mind.

GIRL
(in POLYNESIAN, with subtitles)
Happar good!

The children laugh.

TOBY
(satisfied)
See. I told you. We're in the clear!

Suddenly the path broadens, and in a few paces, the children run ahead and begin to shout for help. Soon, a few **PEOPLE** gather, spot the strangers, and they in turn shout down the path. An echoing chain of shouts now telegraphs through the valley.

EXT. ROAD IN FRONT OF MAHEYO'S HOUSE

The road enters an area with several houses close together. **PEOPLE** choke the street escorting **REDBURN** and **TOBY** who are led by the **BOY** and **GIRL**. A **WOMAN** and **MAN** walk along with the kids.

WOMAN
(in POLYNESIAN, with subtitles)
Where did they come from?

BOY and GIRL
(in POLYNESIAN, with subtitles)
The *annui* tree.

MAN
(in POLYNESIAN, with subtitles)
Did they give you those?

GIRL
(holding it up – in POLYNESIAN, with subtitles)
They said it was a gift!

MAN
(in POLYNESIAN, with subtitles)
What else did they say?

BOY
(excited – in POLYNESIAN, with subtitles)
They love the Happar!

GIRL
(in POLYNESIAN, with subtitles)
**Yes – the strong one said the Happar
are the best!**

The crowd is aghast. This upsetting news spreads among them. The procession comes to a stop. All is still as they see **MEHEVI** standing in the road. **MOW-MOW**, and other **CHIEFS** stand behind Mehevi.

MEHEVI
(in POLYNESIAN, with subtitles)
Take them to Maheyo's house.

As the chief says this, a path through the crowd opens up to the gate of a spacious home. Toby and Redburn are guided in, and the crowd waits for Mehevi, Mow-Mow, and the other chiefs to enter. The crowd swarms up to peer through any available cranny.

INT. MAHEYO'S HOUSE

The women of the house – matron **TINOR**, and daughters **FAAUA, KARLUNA** and **MUNUNI** – lay out mats and motion for **REDBURN** and **TOBY** to sit on them at the dais. Toby sets Redburn down, then plops himself in tired relief. On the other side of the house, **MEHEVI**, bald, one-eyed **MOW-MOW** and the other **CHIEFS** greet **MAHEYO**. The other men and boys of the house —patron **RUNU**, and prime-of-life **KORI-KORI, MARMUNU, KARNUNU,** plus young teenage **MONU** and **RUARUGA** – stand behind Maheyo. **ARVA**, the family dog, runs around. [See Typee Appendix (Volume 1, page 273) for the Maheyo Family Organization Chart]

MEHEVI
(in POLYNESIAN, with subtitles)
I have brought you strangers, Maheyo. They may be enemies.

Tinor gasps. The chiefs and Runu sit at the opposite end of the dais. Slowly, as Mehevi glares at them, the clamor in the house dies to quiet, then the noise outside quiets too. Redburn and Toby exchange an unease over the nature of Mehevi's unflinching stare.

Mehevi rises and re-sits right in front of Redburn, so close their knees almost touch. He holds Redburn's gaze. Redburn pulls out a pinch of tobacco from his pocket and offers it to the chief. Mehevi dourly refuses. Finally, he asks.

MEHEVI
(in POLYNESIAN, with subtitles)
Happar — Good?

REDBURN
(inspired — in POLYNESIAN, with subtitles)
No. No —

Redburn gives an urgent look for support from Toby.

REDBURN (CONT'D)
(in POLYNESIAN, with subtitles)
**Happar are bad; very bad. Typee are good. Typee are
the best!**

Mehevi slowly smiles. He rises regally, and turns to ring-out for the whole house to hear.

MEHEVI
(in POLYNESIAN, with subtitles)
Taipi are the best!

Mehevi walks to Mow-Mow.

MEHEVI (CONT'D)
(in POLYNESIAN, with subtitles)
See, Mow-Mow. I told you.

MOW-MOW
(in POLYNESIAN, with subtitles)
Ask about the French — Are they French...?

Mehevi re-sits in front of Redburn.

MEHEVI
(in POLYNESIAN, with subtitles)
Where are you from, friends?

REDBURN
America.

MEHEVI
(mouthing it — in POLYNESIAN, with subtitles)
A-mer-ri... Oh! *Manika?*

Redburn nods, and Mehevi calls out to the rafters.

MEHEVI (CONT'D)
(in POLYNESIAN, with subtitles)
They're from *Manika!*

MEHEVI (CONT'D)
(to Toby – in POLYNESIAN, with subtitles)
What is your name, friend?

REDBURN
(quietly to Toby)
Name.

TOBY
(smiles)
Toby.

MEHEVI
(mouths the sounds warmly and easily)
TO-bi; Tobi.

Mehevi pats his own chest.

MEHEVI (CONT'D)
ME-HE-VI.

TOBY
Mehevi.

MEHEVI
(in POLYNESIAN, with subtitles)
Your name?

Redburn looks blank. He turns quickly to Toby.

REDBURN
If you're Toby, I should be...

Inspired, Redburn returns to Mehevi.

REDBURN (CONT'D)
...Tom.

MEHEVI
(pained expression)
TA...

REDBURN
Tom.

MEHEVI
TA-ma; Ta-mu; TO-muu...

REDBURN
Tom...

MEHEVI
TO-M-mo; TOMMO?

REDBURN
Tommo. Toby; Tommo!

MEHEVI
(looks kindly)
Mehevi.

REDBURN
Mehevi.

MOW-MOW
(impatiently — in POLYNESIAN, with subtitles)
Ask about the French...

Mehevi gives Mow-Mow an impatient glare, then returns to Redburn with benevolence.

MEHEVI
(in POLYNESIAN, with subtitles)
You know about the French — the 'Wi-Wi?'

Toby chuckles.

TOBY
Did he just call the Frogs — 'Oui-Oui's?'

REDBURN
(mouthing the word for French)
Francee — Franee?

REDBURN (CONT'D)
(in POLYNESIAN, with subtitles)
Ships in Nukahiva. Many ships.

This piece of intelligence stirs Mow-Mow to his feet. Mehevi holds up his hand, silently commanding Mow-Mow to stay put.

MEHEVI
(in POLYNESIAN, with subtitles)
The 'Wi-Wi' are our greatest enemy: do you know that?

REDBURN
(in POLYNESIAN, with subtitles)
Yes.

Mehevi glances between Redburn and Toby.

MEHEVI
(in POLYNESIAN, with subtitles)
**What can you tell us about their plans? The number of
soldiers; weapons?**

REDBURN
(exhausted – in POLYNESIAN, with subtitles)
Water.

MEHEVI
(in POLYNESIAN, with subtitles)
What?

REDBURN
(in POLYNESIAN, with subtitles)
Water – please.

Mehevi feels a great boor. He calls to Tinor.

MEHEVI
(in POLYNESIAN, with subtitles)
The boys need water!

Tinor directs Faaua and Karluna to pour water into several gourd cups. The women
take these to the guests, and as Redburn takes a cup from Faaua, he brushes her hand,
and sees she has blue eyes. As they drink greedily, Tinor croons softly to them.

TINOR
(in POLYNESIAN, with subtitles)
**Drink. It is medicinal water – the best.
Drink it all.**

MEHEVI
(in POLYNESIAN, with subtitles)
Boys – bring some light.

Kori-Kori, Marmuni and Karnunu rush out to the veranda to light torches. Tinor asks
Mehevi.

TINOR
(in POLYNESIAN, with subtitles)
What about food?

MEHEVI
(to Toby – in POLYNESIAN, with subtitles)
Food?

Mehevi pantomimes eating.

TOBY
(emphatically)
Yes –

TOBY (CONT'D)
(self-consciously)
...Please.

REDBURN
(in POLYNESIAN, with subtitles)
We are hungry.

Tinor roars to the girls.

TINOR
(in POLYNESIAN, with subtitles)
Poi-poi! **Go, quickly!**

Mehevi tells Toby.

MEHEVI
(in POLYNESIAN, with subtitles)
It's coming. Please wait.

The young men appear with lit torches and position them along the front of the dais.

MEHEVI
(to Redburn – in POLYNESIAN, with subtitles)
About the French—

REDBURN
(in POLYNESIAN, with subtitles)
Six ships.

REDBURN (CONT'D)
(to Toby)
How many men on the French ships?

TOBY
About...with the crew?

REDBURN
Just the marines.

TOBY
About twenty on the *Blanche*.

Redburn tries to convey the number.

REDBURN
(in POLYNESIAN, with subtitles)
Two – tens – twenty? Twenty on the largest ship...

TOBY
About ten on each on the others.

REDBURN
(in POLYNESIAN, with subtitles)
Three tens on the other ships.

Mehevi looks to Mow-Mow who is doing the mental calculations. He turns back warmly to Redburn.

MEHEVI
(in POLYNESIAN, with subtitles)
Good. It's good you tell us what you know—

The food arrives – two gourd bowls with poi. The guests pick up the bowls, but pause in confusion.

TOBY
No spoons...

Redburn shrugs and sticks his fingers in and scoops up a giant glob. Toby follows suit, and makes an equal mess. The whole house breaks into laughter.

REDBURN
Looks like our uncivilized manners are entertaining our hosts.

TOBY
Aye – we're like a pair of monkeys at tea with the Queen Vicki.

They continue to eat. Mehevi gestures to Tinor for a bowl of poi. He holds it up to his face.

MEHEVI
(in POLYNESIAN, with subtitles)
Toby. Tommo. Like this.

Mehevi delicately takes the fore and middle finger of his right hand, deftly dips it in, and swirls out a dainty portion. He grins at the Americans, and plops it in his mouth. Redburn and Toby try, but continue to make a mess of it. Tinor leads a charge of steaming dishes, which are set down one by one between her guests: dumplings wrapped in green leaves, slices of toasted breadfruit and coconut; and to drink, green coconuts with their tops cut off, and bowls of kava. Redburn and Toby can't believe the feast taking shape before them. They dig in.

MEHEVI
(rising – in POLYNESIAN, with subtitles)
Rest. Eat – enjoy. We'll talk in the morning.

Mehevi walks to Mow-Mow and the other chiefs. He gestures for them to rise and go to the door. Runu stays where he is.

MEHEVI (CONT'D)
(in POLYNESIAN, with subtitles)
We need to strategize, but wait...

Mehevi has a quick unheard word with Maheyo.

MOW-MOW
(to Kori-Kori — in POLYNESIAN, with subtitles)
I don't trust them — you can never trust them—

KORI-KORI
(in POLYNESIAN, with subtitles)
True. They'll all the same — treacherous. And, they stink. Don't those savages wash?

Mehevi comes back quickly and takes Kori-Kori by the arm.

MEHEVI
(in POLYNESIAN, with subtitles)
Kori-Kori — mind our guests. They go nowhere without you. Understood?

Kori-Kori is abhorrent of the idea, but he acquiesces.

KORI-KORI
(in POLYNESIAN, with subtitles)
Yes, chief.

Mehevi leads the way out, and is followed by Mow-Mow and the other chiefs. Kori-Kori catches Redburn's eye, and Redburn starts: there is something suspicious and hostile in Kori-Kori's intent.

[Part 2 – V: The First Full Day]

INT. MAHEYO'S HOUSE – MORNING

REDBURN opens his eyes. Above him, in the rafters, are three bundles about twelve inches round. They are fabric, tied at the top with a rope that rounds the beam, and trails one end down to eyelevel, where it is secured by a peg in the wall. Two of the bundles are of faded and soiled tapa, but the third — hanging right over Redburn's head — is made from a sailor's blue and white striped shirt. Redburn becomes aware of the noises of the house — people are abuzz with their usual activity. He cocks his head. **TOBY** lies next to him, turned on his side facing him, and Redburn realizes he has slept on Toby's extended arm as a pillow. The sailors are down to their tee-shirts and drawers, and a light tapa blanket is kicked down around their heels. He sits up and is unprepared to find **KORI-KORI** sitting cross-legged, staring him down. Redburn blinks a few times, then pokes Toby in the side. Toby groans and rolls over to his other side. Kori-Kori does not flinch, and Redburn pokes Toby again with some force.

TOBY
What...?

REDBURN
Get up.

Toby groggily sits, propping himself on his hands. He sees Kori-Kori's stare. Kori-Kori rises and calls to the rest of the household.

KORI-KORI
(in POLYNESIAN, with subtitles)
They're awake.

Redburn and Toby glance around the house. **RUNU** sits in the same position as last night. **ARVA** is in his lap. **MAHEYO** sits next to him. Teen boys **MONU** and **RUARUGA** are roughhousing near the door to the veranda. **TINOR** sidles up to them, none too amused.

TINOR
(in POLYNESIAN, with subtitles)
Monu; Ruaruga! Take it outside.

The boys stop playing as Tinor pushes past them. She goes to the veranda door and calls out.

TINOR (CONT'D)
(in POLYNESIAN, with subtitles)
Girls! Time to bathe them.

Redburn and Toby have stretched, yawned and come to sit at the front edge of the dais. Now they can see through the open front door. A crowd is there, all the way back to the road, to catch a glimpse of the visitors. **FAAUA, KARLUNA** and **MUNUNI** come from the veranda. The first two girls hold large gourd bowls with water and sponges. Mununi carries a smaller bowl of coconut oil in one hand, while short rolls of tapa are draped across her other arm.

TINOR (CONT'D)
(in POLYNESIAN, with subtitles)
Monu, Ruaruga — undress them.

The boys exchange a funny look, then go to Redburn and Toby. Each takes the hand of one of them, and lifts them to make the guests stand. The boys grab the ends of the sailors' tee-shirts and lift and pull them off. The boys set the shirts aside, making a 'stinky face,' then go to work pulling on the drawers.

TOBY
(squirming)
Oh, no, Pillgarlic. No, no, no....

REDBURN
(to the boys — in POLYNESIAN, with subtitles)
Not those.

The boys stop, and turn to Tinor.

MONU
(in POLYNESIAN, with subtitles)
They want to wear that...

Monu points at Redburn's crotch.

MONU (CONT'D)
(in POLYNESIAN, with subtitles)
...Thing.

TINOR
(in POLYNESIAN, with subtitles)
Leave it — could be a religious thing.

The boys walk away, bumping shoulders, and looking well-entertained. The girls come forward. Faaua bathes Redburn; Karluna, Toby. The girls squeeze out their sponges and moisten the sailors' shoulders and chests. Redburn gazes into her blue eyes.

REDBURN
(in POLYNESIAN, with subtitles)
What is your name?

FAAUA
Faaua.

REDBURN
Fa-au-a.
(to Toby)
Did you ever hear anything so romantic.

The girls raise up the men's arms, and scrub their armpits.

TOBY
What is it? Fay-a-way?

REDBURN
(considers)
Fayaway — equally poetic. Did you see? She has blue eyes — like you.

Toby grows squeamish, and the girls chat merrily.

KARLUNA
(in POLYNESIAN, with subtitles)
Skin so white —

FAAUA
(in POLYNESIAN, with subtitles)
— It feels so smooth —

MUNUNI
(in POLYNESIAN, with subtitles)
I wonder if it smells good?

Karluna pulls Toby's forearm down and brings her nose to it.

TOBY
I don't like this…

KARLUNA
(in POLYNESIAN, with subtitles)
Smells the same –

REDBURN
Afraid of a reaction?

TOBY
As if!

Done with the bath, the girls dip fingers in the coconut oil and rub it in their palms. Karluna smears it evenly over Toby's chest and arms, Mununi over his legs and top of his feet. Faaua extends Redburn's arm and massages the oil into his chest.

REDBURN
(in POLYNESIAN, with subtitles)
You have beautiful eyes.

Faaua looks downcast and blushes.

FAAUA
(in POLYNESIAN, with subtitles)
Don't let Kori-Kori hear you say such things – we are together.
He is very protective of those he loves.

As Redburn digests this, Mununi touches his left ankle. He recoils in pain. The girls back away and look to Tinor.

TINOR
(in POLYNESIAN, with subtitles)
Dress them girls; dress them.

Mununi unrolls a piece of tapa, which is about eighteen inches wide, and she and Karluna approach Toby. Faaua gestures for him to lower his drawers. Toby instinctively clutches onto the waistband.

TINOR (CONT'D)
(in POLYNESIAN, with subtitles)
They want them on.

As the girls wrap the tapa kilt around Toby's waist, Redburn sniffs in his direction.

REDBURN
You smell – tropical.

The girls dress Redburn, and Toby snuffs Redburn's way.

TOBY
You smell like – axle grease.

After the girls leave, Toby starts to dance from foot to foot.

TOBY (CONT'D)
I've got to pee. Don't you?

REDBURN
Um — let's go to the door.

Toby supports Redburn and they move to the front door. Kori-Kori blocks it. Redburn swallows hard.

REDBURN (CONT'D)
I don't know the word...

Redburn points to Toby's crotch, and Toby — getting the idea — clutches at it and springs from foot to foot. Kori-Kori's stern expression falters for a moment, then he leads the sailors outside.

INT. MAHEYO'S HOUSE

Steaming plates of food are laid for the guests. Toasted squares of coconut, and steaming dumplings are stacked on plates. Two green coconuts with their tops cut off stand by. **KORI-KORI** leads **REDBURN** and **TOBY** through the front door. **MAHEYO** rises and gently pushes Kori-Kori aside. Gesturing to the food, he invites to his guests.

MAHEYO
(in POLYNESIAN, with subtitles)
Eat, friends — eat!

Toby sets Redburn on the edge of the dais and climbs up himself. They tuck in. **MEHEVI** enters followed by **MOW-MOW** and other **CHIEFS**. Mehevi looks officious — he wears bold earrings, a red-feathered headdress, and a finely decorated tapa mantle. While Redburn and Toby eat, the chiefs exchange an unheard word with Maheyo and Kori-Kori, who gestures at the guests without looking.

TOBY
Look. It's the tribe's commodore — I guess the one-eyed chap's captain of the ship of state.

REDBURN
What's was baldy's name again?

TOBY
Something like 'Meow-Meow.'

The chiefs settle in the same positions as last night and greet **RUNU**. **ARVA** growls at Mow-Mow. Mehevi's expression is grave and wordless on the Americans. After a pause, Redburn motions for Toby to toss him Redburn's jersey. Toby does, and Redburn fishes out some tobacco. He faces Mehevi, holds up the lump, and speaks softly.

REDBURN
Mehevi?

Mehevi beams, rises, and sits in front of Redburn.

MEHEVI
(in POLYNESIAN, with subtitles)
Tommo! So kind.

Mehevi pushes Redburn's hand back, and pats it warmly. He glances at Maheyo, who springs into action, telling the older boys.

MAHEYO
(in POLYNESIAN, with subtitles)
Quick. Light some pipes, Tommo wants to smoke! Quickly now.

MARMUNU and KARNUNU rush out the veranda door.

MEHEVI
(in POLYNESIAN, with subtitles)
Do you remember, we were talking about the French—
(to Toby)
The 'Wi-Wi....'

Toby involuntarily giggles, and shoulders Redburn.

REDBURN
(to Mehevi — in POLYNESIAN, with subtitles)
Yes.

MEHEVI
(in POLYNESIAN, with subtitles)
What kind of weapons do they have?

REDBURN
(to Toby)
What weapons do you suppose they have?

TOBY
Same as everyone — rifles; cannon.

REDBURN
(just remembering)
Oh, cannon; about forty. Where's our bag? Get it.

Toby roots under their clothes and hands the pack to Redburn. Redburn pulls out his stationary box. Opens it, and quickly takes out a pad and pencil. He draws a sketch of a rifle and shows it to Mehevi.

REDBURN (CONT'D)
(in POLYNESIAN, with subtitles)
What is the word?

MEHEVI
(in POLYNESIAN, with subtitles)

Gun.

Marmunu and Karnunu come up with trays of lit pipes. Toby, Redburn and Mehevi each take one. The young men move on to the other men, and soon all are smoking.

REDBURN
(in POLYNESIAN, with subtitles)
Many guns.

Redburn then draws a cannon in the same scale as the rifle. He shows it to Mehevi, who puzzles over it.

REDBURN (CONT'D)
(in POLYNESIAN, with subtitles)
Big gun. Four tens big gun.

MEHEVI
(to Mow-Mow — in POLYNESIAN, with subtitles)
Look. What does it mean?

Mow-Mow comes up and looks over Mehevi's shoulder.

MOW-MOW
(in POLYNESIAN, with subtitles)
It means they've come to invade.
(to Redburn)
Forty big guns?

REDBURN
(in POLYNESIAN, with subtitles)
Yes. One *cannon* — big gun — destroy this house in single shot.

The men are shocked and pass grave glances at one another. Maheyo looks to account for all his treasured belongings.

MOW-MOW
(hotly to Mehevi — in POLYNESIAN, with subtitles)
And you talk of placating the French — I told you, Mehevi—

Mehevi rises and dresses down his underling.

MEHEVI
(in POLYNESIAN, with subtitles)
Later — not here. Watch what you say.

Mehevi gestures for Mow-Mow to sit in his old position. Mow-mow does so with reluctance.

TOBY
Well, it's what they wanted to know — if only Montezuma had been so warned.

Redburn stands to put his stationary away — he flinches in pain. Toby rises to support him.

MEHEVI
(to the room — in POLYNESIAN, with subtitles)
**Tommo is hurt! Ruaruga — go and fetch the doctor. It's his
ankle. Run, boy. Run.**

Ruaruga dashes out the front door. As Toby helps Redburn sit, he tries to distract his mate from his pain. He motions with his chin towards Arva.

TOBY
**What in the name of Great Danes everywhere do you
think that is?**

REDBURN
Some sort of hairless — rat?

TOBY
**I have a sinking suspicion it passes for a dog of sorts
in these parts.**

Monu, seeing their interest, goes and picks up the dog. He brings Arva to the sailors, and holds it up to their faces — they recoil.

MONU
Arva. Arva!

The boy cuddles his dog.

REDBURN
(smiles a bit)
Arva. Hell of a name; hell of a dog....

RUARUGA comes back holding the doctor's bag and several green coconut leaves. The **DOCTOR** follows him in.

REDBURN (CONT'D)
Toby — look at that old Hippocrates — Don't let them — Don't.....

The Doctor immediately latches onto Redburn's ankle. Mehevi motions for Toby to scoot, and sits himself on the other side of Redburn. The Doctor at first gently palpates all around the perimeter of soreness. Redburn stiffens. Suddenly, the Doctor casually begins to hammer on the tenderest spots. Redburn immediately roars in pain and tries to stand. Mehevi takes his shoulders and pins him to his seat.

TOBY
(springing up)
Oh, God. Oh, my God!

Toby can't figure out what to do. Redburn is nearly screaming now, but Toby doesn't want to lay a hand on the chief, so he begins to sign-language to Mehevi, to Tinor, to

Maheyo, about pain, and letting his mate stand, and on and on. Toby panics. He drops to his knees before Mehevi and the Doctor. He makes supplicant hands to them, and tears of fright roll down his cheeks.

TOBY (CONT'D)
Please stop. Stop....

Mehevi and the Doctor are somewhat puzzled by Toby's tears, but the doc assesses that the ankle is better. He motions for Ruaruga to hand him his bag and plant-leaf bandages.

DOCTOR
(to Mehevi — in POLYNESIAN, with subtitles)
Hold him.

The Doctor pulls out a small gourd bowl sealed with a leaf. Uncovering it, he dips his fingers in a thick salve, which he liberally spreads all around Redburn's left ankle. Toby rises, backhanding his eyes and cheeks. The Doctor bandages Redburn's ankle with leaves and twine. He stands and speaks to Mehevi.

DOCTOR
(in POLYNESIAN, with subtitles)
It's not too bad. It will heal.

The Doctor gives the salve to Tinor with instructions. Mehevi stands, as do the other chiefs.

DOCTOR (CONT'D)
(in POLYNESIAN, with subtitles)
Spread on some ointment every morning and change the dressing mornings and evenings.

Mehevi escorts the Doctor to the door, and they and the chiefs go out together. Toby sits next to Redburn. He puts his arm around Redburn's shoulder from behind.

TOBY
Do you want to lie down?

REDBURN
No — I think I'm going to be sick.

Redburn starts to tremble. Toby freshly panics.

TOBY
You're shaking — you had — Where's your frock? You want your frock?

Redburn nods, his teeth chattering. Toby crawls across the dais behind Redburn. He finds Redburn jersey, and kneels behind him.

TOBY (CONT'D)
Raise your arms.

After he slips it on, Toby sits next to his partner, and supports him — one arm behind, one arm in front. Toby slowly hugs, and rocks Redburn gently. On the other side of the house, everyone watches with the joint recognition of just how close these two young men really are.

[Part 2 – VI: First Bath in the Stream]

INT. MAHEYO'S HOUSE – MORNING

REDBURN opens his eyes. He blinks a few times, recognizing where he is by the bundles above him in the rafters. Redburn becomes aware of the NOISES of the house — people are abuzz with their usual activity. He cocks his head. TOBY lies next to him, turned on his side facing him, and using Redburn's arm as a pillow. They wear only their drawers, and a light tapa blanket is kicked down around their heels. Toby groans, and snuggles in close to Redburn's chest. Redburn looks beyond Toby, and is unprepared to find KORI-KORI sitting cross-legged, staring him down.

> REDBURN
> (to Kori-Kori – in POLYNESIAN, with subtitles)
> **Good morning.**

Redburn gingerly extracts his arm, but Toby groans and rolls onto his other side; almost into Kori-Kori's lap. Toby starts awake. He pushes back sluggishly, and blear-eyed looks around for Redburn. He greets Kori-Kori still half asleep.

> TOBY
> (in POLYNESIAN, with subtitles)
> **Hello.**

> KORI-KORI
> (to the house – in POLYNESIAN, with subtitles)
> **They are awake.**

As Kori-Kori rises and moves off, TINOR bustles up.

> TINOR
> (in POLYNESIAN, with subtitles)
> **Toby! Tommo! – Bathe! In the stream. Go –**

Tinor gestures to the door.

> REDBURN
> **I guess we're going out.**

Toby gets their tee-shirts, and as he does, KARLUNA and MUNUNI come with their kilts. Redburn scoots to the edge of the dais, and sits with his legs on the floor. He stands to test his pain level. He is surprised.

> REDBURN
> **Don't go telling that old Aesculapius of a witchdoctor – but –**
> **my ankle feels better today.**

Toby flings Redburn's shirt to him.

TOBY
Good. Indolent to invalid – that suits you.

INT. FRONT VERANDA OF MAHEYO'S HOUSE

KARLUNA, MUNUNI, RUNU, MARMUNU, KARNUNU, MONU and **RUARUGA** troop out the front door loaded down with bathing accouterments. The girls carry small containers with lotions and oils; the young men, gourd dippers and sponges; the boys, stacks of tapa towels. They chat merrily, and the boys roughhouse, as they move to the road. **KORI-KORI** follows, and is stopped by **FAAUA** grabbing his arm. She is in mid-sentence.

FAAUA
(in POLYNESIAN, with subtitles)
...He can't make it all the way to the stream – you'll have to carry him.

Kori-Kori is amazed at the suggestion.

KORI-KORI
(in POLYNESIAN, with subtitles)
What..?

FAAUA
(in POLYNESIAN, with subtitles)
You heard Mehevi – Watch after them; especially Tommo.

KORI-KORI
(in POLYNESIAN, with subtitles)
Watch them – not watch after them....

REDBURN comes out of the door supported by **TOBY**. Toby holds onto something wrapped in his bandana. **TINOR** follows in a fluster.

TINOR
(to Faaua – in POLYNESIAN, with subtitles)
Tommo's medicine. Use a lot of it, we want him better!
(to the sailors)
Enjoy! Bathe...bathe.

Tinor shoos them away.

REDBURN
(empty repeating – in POLYNESIAN, with subtitles)
Bathe.

Tinor laughs and goes inside. Faaua pokes Kori-Kori in the ribs and gestures to Redburn. Toby repositions his arm for Redburn to grab on to, but suddenly Kori-Kori blocks him. Kori-Kori takes Redburn by the elbow and leads him to the edge of the top step.

Gesturing 'wait a minute,' Kori-Kori deftly steps down in front of Redburn and turns his back to him. Kori-Kori stoops and slaps his sides a few times.

REDBURN (CONT'D)
(to Faaua – in POLYNESIAN, with subtitles)
No – I – I will walk....

FAAUA
(insistent – in POLYNESIAN, with subtitles)
Kori-Kori will take you! You must.

Faaua gently pushes Redburn closer to her partner. Toby laughs; makes riding crop gestures.

TOBY
Ride, Pillgarlic, ride! As I said: from indolent to invalid.

Redburn sighs and grabs onto Kori-Kori's shoulders. The man grabs Redburn's legs behind the knees, and straightens.

EXT. STREAM IN TAIPIVAI

The young **MEN** and **WOMEN** of Maheyo's household crash through clumps of waterweeds in high spirits. In a clearing by the brilliant water moving along the rocky brook, the party sets their things down and the young men and boys immediately strip their kilts and dash in the water to play. Various other **PEOPLE** are bathing already. As the young women arrange their things, **KORI-KORI** appears at the opening with **REDBURN** on his back. **TOBY** and **FAAUA** follow. A chorus of **"Good morning, Toby"** and **"Good morning, Tommo!"** come from the crowd in POLYNESIAN, with subtitles.

EXT. ROCKY OUTCROP IN STREAM

KORI-KORI skirts along the bank with **REDBURN** still on his back to a spot where a large flat rock is lapped by a deep pool of the stream. **TOBY** and **FAAUA** follow. Kori-Kori steps into the water and backs Redburn up to the rock where he puts his charge down. Toby clambers on the rock behind him and tosses his bandana aside. Toby rips off his shirt, then undoes his kilt to show he is still wearing his drawers. He reaches down and pulls off Redburn's shirt, and puts their clothes together in a safe spot. Toby jogs up to the edge of the rock, arcs his back, and with a smiling glance at his mate, dives into the water. Toby's head bobs up from the sunlit water and shakes a moment like a dog. Toby slicks his hair back, and squints a challenge at his partner.

TOBY
You want to mope all day long? Get in!

REDBURN
(self-pity)
I better not....

Faaua reaches down and undoes Redburn's kilt, distracting him from noticing Kori-Kori coming with a big sloshing bowl of water. Standing behind him, he douses it over

Redburn's head. Toby hoots and laughs riotously. **KARNUNU, MONU** and **RUARUGA** wade over to join the fun. The four begin to splash and play as Kori-Kori scrubs Redburn vigorously with a sponge, especially under his arms. After another dousing of water, **KARLUNA** and **MUNUNI** dry him with towels, and **FAAUA** gently pulls his left leg to a dry position on the rock. She undoes his bandage. As the other two girls massage coconut oil into his skin, Faaua dabs on the salve and redresses the wound with new leaves. She makes eye contact with Redburn who smiles at her with tenderness. Kori-Kori, standing above Redburn, stiffens.

EXT. ROCKY OUTCROP IN THE STREAM – MORNING – LATER

Looking down from above, **REDBURN** and **TOBY** lie side-by-side sunning themselves on the rock. They have their hands behind their heads. Sounds of the women **CHATTING** and **GIGGLING**, and of the young men **SPLASHING** and **CALLING** drift in from the sides. Toby suddenly remembers something, and spryly jumps onto his haunches. He reaches over and grabs his bandana.

> **TOBY**
> OH – now it's time for you to do a little work.

Redburn sits up, and Toby unties the cloth to reveal his shaving kit. He opens it and pulls out a bit of shaving soap. He calls to **MUNUNI** who is off a short distance with **KARLUNA** and **FAAUA** combing each other's wet hair.

> **TOBY**
> (in POLYNESIAN, with subtitles)
> Water – water, please.

Toby points to a gourd bowl and Mununi fills it and brings it to him.

> **REDBURN**
> Are you serious?

> **TOBY**
> I need a shave – <u>you</u> need a shave.
> (to Mununi – in POLYNESIAN, with subtitles)
> Thank you.
> (to Redburn – in ENGLISH)
> Now – up, and about your duty.

Redburn kneels and Toby sits back on his heels. In the water right by their rock, **KARNUNU, MONU** and **RUARUGA** pause and watch. Redburn lathers the soap in the palm of his hand and smears it on Toby's face. Opening the razor, he tilts Toby's chin this way and that and shaves his mate. At the end, Redburn wipes off stray soap from Toby's face with his fingers dipped in water.

> **REDBURN**
> How's that?

Toby rubs his cheeks with the back of his fingers.

TOBY
Tolerable... Now, you.

REDBURN
No. I think I'll let my stubble grow *au natural*.

Redburn dabs the razor dry with Toby's bandana, noticing the interest of the boys in the water. He puts the gear away, and turns his legs on the rock. He says to them.

REDBURN (CONT'D)
(in POLYNESIAN, with subtitles)
Good?

Karnunu launches his upper body out of the water, and braces his chest on Redburn's legs. He stretches out an arm towards Toby, who brings his cheek down. Karnunu strokes Toby's grin.

KARNUNU
(in POLYNESIAN, with subtitles)
Smooth. Like a baby!

Karnunu forcefully kicks his torso backwards into the water with his hands. He comes to the surface, and singsongs to the others. They quickly join in.

KARNUNU (CONT'D)
(in POLYNESIAN, with subtitles)
Toby's got a baby face! Toby's got a baby face....

TOBY
What does he say?

REDBURN
(ear-to-ear grin)
Smooth as a baby's backside.

[Part 2 – VII: A Tour of Taipivai]

EXT. VERANDA OF MAHEYO'S HOUSE – NOON

A slow pan of the railing shows items hung to dry: tapa towels, Kori-Kori's kilt, a pair of drawers, more tapa towels, a second pair of drawers, then two tee-shirts side by side.

INT. MAHEYO'S HOUSE

REDBURN and TOBY sit on the dais, smoking. They wear their belts and jackknifes over their tapa kilts. KORI-KORI rushes in.

KORI-KORI
(in POLYNESIAN, with subtitles)
Toby; Tommo – Mehevi is here. Let's tour Taipivai. Up, up!

Redburn tries to rise; Toby helps him.

> **REDBURN**
> **I guess we're being given a tour.**

EXT. GATE TO MAHEYO'S HOUSE

When they get to the bottom of the steps, **MEHEVI** greets **REDBURN** and **TOBY** warmly. Toby is supporting his mate. **KORI-KORI** comes down after them, and Mehevi meets them halfway between gate and house.

> **MEHEVI**
> (in POLYNESIAN, with subtitles)
> **Toby! Tommo – how is the leg?**

Mehevi frowns severely at Kori-Kori, who gently replaces Toby as Redburn's crutch.

> **REDBURN**
> (in POLYNESIAN, with subtitles)
> **It's fine.**

> **MEHEVI**
> (in POLYNESIAN, with subtitles)
> **Good. Now, let's visit the heart of the valley,**
> **and lunch at the men's house. All right?**
> (to Toby)
> **All right?**

EXT. CENTRAL AVENUE OF TAIPIVAI – AFTERNOON

MEHEVI, TOBY, and **REDBURN** – supported by **KORI-KORI** – stroll down the straight, forty-foot-wide road. **PEOPLE** come out of their houses to warmly greet Redburn and Toby. Toby smiles and waves, something the locals do not do, but they receive it as friendly.

EXT. GATE OFF CENTRAL AVENUE OF TAIPIVAI

MEHEVI, TOBY, REDBURN and **KORI-KORI** approach a grand passage formed by woven tree boughs. Beyond it, an impressive one-hundred-fifty-yard-long *allée* of arching coconut trees stretches back. The guards open the gate for Mehevi.

> **REDBURN**
> **I wonder what this could be?**

> **TOBY**
> (swallows hard)
> **Fairground meets execution ground...?**

EXT. HULA HULA GROUNDS

At the other end of the *allée*, a second gate opens onto a clear space one hundred twenty-five yards by two hundred fifty yards. **MEHEVI, TOBY, REDBURN** and **KORI-**

KORI come into the open. The sailors note that the perimeter is marked by any number of shrines in the form of six-foot-square houses raised on five-foot high stone platforms. Each shrine is thatched and completed with narrow steps up to the open front; each features an idol and offerings of fresh flowers, food and water.

TOBY
Like Westminster – walls packed to the brim with the
mighty…and dead.

Straight in front of them is a third and smaller gate. Flanking it on either side are the narrow ends of identical structures with wide verandas. This compound is the *Ti*, or inner sanctuary. The two buildings are about fifty feet by one hundred fifty feet. As they near this third gate, Redburn glances over his shoulder. The trail of women following them begins to dwindle. [See Typee Appendix (Volume 1, page 272) for a scale drawing of the Hula Hula Grounds]

REDBURN
Did you notice? All the women are now falling back. I reckon
they are not allowed any farther.

Mehevi leads them to the structure on the right.

[Part 2 – VIII: Lunch at the *Ti*]

INT. FRONT VERANDA OF THE *TI* – AFTERNOON

MEHEVI, TOBY, REDBURN and **KORI-KORI** mount the steps, and the Americans see a pure-white gravel yard beyond the third gate. It is about one hundred fifty feet square, and two mature trees are aligned with the gate. They have platforms built around their trunks about three feet off the ground. The back of this court is formed by a structure like bleachers.

INT. OF THE *TI*

MEHEVI, TOBY, REDBURN and **KORI-KORI** walk through the vestibule. Hanging on the wall are half a dozen muskets and powderhorns. **BOY** servants greet the party, and show them inside to a wide-open space. The men sit on mats the boys arrange for them facing the yard.

MEHEVI
(in POLYNESIAN, with subtitles)
Boy, where are Mow-Mow and the others?

BOY
(in POLYNESIAN, with subtitles)
At the Rectory.

MEHEVI
(in POLYNESIAN, with subtitles)
Fetch them, and we're ready to eat.

The boy leaves. First he pauses at the veranda to tell something to the other boys, who spring into action by filling dishes, then the boy runs across the yard and up the steps of the identical building.

MEHEVI
(to Toby — in POLYNESIAN, with subtitles)
Are you hungry?

TOBY
(in POLYNESIAN, with subtitles)
Yes!

MEHEVI
(in POLYNESIAN, with subtitles)
**Good. Good! Today is a special day — we have roast pork.
It was cooking all night.**

TOBY
(quietly to Redburn)
What...?

REDBURN
(smiling awkwardly)
No idea.

The boy reappears from the Rectory and runs back across the yard. **MOW-MOW** and the other **CHIEFS** come casually down the steps and make their way to the *Ti*. With them is the high priest **KOLORI** in a red mantle and swaddling something in his arm.

MEHEVI
(in POLYNESIAN, with subtitles)
**Now comes Kolori with the likeness of Manu Atu, our sacred
guardian of Taipivai.**

REDBURN
Manu Atu?

MEHEVI
(in POLYNESIAN, with subtitles)
**A great spirit — Kolori keeps him content, and thereby,
Taipi safe.**

The others arrive and seat themselves; Mow-Mow next to Mehevi. The boys form a line and bring steaming trays of food. First poi, then dumplings, roasted breadfruit, and lastly, a boy with cups of kava. They begin to eat, and Redburn notices Kolori pull back the hood on the idol he is holding. He then holds up a piece of food to the statue's lips. The idol's features are smooth from hundreds of years of touching. It wears a fine tapa mantle, and has a bib made of faded crimson fabric on its chest.

KOLORI
(crooning in POLYNESIAN, with subtitles)
Eat. Eat, or you will get sick.

REDBURN
(nudges Toby diplomatically)
**Don't look now, but it seems the pontiff of these parts
had a baby....**

TOBY
I saw. It's just as lovely as he.

REDBURN
I suppose they always invite God to attend their earthly affairs.

TOBY
Don't all Bishops implore just the same?

MOW-MOW
(aside to Mehevi – in POLYNESIAN, with subtitles)
**Should these outsiders be in the presence of the image of Manu
Atu? They may be planning treachery....**

MEHEVI
(in POLYNESIAN, with subtitles)
**Eat, Mow-Mow. The time to talk is when we have no
guests to attend to.**
(loud baby talk)
Is that not correct, Manu Atu?

Kolori holds up the idol and nods its consent. An odd NOISE arises; a guttural agreement. Redburn and Toby stop chewing and gawk at each other for silent confirmation that they both heard it.

INT. OF THE *TI* – MID-AFTERNOON

The plates of food are pushed aside. The men smoke leisurely. **MEHEVI** begins to absentmindedly sing an old song. Soon the other men join in. Afterwards, **REDBURN** and **TOBY** clap, but become self-aware that the others don't know what this means.

REDBURN and TOBY
(in POLYNESIAN, with subtitles)
Good! Good.

MEHEVI
(in POLYNESIAN, with subtitles)
Toby; Tommo – sing!

The sailors glance at each other, and Toby beats out the time for a drinking song.

REDBURN
(SINGS – chorus section)
"Every voice raise a song!
Every heart then pass it along
Like a free-flowing gift

For every free spirit to lift.

REDBURN and TOBY
(SING — chorus section)
A bottle, a barrel, a flask —
A tankard, a piggin, a glass —
Lift them high where we all may bask
In brotherhood's freed tantalus.

REDBURN
(SINGS — verse one)
A lass loved a lad and was glad,
Though shipped he far away from her,
With every cheer she was not sad,
But knew he drank to only her.

(Redburn and Toby recap: "Every voice raise a song... A bottle, a barrel, a flask — " etc.)

TOBY
(SINGS — verse two)
A lad left his brother on the shore,
Though two men were never more fit.
One the other would not see more,
Until Providence had seen to it.

TOBY
(SINGS — chorus section)
Every voice raise a song!
And let no misery prolong
Hearts a-flow but never adrift
From every spirit's potent drift.

REDBURN and TOBY
(SING — chorus section)
A bottle, a barrel, a flask —
A tankard, a piggin, a glass —
Lift them high where we all may bask
In brotherhood's freed tantalus."

MEHEVI
(in POLYNESIAN, with subtitles)
Amazing! Like the voice of spirit itself.

MOW-MOW
(in POLYNESIAN, with subtitles)
I don't know about that...

The boys reappear, this time all of them toting a large wooden trencher covered in steaming breadfruit leaves. The platter is set before Redburn and Toby, and the boys remove the leaves. The sailors peer in on three small forms, well roasted.

TOBY
(quiet amazement)
I think the tales were true – they are serving us baked babies...

REDBURN
(annoyed)
Oh, Toby, be done with your jokes.

Mehevi gestures, and Redburn reaches into the dish to pull off a small portion of meat.

TOBY
You're not going to eat any of that mess, are you?
How can you tell what it is?

REDBURN
By tasting it, of course.

TOBY
Saints protect us!

MEHEVI
(in POLYNESIAN, with subtitles)
It's Pork. Try the pork!

REDBURN
(considering)
It's oddly familiar – much like....

Toby deftly takes out his jackknife and turns some of the meat over in the dish. It's clearly roast suckling pig.

TOBY
Like, pork?

REDBURN
Like pork!

MEHEVI
(in POLYNESIAN, with subtitles)
Pork.

REDBURN and TOBY
(in POLYNESIAN, with subtitles)
Pork!

MEHEVI
(in POLYNESIAN, with subtitles)
Eat! Everyone, eat.

The men, except Redburn and Toby, stand and move toward the food, but Mow-Mow tugs at Kolori and they step aside.

> TOBY
> I still think they are just fattening us up.

> REDBURN
> Then starve yourself to bone and gristle.

> TOBY
> Too good — can't stop eating....

INT. FRONT VERANDA OF THE *TI*

MOW-MOW and KOLORI talk unobserved.

> MOW-MOW
> (in POLYNESIAN, with subtitles)
> They mock our ways — laugh too freely...they are French spies working with our enemies. They profane our holy grounds — come around, Kolori, to support me. We must make for the French before they make for us. It's do or die.

> KOLORI
> (in POLYNESIAN, with subtitles)
> Mehevi's plan for French appeasement is a popular one. Things will have to change — minds will have to be swayed — before you have a chance to lead us.

> MOW-MOW
> (crafty)
> Perhaps the best mind-changer is cradled in your arms.

Kolori shifts the weight in his arm, and a slow descent onto the idol's face shows its worn and menacing features.

INT. OF THE *TI* — EARLY EVENING

The men sit and smoke as before. **KORI-KORI** restlessly goes to the front veranda, exchanges heated, unheard words with the **BOYS**, then he comes back restlessly to **REDBURN** and **TOBY**'s side. He gets up again, and Redburn gets the idea.

> REDBURN
> It looks like our welcome here has run thin.

> TOBY
> It is getting late.

Kori-Kori comes back, sits and sighs. He attempts a halfhearted smile at Toby.

> REDBURN
> (to Kori-Kori — in POLYNESIAN, with subtitles)
> Home...?

KORI-KORI
(springs up, relieved – in POLYNESIAN, with subtitles)
Oh, all right – if you insist.

Redburn and Toby stand, stretch, and move towards the entry; Redburn with Toby's help. Mehevi suddenly stops them. Kori-Kori rushes past them and out the door.

MEHEVI
(in POLYNESIAN, with subtitles)
Wait. Wait.

TOBY
(low)
Your cauldron, sir, will be ready shortly.

REDBURN
Shush!

Kori-Kori comes back beaming. He takes Toby's place as Redburn's crutch, and Mehevi leads the way.

[Part 2 – IX: The Parade Home]

INT. FRONT VERANDA OF THE *TI*

A spectacle opens up in front of them, and **REDBURN** and **TOBY** gasp. The Hula Hula ground is full of **PEOPLE**, while the head of the parade waits for them in front of the *Ti*. Young **MEN** and **BOYS** stand two by two with woven leaf headbands and anklets.

EXT. HULA HULA GROUNDS

When they clear the last step, **KORI-KORI** motions, and **TOBY** supports **REDBURN**. Kori-Kori links arms with an equally well-built young **MAN**, and the two genuflect before Redburn. Kori-Kori gestures for Redburn to hop on. Another young **MAN** helps, and he and Toby lift Redburn into position. Redburn braces himself with hands on the napes of the two men under him. Before he knows it, Toby is hoisted on the shoulders of two other young **MEN**, and together with his mate, they are matched along the double columns of waiting **MEN** and **BOYS**. As they pass, things happen. At the rear of the troop, a single strong **MAN** lifts a trencher full of roast pork onto his head; then four **MEN** raise ten-foot bamboo poles with green baskets of breadfruit suspended from the ends; then five pairs of **BOYS** hoist five-foot poles, some with bunches of banana, some with strings of green coconut; then ten pairs of **BOYS**, each with a gourd bowl, lift them to the top of their heads; some with roasted breadfruit, some with roasted coconut, some with Tahitian gooseberry, and some with leaf-wrapped dumplings. When Redburn and Toby get to the head of the parade, **MEHEVI** is there and signals. Four young **MEN** hoist fifteen-foot poles with eight-foot-long narrow pennants of pure white tapa. Then the troop begins to intone a chant and stomp their feet as they move through the gate of the Hula Hula grounds.

EXT. CENTRAL AVENUE OF TAIPIVAI

The voices of the **MEN** and **BOYS** of the parade ring down the vale. **PEOPLE** and **CHILDREN** laugh and march along with **REDBURN** and **TOBY**.

EXT. GATE TO MAHEYO'S HOUSE

MAHEYO and **TINOR** come out to see what the ruckus is. The gate is opened, and **REDBURN** and **TOBY** are deposited in front of them with the last crescendo of the chant.

> **MAHEYO**
> (in POLYNESIAN, with subtitles)
> **Toby! Tommo! Welcome home.**

> **REDBURN**
> (in POLYNESIAN, with subtitles)
> **Home.**
> (to Toby – in ENGLISH)
> **You, and your dark thoughts....**

Toby shrugs, and is immediately pulled aside as a torrent of food begins to enter the yard. Maheyo and Tinor instruct the men and boys where to put it all.

[Part 3 – Settling In – I: A Day in the Life]

INT. MAHEYO'S HOUSE – MID-MORNING

TOBY sits near the veranda working with **MARMUNU** and **KARNUNU**, who decorate paddles and spears. Toby uses his jackknife to carve scrimshaw-like decorations on a gourd bowl. They chat, and the men of the household offer Toby encouragement. **REDBURN** lies on his stomach on the dais, scanning the room. In front of him is an open notebook; a pencil varies from writing to resting on his lower lip in contemplation. To his right, he can see out of the house, and **MAHEYO** rambling back and forth to his 'tool shed.' Far to his left on the dais, **RUNU** naps in a sitting position. Redburn now sports a short and youthful beard and mustache; Toby remains clean-shaven.

> **REDBURN (V.O.)**
> In Typee the history of a day is the history of a life. One tranquil period of ease follows another in quiet, and happy, succession. After the morning repast, and the social passing of pipes, Marheyo inevitably retreats to the little hut he is forever building, and Tinor busies herself in the inspection of her rolls of tapa, or employs her industrious fingers in the plaiting of grass mats. Fayaway and the other girls ready themselves for rounds of mid-morning visits by dressing each other's hair, and dabbing fragrant oils here and there. The young men of the household retreat to the veranda and produce their personal possessions. They number few, but are greatly treasured handiworks, like paddles, clubs, spears, fishing gear, and a few ornaments for around the neck or ears. My companion sits amongst these intent-but-smiling men as they endeavored to permanently mark their goods as their own. Using a honed bit of shell, or a

holstered shark tooth, they – and Toby with his jackknife – carve
motifs unique to themselves; unique so that all Typee-vie will
know instantly to whom this treasure belongs.

Maheyo comes in and goes to his usual spot where he slips in his 'going out' earrings.
Redburn rises to a crossed-legged position, and Maheyo notices his intent. After his
jewelry is in, Maheyo nods to Redburn and picks up a fan. He sits next to Redburn and
begins to gently cool his guest.

MAHEYO
(in POLYNESIAN, with subtitles)
Poor Tommo. How is your ankle?

REDBURN
(in POLYNESIAN, with subtitles)
It hurts, but I can walk better now.

MAHEYO
(in POLYNESIAN, with subtitles)
Poor Tommo. So far away from family.

REDBURN
(not knowing the word – in POLYNESIAN, with subtitles)
Family?

MAHEYO
(smiles, gestures around – in POLYNESIAN, with subtitles)
Family. Here, we!

REDBURN
(gets it – in POLYNESIAN, with subtitles)
Family.

MAHEYO
(prosaic – in POLYNESIAN, with subtitles)
But – you have Toby. You are family, right?

REDBURN
(in POLYNESIAN, with subtitles)
Toby; my family, yes.

MAHEYO
(in POLYNESIAN, with subtitles)
**Good. It's very good not to be alone. In *Manika*, how do
you say family?**

REDBURN
Fa-ma-ly

MAHEYO
FA-MA-Li

REDBURN
Family.

MAHEYO
Family—
(in POLYNESIAN, with subtitles)
Good. Family!

REDBURN
(in POLYNESIAN, with subtitles)
Who is family here? So many people....

MAHEYO
(in POLYNESIAN, with subtitles)
Oh. Runu is head. He married Tinor and me when we were young — then we three built this house together. We have sons — Mowanna, who is married with his own house; then Marmunu and his girlfriend Karluna; Faaua, our daughter with Kori-Kori; Mununi, our daughter, with Karnunu — and our youngest son, Monu with his boyfriend, Ruaruga. Do you understand? Monu and Ruaruga are like you and Toby — together.

REDBURN
(smiles — in POLYNESIAN, with subtitles)
Yes. Together.

MAHEYO
(in POLYNESIAN, with subtitles)
So we were blessed with sons and daughters, and soon, older men will marry them. Monu and Ruaruga need an older woman with her own house — the others, an older man. Do you understand?

REDBURN
Family!

MAHEYO
(laughs)
Family.
(in POLYNESIAN, with subtitles)
Tinor is looking for a good woman for you and Toby to marry. Then you can settle down in a big home and have your children. Don't tell her I told you, right?

Maheyo chuckles to himself, rises and walks out the front door, repeating 'family' to himself several times. Toby comes up and jocularly slaps his partner's back.

TOBY
Well, my brother — are we in for the day, or what?

REDBURN
No. Let's take a walk. I have a lot to relay.

[Part 3 – II: They Know]

EXT. CENTRAL AVENUE OF TAIPIVAI – NOON

TOBY and **REDBURN** stroll along. They wear their kilts, belts, hats and borrowed sandals. Redburn uses a paddle as a crutch. Behind them, **KORI-KORI** and **FAAUA** follow, enjoying a lover's tête-à-tête.

TOBY
...So you say, young couples are 'married' by an older, more established, man – polygamy, in multiples of husbands?

REDBURN
Yes. Just two men, one woman.

TOBY
Good for the women folk here – it makes sense. If one man is killed or crippled in one of their wars, then the children are still looked after.

REDBURN
But sometimes the older, better established, is a woman.

TOBY
Huh?

REDBURN
Two men and a woman – same arrangement, only she marries the young men who are the couple.

TOBY
Oh.

REDBURN
They know about us, Toby. Maheyo says those young ones – Monu and Ruaruga – are like 'Toby and Tommo.'

TOBY
Those lazy scapegraces?

REDBURN
Monu is their son; Ruaruga is his partner.

Toby stops Redburn with a hand and a slack jaw.

TOBY
What does that mean?

Redburn glances over his shoulder at Kori-Kori and Faaua several paces behind them. Toby gapes at them too.

REDBURN
It means, they know, and...they don't care.

TOBY
(blurts)
But, how can that—

Redburn grabs Toby's arm and compels forward.

REDBURN
It can, and it is. Their traditions are open. The way we
were raised is not the way it has to be.

CHEERS drift from beyond the line of trees. In a few steps, an opening to a clearing shows a **CROWD** gathered in a circle watching something. Kori-Kori runs up excited and pulls them in.

EXT. A CLEARING

REDBURN, TOBY, KORI-KORI and **FAAUA** make their way to the back of the **CROWD,** and as they are seen, people call out 'Toby' and 'Tommo' and push them to the front. Two young **MEN** are wrestling. Finally, the sweaty and smiling victorious **WRESTLER** comes up to Toby.

WRESTLER
(in POLYNESIAN, with subtitles)
Wrestle with me!

TOBY
(in POLYNESIAN, with subtitles)
No – I....

The Wrestler pulls Toby's arm, and Toby lets himself be led to a match. He quickly pops his hat on top of Redburn's. In the ring, Toby puts on his war face and wrestles. Eventually he pins his opponent, and the crowd calls out: '**Toby; Toby; Toby.**' After the match, Toby extends a hand and lifts the young man to a standing position. He slaps the Wrestler's shoulders in good fellowship, then Toby jogs over to Redburn.

TOBY
Come on lad! Let's show them how to box.

REDBURN
I can't—

Toby picks the hats off of Redburn and drops them on Faaua's head. He takes Redburn's paddle and gives it to Kori-Kori.

TOBY
Sure you can. I know you only half rely on that crutch. Don't
worry — exhibition match only.

Toby pulls Redburn out, and they strike a boxing pose. The crowd is in hushed awe as
the Americans begin a dance with feet and fists. Toby jabs right; Redburn ducks left,
etc. Some playful punches are landed by Toby, and the crowd again chants his name.
Redburn gives as good as he gets, but becomes distracted by pairs of small **BOYS**
running around the inner perimeter of the ring putting up their dukes. Toby lands a
punch that is too hard. Redburn falls on his backside. Toby rushes to help him stand.

TOBY
Are you all right?

REDBURN
(grimace)
I think I twisted it again.

Toby motions desperately for Kori-Kori to come to them. Kori-Kori presents his back,
and Toby and the Wrestler help Redburn mount piggyback style. As Kori-Kori rushes
back to the road, Toby calls after them.

TOBY
I'm sorry — I'm sorry. Damn my hot head!

[Part 3 — III: Toby Must Go]

INT. MAHEYO'S HOUSE — MID-AFTERNOON

It is the hottest part of the afternoon. The **HOUSEHOLD** is in deep siesta, arranged on
the dais in quiet pairs. **REDBURN** and **TOBY** sit at the edge of the dais and chat in
hushed tones. Toby looks miserable. He reaches up and strokes his mate's cheek with
the back of his fingers.

TOBY
I hurt you.

REDBURN
It's not you. But, I am worried. If that witchdoctor deems my
foot has to come off — off it comes!

TOBY
I won't let them....

REDBURN
You can't stop them. No. I need medical attention. I have
to get to Nukahiva.

TOBY
How! You can't walk. You expect Kori-Kori to carry you there?

REDBURN
(swallows hard)
**No. It's up to you to get there and come back with a doctor, or
at least, some medicine.**

TOBY
**Never. I will never leave you alone, in the hands of
these...these—**

Redburn picks up Toby's hand.

REDBURN
You have to go. It's the only way.

TOBY
**It's my fault — just — just hold on for a few weeks. I know you
can. Then you'll be better, and we can walk out of here, together.
What makes you think they'll let me leave anyway?**

MAHEYO rouses. He rises and looks around for his fan.

REDBURN
**They know you will return. They know as well as I do, you will
never leave me here without you.**

Maheyo, fan in hand, sits on Redburn's other side. He fans both his guests in a gentle
back and forth with his wrist in his lap.

REDBURN (CONT'D)
(in POLYNESIAN, with subtitles)
**Maheyo — my ankle is bad. I need a French doctor; French
medicine. Let Toby go and bring it back to Typee.**

Maheyo is saddened, but then he sees Toby's moist eyes.

MAHEYO
(in POLYNESIAN, with subtitles)
**Poor Toby. Poor Tommo. You are both in pain. I will help you
ask Mehevi. Toby? You will come back....**

TOBY
(vehemently — in POLYNESIAN, with subtitles)
I will come back.

MAHEYO
(in POLYNESIAN, with subtitles)
Good. I know.

[Part 3 — IV: No Treachery]

INT. OF THE *TI* — EARLY EVENING

REDBURN, TOBY, MAHEYO, KORI-KORI, MOW-MOW and MEHEVI are lounging
and smoking.

MAHEYO
(in POLYNESIAN, with subtitles)
Mehevi – Tommo's leg is worse. Toby must fetch medicine so
all will be well with them. Toby will return.

MOW-MOW
(in POLYNESIAN, with subtitles)
French medicine? What's wrong with Taipi medicine!

MAHEYO
(in POLYNESIAN, with subtitles)
Nothing – for us. For Tommo, it does not work. I suspect his
spirit is suited for other medicine, not ours.

MOW-MOW
(in POLYNESIAN, with subtitles)
Bull. They just want to leave. They care nothing
about our hospitality—

Mehevi tersely cuts him off.

MEHEVI
(in POLYNESIAN, with subtitles)
There is no treachery in love. If Tommo is ill, Toby will not
abandon him. You have eyes!

Mow-Mow fumes in silence. He looks to Kori-Kori for support, but it seems Kori-Kori has
had a change of heart. Mehevi turns to Toby with affected lightness.

MEHEVI (CONT'D)
(in POLYNESIAN, with subtitles)
You will return to Taipivai; to Tommo?

TOBY
(in POLYNESIAN, with subtitles)
I will not leave Tommo for long. I'll get the medicine and
come back quickly.

MEHEVI
(to Mow-Mow – in POLYNESIAN, with subtitles)
See. No treachery.
(to Maheyo)
Only love. You, Maheyo, will provision Toby – food, water,
whatever he needs.
(to Redburn)
But Toby must stay for a few more days for the festival. That
way, we have time to plan. Yes?

REDBURN
(in POLYNESIAN, with subtitles)
Yes.

TOBY
What does he say?

REDBURN
You can go in a few days — something about a holiday.
Maheyo will help us prepare.

Toby beams, thanking first Mehevi, then Maheyo by taking his host's hands.

TOBY
(in POLYNESIAN, with subtitles)
Thank you. Thank you!

[Part 3 – V: Feast of the Calabashes]

EXT. COCONUT TREE *ALLÉE* – NOON

MUSIC fills the air; **PEOPLE** in holiday mood **LAUGH** and **CHAT**. The crowd moves toward the second gate to the Hula Hula grounds. The crowd treats Maheyo's family like honored guests, and warm greetings **RING** out. First, **MARMUNU** and **KARLUNA** lead a tottering **RUNU**, closely followed by a beaming **TINOR** with **MAHEYO** and **FAAUA**. Next **REDBURN** is walking, braced by his arms over the shoulders of **TOBY** and **KORI-KORI**. Then, **MUNUNI** with **KARNUNU**, and trailing arm in arm, **MONU** with **RUARUGA**. The women of the family are wearing the calico brought by Redburn and Toby. The men wear kilts with mantles on their shoulders. Everyone is decked out with green head wreaths, collars, and anklets. The crowd swells, and everybody is compelled through the gate into the Hula Hula grounds.

EXT. HULA HULA GROUNDS

The rhythm of the **MUSIC** becomes acute, as **PEOPLE** swirl around the transformed yard. Each of the shrines is festooned in garlands of flowers and foliage, and each idol is freshly dressed in bright white tapa. The narrow end of the grounds, to the right of the gate, is centered with a hundred-foot-long stage raised three feet off the ground. Here **WOMEN** dance while **MEN** on the flanks intone the legends of their peoples. Behind the stage, a platform rises ten feet above it. Massive fifteen-foot-long drums are propped with one end on stage and the other on the raised platform, where young **MEN** play them in unison. Behind the drum platform rises a tiered hundred-foot-high pyramidal tower. Each level is dotted with hundreds of hanging lanterns cut from the round bottoms of green gourds. Each is incised with decorations, so white shows through when lit. The left end of the yard is a grandstand that rises thirty feet in the air. People are sitting here, watching the dance, chatting and eating. The women of **MAHEYO**'s party head to the grandstand, while the men move to the *Ti*.

INT. GARDEN VERANDA OF THE *TI* FACING THE INNER COURT

The rear bleachers connecting the *Ti* and Rectory are dotted with visiting **MEN** who are neighboring dignitaries. The yard is decked with a dozen green bamboo poles equally spaced and each sporting a spotless white tapa pennant. The platforms around the trees each have four **PRIESTS**, sitting cross-legged with their backs on the trunks. They have closed eyes, and hands folded in prayer. They chant in unison.

INT. OF THE *TI*

Front and center, facing the court, **MEHEVI** entertains **REDBURN** and **TOBY**. Around, and behind them, all the **MEN** of Taipivai sit, chat, eat, smoke. Before the Americans, a trencher of roast pork steaming invitingly. They help themselves with casual languor.

> **REDBURN**
> **What do you think of this description: 'They convert rebellious and hostile hogs into the most docile and amiable pork — a morsel of which, placed on the tongue, melts as helplessly as a soft smile fades from the lips of beauty.'**

> **TOBY**
> (lip-smacks)
> **Rhapsodic — and all for a pork chop.**

> Redburn is crestfallen.

> **TOBY (CONT'D)**
> **But — it's beautiful. You have a way with our glorious 'mongrel tongue.' You'll be famous one day; I know it.**

> **REDBURN**
> **I wish I had my journal.**

> **TOBY**
> **You'll remember it. You won't forget any of this.**

[Part 4 — Do or Die — I: Spiky Shadows]

EXT. MAHEYO'S HOUSE — NIGHT

Full-moon brilliance shines light on a sleeping Taipivai. The light is sliced into spiky shadows by coconut leaves as a gentle breeze animates them on Maheyo's veranda floor.

INT. MAHEYO'S HOUSE

Sounds of the household asleep calmly measure out a beating rise and fall. **REDBURN** and **TOBY** lie in each other's arms and kiss. Toby's left arm is under his mate's head, and he hovers above Redburn. Redburn's right-hand laces up through Toby's armpit to grip Toby's shoulder, while his other hand moves below the line of the tapa blanket below their waistline. As they continue to kiss, Redburn pleasures his partner, and soon Toby has to pause for air. Toby continues to hover over Redburn, even though his breaths become short and sharp. As Toby reaches orgasm, Redburn greedily lifts his head to catch these breaths. Toby falters, like he is going to collapse on Redburn, but instead, he executes a measured and slow descent. He kisses his mate passionately. He stops and strokes Redburn's short beard, smiles, then rests his head on Redburn's chest. Redburn brushes Toby's curly hair out of Toby's eyes, and unaccountably looks above him. The three bundles loom in the eerie light with more menace than ever.

[Part 4 – II: Goodbyes]

EXT. GATE TO MAHEYO'S HOUSE – MID-MORNING

TOBY is outfitted for his mountain hike. He is back in his sailor clothes and hat. His escorts, **MARMUNU, KARNUNU** and **MONU**, are checking their spears and generally horsing around. Marmunu, as leader, is anxious to get on the road. **MAHEYO** comes up with parental concern.

MAHEYO
(in POLYNESIAN, with subtitles)
**Toby! Be careful. The Happar are treacherous – you
understand? Enemies!**

TOBY
(in POLYNESIAN, with subtitles)
I'll be safe with your sons.

MAHEYO
(in POLYNESIAN, with subtitles)
**They can't enter Happar territory. If they see Happar, they will
explain you need to pass through. Then they will come back.
Toby, you are brave. You are a son to me. Understand?**

TOBY
(nods)
I need a spear – to fight the Happar!

Karnunu puts up his dukes.

KARNUNU
(in POLYNESIAN, with subtitles)
**You don't need a spear. For a hothead like you, strong fists
are all you need!**

Monu comes up and play-punches Toby's gut.

MONU
(in POLYNESIAN, with subtitles)
Yeah! Give the Happar your 'one-two; Pow. Pow!'

Toby smiles and weaves in play-defense.

TOBY
Brat. Pow. Pow, yourself.

TINOR comes bustling with a lashed pair of green coconuts. Behind her, **REDBURN** ambles from the house with his paddle crutch.

TINOR
(in POLYNESIAN, with subtitles)
Monu! Take these. Come get more.

Tinor leads Maheyo, Marmunu, Karnunu and Monu back to the veranda, leaving Toby and Redburn alone.

TOBY
No emotion now. I will be back by three-days at the longest. You
rest yourself – be strong and ready in case we can get you out
by boat. You might need to make a run for it.

There is silence from Redburn. The boys come back with strings of coconuts draped over their necks. Their respective partners: **KARLUNA, MUNUNI** and **RUARUGA**, follow. Paired up, they pause. They are moved watching the Americans' parting.

TOBY (CONT'D)
Keep your spirits up. I'll be fine.

MARMUNU
(in POLYNESIAN, with subtitles)
Toby. Let's go.

Toby looks sad. He picks up Redburn's hand a moment, and pulls him into a brief smack on the lips. Suddenly, Karluna takes her partner's hand and pulls him down into a kiss. Karnunu turns and plants a peck on Mununi's cheek. Ruaruga titters, but Monu puts his arm around his neck, and soon the boys kiss like they mean it. Inspired, Redburn kisses his partner like he means it too.

REDBURN
Well, brother, looks like we've started
a trend.

Before Toby can respond, the young men are out the gate and motioning for Toby to follow. As they troop up the road, Redburn moves to the gate; the women go into the house, chatting. Toby turns and gives a jocular wave. As he watches his mate disappear, Redburn can feel **KORI-KORI** and **FAAUA** come up, and stand behind him. Redburn gives a final, desperate wave.

[Part 4 – III: Trouble Ahead]

EXT. MOUNTAIN PASS – AFTERNOON

A narrow pass cuts through deep woods. **MARMUNU** comes along as quietly as possible. He is followed by **TOBY**, then **KARNUNU** and **MONU**. Marmunu stops and motions for everyone to crouch down and be still. They hear no sounds of people.

MARMUNU
(low — in POLYNESIAN, with subtitles)

Toby, this is as far as we can go. We are in Happar territory, and there is no one around. You just quietly follow this path. It goes around behind the Happar valley, and by the end of the day, you will cross into Nuku Hiva.

Monu is impatient with his brother.

MONU
(in POLYNESIAN, with subtitles)
We can't leave him — those barbarians will kill him.

MARMUNU
(authoritative — in POLYNESIAN, with subtitles)
**We can't be caught here. Toby is safer without us. Goodbye,
Toby. We will look after your Tommo until you can return.**

The young men transfer two strings of coconuts to Toby's shoulders.

TOBY
(in POLYNESIAN, with subtitles)
All right. Good-bye.

The other young men make a retreat the way they had come. Toby stands erect, tips his hat brim back, and eyes the path ahead warily.

INT. MAHEYO'S HOUSE — EARLY EVENING

REDBURN sits alone on the dais. **FAAUA** brings him a gourd bowl with steaming dumplings in it. She sits next to him with the food in her lap.

FAAUA
(soft — in POLYNESIAN, with subtitles)
Tommo, you didn't eat anything today. Have something.

REDBURN
(in POLYNESIAN, with subtitles)
Eat...? No — but, stay awhile.

After an awkward pause.

FAAUA
(in POLYNESIAN, with subtitles)
Toby is a good man. He will return.

REDBURN
(in POLYNESIAN, with subtitles)
You love Kori-Kori, don't you?

FAAUA
(in POLYNESIAN, with subtitles)
Kori-Kori is a good man too.

REDBURN
(in POLYNESIAN, with subtitles)
He doesn't like me, does he?

Faaua reflects before answering.

FAAUA
(in POLYNESIAN, with subtitles)
**Kori-Kori is slow to trust — But once his confidence is gained,
he'd sacrifice anything for those in his heart.**

REDBURN
**You're like Beauty itself — you bring out the best in
every human heart.**

FAAUA
(puzzled — in POLYNESIAN, with subtitles)
What...?

REDBURN
(in POLYNESIAN, with subtitles)
I say — you are beautiful.

Faaua blushes, and is miffed.

FAAUA
(in POLYNESIAN, with subtitles)
Don't tease. I know you don't like girls.

Redburn is a bit shocked that the subject is talked about so openly, and so lightly.

REDBURN
(in POLYNESIAN, with subtitles)
Well — still, you _are_ beautiful.

An odd **SOUND** arises, and pours in from the front door and verandas. People on the road are shouting. A telegraphing message in horrifying timbre comes down the valley. Redburn and Faaua stare at each other in rising, but stymied, alarm as they make out the words (in POLYNESIAN, with subtitles): **"Oh, no! Oh, no! Toby has been killed!"**

EXT. GATE TO MAHEYO'S HOUSE

TINOR, MAHEYO and **FAAUA** come running up the gate. An agitated throng of **PEOPLE** point up the road. **REDBURN** is helped by **KORI-KORI**, and by the time they make it to the gate, a dusty cloud resolves itself into **TOBY**'s white duck-covered legs swinging off the ground as **MARMUNU** and **KARNUNU** run sideways. Their arms are linked, and support the front half of Toby. **MONU** struggles behind them to support

Toby's torso. Soon, two other young **MEN** relieve him, and Monu runs ahead. Kori-Kori shouts to Monu.

KORI-KORI
(in POLYNESIAN, with subtitles)
Go fetch the doctor!

Monu continues past the house. The young men bring Toby through the gate, and Redburn sees Toby's head and shoulders are covered in blood. Kori-Kori picks Redburn up and takes him into the house before anybody else gets there.

INT. MAHEYO'S HOUSE

KORI-KORI sets **REDBURN** down by the dais. As the young **MEN** bring **TOBY** in, Redburn takes charge. He points to where Toby is to be deposited. Then roars to **TINOR** and **FAAUA**.

REDBURN
(in POLYNESIAN, with subtitles)
Water!

As the women gather bandages and bowls of water, the young men group with Kori-Kori and Maheyo.

MAHEYO
(to Marmunu – in POLYNESIAN, with subtitles)
What happened?

KARNUNU
(in POLYNESIAN, with subtitles)
Damn Happar!

MARMUNU
(in POLYNESIAN, with subtitles)
**We just left Toby on the Happar side, when we hear some angry
voices demanding to know who Toby is. Toby has no time to
say anything before they attack him.**

KARNUNU
(in POLYNESIAN, with subtitles)
**We rushed back to help him, and the Happar cowards ran
away. We found Toby bleeding from—**

MARMUNU
(in POLYNESIAN, with subtitles)
Savages! They attacked him for no reason.

Redburn positions himself behind Toby and puts Toby's head in his lap. He gently rotates it so the open gash is facing upwards. Toby shows no signs of life. Redburn puts his hand through Toby's jersey and under his tee-shirt to rest on his heart. Faaua rushes up with sloshing water.

REDBURN
(to Faaua)
He's alive. Thank God, he's still alive!
(in POLYNESIAN, with subtitles)
Alive!

Redburn dips his fingers in the water and drips it over the wound. Now he can see some of Toby's hair is in it, so he gently extracts it, and pours a stream of water to wash it. The **DOCTOR** arrives with **MONU** holding his bag. The Doctor calmly goes over to Toby and waves for Redburn to move. Redburn grits his teeth and shakes his head. The Doctor shrugs, and calls for his bag. From it, he extracts a thick succulent pad. He snaps it in two and holds the oozing ends to Toby's wound. Toby starts in pain. Redburn grabs his shoulders.

REDBURN
(shushes)
Be still now. Just wait.

Toby's wild eyes settle on Redburn, then on the Doctor, and a current of relief washes over him in relaxation. Toby closes his eyes, and a devilish grin creeps across his lips.

TOBY
A fine invalid pair we make.

REDBURN
(shushes)
Thank you, God.

[Part 4 – IV: Taipivai's Washington]

EXT. CENTRAL AVENUE OF TAIPIVAI – NOON

KORI-KORI and **REDBURN** stroll. Redburn wears his kilt, belt, borrowed sandals and his hat. He neither leans on Kori-Kori nor has his paddle crutch; he limps slightly.

KORI-KORI
(in POLYNESIAN, with subtitles)
Toby is brave. He is a strong man. You are lucky.

Redburn is distracted by an opening coming up. A thicket of bamboo poles with white tapa pennants mark the entrance to a clearing. He points.

REDBURN
(in POLYNESIAN, with subtitles)
What is this place?

KORI-KORI
(in POLYNESIAN, with subtitles)
Come.

Kori-Kori leads Redburn through the tapa-strewn poles.

EXT. SHRINE COMPOUND

A perimeter of palm trees edges a clearing of about fifty square yards. To the left side from the entry, a stone platform rises about three feet, and supports a building about ten feet square. The front is open, and a tall idol rides a full-size canoe. The idol is dressed in a red mantle, and an offering table by the prow of the boat is full of food, flowers and drink. **REDBURN** forgets his host and walks right up to the canoe. **KORI-KORI** is impressed by Redburn's interest.

KORI-KORI
(in POLYNESIAN, with subtitles)
**This is Kikiruaru — Great Chief of Taipivai. He built the Ti and
Hula Hula enclosure ten generations ago.**

Redburn sees the limbs of the statue are glistening. He sniffs at it, and makes a puzzled look to Kori-Kori.

KORI-KORI (CONT'D)
(in POLYNESIAN, with subtitles)
**Every day the chief is bathed by women, then dressed with
coconut oil and given a new mantle to wear.**

REDBURN
(in POLYNESIAN, with subtitles)
He's in a boat.

KORI-KORI
(in POLYNESIAN, with subtitles)
**To travel from Taipivai to heaven — in the stars — and back to us
again. He could never leave Taipi. We love him. We never allow
the loved one to leave here — the place where he is best loved.**

REDBURN
(in POLYNESIAN, with subtitles)
Your heaven is in the stars?

KORI-KORI
(in POLYNESIAN, with subtitles)
Yes — see the paddle?

Redburn looks again, and at the side of the figure, held by both his hands, is a broad paddle.

KORI-KORI (CONT'D)
(in POLYNESIAN, with subtitles)
**He paddles through the waters of the sky where all is rest and
comfort. Whenever he wishes for breadfruit, ripe ones fall to his
feet. When he thirsts, green coconuts open themselves to his lips.
If he rests, it is upon mats much finer than those we use. And he
has an endless selection of plumes, boar tusks, whale teeth, to
decorate his body. And there, among him, are young men and
young women, lovelier than the sons and daughters of our earth.**

REDBURN
(in POLYNESIAN, with subtitles)
A very pleasant place – But, it sounds exactly like Typee.

Kori-Kori comes up and whispers a secret in Redburn's ear.

KORI-KORI
(in POLYNESIAN, with subtitles)
It is.

Redburn turns into an unaccountably near Kori-Kori.

REDBURN
(in POLYNESIAN, with subtitles)
Do you, then, wish to accompany the chief on his travels?

KORI-KORI
(in POLYNESIAN, with subtitles)
**In time. If I do no harm here among my brothers and sisters
while living, I will join him; but not now.**

TOBY, supported by **FAAUA**, walks into the sanctuary unnoticed. Toby's head is bandaged with tapa, and his beard is growing.

TOBY
Ahoy, matey!

Redburn rushes over to him, relieving Faaua of her duty.

REDBURN
Toby. What are you doing? It's only been a week—

TOBY
Air, my boy. Air. Fayaway makes pleasant company.

Redburn puts his hat on Toby's head.

REDBURN
I told you not to go out in the sun.

TOBY
(to Faaua – in POLYNESIAN, with subtitles)
Mother-hen.

Faaua and Kori-Kori laugh heartily, and Kori-Kori slaps Redburn's shoulder, repeating.

KORI-KORI
(in POLYNESIAN, with subtitles)
You're a mother-hen!

A chorus of voices telegraphs up the valley road from the beach (in POLYNESIAN, with subtitles): **"A boat is approaching – gather fruit!"**

REDBURN
(quietly to Toby)
A boat. There's a boat coming.

PEOPLE are seen on the road, many carrying coconuts and other produce. They run towards the beach.

TOBY
(to Redburn with affected glibness)
I have to go. I can get help.

Kori-Kori becomes authoritative, and moves towards the road.

KORI-KORI
(in POLYNESIAN, with subtitles)
We should go home.

Redburn blows his cool. He nearly pleads to Kori-Kori, until Toby stops him.

REDBURN
(in POLYNESIAN, with subtitles)
Take us to the beach....

TOBY
**Calm yourself. This is the time you take my advice. Stay
calm; stay here.**

He turns lighthearted to Kori-Kori.

TOBY (CONT'D)
(in POLYNESIAN, with subtitles)
**Tommo will stay here — I want to see the fun! Faaua and I can
go, and we'll meet you back at the house.**

So saying, Toby spins around and puts his arm around Faaua's shoulder. They make for the road before Kori-Kori can object. Redburn walks back to the shrine and Kori-Kori must follow. Redburn looks the old wooden idol in the eye, and the noise of people fade as natural sounds call for his attention. The palm trees around the enclosure rustle; birds call in pleasant song; and the stream chops itself over smooth stones. From the food and flowers on his offering table, a slow draw leads up to the chief's wooden eyes. Redburn leans in as close to the idol as he dare, while Kori-Kori drifts up behind him, not knowing what's happening.

REDBURN
**God speed, brave one. May you have a pleasant voyage to the
beyond. To the outward eye, you make but little progress, but to
the inner eye of deep abiding faith — you cleave the bright waters
and cut the foaming waves into brilliant shards with never-
forgetting fingers. You never leave those you love.**

[Part 5 – Fayaway's Love – I: In the Name of David and Jonathan]

INT. MAHEYO'S HOUSE – MID-AFTERNOON

As most of the household sleeps in cozy pairs, **REDBURN** lies on his stomach, his journal in front of him. His beard is longer now.

INT. VERANDA OF MAHEYO'S HOUSE

FAAUA and **KORI-KORI** glance at Redburn and chat quietly. They speak in POLY-NESIAN, with subtitles.

> KORI-KORI
> Toby's not coming back... He's betrayed his partner.

> FAAUA
> It's only been a few weeks; if he could come back, he would. I
> just hope – he's not dead.

> KORI-KORI
> He's not coming back—

Faaua is unaccountably forceful.

> FAAUA
> You were not on the beach with Toby. If he can come back, he
> will. You did not see the fear in his eyes. He didn't want to leave,
> but....

> KORI-KORI
> But, what?

> FAAUA
> Mow-Mow.

She leaves the rest unsaid, as if Kori-Kori would understand, but he does not.

> FAAUA (CONT'D)
> Mow-Mow wanted Toby gone, so he is gone.

> KORI-KORI
> He must be far away, not to come back...he's broken his heart,
> but Tommo must think of the here and now, not the past.

INT. MAHEYO'S HOUSE

REDBURN writes in his journal. During the following voiceover, the typical sights of the house in the afternoon are shown: Arva doing some person grooming; Kori-Kori and Faaua chatting quietly on the veranda; Tinor rises first, proceeding to tidy up a bit; Maheyo getting up next and busying himself with his 'tool shed' outside; etc.

> REDBURN (V.O.)

In the history of the day, the luxurious siesta is almost never omitted. When mid-day has crept a near-shadowless apogee, peace fairly comes to the vale and not a sound is to be heard, while deep sleep falls upon one and all. The post-meridian heat of afternoon is often cut with meandering strolls to the little lake. Here Fayaway, Kori-Kori and I row the canoe I asked to be placed there, or swim, and this is where Kori-Kori will inevitably play and tumble in the water — his pranks designed for the sole purpose of diverting my sadness. For the one thing that stands out in contrast to our so-called 'civilized,' and our so-called 'christian,' world is that here, there seem to be no cares; no grief; no trouble, or jealousy; not in all the valley of the Typee. I, in my self-contemplating doubt, stand out like a sore thumb — or ankle — while they trip the hours along as gaily as a laughing couple down a country lane. I am the only thing they have to worry about.

Redburn's pencil goes to rest on his lower lip as he recalls a memory.

BEGIN 'KISS IN THE GRANDSTAND' FLASHBACK:

EXT. HULA HULA GROUNDS GRANDSTAND — NIGHT OF FESTIVAL

The gourd lanterns are all lit. Torches mark the boundaries of the stage as men chant and play drums on the platform. women dance on the stage. Redburn sits next to Toby and both are taken with the beauty of the scene. They are happy. Toby leans in.

TOBY
Have you ever seen the likes? Now, <u>this</u> is adventure.

Toby scans his partner's face, hoping to make him smile. Redburn won't look at him.

REDBURN
You are coming back for me, right?

Toby gulps in choked sorrow. He turns Redburn by the cheek to him.

TOBY
And, what in name of David and Jonathans everywhere
would I do without you...?
(in POLYNESIAN, with subtitles)
I <u>will</u> come back for you.
(in English)
Idiot.

They turn to watch the festivities. Redburn quietly slips his fingers into Toby's grasp. After a while, Toby lifts it, and gently kisses the back of Redburn's hand. Redburn is amazed.

REDBURN
Don't you care who sees?

TOBY
(amazed back)
**You are right – They know. And, they don't care, except
to be happy for us.**

Redburn leans in, and plants a peck on Toby's cheek. Toby seems sadder than ever. He glances around, and catches the eye of Faaua, who has a dreamy look for him. Next to her is Kori-Kori who seems only mildly interested. Then he glances to find Tinor and Maheyo with hand-in-glove affection for each other. Redburn notices Toby's inspection, but is not prepared to see the soul-searching ache he turns on Redburn.

TOBY (CONT'D)
It will be all right. Trust me.

Toby puts a hand on the back of Redburn's head and draws him into a sustained and tender kiss. As they kiss, they draw attention – Karnunu with Mununi; Marmunu with Karluna; and especially Monu with Ruaruga – are all moved by the genuine love of their houseguests.

END 'KISS IN THE GRANDSTAND' FLASHBACK.

INT. MAHEYO'S HOUSE

KORI-KORI stands in front of **REDBURN**.

KORI-KORI
(in POLYNESIAN, with subtitles)
Tommo – let's go for a swim.

Redburn sees **FAAUA** is waiting at the door with towels. He nods and put his pencil down.

[Part 5 – II: Lake Scene]

EXT. LAKE IN TAIPIVAI – MID-AFTERNOON – LATER

A sheet of clear water, with lush foliage coming straight down to its margins, is disturbed by a coming wake. At water level, the prow of a canoe glides into view. Behind the prow, **REDBURN** reclines in the bow with hands behind his head. Next, **KORI-KORI** lazily paddles from the center of the boat, while standing in the stern, **FAAUA** has taken the hem of her long skirt and lifted it above her head. She holds it there, and the gentle breeze on her face billows the fabric out behind her like a living 'Spirit of Ecstasy' figure.

EXT. FLAT ROCKY OUTCROP IN LAKE

In a large sunny area **FAAUA**, with glistening skin and wet hair, lightly fans the face of **REDBURN** lying by her tucked-in legs. Redburn also glistens from his swim, and he is naked except for a wet strip of thin tapa draped over his crotch. Redburn rotates his head to watch **KORI-KORI**'s antics in the water by their side. He bobs straight up with his hands by his sides, and then topples over like a felled tree, making a big splash. Redburn turns, and arrests Faaua's fan. He holds it gently, and quietly pleads with her. They speak in POLYNESIAN, with subtitles.

REDBURN
Tell me again.

FAAUA
(sighs)

A man like you in a boat talked to Toby. Toby did not want to go — he made me promise I would tell you he would come back in three — no, no — sooner. <u>Before</u> three days. He didn't want to leave you, you know that...but....

REDBURN
But, what?

Faaua is visibly nervous. She glances around, like she shouldn't say this, and is barely audible.

FAAUA
Mow-Mow is not your friend.

Kori-Kori comes up to the rock with a sly grin and with a mouthful of water. He aims a stream on Redburn and Faaua, who both start. Redburn sits and puts out his hand as a shield. Kori-Kori launches himself onto the rock next to Redburn. Faaua sits on Redburn's other side. In a moment of quiet, Redburn sees a lingering sadness in Faaua be answered by a bit of awkwardness from Kori-Kori. Faaua's hand comes up and gently pulls Kori-Kori into a lingering kiss before Redburn's face. After they part, they stay close to him. Faaua kisses Redburn with equal tenderness, then both glance at Kori-Kori. With subtle urging from Faaua, Kori-Kori puts a placid hand on Redburn's cheek, and gradually draws him into a kiss with increasing warmth, and lingering desire.

EXT. MAHEYO'S HOUSE – NIGHT

Full-moon brilliance shines light on a sleeping Taipivai. The light is sliced into spiky shadows by coconut leaves as a gentle breeze animates them on Maheyo's veranda floor.

INT. MAHEYO'S HOUSE

Sounds of the household asleep calmly measure out a beating rise and fall. **REDBURN** lies awake between **FAAUA** and **KORI-KORI**. They sleep peacefully turned towards him, their arms meeting across his abdomen. Redburn's hands are behind his head, and he contemplates the mysterious three bundles. A slow descent on Redburn's face shows a single tear pressed out as he closes his eyes.

[Part 5 – III: Tattoo scene – Love in the Grass]

EXT. CENTRAL AVENUE OF TAIPIVAI – NOON

REDBURN is helped along by his paddle crutch and **KORI-KORI**. His ankle is noticeably worse. Redburn is distracted by a path; faint **TAPPING** accompanies low **CHANTING**.

> **KORI-KORI**
> (in POLYNESIAN, with subtitles)
> **Tattoo; you want to see?**

EXT. A CLEARING

REDBURN and **KORI-KORI** enter. In the center is a tall canopy of palm leaves. Moving closer to it, they see a **MAN** lying on his back, his arm covering his eyes, and a **TATTOOIST** working on the man's leg. The Tattooist intones a prayer to the beat of his stylus.

INT. TATTOO SHELTER

REDBURN, supported by **KORI-KORI**, comes in for a closer look. The **TATTOOIST** becomes distracted, and his work and chant slows down. The **MAN** looks up, and smiles at the visitors. The Tattooist asks Kori-Kori with mild interest.

> **TATTOOIST**
> (in POLYNESIAN, with subtitles)
> **Does Tommo want one – is he ready to become Taipi?**

> **KORI-KORI**
> (shrugs – in POLYNESIAN, with subtitles)
> **I don't know. Do you want?**

Redburn jumps as if awoken from dream by a bee sting.

> **REDBURN**
> (in POLYNESIAN, with subtitles)
> **No! No – I was just watching.**

The Tattooist rises and latches onto Redburn's arm.

> **TATTOOIST**
> (in POLYNESIAN, with subtitles)
> **Yes – good face; it will make nice lines....**

Redburn pleads to Kori-Kori.

> **REDBURN**
> (in POLYNESIAN, with subtitles)
> **I was just looking—**

> **KORI-KORI**
> (fatherly – in POLYNESIAN, with subtitles)
> **This is a big step, Tommo....**

REDBURN
For God's sake — hands off.
(to Kori-Kori — in POLYNESIAN, with subtitles)
No. Not now; he's hurting me.

At this information, Kori-Kori grows stern and picks the fingers of the tattooist one by one off of Redburn's flesh. He shields Redburn behind him.

KORI-KORI
(in POLYNESIAN, with subtitles)
Not now — we must ask Mehevi first.

Kori-Kori deftly turns and picks up Redburn, honeymoon-fashion. He speeds away towards the road, but as soon as they are out of sight of the Tattooist, Kori-Kori gently sets his charge down, but he does not let go. He looks angst-ridden, like a parent who has just exposed his child to some potential harm.

KORI-KORI
(in POLYNESIAN, with subtitles)
I am sorry. You do not want a tattoo, do you?

REDBURN
(in POLYNESIAN, with subtitles)
No.

KORI-KORI
(in POLYNESIAN, with subtitles)
No. That would mean you had decided — to become.... It's a big decision. I'm sorry, I would never let anyone hurt you. Do you understand? You are family now. I will protect you in everything, because.... Because.

Redburn cannot account for the depth of sadness showing on his companion's face, but he smiles a bit in an effort to comfort. Kori-Kori responds by taking Redburn's hand and leading him into the tall grass off the path.

EXT. TALL GRASS

In a bit of a wide spot, **KORI-KORI** stops, turns, and leans down to kiss **REDBURN.** An initial awkwardness is soon lost in mutual and reciprocal passion. After a few moments, Kori-Kori gently pushes Redburn back a bit, and slowly reaches down to the slit in Redburn's kilt. As Kori-Kori begins to work his hand, Redburn moans and Kori-Kori resumes kissing him. As the tension builds, Redburn slowly leans back, and Kori-Kori follows, using his other hand and arm to brace his lover at the small of his back. As Redburn's breath grows rough and ready, Kori-Kori slides his supporting hand up to, and behind Redburn's neck. He raises the American so his lips press his, but Redburn's pleasure is such, he continues to glide forward, and Kori-Kori steers Redburn's head to rest on his chest. Redburn's hand reaches up to steady himself, and holds onto Kori-Kori's working bicep. As Redburn climaxes, his parted lips blanket heavy breaths on Kori-Kori's erect nipple. After he feels Redburn relaxes the tension in his grip, Kori-Kori gradually lowers his mouth and kisses the top of Redburn's head.

KORI-KORI
(in POLYNESIAN, with subtitles)
Because. Rest now.

INT. VERANDA MAHEYO'S HOUSE – MID-AFTERNOON

REDBURN sits with **KORI-KORI** at his side. He has Toby's yellow bandana, from which he extracts their photo. He pops open the case and holds it for Kori-Kori to see. Kori-Kori smiles and goes about his business of lighting a pipe for them. As Kori-Kori works at this, Redburn set the open photo aside and writes in his journal.

> **REDBURN (V.O.)**
> And what of my companion, Toby? For that is the name he goes by among us sailors – and a fitter *nom de mer* he could not have chosen. 'Tobias' is worthy of him – the Biblical man touched by an angel – matches the grace and conduct of my mate. Toby has a remarkable ability, unseen in most other men, to be fearless in the expression of his feelings. When those feelings are hot, brawny follows – with no lack of ordinary courage – will fairly quail before this stripling.

Redburn notes that Kori-Kori has arranged his loaded pipe and tinder and is now beginning to rub a fire stick in a wooden channel. Kori-Kori begins to inhale sharply, and work with increasing speed.

> **REDBURN (CONT'D – V.O.)**
> His shipmates, other than me, view Toby as a strange and wayward being, proceeding through the world fists-first. They look upon me to smooth out the rocky course his frankness leads him. But, when those feelings are tender, the tenor of his private conversations will reveal all, that is, until a nagging creep of conscience concerns him, and makes him anxious to conceal them, from all but me. Our future it seems is destined to be encountered together. We move in a different sphere – the one that is active, ready with fearless courage, obliging to duty, and so too, to love. We are the type of sailor never to allude to home or origin; never to list lacking comforts; never to brook much closeness with those different; or for even those 'others' to manipulate our names in their work-a-day mouths. We give false names, changeable as our moods, so none can guess who we really are. Toby and I are they – the wayward, the strange beings – prone to go rambling over the world as if pursued by the same mysterious fate that drives some captains to try to outdo the Word of God Itself. This compelling fate is never to be eluded; never to be satiated; but at least Toby and I were fated to row our divided quests into the common oar of a union brave – two fates to be sought out as one.

Sweat beads Kori-Kori's forehead as he continues, and his limbs begin to glisten, much to Redburn's visual delight.

REDBURN (CONT'D – V.O.)

And what of Toby's looks? In navy frock and duck trousers, he cuts as fine a figure as any sailor ever had. Sixteen months my senior, I nevertheless stand a few inches taller, and have a few pounds on him, but his great freedom of movement as he springs to action is envied by all sailors. His naturally dark complexion is bronzed to perfection by the tropical sun, and his dark hair, with its rakish curl, clusters about his temples to throw a deepening mystery of shade across his large blue eyes. This Toby – fearsome and fearless; slight and mighty – is mine, and the very one I choose as my partner. What solace, I ask myself, could there be on land, nay, even in the Garden of Eden itself, without my companion? None. And so he must have asked himself of me, because I had to convince him to escape without me....

Redburn can't go on. He turns sad eyes on Kori-Kori, who is in a radiant halo of smoke. Kori-Kori leans back on one hand, and his body glows like a post-coital partner, smoking. He presses his pipe to Redburn's lips, who inhales and smiles devilishly.

KORI-KORI
(in POLYNESIAN, with subtitles)
What?

REDBURN
(in POLYNESIAN, with subtitles)
Nothing...

Redburn sidles up so their thighs touch.

REDBURN (CONT'D)
(in POLYNESIAN, with subtitles)
But this.

Redburn holds his lover's eyes, and he spits into his left palm. He reaches down and begins to pleasure Kori-Kori, who quickly turns to look over his shoulder. The house is still asleep, so he lolls back to Redburn with heavy eyelids. Soon Kori-Kori's breaths become jagged and spasmodic. He lowers his head into Redburn's waiting mouth. Redburn muffles the sound, and then greedily takes Kori-Kori's gasps of pleasure into his mouth as his partner climaxes. The two finish with an extended and gentle kiss. In his other hand, Redburn presses Toby's picture tight to his heart.

[Part 5 – IV: Polynesian Apollo]

INT. MAHEYO'S HOUSE – MID-MORNING

REDBURN sits on the edge of the dais writing in his journal. **RUNU** sits in his usual position with **ARVA** in his lap. **MAHEYO** rushes in, excited and breathless.

MAHEYO
(in POLYNESIAN, with subtitles)
Marnu is coming!

REDBURN
(puzzled)
Marnu?

MAHEYO
(in POLYNESIAN, with subtitles)
Yes. Yes, Marnu!

REDBURN
(in POLYNESIAN, with subtitles)
Good.

Maheyo exits again and Redburn can hear voices on the road telegraphing (in POLYNESIAN, with subtitles): **'Marnu is coming!'**; then **'It's Marnu!'** In a minute, **CHIEFS** enter the house and greet first Runu, then Redburn. **MEHEVI** and **MOW-MOW** come next, and Redburn rises, having trouble putting weight on his ankle. Mehevi and Mow-Mow pay no attention to him, and instead turn expectantly to the door. **MARNU** enters like a king, and all the chiefs make a great fuss to show him to the seat of honor. Marnu completely ignores Redburn, but the American is instantly taken with the young man's beauty. The chiefs, Maheyo and Marnu sit removed from Redburn and soon are engaged in lively conversation, during which Marnu jocularly stretches his legs in front of him and generally coveys youthful animation. As they talk, Redburn returns to his journal with a new subject.

MOW-MOW
(in POLYNESIAN, with subtitles)
What about the French?

MONU
(looking grave – in POLYNESIAN, with subtitles)
They have built a *prison* in Nuku Hiva – this is a house with metal windows and doors. They lock in here warriors whom they say fight the French.

MOW-MOW
(in POLYNESIAN, with subtitles)
Like a cage, for chickens?

MONU
(in POLYNESIAN, with subtitles)
Yes – but strong – no man can get out. The French are bad. They do not care if warriors bathe, have blankets, or even food.

Mehevi offers a gentle scoff.

MEHEVI
(in POLYNESIAN, with subtitles)

It can't be that bad....

MOW-MOW
(in POLYNESIAN, with subtitles)
You haven't seen it with your own eyes — Marnu has.

Marnu plays the peacemaker.

MARNU
(in POLYNESIAN, with subtitles)
**Why they do these things, we cannot understand. They have
a word: crime...**

Marnu pauses to glance at Redburn writing.

MARNU (CONT'D)
(in POLYNESIAN, with subtitles)
...They expect people to do bad things....

The men continue to talk.

REDBURN (V.O.)
**The stranger could not be a day over twenty-five, and tall — yet,
if a hair's breadth taller, the matchless symmetry of his form
would be destroyed. His unclad limbs are beautifully formed;
while the elegant outline of his figure, together with his
beardless chin, entitles him to be called a Polynesian Apollo.
Never before have I beheld such a powerful exhibition of natural
eloquence as this Marnu displays. The grace of his attitudes, the
ease of his flexible and exposed limbs, and above all, the fire
which shoots from his brilliant eyes...**

The crowd laughs at Marnu's joke — he rises and mimics a 'Oui-Oui' with a fishing rod
— to general hilarity.

REDBURN (CONT'D — V.O.)
**...Imparts varied accents to a voice any orator would be proud
to possess. One moment, calm and poised, he reclines on a bent-
elbow — legs outstretched and crossed before him — the next,
standing mightily and contorting his face with the passion of his
tales — he commands his audience with lofty attitude. Marnu —
how the island cooed the dulcet name, and soon I breathlessly
followed suit — Marnu. This all-attractive personage, has hair of
rich coiling brown, that twirls about his temples and neck in little
close-fitting ringlets; which dance up and down continually as
he is animated in speech.**

Marnu casually enquires about Redburn.

MARNU
(in POLYNESIAN, with subtitles)
So, there is the famous Tommo. Does he content himself

in Taipivai?

MOW-MOW
(in POLYNESIAN, with subtitles)
Yes, he is very happy—

MEHEVI
(in POLYNESIAN, with subtitles)
Well, his partner abandoned him. He is still sad about that.

MARNU
(in POLYNESIAN, with subtitles)
With your permission, I would speak with him.

Mehevi heads to Redburn.

REDBURN (V.O.)
**His light olive skin is free of the least blemish, and his soft
cheek rides the tides of his smiles with flawless grace....**

Marnu sits by his side without the American's knowing it. When Marnu continues to
speak to the chiefs, he startles Redburn, but still refrains from looking towards him.

MARNU
(in POLYNESIAN, with subtitles)
Well, this valley grows more lush each time I visit...

Marnu holds out his hand for Redburn to take.

MARNU (CONT'D)
(in POLYNESIAN, with subtitles)
...Too bad I missed the festival...

When he feels Redburn take it, he looks him in the eye for the first time, and then pulls
him in so close his lips nearly touch Redburn's ear.

MARNU (CONT'D)
...And, how do _you_ do?

Redburn stares back in astonishment.

REDBURN
I...I do fine – you speak English?

MARNU
(to others – in POLYNESIAN, with subtitles)
He wants to converse in his language.

Marnu shrugs like 'what can I do?'

MARNU (CONT'D)
Watch your tone – no animation now. We are being

watched. Smile.

Redburn gathers himself and turns a grin on the others, who seem to relax.

REDBURN
What do you know about my companion, Toby?

MARNU
(half sighs)
Rumors, only. Some say he was kidnapped by other islanders, and taken away at night. Some say the French put him in irons and sent him to Tahiti for prison — others say he shipped on a whaler. I am sorry — whichever is true, his is not on Nuku Hiva.

REDBURN
How can you travel freely?

MARNU
I am *taboo* — no one will harm me. It is a 'sin,' as you call it.

Redburn glances at the men, while desperately attempting to control his tone.

REDBURN
Take me with you.

MARNU
There is nothing I can do. I have no influence here — these people rave about you — these people love you — they will never let you go.

REDBURN
You must help me—

MARNU
Watch your tone.

Mow-Mow rises in anxious suspicion. He addresses Mehevi.

MOW-MOW
(in POLYNESIAN, with subtitles)
They talk of French spying.

Mow-Mow puts on a fake smile and walks up to Marnu.

MOW-MOW (CONT'D)
(in POLYNESIAN, with subtitles)
Tommo must rest. Marnu, come to the Ti. We must further discuss important matters, and eat.

The chiefs rise and pressure Marnu to do the same. The valley's leaders make for the door, and Marnu, standing over Redburn, warns him.

MARNU
They will never let you leave.

[Part 6 – Shadow of Death – I: A Man Amongst Us]

EXT. CENTRAL AVENUE OF TAIPIVAI – MID-AFTERNOON

The sun beats down; the stream rolls over smooth rocks. **REDBURN** and **KORI-KORI** slowly walk along.

INT. GARDEN VERANDA OF THE *TI*

REDBURN writes in his journal. **KORI-KORI** sits next to him smoking. Kori-Kori bumps Redburn's arm and passes the pipe. Redburn takes a drag and passes the pipe back with a grin. He slowly exhales as he resumes writing, a twinkle on his lips. During the following voiceover, the white gravel of the yard, flowers, birds, etc. are interlaced with glimpses of Kori-Kori's glorious physique and handsome face. He glows in that 'post-coital' exertion Redburn has already written about.

> **REDBURN (V.O.)**
> **Kori-Kori is quite expert at striking a light – a necessary effort when one is ready for a smoke. At first Kori-Kori goes to work quite leisurely, but gradually, his pace quickens – and waxing warm in his employment, drives the stick furiously along the smoking channel, plying his hands to-and-fro with amazing rapidity, the perspiration starting from every pore. As he approaches the climax of his efforts, he pants, and gasps for breath, his eyes almost closing with near faintness from the violence of his exertions. This is the critical stage of the operation – all his previous labors are in vain if he cannot sustain the rapidity of movement until the spark is produced. Suddenly, he stops. He becomes perfectly motionless. His hands still retain their hold on the smaller stick, which is pressed convulsively against the further end of the channel – the channel where a fine powder has accumulated – as if it had just been pierced through and through. The next moment, a delicate wreath of smoke curls spirally in the air, the heap of dusty particles glow with fire, and Kori-Kori almost breathless, passes me his smile, and, his pipe.**

Redburn puts his pencil down and turns a half-lecherous grin on Kori-Kori. After he pushed down on his erection a bit, Redburn places his hand on Kori-Kori's knee and motions for the pipe. Kori-Kori, grinning, holds it to his partner's lips, and Redburn inhales. Redburn tilts his head back and slowly exhales to the rafters.

INT. OF THE *TI*

MEHEVI, MOW-MOW and **MAHEYO** enter and sit on the mats. **REDBURN** and **KORI-KORI** rise and join them with smiles. Mehevi calls for a servant. They speak in POLYNESIAN, with subtitles.

> MEHEVI
> **Boy! Pipes!**

A **BOY** appears, nods and disappears.

> KORI-KORI
> **Marnu is safely on his way back home?**

Mehevi nods.

> MEHEVI
> **He is.**
> (to Redburn)
> **I hear you have taken an interest in the tattoo?**

Redburn elicits a nervous call for help from Kori-Kori.

> REDBURN
> **I saw the artist work....**

> MAHEYO
> (proudly)
> **You don't know how it honors our hearts that you consider taking this final step.**

> REDBURN
> **Final?**

> MEHEVI
> **To become a man, amongst us —
> to be Taipi.**

> KORI-KORI
> **He is injured—**

> MEHEVI
> **Naturally — all in good time. First, my boy — First, the face—**

> REDBURN
> **Face!**

BOYS arrive with pipes. This gives Redburn time to think. He draws a pair of lines around his bicep.

> REDBURN (CONT'D)
> **Face, no. A band — a bold design, here.**

Mehevi intones loud and proud towards Mow-Mow.

> MEHEVI
> **Good.**

MAHEYO
Brave lad. Brave.

MEHEVI
But first — the face.

Redburn again looks for Kori-Kori's support.

KORI-KORI
That's the way it is — a few dots — a few lines....

REDBURN
Later. Later.

Mow-Mow is done with chitchat.

MOW-MOW
Marnu's intelligence should prompt us to take preemptive action.
Our boats can make a night raid and be gone before the *Wi-Wi's*
know about it.

Mehevi broods in silence — smokes. Mow-Mow grows angry.

MOW-MOW (CONT'D)
Time is not on our side. Damn it — do something about this.

MEHEVI
(calmly)
The French stay away from Taipivai. If they came here, they
know they wouldn't make it back to France again.

MOW-MOW
But—

Mehevi cuts him off curtly.

MEHEVI
Quiet.

As Mow-Mow fumes in impotent rage, Mehevi speaks softly to Redburn.

MEHEVI (CONT'D)
Tommo, what is on your mind? Please sing for us. Please.

BEGIN 'LOVE IS A STREAM' SERIES OF SHOTS:

As Redburn sings in English, views of his face, and of the men transfixed around him,
fade to a series of flashbacks of Toby in Redburn's memory:

A) Toby on ship

B) Toby squinting up at him from the rock during the escape

C) Face of Toby smiling by the cave fire

D) Toby seeing Redburn enter the longboat

E) Face of Toby as Redburn kisses his fist in the cave

F) Toby jubilant in the palm tree

G) Toby giving beads to the children

H) Toby dancing his 'pee' dance

I) Toby glistening in the stream, slicking his hair back

J) Toby putting up his dukes

K) Toby kissing Redburn in the grandstand

L) Last night of lovemaking before Toby's trip overland

M) Toby's bloody face in Redburn's lap

N) Redburn putting his hat on Toby — his last sight of him

REDBURN
(SINGS)

"Love is a stream that always flows —
It roils, it tumbles
But smoothly over strife it goes
It pains, it humbles
Yet love is love; it always flows.

Once I loved a one, who loved me —
A greater gift never was,
For his love was deep as the sea,
To wash me as the ocean does.

I the lucky one, who loved him,
Riding the tide of swelling grace,
Showing me just where to begin,
To match his flow with my own pace.

Love is a stream that always flows —
It rails, it grumbles
Yet calmly over grief it goes
It falls, but won't stumble
For love is love; it always flows."

END 'LOVE IS A STREAM' SERIES OF SHOTS.

As the song ends, all are lost in thoughts of their own mortality, when suddenly the still is broken by a gun **SHOT** a half-mile off, up the flanks of the mountains. The men rush to the garden veranda. Several muffled voices and angry **CRIES** ring out, then several more **SHOTS.** Puffs of smoke rise from the top of trees up the hill. Kori-Kori whispers in Redburn's ear.

KORI-KORI
Happar.

SHOUTS come from the entry of the *Ti.*

INT. FRONT VERANDA OF THE *TI*

MEHEVI gives orders. **MOW-MOW** hands out the guns and powderhorns to several young **MEN** who have answered the call to arms. **MAHEYO** dithers, telling the **BOYS** to make coconut canteens. **REDBURN** and **KORI-KORI** lag behind. The men rush down the steps with their weapons, and Kori-Kori sits Redburn down on the top step.

EXT. HULA HULA GROUNDS FACING THE *TI*

The **BOYS** come rushing to the men with green coconuts on cords, which the men fling on their backs. Several other young **MEN** haul the long drums from their storage places underneath the *Ti's* front veranda, and jostle them into position in the yard. As Mehevi and his fighting party jog under the gate, the drums begin to sound.

EXT. TREES ON THE HILL – LATE AFTERNOON

As the war drums continue to **BEAT, MEN SHOUT** from far away. Several **SHOTS** ring out, followed by **WHOOPS** of joy and victory. The voices begin to telegraph down the valley.

EXT. HULA HULA GROUNDS FACING THE *TI* – EARLY EVENING

A large **CROWD** is gathered. They pause to hear the content of the message approaching them. They become jubilant. Kori-Kori explains to Redburn. They speak in POLYNESIAN, with subtitles.

KORI-KORI
Some Happar bastards are caught. They are being dragged
here. Mehevi is a great leader!

MEHEVI appears at the vanguard of his troops. The crowd presses around him with congratulations. As he nears the center of the grounds, a young **WOMAN** with a young **MAN** push through the crowd to him. Mehevi pauses, and the woman hugs his waist. The teenager slaps Mehevi in an all too familiar way for a chief. Kori-Kori explains.

KORI-KORI (CONT'D)
Mehevi's family – his wife and partner. They are glad he is safe.

Mehevi stops and turns to face the outer gate. The crowd pushes back to clear an area, and a pitiful line of four bound and bleeding **HAPPAR** stagger to the center of the yard. Young **MEN** with guns force them to kneel before Mehevi. The children taunt the captives cruelly. Mehevi majestically holds up his hands for silence – the drums stop. They speak in POLYNESIAN, with subtitles.

MEHEVI
And so, here we see the fate of every invader of Taipivai.

The crowd cheers. Kori-Kori leaps to his feet in joy. **MOW-MOW** comes up to him in agitation.

MOW-MOW
Take the outsider home! Now. He can't see this. It is forbidden.

Mow-Mow storms off. Kori-Kori helps Redburn stand.

REDBURN
What's happening?

Kori-Kori latches onto him.

KORI-KORI
Let's rest at home.

REDBURN
I want to stay.

For the first time ever, Kori-Kori is curt with him.

KORI-KORI
NO.

Redburn folds his arms; stands his ground.

KORI-KORI (CONT'D)
Don't make me carry you! Because, I will.

Redburn blinks, then as slowly as possible, descends the steps, watching the captives. Kori-Kori rushes him along.

EXT. GATE TO THE HULA HULA GROUNDS

As **REDBURN** and **KORI-KORI** get to the gate, the drums start again, this time with a slow heartbeat menace. Redburn turns one last time and catches the inner gates opening, and the captive being dragged bodily into the holy sanctuary.

INT. MAHEYO'S HOUSE – NIGHT

Out on the road, a holiday mood prevails. **PEOPLE** rush about, both to and from the Hula Hula Grounds. The house is empty except for a brooding **KORI-KORI** who looks sore to miss the doings, and **REDBURN** who tries to get into his journal. A torch is lit near where he sits on the dais, and casts eerie shadows on his minder's already moody face. The drums **DRONE** on in the distance with their unvaried, hair-raising rhythm.

REDBURN (V.O.)
There is not a single padlock in all the valley – nor even anything that could answer for one. Indeed, there seem no rogues of any type in Typee, and deep in the darkest nights, the natives sleep soundly – their worldly wealth...

Redburn looks up at the three packages also casting odd moving shade onto the rafters above them.

REDBURN (CONT'D – V.O.)
...Dangling freely in the rafters above their night-dreaming heads; their hands by doors that are never barred. In my few

months among them, I never saw a hostile exchange, never witnessed even an unkind word or look — they live as true Christians — without envy, without holier-than-thou pronouncements; without hate in any of its many polite forms so admired among us 'civilized' — they live with only love, and share in the capacity that Christ, when with us, deemed fit for all of us. The only enmity they ever showed was reserved for their valley's hostile neighbors, and show it they inevitably did.

The drums **BEAT** quicker; the voice of the crowd **RISES** along with them, and both reach a sudden crescendo; followed by stillness. A glance at Kori-Kori reveals nothing, only that the local has now officially missed 'the good part.'

EXT. CENTRAL AVENUE OF TAIPIVAI — MORNING

A hazy sun seems not to want to shine. Chickens lazily peck down the center of the abandoned road. Dogs root and scratch up tidbits. After its long night, the valley is sleeping in.

EXT. GATE TO THE HULA HULA GROUNDS

REDBURN leans heavily on **KORI-KORI**. They speak in POLYNESIAN, with subtitles.

REDBURN
It really hurts — it doesn't get better, it only grows worse.

KORI-KORI
Give it time. You should rest at home.

REDBURN
I want to see.

Redburn looks around. The yard looks used, but in order.

INT. GARDEN VERANDA OF THE *TI*

MOW-MOW and **KOLORI** hold a secret conference. Manu Atu is in the priest's arms. At their feet are serving bowls, and a large wooden trencher covered with fresh leaves. They speak in POLYNESIAN, with subtitles.

MOW-MOW
Now is the time. The people are ready for war — we need only one hostile suspicion that the French are in our midst. The tool we need is here already. Will you help? It is for the people.

KOLORI
But, is it right to do so?

MOW-MOW
I may be wrong. If I mistake, future generations will know me as a fool. But, if I am right — there may be no future generations to remember any of us. Now, will you help?

Before Kolori can answer, there are sounds at the entry of the *Ti*. Mehevi loudly **GREETS** Redburn and Kori-Kori. Mow-Mow and Kolori decide to retreat to the interior of the *Ti*. They carefully step around the trencher.

INT. OF THE *TI*

MEHEVI leads **REDBURN** and **KORI-KORI** to the dais. **MOW-MOW** and **KOLORI** are just seating themselves. Redburn's eyes snoop around, immediately spotting the trencher as out of place. They speak in POLYNESIAN, with subtitles. Other **CHIEFS** drift in and sit.

> **MEHEVI**
> (to Redburn)
> **Will you eat?**

> **REDBURN**
> (good-natured)
> **No, not yet. Later.**

> **MEHEVI**
> (paternal)
> **Tommo, your indication to become tattooed has touched
> my heart...**

Mehevi looks around, grows loud.

> **MEHEVI (CONT'D)**
> **Touched all our hearts. You must get well, so you can join the
> men of Taipivai, as our equal.**

> **MEHEVI (CONT'D)**
> (quietly to Redburn)
> **Later, I have a special gift for you.**

Mehevi nods at Kori-Kori, as if in recognition that it was his idea. Kori-Kori unaccountably smiles contentedly.

> **MEHEVI (CONT'D)**
> **Kolori! I see you have brought your 'baby.' Tommo, have you
> seen the image of our Lord Manu Atu being nursed by Kolori?**

> **REDBURN**
> **Nursed?**

> **MEHEVI**
> **Show us.**

While Kolori takes a position in front of them, Kori-Kori whispers to Redburn.

> **KORI-KORI**
> **This is how God instructs us — he tells us what to do.**

REDBURN
(in ENGLISH, to himself)
A wooden oracle....

Kolori begins to perform the ritual, spurred by a half-pleading, half-commanding glare from Mow-Mow. First he cuddles the icon, cooing.

KOLORI
What a good boy you are.

He rocks it, and whispers some question in its ear. All lean in to hear; the question is private. After another cuddle, Kolori holds the idol's lips to his ear. His face goes blank in expectation, then cross, as neither he nor the room hears a peep. Kolori scolds.

KOLORI (CONT'D)
Now, don't be that way. I asked you
a question.

He whispers again into wooden ears, and lingers as he draws holy lips to his head. Kolori says to the crowd.

KOLORI (CONT'D)
Tell us what you know. Will you speak?

Kolori holds Manu Atu forward.

MANU ATU
(faint)
Yes.

Redburn starts; he can't see any ventriloquy, though Kolori looks like his energy is being sapped. Redburn wants to rise and flee, but he is equally determined to see this. The other men are excited and awed.

KOLORI
Tell us what we need to know.

MANU ATU
(voice grows louder)
The French will kill you all. You must fight them first.

The icon's cold wooden features slowly turn to lock onto Redburn.

MANU ATU (CONT'D)
(shrieking)
An enemy is among you — Treachery. Treachery. Treachery.
Look to eliminate the French spy. Treachery!

Redburn covers his ears; Mehevi and Kori-Kori look sick; Mow-Mow, relieved. The godhead is spent. Kolori collapses as if he's fainted. From the floor, he locks eyes on Redburn, and faintly coos.

> **KOLORI**
> **Good, boy. Good, boy.**

Mehevi pulls together his considerable poise.

> **MEHEVI**
> **Well. Quite a lot to say today.**

Kori-Kori laughs and pokes Redburn to join in, for his own good.

> **MEHEVI (CONT'D)**
> **Manu Atu will no doubt keep us informed as to who
> this spy can be—**

Mow-Mow storms to his feet; throws his whole arm towards Redburn's head.

> **MOW-MOW**
> **It's him!**

> **MEHEVI**
> (rising to meet the challenge)
> **Did Manu Atu say that?**

Mow-Mow is floored.

> **MOW-MOW**
> **...Na...no...**

> **MEHEVI**
> **No.**

Mehevi glares at Kolori.

> **MEHEVI (CONT'D)**
> **No, he did not reveal who the enemy is, and we must search
> for him. It must be someone absent from this group.**

Mehevi walks to the veranda, shouting for the servant.

> **MEHEVI (CONT'D)**
> **Boy! Bring it; it's time.**

Mehevi comes back to the assembled with moreauthority than ever.

> **MEHEVI (CONT'D)**
> **Not a word of this leaves the Ti. Not until we suss out who is
> working for our enemies. Swear. Swear it!**

Kori-Kori and the other Chiefs swear readily; Mow-Mow and Kolori halfheartedly. Two **BOYS** come holding a green kilt between them. It is made if carefully cut breadfruit leaves, woven into a band at the top and flowing loose below. On top of the leaves are several strips of white tapa that zigzag in broad bolts of lightning from waistband to hem. Kolori and Mow-Mow grow belligerent the moment they see it.

MOW-MOW
Wait – you can't do this!

Mehevi glances at Kori-Kori, who positions himself between Mow-Mow and Mehevi. Mehevi helps Redburn to his feet. The chief then kneels before him, and the boy servants come to his side. As he places the mark of Taboo around the American's waist, Mehevi intones a prayer.

MEHEVI
(CHANTS)
"Now amongst the foliage,
Now amongst the walks of man,
Now upon the face of the waters,
Of the sky,
Of the air and stars –
You are sacred,
You are untouchable,
You are Taboo."

Mehevi rises in awe of the divinity before him. He bends into Redburn's ear a worried whisper.

MEHEVI (CONT'D)
Fear not, loved one, you are protected.

As Mehevi pulls away, Redburn reels; all eyes are upon him.

REDBURN
I...I am feeling tired. Kori-Kori, let's go home.

The other men rise. Mehevi and Kori-Kori try to placate Mow-Mow and Kolori. In the distraction, Redburn goes towards the garden veranda and trencher. With a quick glance, that Kori-Kori catches, Redburn kicks off the leaves. In horror he looks down on a few flies walking across tattooed flesh – raw human meat in the form of thighs, a lower leg and foot, and a half a forearm with hand still attached.

KORI-KORI
(yelling)
Tommo, NO!

As Kori-Kori runs up to his side, all the men are stunned. Kori-Kori puts the leaves back in order, and singsongs in a demanding way to Redburn.

KORI-KORI (CONT'D)
Roast pork – Roast Pork!

As Kori-Kori leads him away hurriedly, Redburn gets it and sings out.

REDBURN
Yes. Just roast pork. Roast Pork!

EXT. CENTRAL AVENUE OF TAIPIVAI – NOON

REDBURN and **KORI-KORI** plod their way home. Redburn has more trouble walking now. He wears the kilt of taboo. **PEOPLE** on the road greet them, then stand back in awe at the sign of Redburn's sacred investiture.

INT. MAHEYO'S HOUSE

As **REDBURN** and **KORI-KORI** enter, they see all the **MEN** of the household huddled together in Redburn's regular spot in animated chatting. They come up to them without a word, and Redburn peers over **MAHEYO**'s shoulder. The three bundles from the rafters are laid open, one human head rests on each piece of fabric. The head on the cloth from a sailor shirt is a strawberry-blond Irishman; his face is still severely freckled, even in death. **MARMUNU**, still in mid laugh, glances up, and whispers in disbelief.

MARMUNU
Tommo...

The others look, and Maheyo tries to block Redburn's view with his body. Several hands push Redburn back, and as if in slow motion, Redburn extends a pleading arm towards his host father for silent explanation.

INT. MAHEYO'S HOUSE – NIGHT

Moonlight slants in from the front door. The sounds of the household asleep rise up to **REDBURN** sitting on the dais. He is wide-awake in stymied panic. **FAAUA** and **KORI-KORI** lie close to him. He glances up to the rafters. The three bundles are missing, leaving a void in his vision. He looks down again, and straight out at nothing.

REDBURN (V.O.)
My hosts were all the worst things Jim feared — yea, worse. Escape became my only concern. But how? I could not run. I could not escape without the implicit help of one or more of my captors, and that was not likely. Perhaps one European head hung from every house-beam in Typee. Perhaps my shipmate's tale of a whole crew dispatched by these people was not a tale at all: I resolved to redouble my acceptance while I bided my time. I must act as if none of these revelations affected me in the least — I must play with their children, must compliment their food, I must live their dream of an earthly heaven until I can awake from my nightmare of Hell. For surely, I walked among them as if in the valley of the shadow of Death.

BEGIN 'LOVE IS' FLASHBACK:

INT. VERANDA OF MAHEYO'S HOUSE – NIGHT BEFORE TOBY LEFT

REDBURN and **TOBY** sit and look up on a full moon. The valley is quiet; the house at their back, asleep. Toby has a tapa bandage on his head. Soft **MUSIC** re-introduces Toby and Redburn's love theme.

TOBY
I lost my hat.

REDBURN
You'll use mine from now on. It's been a week, but you can't
go out in the sun until your head heals.

After a pause.

TOBY
What will we do now?

REDBURN
Wait. You recover; I recover; and it's just like you said:
we both walk out of here.

After a pause.

REDBURN (CONT'D)
You were right. I should have listened to you. We should be in
our bunk on board the *Dolly*.

TOBY

That seems a thousand years ago. If I had listened to me, I never would have seen the parade; the lanterns; met these people; had this experience...with you. Maybe one day you will take my advice, but maybe it's not so bad here. They treat us like, like — I was going to say 'kings,' but they treat us better than that — they treat us like men.

REDBURN
(lost in his own thoughts)

'It is patient; it is kind. It does not envy others; it does not boast of its own — it never offends. It does not seek to disgrace others, or promote its own — it is never angry and it never tallies wrongs. It does not exalt the unfair, and will ever uphold the truthful—'

TOBY
'Love always defends; always trusts; always believes; and
love will always persevere.'

Redburn puts his hand on Toby's far shoulder and draws him to rest Toby's head on his shoulder. After a long choking pause, Redburn is able to say.

REDBURN
Too bad men don't say 'I love you.'

TOBY
No. Men don't say 'I love you' — they don't have to.

END 'LOVE IS' FLASHBACK.

INT. MAHEYO'S HOUSE – NIGHT

Kori-Kori sits up, looks for Redburn, then swings his legs to sit on the dais with him. Kori-Kori yawns, stretches and places a hand across Redburn's shoulder. He speaks to him with gentle concern; with love.

KORI-KORI
(in POLYNESIAN, with subtitles)
**Rest, Tommo. None of what you have seen matters — Mehevi
has protected you, so we may keep you forever.**

Kori-Kori rocks his charge and softly intones a lullaby his mother would sing to him.

KORI-KORI (CONT'D)
(in POLYNESIAN, with subtitles)
(SINGS)
*"In the vale of the Taipi,
The water runs clear,
The breadfruit falls —
There is plenty to eat
There is plenty of sleep —
So rest little one,
Rest your head in peace."*

Kori-Kori tenderly pulls Redburn's head to rest on his chest. He closes his eyes as he rocks, but Redburn does not. In Redburn's hand is Toby's bandana and picture.

[Part 7 – Family – I: Solemn Prayer]

BEGIN 'FITTING IN' MONTAGE:
■ **EXT. MAHEYO'S HOUSE – MORNING**
Redburn makes a popgun out of a piece of cut bamboo. At first a few children are gathered, and he shows them how to play with the gun. They run off, and soon more children gather, each wanting their own. More children and adults gather too, and Redburn teaches Karnunu how to make them. Everyone loves this new toy, and the valley rings, high and low, to the sound of **"POP; POP; POP."**
■ **EXT. CENTRAL AVENUE OF TAIPIVAI – NOON**
Redburn strolls along supported by Kori-Kori. He looks up a coconut tree and unaccountably sees Maheyo smoking in the top just as content as can be. Redburn hails him, and Maheyo looks down and gestures in friendly acknowledgement.
■ **INT. MAHEYO'S HOUSE – AFTERNOON**
Redburn sits on the dais. Sitting on the floor with his shoulders between Redburn's knees, is Marmunu. The young man's head is mildly lathered, and Redburn is carefully shaving him. There is a bowl of water by Redburn's side, and halfway through, he gestures for Karluna to sit in his place. He teaches her how to shave her man. Afterwards, a beaming

Marmunu rubs his head and looks deeply indebted to Redburn. Once he presents the razor and soap to the young man, Marmunu looks like he is going to cry, which makes the American smile and play-polish Marmunu's clean pate.

■ **EXT. CENTRAL AVENUE OF TAIPIVAI – MID-AFTERNOON**

Redburn strolls along supported by Faaua. Kori-Kori trails behind with their swimming gear. Redburn stops and points up a particular coconut tree. The top leaves have been artfully interwoven to form a sort of basket like a balloon gondola. Redburn expects to find someone at home, and shouts up: **"Talu!"** A small boy peeks over and laughs in high spirits. Talu cries out (in POLYNESIAN, with subtitles): **"Tommo! Get better, so you can see my view from up here!"** Redburn mutters to himself: **"Little cherub a tree sits aloft; Singing bright from his entire toft."**

■ **EXT. ROCKY OUTCROP IN THE LAKE – EARLY EVENING**

Kori-Kori performs antics in the water and Redburn and Faaua laugh and shield themselves from his splashing. Kori-Kori launches himself on the rock next to them and glistens like a Greek god as he smooths his hair back. Their attention is drawn to a woman holding a baby enters the water in front of them, and soon she carefully puts the infant to float, then releases it, and the baby swims with perfect felicity. Redburn is amazed; Faaua and Kori-Kori chuckle that their companion has never seen a baby swim before.

■ **INT. MAHEYO'S HOUSE – NIGHT**

Supper is finished. All the males of the house lounge, smoking. Kori-Kori nudges Redburn, and with a near-lecherous grin, passes his pipe. Redburn flushes at the import of this inside joke. Across the room, the women of the house are getting dolled up in breadfruit leaf skirts. They have flower wreaths on their heads, wrists and ankles.

■ **EXT. MAHEYO'S HOUSE – NIGHT**

All the males of the house sit on the grass looking up to the veranda; several other people from the road join them. Close to the house, a line of low, lit torches serve as footlights for the veranda. Here the women of the house dance, while Monu and Ruaruga – regaled like the young women – sit to one side playing drums and chanting.

■ **INT. MAHEYO'S HOUSE – NIGHT**

The memory of the boys' chanting fades into a broader and solemn prayer. Led by Runu, the men and women of the household huddle in a large circle with lowered heads. Redburn joins in by taking the hands of Faaua and Kori-Kori. Maheyo and Tinor exchange a happy glance knowing all their children are safe and content.

END OF 'FITTING IN' MONTAGE.

[Part 7 – II: Siesta and Maheyo's Assessment]

EXT. MAHEYO'S HOUSE – MID-AFTERNOON

The sun is hot; shadows are shimmering on the roof and yard, and on Maheyo's tool shed.

INT. MAHEYO'S HOUSE

KORI-KORI's body is curled up in sleep. Facing him is **FAAUA**. Their hands touch. Sitting on the edge of the dais next to them is a wide-awake **REDBURN**. He casts worried eyes out over the back veranda where **MAHEYO** is busy piling up bamboo by his tool shed. Maheyo pauses and sees Redburn. He putters some more; then comes into the house. Taking a fan, he sits next to Redburn, and fans him slowly. Maheyo offers a sad assessment. They speak in POLYNESIAN, with subtitles.

MAHEYO
You miss your home, don't you?

Redburn nods.

MAHEYO (CONT'D)
You miss your Toby – your family.

Maheyo blinks a moment, then remembers the English.

MAHEYO (CONT'D)
Family.

Redburn takes the fan and cools his host in gratitude.

REDBURN
You are a good father. Your children are so lucky.

MAHEYO
Poor Tommo. Surrounded by those who love you, but still so
lonely. If you cannot feel un-alone here, I think you will always
feel alone.

Redburn's face suffers a slow-motion recognition of the truth of the statement.

MAHEYO (CONT'D)
Poor Tommo.

[Part 7 – III: Marnu's Help]

EXT. CENTRAL AVENUE OF TAIPIVAI – DAY

Routine life continues uninterrupted: chickens scratch in the morning; **PEOPLE** stroll to bathe mid-morning, and visit friends later in the day.

EXT. GATE TO MAHEYO'S HOUSE – AFTERNOON

REDBURN leans heavily on **KORI-KORI** as they walk. As Kori-Kori bends forward to open the gate, voices telegraph down the valley behind them: **"Marnu is back."** This time they are not joyful shouts, but veiled in suspicion. **PEOPLE** come down the road with **MARNU** as their locus. Redburn has to step into the man's path, and take a hold of his arm for Marnu to acknowledge him.

REDBURN
(low tone)
You have to help me escape.

MARNU
Impossible. There is rumor of a French spy among the Taipi. They
suspect both of us. There is a lack of trust; nothing can be done.

The crowd grows concerned. Marnu tries to move on.

MARNU (CONT'D)
I can't be seen talking to you. It puts both of us in danger.

REDBURN
What about Taboo? We're both Taboo....

MARNU
(laughs)
It may be a sin to harm us, but sinners are as common as dark thoughts, my friend — dark thoughts.

Marnu laughs again and turns to continue on his way.

REDBURN
(loud)
You have to help me escape!

Marnu turns angrily.

MARNU
Don't you see? You are a pawn for the French-haters. There is nothing I can do.

Marnu walks on, and Redburn leans on the gate, devastated. Marnu walks back-wards, and shouts back to him.

MARNU (CONT'D)
Note the path I take. Follow it when you can.

Marnu turns off the road and begins to ascend a trail through the upper woods. Redburn watches him disappear.

[Part 7 — IV: Finale — Family]

EXT. CENTRAL AVENUE OF TAIPIVAI – DAY

Routine life continues uninterrupted: dogs nap and pant in the shade of verandas during the hottest part of day; **PEOPLE** take siestas while youngsters fan their elders.

EXT. SHRINE COMPOUND – LATE AFTERNOON

REDBURN stands completing the great chief's statue. Behind him, **FAAUA** and **KORI-KORI** lounge on the grass and act as much in love as they are. Redburn speaks quietly to the effigy.

REDBURN
Guide me, great chief — Washington of your people. There are no snakes naturally on this island, but waterborne vipers in the guise of the French are the serpents in your Garden of Eden. They

> will not leave Typee uncorrupted — they will not allow your
> practices; but they will introduce envy, greed and addictions to
> drink and dope. Help me, sage one, to leave. I don't belong here.
> I was born into the unstable, and need it to survive. Typee is too
> perfect a place for an imperfect being like me.

Redburn looks around. An odd breeze rustles the tops of the coconut trees enclosing
the holy compound. The tapa banners bellow and snap suddenly. With anticipation,
Redburn studies the painted eyes; the marks of the sea as cut by the chief's celestial
prow.

REDBURN (CONT'D)

> You, running your hands through the great sea of stars —
> sparkling the firmament with your cutting fingers — Will you help
> me?

The wind makes another round; the tapa snaps, and for a wild second, all is perfectly
still. Redburn hears a hoarse voice whisper: **"Yes."** Redburn straightens up. This voice
seemed like the one of Manu Atu. A quick glance at Faaua and Kori-Kori proves it was
not they who did it. He leans and listens again. In the wind — cut by it — a throbbing cry
rises and falls; it grows louder. In a moment, he can pinpoint it as coming up the central
road from the beach. His companions hear it too. Voices telegraph the almost
incomprehensible (in POLYNESIAN, with subtitles): **"A Boat"** and then **"Toby is back!"**
"Toby has returned to his Tommo!" Stumbling, Redburn nearly falls into Kori-Kori's
open grip. They make their way with beaming smiles to the road. Over his shoulder,
Redburn casts a parting, and thankful, glance at the man in the canoe.

EXT. CENTRAL AVENUE OF TAIPIVAI

There is commotion as people run up the valley to gather supplies for bartering with
the boat. **REDBURN** ambles along supported by **KORI-KORI** and **FAAUA**. **PEOPLE**
stop and joyfully congratulate Redburn (in POLYNESIAN, subtitles): **"Toby is on the
beach"; "Go to him"; "I knew he'd come back to you."**

REDBURN
(to himself)
Oh, God, please let it be true.

EXT. CENTRAL AVENUE NEAR BEACH

The sound of the **SURF** greets **REDBURN** before he can see any sign of beach. The sea
greets his sense of smell, and invigorates. More **PEOPLE** crowd around him and **FAAUA**
and **KORI-KORI**, but as they get to the last house before the beach, voices from in
front of them turn confused and disappointed (in POLYNESIAN, subtitles): **"It's not
Toby"; "Tommo — poor Tommo"; "Tommo, turn back!"; "Go home — let's rest."** The
crowd stands shoulder to shoulder to close off the road and stop Redburn from
advancing. Kori-Kori pulls Redburn to the door of the nearby house. As they get there,
he instructs Faaua.

KORI-KORI
(in POLYNESIAN, subtitles)
Watch him. I'll be back soon.

Faaua and Redburn watch Kori-Kori run back up the road. The crowd pushes the two into the house.

INT. HOUSE BY THE BEACH

FAAUA guides **REDBURN** to sit on the dais across from the door. **PEOPLE** linger outside, looking in. They speak in POLYNESIAN, with subtitles.

> **REDBURN**
> (pleads to Faaua)
> **I have to get to the beach – Toby!**

> **FAAUA**
> (saddened)
> **No, Tommo. Toby is not there.**

The crowd parts and MOW-MOW steps into the house.

> **MOW-MOW**
> (low)
> **Well, you think your treachery can escape these people? Run. Run to your freedom – if you can. I can use you equally well, dead or alive.**

Faaua shields Redburn from Mow-Mow with her body. As she fumes, Redburn gently slips his fist into her open palm. She turns, and in a still moment of acute pain, knows what she must do. She helps him stand, and they move for the door. Mow-Mow precedes them out of it with an arrogant swagger.

EXT. CENTRAL AVENUE NEAR BEACH

As **REDBURN** and **FAAUA** appear in the doorway, **MOW-MOW** shouts to the crowd. They speak in POLYNESIAN, with subtitles.

> **MOW-MOW**
> **No one help him. No one hinder him.**

The crowd parts. Redburn and Faaua make it to the road. Again, the way opens up for them, but Faaua falters under his weight. **MARMUNU** and **KARNUNU** stand at the edge of the crowd. Faaua beckons to them to help her. Karnunu starts to, but Marmunu forcefully takes his arm. Faaua and Redburn stumble to the edge of the beach.

EXT. HEAD OF THE BEACH

The surf crashes; seagulls cry and circle in the air. A hundred yards ahead is a shocking plate of blue with whitecaps rolling onto white sand. **REDBURN** hasn't seen the sea in four months. He and **FAAUA** pause, not knowing where to go. **MAHEYO** and **TINOR** run up behind them. Then **MOW-MOW** angrily steps in front. He commands some young **MEN**. They speak in POLYNESIAN, with subtitles.

> **MOW-MOW**
> **Sit him down!**

Several hands come out and pull Faaua away, then force Redburn to sit painfully on his haunches. **KORI-KORI** forces his way in, and fends off these men. He now has a cord with a folded leaf pendant around his neck. He is breathless, and worried about Redburn.

KORI-KORI
Hands off, or you'll hurt him!

Redburn struggles to see down the beach through the legs of the men around him. While Kori-Kori fends them off, he pulls himself up using Kori-Kori's leg, then waist and finally, his shoulders. The young men and Kori-Kori are exchanging accusations, but Redburn can hear English. He pinpoints where it is coming from. There is a longboat two hundred yards away. **SAILORS** are in the water turning its prow seaward. It is moving off the beach. Next he spots a flash of green. **KARAKOI'I** instructs the sailors.

KARAKOI'I
(English)
Tack her here, lads — and steady with the oars — this is
going to be touch and go!

MARMUNU joins Kori-Kori in pushing back and squabbling with Redburn's detainers. Tinor encourages them, and **MONU** and **RUARUGA** step up too. The bickering grows louder and more heated. Redburn can see Karakoi'i pulling a pair of rifles out of the longboat; he has several powderhorns around his neck. As he comes up the beach, four **CHIEFS** stop him. He offers the guns, but they refuse to take them.

REDBURN
Karakoi'i!

He waves. Karakoi'i waves back with a rifle in the air. **MOW-MOW** takes this as a bad sign. He shouts to the chiefs.

MOW-MOW
Push him back to the boat!

Half of Redburn's detainers rush off to help the chiefs.

REDBURN
(English)
They're holding me here — come get me!

Several angry hands come out and push Redburn back to the sand. Maheyo has had enough and angrily chides them.

MAHEYO
Tommo is Taboo! Don't lay a hand on him! Taboo!

Marmunu, Ruaruga and Monu push them back with louder and louder threats. Kori-Kori and Maheyo help Redburn rise. He leans on his host father, and Kori-Kori returns to the fray. Karakoi'i is pushed back towards the boat and into the surf by the chiefs and young men. Redburn's opportunity is fading. He chokes out a stifled cry, then feels Maheyo's gentle touch at his elbow.

MAHEYO (CONT'D)
Poor Tommo. You must go home; home to your Toby; home to your family.

Maheyo calls out to Kori-Kori.

MAHEYO (CONT'D)
He must go home! We have to help him.

Kori-Kori looks shell-shocked. He stands a moment in selfish indecision. His eyes glaze over.

MAHEYO (CONT'D)
(softly)
Pick him up, and take him to the boat.

Faaua falls to her knees and grips Redburn's legs. She whips her head back and forth. Tinor bends and takes her into her arms. Kori-Kori purses his lips and shakes his head in slow defiance of Maheyo's order. Maheyo silently pleads, and slowly a change overcomes Kori-Kori. The sounds of arguing fade; the cry of birds and the pounding of the surf return. Kori-Kori inhales sharply, trying to regulate his pounding heart to the stillness of these rhythms. He knows what he has to do. Tears need to be wiped from his eyes, but he stumbles to Redburn and picks him up bodily, over his shoulder. Tinor, **KARNUNU, MUNUNI** and **KARLUNA** now join the rest of the family in angrily pushing back the crowd. Kori-Kori stumbles forward, having a hard time seeing. Redburn holds out his hand towards Maheyo, who latches onto his fingers for a moment.

MAHEYO (CONT'D)
(English)
Family.

EXT. BEACH

KORI-KORI carries **REDBURN** over his shoulder. He moves as fast as he can on the giving sand towards the boat. Now two factions have formed. **MONU** and **KARNUNU** run up to the young **MEN** and **CHIEFS** closest to the boat and reason loudly with them, keeping them away from Kori-Kori. They shout (in POLYNESIAN, with subtitles): **"Tommo must go home" "Tommo must help Toby."** The rest of the young men turn against the Chiefs. **MOW-MOW** calls from the beachhead.

MOW-MOW
Foreigner! Good riddance!

The pro-Mow-Mow faction starts shouting (in POLYNESIAN, with subtitles): **"French spy!"; "He betrayed us!"; "Ungrateful!"**

As Kori-Kori struggles with great perseverance, **MAHEYO, TINOR** and **FAAUA** begin to trail behind him. They stop at the water's edge, but Kori-Kori wades in towards

KARAKOI'I waving at him from inside the boat. The **SAILORS** peer over their shoulders, oars in the air, ready to row.

INT. LONGBOAT

KARAKOI'I steps back from the stern, and **KORI-KORI** hoists **REDBURN** in. Redburn can't express any thanks, but lingers a hand on Kori-Kori bicep. Kori-Kori rips off the leaf from his chest and presses it into Redburn's hand. As the oars lower to the water, Kori-Kori reaches his hand behind Redburn's head and draws him into a passionate and tear-stained kiss. The boat lurches Redburn out of his grip and he stands there, sobbing. Redburn sees **FAAUA** run up to him, and they console each other in a gripping embrace. Behind them, **TINOR** and **MAHEYO** likewise stand together in sorrow. Redburn rotates in the boat. Karakoi'i flashes an astonished and devilish grin.

KARAKOI'I
And what, exactly, have you been up to in Taipi?

Redburn thinks a moment, smiles, then winks at Karakoi'i.

REDBURN
But, how did you know to rescue me?

KARAKOI'I
Marnu told me.

REDBURN
(quietly)
Marnu?

REDBURN (CONT'D)
(shouts)
Marnu! You did help me after all!

Redburn feels something in his hand. He pulls back the leaf and spots a bit of yellow bandana. He unwraps it, and finds himself holding Toby's picture. Now he can't help but feel all the pressure of the escape in one terrible instant. He shudders. Sobs rack him; he holds the picture case to his lips. He turns and waves at the receding figures of his Taipi family in profound appreciation; and they wave back.

END CREDITS.

While credits roll, there are shots of: oars cutting sparkling water; the sound of men's exertion; the boat rounding a rocky promontory; The *Julia* lying at anchor; Redburn's hand reaching down from the boat; his fingers cutting the sparkling water into diamonds.

Typee Appendices

The updateable nature of the internet means some material documented here may have been moved or deleted. If so, copy the name of the content & content-creator and search online. Alternates will most likely be easy to find.

Typee Script Notes

1) Time Setting: April to August, 1842.

2) Character and Costume Notes:

On the *Dolly*

JIM: A New Englander; early-40s. A haggard and careless dresser, Jim is the kind of sailor who will take a mentoring position with a young sailor he feels is properly respectful to his authority. He likes Redburn because he is bright and well-mannered; he keeps his distance because Toby is not so well-controlled. He would fancy Redburn if Toby was not in the picture. He knows Redburn is prone to rash decisions, and tries to dissuade – he admires that Toby does the same.

TOBY: Born and raised in New York City; 24 years old. Toby is the type of self-contained person others must pursue to form a friendship with. Once the outer shell is penetrated, and an honest relationship is exchanged, he will fight tooth and nail against all odds to hold that friendship. Lacking in patience, his dealings with the world often seem to have a 'chip on their shoulder,' but when comfortable with someone, his wicked and witty sense of humor endears all close to him. Redburn is the love of his life; he never imagined he could fall for someone so completely. Married in mind, he cannot picture a day of the future not spent with Redburn. The sea is both escape and retreat for them to build a life together. Part of the reason the other sailors "quail before this stripling" is because of his physical beauty. He is lithe and jocular in the extreme, but also handsome in face, with fine dark curls and placid blue eyes that melt all hearts set against him. [4]

CLOTHES: On the *Dolly*, he is meticulous and trim, and he makes sure Redburn and his wardrobes are ship-shape. He learned this fastidiousness from his first sea protector who did the same for him when he was sixteen. He takes pride in his appearance, and in the appearance of his mate, and looks down on his shipmates who are more slovenly inclined. He likes colorful and youthful sailor attire: striped French and Russian style shirts; indigo jerseys; duck trousers; colorful scarves and bandanas; and various brimmed hats with bright-colored ribbons trailing down. On the island, he quickly dumps the wool and goes native with two additions – his belt so he can have his jackknife handy, and his hat to keep the sun off his face.

REDBURN: (aka *Tommo*) From the Hudson River Valley; 23 years old. Redburn loves Toby as he loves himself. Like two hands fitted together, their love-at-first-sight was a perfect match. So much alike, yet tempered to bolster the weak spots of the other, neither can see a day in the future when they are apart. Life on ship offered that 'place apart' where two men could build a life together, and neither expected to stumble into a land where they and their love is not only recognized, but seen as ideal because of its purity. As a poet, Redburn idolizes Faaua as the personification of beauty itself. He abstracts her into all that is good and kind locked with the human spirit. He loves her with a tenderness that speaks of his love of the force of life; or put another way, of his love for himself. His natural lack of a physical attraction to her aids him in rendering her in an objectified context, but via the trauma of losing his partner, he begins to sense the intensity of her feelings towards him. If conditions were right, he could imagine a life with Faaua and Kori-Kori, but their love for him is not enough to compensate for a lack of love from Redburn. He is confused. All he knows for sure is that he must find Toby. He has longish brunette hair which he sometimes wears tied back.

> **CLOTHES:** On the *Dolly* and island alike, he wears what Toby wears. On the island, he too goes native with two additions – his belt so he can have his jackknife handy, and his hat to keep the sun off his face.

KARAKOI'I: Hawaiian from Oahu; late-20s. The harbor pilot and diplomat between the French and visitors to Nuku Hiva, he is suave, adept at reading people and situations, and quick to pick up cultural signals – like the French habit of bowing, and the American wink. He has many admirers to pick and choose from; a situation he is used to from years of sailing. He is suffused with a Polynesian *joie de vivre* which angers Jim's naturally pessimistic nature when they clash. The love between Redburn and Toby, which he is quick to pick up on, reinforces his belief in the solidity of 'his kind.' He has long hair worn up and goes about hatless.

> **CLOTHES:** His most distinctive article of clothing is a grand hunting jacket given to him by an officer of la *Reine Blanche*. He wears this green coat with pride, knowing most others know who gave it to him, and thus to whom Karakoi'i is romantically attached. Under it he wears tidy sailor trousers and tee-shirts open at the neck to proudly display a shark tooth pendant on a string of chunky coral beads.

Chiefs and Priests of Taipivai

MEHEVI: Son of a chief who rose to preeminence through merit; mid-30s. A man's man, Mehevi jumps into situations with both feet. Having grown up in a courtly life, he manipulates courtiers masterfully, but only for benevolent goals. He is deeply conflicted concerning the French. Part of him wants to act rashly and strike the first blow. But mostly he believes, or wants to believe, that French interest will always remain remote from Taipivai. Pending further information, his wait-and-see policy is a sage one. He is Redburn's "beau ideal warrior" as dreamed about on board the *Dolly*, but Redburn never could have imagined a man so accomplished in both war and politics; a native Washington for his people. His profound instincts tell him Toby and Redburn are harmless, then he grows to like both of them, and finally to respect them as a devoted couple. He has a young wife and husband who come to him after the battle with the Happar. [5]

> **CLOTHES:** He wears everyday clothes: kilts, tastefully decorated mantles, and subtle earrings. His state raiment are the same form, but rich in color and scope. During these occasions, he wears commanding earrings, heavy pendants and headdresses of colorful bird feathers.

MOW-MOW: Son of a chief who grew up in the shadow of a commander in 'George W. Bush' type insecurity and curt behavior; 45 years old. He feels self-important and somehow placed on Earth to fulfill a mission. Ineffectual at leadership, his mature years have been an exercise in frustration and internalized anger at his failures. He looks upon the appearance of the French as a 'godsend.' His mission, as one divinely self-appointed, will be carried out come hell or the extermination for his people. He wants to be remembered, and he doesn't care how. He is shorter than Mehevi, completely bald, a tad overweight, and lost an eye in a battle twenty years ago.

> **CLOTHES:** He wears his kilts a bit too high in a vain effort to cover his noticeably flabby midriff. He too has special-occasion attire, but looks awkward in it; like someone with no style or self-confidence overcompensating with frills and gewgaws.

KOLORI: Pious son of a priest with a deep abiding faith; mid-50s. He does not regard the world as a changeable place, thus he is unable to see the French as much of a threat. He is swayable when it comes to matters of true catechism being diminished by outsiders. Mow-Mow finally hits upon this and is able to swing Kolori over to his antagonistic approach towards the French. Theirs is not a hands-off religion: the gods are present on a continual basis; the purpose of religious practice is to tap into this current and bring its existence forward to the minds trapped in outward consciousness. Thus Manu Atu, treated like a plaything, is deadly serious.

> **CLOTHES:** The color of priesthood is red. He wears kilts and mantles of this color every day.

MARNU: Youngest son of a Nuku Hiva Chief; 25 years old. According to Melville, he is a Polynesian Apollo, or put another way, a nature boy of the most intense self-possession, charm and manly calm. Tall, well-built, jocular, and an all-around jolly fellow, he travels freely throughout the island collecting and dispersing news. His sacred *taboo* status means he can be everybody's friend; enemy to none. He has longish hair with a soft curl to it.

> **CLOTHES:** He wears kilts and bold pieces of jewelry.

Maheyo's Household

RUNU: Senior head of the house, retired; 60 years old. In typical Polynesian tradition, he married a young couple some 25 years ago, and together they raised a houseful of wonderful children. Several years ago he passed the day-to-day management of the household to his husband Maheyo. Now, he basks in the comfort of hearth and family. When young, he was dashing and brave. The three trophy heads in the rafters are due to his youthful prowess. Jim's tale on how the strawberry blond came to reside above Redburn's head is accurate.

CLOTHES: He wears the typical kilt and mantle of his age and status when he leaves the house, which is not very often.

MAHEYO: Husband to Runu and Tinor; 46 years old. Tall, virile and well-built, he is a father figure to Redburn. A bit of an eccentric, caught in the middle of not liking to spend too much time with his grown children, and not yet having grandchildren to dote over, he likes to be out of the house. He spends time in his 'tool shed,' or visiting friends in the afternoon. He is extremely pleased with his children and looks on Toby and Redburn as sons. He is proud to see the Americans' commitment to each other, and naturally thinks they need an unassailable woman to allow them to have their own home and children, but Maheyo will let Tinor do the matchmaking. He has a pair of commanding earrings which he wears only when visiting others. Since he is in and out all day, the earrings are constantly coming on and off. He has a penchant for bathing in the still of midnight; just he and Tinor. He plucks his beard hairs with a pair of mussel shell tweezers; smokes in the top of a nearby coconut tree; and keeps the matrimonial fires kindled with discreet nocturnal hand-jobs for his mate. Tinor and he make love on the flat rocks by the stream at midnight.

CLOTHES: He dresses unceremoniously, except for his 'going out' earrings, which are made from whale teeth. He wears kilts and goes about without any shoulder coverings or headgear.

TINOR: Wife to Runu and Maheyo; 43 years old. A kindly mother figure to both Toby and Redburn, she is a formidable woman. Most of her tireless day is spent directing the other women of the house in food preparations, tapa making, et al. She prefers to pound the poi herself, as the girls are too namby pamby about really smashing it. She is suitably overjoyed and distracted from domestic concerns by the 'problem' of finding a good match for Toby and Redburn. When she rouses her boys from their afternoon siestas, she sneaks up and places a treat into each sleeping hand. She knows what each prefers. [6]

CLOTHES: Her work clothes are typical: skirt to lower calves, and an outer layer that consists of a pair of long cloths tied attractively at the shoulders, and cinched at the waist with a sash. This outer piece comes down to the knees in front, and to the ankles in back. The sash is in a contrasting color and tied with a big bow at the side on the hip. Tinor only wears jewelry on special occasions. She made outer garments with the calico that Toby and Redburn presented to her for her girls and herself. They wear the calico during the feast of the calabashes, to general envy. In the custom of married women, her long hair is tied up in a bun at the back by means of a headband. This strip of colorful cloth is worn on the forehead and tied at the back around the hair.

MARMUNU: Family son; 23 years old. As the second eldest son, he expected the departure of his older brother to his own home would mean his elevation in the household hierarchy. This did not happen due to the presence of Kori-Kori.

He is not jealous of the confidence shown to his sister's boyfriend, mainly because he respects Kori-Kori too much. Nevertheless, he relishes the task of conducting Toby to the Happar frontier to show his mettle as leader. He is youthful, confident, fun loving, and has ambitions of rising to a chief one day. He likes to keep his hair very closely cropped, and later asks Redburn to shave his head for him, mainly because Redburn shaved Toby and Marmunu wants to be closer to him; give him a job to replace the one he lost.

> **CLOTHES:** He wears kilts and goes about without any shoulder coverings or headgear.

FAAUA: Family daughter; 18 years old. She is an attentive student to her mother's teaching. She is fully ready to strike out on her own with Kori-Kori and another man. Her mother had her first child at the age of eighteen, and wishes to follow suit. Kori-Kori is an imposing figure who makes her swoon to her very marrow, but feels this quality of his personality may be holding back potential suitors for their hands. With Toby's disappearance, she grows to love Redburn as an adoptive mother might. She knows he is heartbroken, but she also knows that over the months Kori-Kori has developed a protective affection for his charge, the same kind he has for her. Hope against hope, she witnesses Kori-Kori's affection blossom into love. With the three of them, the community will rally to build them a home and make sure their married life starts off right. When she lets Redburn go at the end, she is giving up much more than the man she loves; she is giving up a future she had already mapped out. She has pale blue eyes. [7]

> **CLOTHES:** She dresses like her mother, only with more youthful flourishes. She lets her long hair flow free, and likes to arrange flowers and foliage as a crown after her morning bath.

MUNUNI: Family daughter; 16 years old. She acts the middle child, which she is; reserved, neither daring nor needing attention. She spends much of her time thinking about and caring for Karnunu. She knows he will be great one day, and is proud of him already. She is the type, rare among her people, who wants her man all to herself. A poly marriage has less appeal to her, even though she sees happy examples all around her. If Karnunu keeps pace with out-braving all the other warriors, she knows they will be content in a home just built for two.

> **CLOTHES:** She dresses like her mother, only with more youthful flourishes. She lets her long hair flow free, and likes to arrange flowers and foliage as a crown after her morning bath with Faaua.

MONU: Family son; 15 years old. The doted-upon youngest, he is let loose to do as he sees fit. More scolded from the young men of the house than his parents, he nevertheless gets away with a great deal. The only thing he takes seriously in life is Ruaruga. They had been close friends from early childhood, and when puberty struck both boys, an abiding love was born and reciprocated. Edging seamlessly from boys to young men, from friends to partners, they while away the time in play and playful attention to each other's needs. He and Ruaruga are both not quite ready to set childhood aside, except when the other is ready.

Though without acknowledgement, Redburn and Toby set the example they want their evolving relationship to mature into. He is accomplished at music, has a fine voice, and relishes his father's storytelling and prayers. This talent is encouraged, and it will probably be his calling for life. He keeps his curly hair long and boyish.

CLOTHES: He wears kilts and never thinks about jewelry or anything to cover his shoulders or head.

KARLUNA: Girlfriend to Marmunu; 17 years old. She looks up to Faaua and to the certain seriousness with which that girl goes about life. She's more of a free spirit and often wonders why Faaua suffers Tinor's pedantic ways; then she remembers Marmunu. She loves the nature-boy in him, like a learning lad who sometimes needs protection from himself. She too is anxious to be 'discovered' and have her and her man swept off their feet. She feels she will be an excellent mother, well-armed with what not to do.

CLOTHES: A fashion plate, she has several outfits of the most daring cut and color. She too likes things in her hair, and likes playing master hair-styler to the other young women of the house. She favors chunky coral necklaces and bangles.

KORI-KORI: Boyfriend to Faaua; 25 years old. A natural-born leader, he neither studies how to flatter, nor makes enemies with his frankness. People flock to his inner strength, which makes him a bit standoffish. If it were up to him, his life would be one played on the sidelines, but everybody has confidence in him, which propels him on the 'world stage' of Taipivai. Mehevi is secretly grooming the young man to be his right hand man and successor. Kori-Kori is aware that he is smarter than most others, but he tries to hide this. He is aware that his physical prowess is greater than most others, so he tries to play down to their levels. With Redburn, the change over from playful affection to committed love is tied up subconsciously to a commitment to stop holding himself back. If fate has put he and Faaua and Redburn together, then Kori-Kori is willing to let fate lead all aspects of his life. As Faaua says, Kori-Kori is slow to commit, but once confidence is given, mountains or seas cannot keep him from honoring and protecting that love. Losing Redburn was like having to lose himself; for him to be the instrument of this loss is like a commitment to doing what's right no matter the consequences. He is tall, well-built, and in many ways a physical match for Marnu, though contrasting to him in having a taciturn demeanor, in which regard he is like Toby. He has straight hair, which he wears fairly short.

CLOTHES: He dresses with no muss, in kilts and without mantles or head-gear.

KARNUNU: Mununi's boyfriend; 18 years old. A jovial lad focused on the future, he is courageous, sporty, attentive to his elders, and takes the greatest offence at Monu's 'bad boy' image. He can't wait to be Kori-Kori's age, for that age seems a golden time when 'adults' take a man seriously because he has had time to prove himself. With Marmunu, Kori-Kori and him in the same house, he knows he is going to the top of local leadership. He is clever but conflicted over which faction to back. Perhaps a pessimistic strain knows Mow-Mow is right, but Mehevi is the type of leader he wishes to be, so he is naturally drawn to Mehevi's position. He has fairer hair, which is long and wavy.

CLOTHES: He dresses in flashy kilts and mantles that make him seem older than he is. His girlfriend, and her fashion-forward drive for being noticed, selects the decorations on his clothes. He often wears something flashy, life feathers, in his hair, and sports a rakish choker of cowry shells and bone beads.

RUARUGA: Monu's boyfriend; 14 years old. Though a few months younger, he is more mature than Monu, and quickly growing to see himself as a positive influence on his partner's development. He still likes to horse around, but increasingly feels pangs of guilt creep over him when he sees how focused and intent Mununi and Marmunu are. Though young, he has already stopped thinking in terms of 'me,' and shifted effortlessly into only thoughts of 'we' in regards to Monu.

CLOTHES: Like Monu, he wears plain kilts and the rest, but recently he's been drawn to the flashy stuff Karnunu is wearing, mainly because it makes him more handsome than he already is. He wants to ask Mununi to start dressing him too, but doesn't want Monu to harangue him about it. He's going to get Mununi to start dressing both of them.

ARVA: Family dog; 6 years old. Most Polynesian breeds of dogs are considered extinct due to interbreeding with imported European examples. Melville's reaction to local canines is piquant: "Dogs! — big, hairless rats rather; all with smooth, shining, speckled hides — fat sides, and very disagreeable faces." (Chapter 28). Hairlessness is a unique feature, and that coupled with small size, leads one to think of Asiatic / Mesoamerican breeds like the Chinese Crested and Tepeizeuintli. The better known Xoloitzcuintli is not a candidate, because these are large dogs and do not qualify for Melville's "big rat" status. (see the Visual Key for a Marquesas dog drawn in 1844, and looking remarkably like a Chinese Crested.)

3) Hula Hula Grounds, Ti, Rectory and Surroundings:

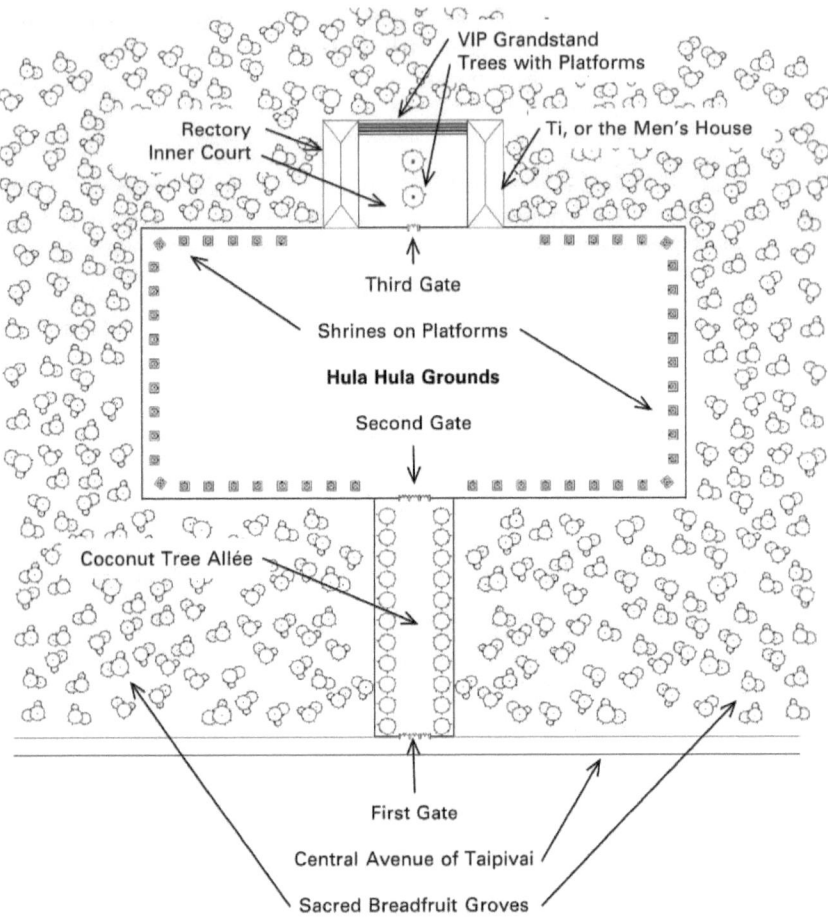

4) Maheyo Family Organization Chart:

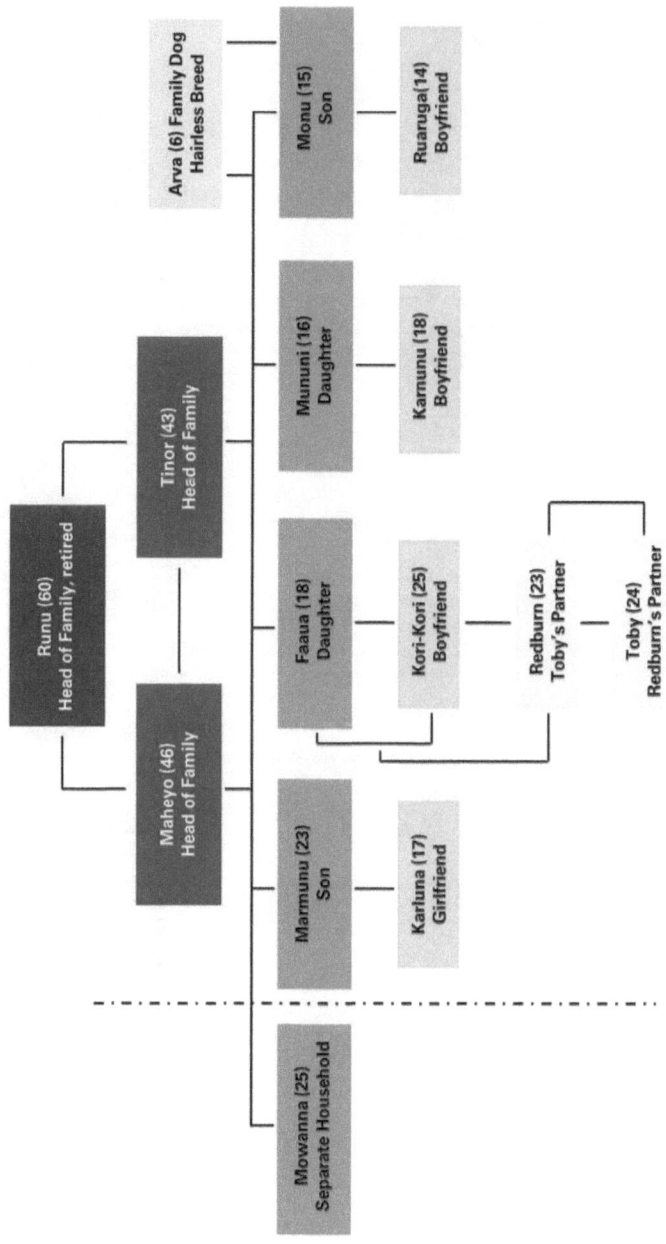

5) For an introduction to the history of the Marquesas and its general place in Polynesia culture, see Dr. Janet Sumner-Fromeyer's article here:

http://www.ms-starship.com/sciencenew/marquesas.htm

6) Eliot Rifkin provides an excellent summary of traditional same-sex love in Polynesia. See his September 12th, 2010, article here:

http://madikazemi.blogspot.com/2010/09/polynesias-ancient-same-sex-acceptance.html

7) Also of interest is the Aikane article, which is the term for committed same-sex partners and their marriages, on the webpage *Marriage Project – Hawai'i*. See here:

http://mphawaii.tripod.com/

Typee Extra Scene – Toby's Story

The following scene appears in Secret Melville 7, "Pierre, and the Ambiguities." But it is to be filmed with "Typee."

EXT. CENTRAL AVENUE OF TAIPIVAI – NOON

There is commotion as **PEOPLE** run up the valley to gather supplies to barter with the boat. **TOBY**, leaning on **FAAUA**, heads down to the beach. Several young **MEN** stop and begin to try and delay them. Some run ahead and disappear off the road in the overgrowth. **KNOCK; KNOCK; KNOCK** – a tree off the road is hit. The young men **HOOT** and cry towards Toby: **"Happar!"** They speak in POLYNESIAN, with subtitles.

FAAUA
Don't listen – they are playing with you....

YOUNG MAN
Toby! Happar *bastards!* They are close.

He points into the overgrowth.

TOBY
Happar? Here?

Toby winks at Faaua, then reaches for the spear of the young man.

TOBY (CONT'D)
Lend it over. I'll take care of the Happar!

YOUNG MAN
No. No – no need. A short-temper like yours, it's best
you use your fists!

He puts up his dukes, and Toby play-swings at him. Toby and Faaua hurry down to the beach. The young men follow.

EXT. HEAD OF THE BEACH

The surf crashes; seagulls cry and circle in the air. One hundred yards ahead, whitecaps roll onto white sand. **TOBY** and **FAAUA** pause, not knowing where to go. **PEOPLE** rush past them laden with fruit. These folks are running to where a longboat is pulled on the beach. Four **SAILORS** stand by and barter with the locals. **JACK**, the leader is conversing with **MOW-MOW**. Toby and Faaua head that way, but now the crowd's attention begins to shift to Toby's presence.

EXT. BEACH

TOBY, supported by **FAAUA**, calls to **JACK**.

TOBY
Ahoy, there!

MOW-MOW glares at them; angry at Faaua's presence. He commands the **CROWD**.

MOW-MOW
(in POLYNESIAN, with subtitles)
Take him to the shrine!

Mow-Mow gestures to a structure at the tree line. The crowd closes in and forces Faaua and Toby to go there.

EXT. BEACH SHRINE

As they near it, **FAAUA** is forced to let **TOBY** go; the shrine is Taboo for women. She hangs back as close as she dare, nervously pacing. Young **MEN** force Toby to sit on the steps of the stone platform, and then crowd about him. Toby bobs and weaves, trying to see around their legs.

TOBY
Sir! Oh – sir!

JACK appears, and Toby leaps up to greet him.

JACK
So – The tales are true!

TOBY
What tales?

JACK
Of a pair of tars in Typee. Your companion...?

TOBY
He's – he needs a doctor. His ankle is bad.

Jack inspects Toby's bandage by knocking Toby's brim back.

JACK
You need a doctor, son. You better come with me.

TOBY
No. Not unless you can fetch Redburn.

JACK
They'll be no fetching. I'll be lucky to pry you away.

TOBY
I'm not leaving — send help back.

JACK
(lies)
Ah — but, well here's the rub. These here natives are telling me you're not allowed to be on the beach. Seems they take these matters much too seriously — If you read me? Now, it seems they won't let you go back into the valley either.

Confused, Toby looks for Faaua.

TOBY
That can't be. Faaua!

JACK
(lies)
I will come back tomorrow for your Redburn — this Tommo they tell me of. Trust me.

TOBY
Faaua!

He can see her being held back by the crowd. His temper flashes at Jack.

TOBY (CONT'D)
Hell no! I cannot leave this island unless my partner goes with me. Go get him, now!

JACK
Man — does it look like I brought an army! Use your head.

TOBY
I only left him in the vale because they wouldn't let him come down with me.

Toby falters. His hand goes to his bad temple.

JACK
Reason, boy. Take reason — you need medical care.

Confused and in pain, Toby scans the crowd.

TOBY
Faaua.... Fayaway!

Toby bolts for it.

JACK
(in POLYNESIAN, with subtitles)
Seize him!

Faaua screams as young men grab violently onto Toby, who is trying to get to her. He is out of the shrine compound, so she runs to him. The young men force Toby to sit on the sand.

FAAUA
(in POLYNESIAN, with subtitles)
Toby! Don't be fooled by them.

Faaua drops to her knees by Toby. She holds onto his trembling hands, barely able to see. **TINOR** pushes her way through the crowd and supports her daughter. They both help Toby stand.

FAAUA (CONT'D)
(in POLYNESIAN, with subtitles)
Don't let them take you....

MOW-MOW strides cockily up behind Toby to stand with Jack.

JACK
Come on, Pillgarlic! It's getting late – We must shove off!

TOBY
(in POLYNESIAN, with subtitles)
I want to go home....

Tinor interrupts him, choking up.

TINOR
(in POLYNESIAN, with subtitles)
Toby, don't you like Taipi?

TOBY
(sobbing - in POLYNESIAN, with subtitles)
Home to Tommo; home with you! Typee is the best—

Rough hands shove Toby towards the boat. Again Faaua screams, this time in anger.

TINOR
(in POLYNESIAN, with subtitles)
Wait!

Faaua runs up to him. Toby takes his shaking palm and smears it across his eyes so he can see her.

TOBY
(in POLYNESIAN, with subtitles)
**Tell him. Tell Tommo, I will be back for him before three days
have passed. Tell him! Please—**

Toby is shoved again.

FAAUA
(in POLYNESIAN, with subtitles)
I will tell him! You <u>will</u> be back....

She reaches out for him, and just as their fingers meet, the young men pick Toby up and carry him to the boat.

INT. LONGBOAT

TOBY is tossed in, and tumbles to the boat floor. **FAAUA** and **TINOR** run up. Faaua desperately grabs onto the side of the boat, and Tinor hangs onto her. **JACK** tosses strings of beads at Tinor, who lets them fall repulsively into the water. The **SAILORS** begin to shove off, and Faaua is pushed aside. As the boat starts to float, Toby rises in the stern and looks back at Tinor and Faaua. Behind them, **MOW-MOW** stands with folded arms and a 'good riddance' smirk.

~

Typee Text Endnotes

[i] Unpublished portions of Typee: there is a total dearth of Melville manuscripts surviving for his books. The only two exceptions are Billy Budd, the corrected draft of which he completed only weeks before his death, and a mysterious, 100-or-so-page chunk of Typee recovered from a barn clearing in 1983. Melville seems to have given this section (or the complete work) to a young man he fancied whose family once owned the property. Analysis of this rare artifact includes many sections that are even more frank concerning Toby and Melville's love than the entirely open passages he did publish. For an introduction to this manuscript material, see John Bryant Melville Unfolding and Beyond: Looking at Culture, Sexuality, and the Fluid Text, National Sexuality Resource Center, February 2nd, 2009:

https://rotunda.upress.virginia.edu/melville/links.html

[1] Toby and Redburn's photograph case: early 19th century gutta-percha case with scallop shell design:

https://i.ebayimg.com/images/g/2YEAAOSw3WxaMzkv/s-
l500.jpg

[2] Toby and Redburn's love theme: Domenico Zipoli's *All'Elevazione N.1* —
adagio for cello, oboe, orchestra and pipe organ:

https://youtu.be/Cz7BKFwJJCc

[3] Glass oil lanterns: early 19th century "fairy lights" hanging in the rigging of
the *Dolly*:

https://www.lassco.co.uk/lassco-news/wp-
content/uploads/sites/2/2013/12/Victorian-fairy-light1.jpg

https://4.bp.blogspot.com/-
v28eR14paHo/TcHnaUePRwI/AAAAAAAAD60/XqhFStc2im8/s16
00/5274858651_e0d2fd89e3.jpg

[4] Toby: 1846 photograph of Richard Tobias Green, 4 years after his stay on Nuku Hiva:

https://upload.wikimedia.org/wikipedia/commons/1/16/Richard
Tobias_Greene.jpg

[5] 1842 French portrait of a young man from Nuku Hiva:

https://upload.wikimedia.org/wikipedia/commons/5/5f/Atlas_pi
ttoresque_pl_058.jpg

[6] 1837 French portrait of a Nuku Hiva matron. Note the characteristic hair bun and tie showing her status as a mature woman:

https://www.pinterest.com/pin/40954677848496677/

[7] 1843 French engraving of young lady from Nuku Hiva:

https://cdn.shopify.com/s/files/1/1021/8371/products/CW1_0
20_ba470580-b5e2-4162-9e53-
d626a4459c1c_590x.jpg?v=1569786333